BISON BOOKS

Our Voices

NATIVE

STORIES

OF ALASKA

AND THE

YUKON

Edited by
James Ruppert
and
John W. Bernet

University of Nebraska Press, Lincoln and London

Acknowledgments for the
use of copyrighted and
previously published ma-
terial appear on pp. 385–
88, which constitutes an
extension of the copyright
page.
© 2001 by the University
of Nebraska Press
All rights reserved
Manufactured in the
United States of America
⊗
Library of Congress Cata-
loging-in-Publication
Data
Our voices : Native Stories
of Alaska and the Yukon /
edited by James Ruppert
and John W. Bernet.
    p.   cm.
"A Bison Original"
Includes bibliographical
references and index.
ISBN 0-8032-8984-7
(pbk. : alk. paper)
1. Athapascan Indians –
Folklore. 2. Athapascan
Mythology. 3. Tales –
Alaska. 4. Tales – Yukon
Territory. I. Ruppert,
James, 1949– II. Bernet,
John W., 1929–

E99.A86 087 2001
398.2'089'972 – dc21
00-069096

Contents

Illustrations

Preface and Acknowledgments

One century ago, Alaska and the Yukon were associated in the public mind with the great Klondike gold rush. Through the works of poets and writers of fiction and nonfiction — for example, John Muir, Jack London, and Robert Service — the North Country became a place of awesome wonder, scenic splendor, hostile nature, and vast white space to readers in the "civilized" regions of the United States and Canada. As "progress" came to areas of Alaska and northwestern Canada through the building of railroads and the Alcan Highway and through the construction of military bases, the traditional ways of life of the Native peoples were badly disrupted, in some places destroyed. Because they were regarded by Euro-Americans as negligible supporting players, even as expendable extras, in the grand drama of America's manifest destiny, their plight, if reported at all, was dismissed with little understanding.

During the past four decades, certain political, economic, natural, and man-made events have held Alaska in the public eye and kept interest strong: statehood in 1959, the great earthquake in 1964, exploration for oil on the Kenai Peninsula and the North Slope in the 1960s, Alaska Native [Land] Claims Settlement Act in 1971, construction of the Trans-Alaska Pipeline in the mid-1970s, Alaska National Interest Lands Conservation Act in 1980, and the grounding of the *Exxon Valdez* in 1989 with its pollution by petroleum of Prince William Sound. Recently the secretary of the interior recognized two hundred Alaska Native villages as tribes, an action of uncertain implications for issues of vital importance to all Alaskans, Native and non-Native alike, such as rights to subsistence hunting and fishing and relationships between federal, state, and tribal governments. Even more recently, the United States Supreme Court has ruled in several cases bearing upon these issues. In the Yukon Territory as well, effects of the Klondike gold rush, of the Alaska (Alcan) Highway, and of other economic and political developments continue to reverberate in the lives of First Nation peoples.

More, we believe, than in most of the older states and provinces, people in Alaska and the Yukon are vitally interested in correcting the longstanding stereotypes about the land and its inhabitants. Both old-timers (sourdoughs) who know the reality and newcomers (cheechakos) who want to learn it share this interest. Visitors to Alaska and the Yukon, who have increased greatly in numbers in recent years, also want to become accurately informed about the North Country, its people, and their ways of life. Tour companies now offer attractions, and Elderhostel programs offer courses, which explain the diversity of Northern life, ranging from presentations of gold mining by panning, sluice boxes, and dredge to demonstrations of fishing by river wheel, smoking salmon, tanning moose hides, and sewing animal skins. Native peoples of Alaska and First Nation peoples of the Yukon are frequently involved in the presentations having to do with their own cultures, and some Native villages or groups conduct their own tour operations.

Thus, the principal objective of *Our Voices* is to contribute to this corrected image of the North Land and its people by drawing from one group — the Athabaskans of south central and interior Alaska and the Yukon Territory — representative narratives that they have told about themselves and their culture. Fulfillment of this objective should attract a wideranging audience to this book — all those within and outside Alaska and the Yukon who may be interested in the worldview, the human condition, and the literary accomplishments of some of the earliest known inhabitants of the North.

A second objective is to collect in one volume a number of the best narratives by Alaskan and Yukon Athabaskan storytellers, as differentiated from books representing only one language or one storyteller, of which a number of excellent examples have been published over the past quarter century. Our book attempts to illustrate the richness and variety of Northern Athabaskan literature in general and the specific artistry of each of a score of narrators recognized as masters by their people. It should appeal to teachers and students of Native American subjects not only in Alaska and the Yukon but in other Athabaskan areas of Canada and the United States, such as the extensive Navajo and Apache region of the southwestern States. The book may find use in classes at various levels of education — certainly college and secondary.

A third objective is to add to the increasing library of material on Native American cultures a volume that comes essentially from the spirits, minds, and artistic talents of Northern Athabaskan people themselves. In English translation, it is not only a book about them but, more important, a book by them — a view opening from within, not a picture framed from without. Achievement of this objective should attract specialists in all branches of Athabaskan studies for the light the book might shed on the anthropology, history (or prehistory), political and economic situations, and imaginative and artistic genius of the people.

During the past four decades, the Native languages of Alaska and the Yukon have received a great deal of attention. They have been studied and documented by linguists; they have been introduced by educators into the schools from which they had earlier been banished; and they have been embraced by Native people themselves as a treasured, vital part of their cultural heritage. Most of the best collections of Native narratives that have been published are the result of close and careful collaboration between oral storyteller (or writer) and linguist/translator. These books emphasize the Native-language text because it preserves the story as traditionally told and because it documents grammatical, lexical, and stylistic features of languages that have not been written until recent historical time. Speakers of a Native language who also read it (not all of them do) and write it (not many of them do) form one audience for the Native-language text, and scholars of languages and linguistics constitute another.

We have chosen not to include in this book the Native-language texts of the narratives originally told or written in Alaska and Yukon Native languages. To have done so would have meant decreasing the number of narratives, the number of storytellers, and the number of Native cultures we present. Yet given our expected audiences, probably no more than 5 percent of our readers would have tried to work with or to appreciate the many pages of Native-language text. Indeed, we believed that including the text would have limited our readership. And the small audiences that could have read or appreciated the text would not be attracted to the book for that purpose. People who read Gwich'in, for instance, would not be interested in the book for its Gwich'in texts; they would already know and probably own the source material.

Saying this does not detract from our recognition of the culture-specific nature of the Native-language texts; nor does it deny that the Native-language originals are every bit as valuable as the English translations — and for the linguists and Native people who know the languages, more valuable.

The English translations of the stories told by thirteen of the narrators represented here were all made by linguists fluent in the respective languages, who worked with the storytellers in transcribing the spoken narratives and then in translating them. (Four oral narrators told their stories in English.) The English translations of the narratives by three writers in their Native languages whom we include were made for the most part by the writers themselves, assisted in varying degrees by linguists with whom they worked. In our headnotes we have attempted to explain as completely as we can the nature of the transcribing and translating processes as followed for each storyteller and her/his linguist or linguists.

This book has been in progress for nearly a decade. During that time a number of individuals and organizations have helped us, through their interest and support, to improve it in various ways. We take responsibility for its shortcomings, which we hope are few. But we owe our gratitude and express our appreciation to the following:

Arnold Krupat and Brian Swann for initially suggesting the project and for early guidance; Irene Roberts of Doyon Limited and Norma Dahl of Tanana Chiefs Conference for assistance with certain factual information; Adeline Raboff Kari for a contribution that had to be left on the cutting-room floor but for which we are nevertheless grateful; Frederica de Laguna and Torben Lundbæk, Director of the Danish National Museum, for allowing us to reprint the 1933 versions of three of Anna Nelson Harry's stories.

We also wish to thank all holders of copyright who have granted us permission to reprint stories, acknowledging in particular the Iditarod Area School District, the Yukon-Koyukuk School District, and the Copper River Native Association; and storytellers Katherine Peter and Mary Tyone.

We thank another of our storytellers with whom we have had personal contact — Catherine Attla; we are grateful to representatives of the families of three of the storytellers who have approved our use of the material — Mary Jane Jim for the stories of the late Annie Ned, her grandmother; Judy Gingell for the stories of the late Kitty Smith, her grandmother; and Ida Calmegane for the stories of the late Angela Sidney, her mother; and we thank Julie Cruikshank, not only for concurring in our reprinting the stories that she collected from Mrs. Ned, Mrs. Smith, and Mrs. Sidney but also for the thoughtful comments and helpful suggestions she has given us through an always pleasant exchange of letters.

We are also grateful to a number of individuals who contributed their knowledge and expertise to the project: Eliza Jones, transcriber and translator of Catherine Attla's stories, for clarifying certain features of Koyukon orthography; Jeff Leer, of the Alaska Native Language Center, for information on Tagish orthography and speakers; Michael E. Krauss for granting us permission to reprint the many stories under copyright to the Alaska Native Language Center, of which he has been longtime director, for his steadfast interest in and encouragement of our work, best demonstrated in several long discussions in his office and by phone, and, as transcriber and translator of the works of Anna Nelson Harry, for his ever-fascinating, ever-evolving insights into the philosophical perceptions and narrative genius of this last Eyak artist.

Others who, in like manner, gave us the benefit of their expertise and skill and therefore have our gratitude are John Ritter, Director of the Yukon Native Language Centre, for engaging Gertie Tom in our project by allowing us to use three of her narratives and for his helpful, encouraging phone conversations and letters; James Kari, transcriber and translator of five of our storytellers (Belle Deacon, Mary Tyone, Fred and Katie John, Huston Sanford) and editor of the works of Peter Kalifornsky, not only for the extent of this contribution but also for his continuing interest in our work and for his recommendations concerning accuracy and consistency in the spelling of certain words from several of the Native languages; and Millie Buck for the revisions in her translations of the stories of John Billum, for the biographical information on Mr. Billum that she provided us, and for her patience and cooperation during phone calls.

Finally, we express our deep appreciation to the linguists who contributed three of the sections to our anthology, including their headnotes: Ron Scollon for the section on Tanacross storytelling (and to Amy Linda Modig for providing him with biographical facts on Gaither Paul, her father); Pat Moore for the Kaska section and, with the concurrence of John Dickson before his death and Chief Hammond Dick, for letting us publish a story by Mr. Dickson and one by Maudie Dick in a new format designed for this anthology; and Ray Collins and Betty Petruska for the Upper Kuskokwim section, for securing permission for us to reprint the stories of Miska Deaphon, and for preparing the stories of Lena Petruska for initial publication in our book.

It has been a special privilege and pleasure for us to work in person with Katherine Peter in preparing her writings for republication. Her joy in explaining features of her language, Gwich'in, to others is great.

Our largest debt is to the narrative artists themselves — the twenty represented in this volume and the very many, down through the ages, who have preserved the traditional tales of their cultures through memory, oral teaching, and performance.

In the hope of helping to perpetuate this legacy and of contributing to the further study and documentation of the Native languages of the North, we donate all royalties from sales of this book to the Alaska Native Language Center, to the Yukon Native Language Centre, and to a scholarship fund established for Yukon First Nation youth by Annie Ned, Kitty Smith, Angela Sidney, and Julie Cruikshank. Our compensation comes in the belief that the audiences for our book will gain better, truer understanding of Northern Athabaskan peoples, their ways of life, and their remarkable achievements than they may have held in the past.

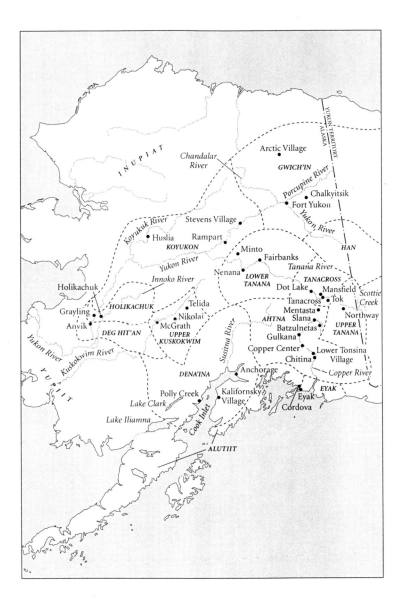

1. Native Peoples and Languages of Interior Alaska

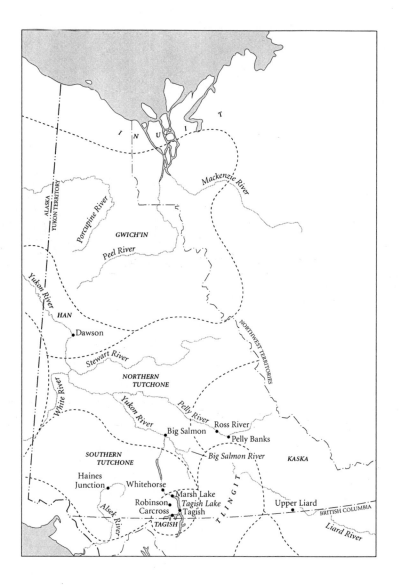

2. Native Peoples and Languages of the Yukon Territory

Our Voices

Introduction

Native American oral narratives have been collected, written down, and published for several centuries. In Alaska and the Yukon Territory, the collection of such material has proceeded for somewhat less than two hundred years, but an exceptional body of written material has been produced during the last twenty-five years by Native storytellers and writers, working with linguists, school districts, and community organizations. Some of the material transcribes and translates oral tradition for use in communities or classrooms, some of it documents and archives the achievements of Native oral literature, and some of it extends the range of oral tradition by regenerating verbal creativity in print. At the center of much of this activity has been the dedicated involvement of the Alaska Native Language Center and the Yukon Native Language Centre. Common to their work is the high degree of collaboration between the linguists and the storytellers, the authenticity and reliability of the English translations created by bilingual publications, and the significant level of community support. Moreover, current work recognizes the performance dimension of oral narrative and its nature as dialogic discourse. Sparked by the theories and practices of such scholars as Dell Hymes, Dennis Tedlock, Robin Ridington, and Julie Cruikshank, this work has been completed in an era of much greater awareness of the literary value of oral narratives and of their spiritual and social roles. Consequently, these contemporary publications have been able to reveal the valuable contributions that Native peoples from south central and interior Alaska and from the Yukon Territory have made to world literature.

As map 1 shows, the Alaskan Athabaskan peoples represented in this book are bordered by Eskimo-speaking peoples to the north and the west and even to the south, along part of the Gulf of Alaska. Also to the south lived the Eyaks, not Athabaskans themselves but distantly related. To the southeast, the major cultures bordering both Alaskan and Yukon Athabaskans are Tlingit and Tsimshian. Map 2 shows the distribution of Athabaskan groups within the Yukon Territory, bordered on the north by Inuit. But in Canada, Athabaskans inhabit territory far beyond the drainage of the Yukon, both to the east and to the south. In lifestyle, culture, and narrative tradition, Athabaskan peoples have much that is similar.

In organizing this book, we have arranged our selections to follow the major rivers in Alaska and the Yukon Territory because they organize the lives of the people there. We move up the Yukon River from Alaska into Canada and the river's headwaters and then return to Alaska. After following the Tanana River downstream, we enter areas whose lifelines are three other important rivers. We conclude with a group of Eyak narratives. Though the Eyaks are not Athabaskan, their traditions tell of a migration from the interior, and their language has been traced back to an ancestral language common to both Eyak and Proto-Athabaskan. To show the diversity of material in the oral tradition, we have chosen from a variety of genres and forms. While most of the material in this book has been previously published, much of it has been in small publications with limited circulation; and we are pleased to be able to offer two hitherto unpublished narratives and two others in a new format prepared by the translator especially for this edition. We are certain that this volume will bring this rich literary tradition to a larger readership.

We have decided to focus most of our sections on one representative storyteller. Some sections, however, will present the work of more than one verbal artist. All these storytellers together have produced a significant body of traditional narrative both on tape and in print, and their work has been accepted by their communities. Eight sections comprise stories narrated orally in Native languages and translated into English. Three present stories narrated orally in English (no less authentically Athabaskan in character, however, for this choice of language by the Native storytellers). And three others feature narratives written in Native languages and translated into English by the writers themselves; these testify to the creative power of Native verbal artists and their desire to move onto the printed page with the same authority and force as a commanding oral storyteller.

CONTEXT OF STORYTELLING

In south central and interior Alaska and the Yukon Territory, distant-time stories were told almost exclusively during the winter, especially in early and midwinter. While other genres might be told at other times — mountain stories only during the summer or personal narratives told anytime — these ancient stories were reserved for night as the long cold winter was coming on. Distant-time stories could be told by both men and women, and many oral traditions expected that a second elder would guide and correct the storyteller. Generally the audience was expected to verbalize its appreciation of the narrative while the narrator spoke, but not to interrupt him or her.

Folklorist Anna Birgitta Rooth documents the existence of two storytelling voices or styles of presentation. One uses a monotone that hypnotizes and transfixes the listeners, transporting them into an otherworldly experience. The second style uses gesture, dramatic mood changes, and the assumption of the voices of different characters (*Importance* 75–76). This style tries to act out the story and entertains through dramatization. Some cultural traditions emphasize one or the other, but examples of each have been found in most groups.

Common to most storytellers in the region is the use of what has been termed "high language." High language raises the level of formality by using many archaic words restricted to storytelling. It is also very metaphoric, in the manner of Athabaskan riddles, songs, and orations (Thompson 20–25). Many of the Athabaskan oral traditions had a formulaic ending for distant-time narratives that amounted to a prayer for a short winter.

Local storytelling traditions have flourished, and often there are rules that might not extend to all the traditions in this book. For instance, Jetté mentions Koyukon storytellers dropping sticks into a pile to mark sections of stories. Koyukon storyteller Catherine Attla notes that storytellers should not interrupt their recounting of a tale for fear of bad luck. Chad Thompson has commented that bad luck could befall the Koyukon listener who fell asleep or left before a story ended. While these expectations might influence specific Koyukon groups, they do not necessarily represent the oral traditions of all the Indian peoples in south central Alaska and along the Yukon River.

While these specific contexts might surround narrative performance, these conventions form a framework that individual storytellers use as means to engage important cultural discourses having both historical and political dimensions. Cruikshank suggests that for some of the storytellers with whom she has worked "an oral tradition is better understood as a social activity than as a reified text" (*Social* xv). Such conventions help structure the interaction between the storyteller and the audience rather than form a set of abstract rules.

ETHNOGRAPHY AND NARRATIVE ART

Our statement about the context of Northern Athabaskan storytelling, its styles, and its traditions is made against an awareness of views by a number of cultural anthropologists and linguists that, as Dennis Tedlock and Bruce Mannheim put it, "any given speaker at any given moment is immediately an actor within a social and cultural world that is always in process" (12). They maintain that acknowledging this fact in publishing "a collection of native texts or a native life history . . . is no mere matter of adding statements about 'context'" (12). Their rigorous criticism, as well as that of their colleagues, is directed at the published works of earlier ethnographers, which, as we point out in a subsequent section of this introduction, include a number of collections of Northern Athabaskan narratives.

The great error in conventional ethnographies, these scholars argue, is that they have appeared in print as monologic treatises in the third person, that is, discussions of indigenous cultures not only as they have been observed by ethnologists in field activity but modified as the ethnologists have reflected further upon them in the serenity of their offices in academe. The many Native participants who contributed in the field to the gathering of knowledge have generally vanished from the published accounts, and even the principal informants are represented in print only by brief quotation or paraphrase and usually by way of supporting the arguments or conclusions of the ethnographers.

Influenced by literary theorist M. M. Bakhtin, the critics argue instead for what Tedlock and Mannheim call "a dialogic ethnography" (8) and "the ethnography of performance" (13). By these terms they mean that the true picture of a culture "emerges" only through multivocal dialogue among indigenous peoples and exogenous field workers. Many current anthropologists believe that the voices of all indigenous participants in the conversation need to be heard, as well as that of the ethnologist. The resulting ethnography will contain as many first- and second-person pronouns (as the several voices express themselves and address the others) as it does third-person pronouns (as those voices explicate features of the culture and tell stories). And Tedlock maintains, "Spoken stories are always interwoven with the larger dialogue that surrounds them" ("Interpretation" 280).

Much of what these cultural anthropologists and linguists say is relevant to our collection of stories. Yet our book is not an ethnography; it is a selection of narratives. Its purpose is not to describe various Athabaskan groups in Alaska and the Yukon and to explain their cultural practices. It seeks, rather, to illustrate the art of Northern Athabaskan storytelling as practiced by a number of gifted narrators in speech and in writing.

Whereas Tedlock and Mannheim maintain that "a narrative told to an ethnographer is a joint construction of the ethnographer and the storyteller" (13), we regard each story in our book as basically an individual performance. If this makes it "monologic," it is nevertheless, as Tedlock himself says of all narratives, "internally dialogical" ("Interpretation" 280), in the sense that the storyteller often presents his or her characters engaged in exchanges of spoken language.

Tedlock and Mannheim note that in ethnographic field work a Native informant may reveal significant information about "social differences ... based on sex, age, kinship, acquired statuses ... solely by represented voices" rather than by expository statements (17). They go on to describe these "represented voices" further: "At a smaller scale are vocal characteristics that identify a particular person rather than a category of persons, and at a still finer scale are changes of voice that signal changes in the emotional state of the 'same' character. Aspects of voicing, at whatever level, may spread from quotations into the surrounding discourse, as when a narrator describes the actions of a character in a way that echoes the identifying voice of that character, thus producing the oral counterpart of free indirect style in written fiction" (17). These are exactly the techniques used by oral narrators of distant-time stories to develop character. One who listens carefully to the taped recordings of Belle Deacon, Catherine Attla, John Dickson, Maudie Dick, Mary Tyone, Gaither Paul, Miska Deaphon, Lena Petruska, John Billum, Anna Nelson Harry — half of the storytellers in our book — may detect these modulations in voice. Certainly the linguists working with them in transcribing and translating their stories have done so.

In other ways as well, the narratives in this book meet other criteria to which Tedlock believes ethnographies should adhere. For example, in giving informants and field workers their deserved voices in the principal text, "there will be local places with proper names as well, and named individuals, and references to nearby objects and recent events ... direct reminders of the human life world" ("Interpretation" 257). The narratives of the three writers in our book — Katherine Peter, Gertie Tom, and Peter Kalifornsky — are replete with such features, as are a number of the oral accounts by Peter John and by Fred and Katie John.

Clearly, many voices throughout the ages have contributed to the making of each story as it has been told in recent times: the voices of audiences responding to and commenting upon individual performances of the tale and the voices of elders prompting, correcting, perhaps amplifying a given rendition by an emergent storyteller. The multivocal settings of these thousands of retellings are no longer retrievable, the influence of the dialogues no longer traceable. Certainly, translators of the narratives in recent times have had their influence upon the transmutation of the stories not only from Native languages to English but also from oral to printed form. Yet we believe it is the individual storyteller who maintains control of the basic elements of the narrative that have come as a legacy out of the past — its concept, its structure, its characters — but who applies to those elements her or his own narrative talents to create a unique work of art.

FUNCTIONS OF STORYTELLING

Perhaps the best way to begin to understand something about Northern Athabaskan oral narratives is to review how they function in their own social frameworks. Tedlock and Mannheim see oral traditions as "a discourse whose intertextuality spans the differences between generations, between rural and urban life, and between vastly different languages ... moving through the remembered past and constructing, in the present, a possible future" (19). Oral narratives are individual performances that engage cultural conversations, ongoing discourses, and group values. They have been compared to Western forms such as parables, fables, and fairy tales; however, these forms prove to be poor analogs because they function much differently within their cultures. One useful way to think about the narratives in this book is to see them as serving three functions in their communities. First, they entertain in ways common to most verbal communication. Second, oral narratives enlighten listeners with cultural, social, and practical wisdom. Last, many storytellers themselves speak of how important the act of telling the narratives can be. They see it as an essential link between the human and the spiritual worlds. The act of telling stories creates a harmony between all realms of life, often by creating healing in the human community and harmony between the human and animal realms demonstrated by luck in hunting. Equally important is that hearing and contemplating the old stories promotes the proper method of thinking about the world.

Undoubtedly, oral narratives entertain in a fashion everyone can understand. To have survived for centuries, distant-time narratives had to be entertaining. They have humor, tragedy, suspense, adventure, horror, mystery, and satire. They tell of heroes and monsters, epic journeys, fantastic creatures, strange lands, and familiar relationships. Raven's foolish acts can make a listener laugh, the existence of a giant rat can tease the imagination of the listener, and a woodpecker's marital jealousy can lead to a tragedy that shocks the listener with its passions. During the dark winter nights, storytelling brought the community and family together. While other goals might exist, storytelling made life richer and happier as it reinforced common ties.

Often Native elders will speak of the vital importance of traditional narratives. They fear that if their children do not hear the stories, they will not turn out to be good, moral people and will not understand their Native identities as Koyukon, Gwich'in, and so on. Such elders emphasize the educational character of the stories. This instruction through narrative continues throughout an individual's life and helps clarify the ways in which the spiritual and human worlds interact. Central to the instructional purpose is the necessity of charting the complex relationships between the human, animal, and spiritual worlds: to show what was, how things started, what processes made them change, and how those processes exist today. Ridington has commented that these elders have lived in "a world of storied experience" and they understand that power comes to those who listen carefully to "the storied world around them" (468, 471).

Undeniably, much cultural wisdom is encoded in the narratives. Desirable personality traits, such as being observant, respecting elders, being truthful, avoiding excessive revenge, controlling one's desires, and not being gullible, can be encouraged. Though it is important that young people hear the old stories, their value is not limited to the young. Older people listen to oral narratives too, and as they grow, often their understandings of the tales grow too. To be successful, oral narratives must resonate on several levels at once. For example, a young person might appreciate a story such as Belle Deacon's "Polar Bear" as an account of the origin of some interesting and powerful animals. However, more mature consideration of the same story might reveal wisdom about the uses of spirit power and the processes of transformation.

In many of the narratives, one may find a wide variety of practical information and insight especially useful for hunting and general survival. They may create cognitive maps of the local terrain and link sites to personal and tribal use, or they may direct the listener to unfamiliar locations or sacred sites. Many stories are developed with accurate observation of the nature and characteristics of animals and natural phenomena. Taken together all this information builds for the attentive listener a knowledge base derived from the pragmatic collective experience of ancestors and relatives, knowledge vital to living in a specific area such as interior Alaska and the Yukon.

The stories might also function to illuminate the lines of social interaction when they explore what Barre Toelken calls "culturally moral subjects" (86) such as the execution of social duties, the relationships between kin, the difficulties and responsibilities of marriage, the conflict of loyalties between clans and spouses, the necessity of cooperation, and the pitfalls of relying on others. Many stories tell of the origin of a social custom or of the establishment of an institution such as the potlatch or council of elders.

A significant number of the distant-time stories include animal actors. Through such narratives, the bonds of relationship are extended into the animal/spiritual world. Since animal and human societies are structured similarly, social instruction can merge seamlessly into spiritual instruction. The stories can reveal and reinforce some of the basic elements of a worldview, such as the awareness that humans will find truth and knowledge in the animal/spiritual world or that one must obey spiritual directives over human ones. The stories remind the listener that since human perception is so limited and the animal/spiritual world so powerful, one must be careful not to mistake illusion for reality. What humans perceive as real may be a misapprehension based on their lack of proper thinking about culture, society, and the world around them.

A more elusive function of storytelling is its ability to promote healing, harmony, and hunting luck. Many storytellers believe that the very act of storytelling, whatever its content, serves to keep the community in harmony with the sacred processes of the world. Indeed, for most Native groups the stories of the distant time function like a body of sacred texts that describe sacred history, as Mircea Eliade suggests. Their recounting can have a religious flavor even if they are not told in a ritual context. Mrs. Attla, who compares the distant-time stories she was told to the Bible, says, "Long ago, when times were hard, people would appeal for mercy by telling stories. It was their way of praying." Though Rooth does not report on the religious dimension of storytelling, she does recognize that the recitation of oral narratives and the singing of songs associated with them are believed to have an influence on hunting: "These stories were not only told for entertainment, they were probably also told to procreate game, good weather and good hunting" (*Importance* 31). While the religious function of the narratives may be highlighted by one storyteller or downplayed by another, the basic assumption is that storytelling promotes a connection to a spiritual reality in ways written forms do not. Orally transmitted stories heal, reestablish spiritual/human balance, and foster hunting luck.

Ridington has written that Native American spiritual traditions "live in song, story, and ceremony" (468) and include as "conversational communicants . . . all sentient beings: animal persons, the voices of natural places and forces, and the voices of those who have gone before" (470). In discussing stories about the vision quest in various Native American groups, Ridington cites a story by the Okanagan elder Harry Robinson in which "spirit helpers appear as voices in conversation" (477) — voices of a chipmunk and of a tree stump, which take human form in order to empower a boy. "Because the stump has survived for a long time," Ridington writes, "it has the authority of an elder. Because it is home to a chipmunk, it shares in that animal's life. . . . As in the other vision quest stories, power comes through a person's storied conversation with the spiritual powers surrounding him" (476–77). One of our stories, though not concerned with vision quest, is similar in basic imagery and in its merging of natural and spiritual situations. Mary Tyone recounts "When Horsefly Was Living in a Stump." The stump is part of a dead tree, but as an "egg stump" in which birds nest, it harbors imminent life. As a central participant in the story, Raven is the one who, after engaging Horsefly in dialogue, retains power and changes the physical nature of Horsefly. James Kari, transcriber and translator of Mrs. Tyone's stories, has called this one "a funny story about the bothersome horsefly," thus attesting to its appeal as entertainment. In showing where birds' eggs might be found, it also has instructional benefit. Together with its joining of the natural and the spiritual worlds, the story thus functions in all three basic ways.

GENRES

When we look at the body of oral narratives of the Eyak and Athabaskan people of south central and interior Alaska and the Yukon Territory, we can identify two broad categories by which the people think of these stories. The first genre we will refer to as distant-time stories, taking the name from the translation of the Koyukon term *kk'edonts'ednee*. These stories tell of the origin of the world and all its inhabitants, and they function in the manner of sacred history. A second grouping clusters what we might call "historical" narratives that recount events of known people in specific locations. Many of these stories may be personal experiences or descriptions of events that have come to an individual storyteller from a trusted source. Other, more specific narrative genres might be established by context, such as Dena'ina Athabaskan mountain stories that are defined by the place and the season in which they are told. The two broad classes seem to be common for all the peoples included in this anthology, though some commentary has questioned the pervasiveness of this distinction.

These Native oral genres are not defined by immutable criteria, however, and the dividing line between them varies according to the oral tradition consulted. Indeed, we might think of the body of oral tradition as a spectrum representing the content of the stories, as illustrated by the figure be-

ORIGIN ERA	TRANSFORMATION ERA	HISTORICAL ERA
DISTANT TIME	MOVEMENT TOWARD SOCIAL FORMS	PERSONAL AND COMMUNAL MEMORY
FLUX		FIXED NATURES

Spectrum of Narrative Content

low. This figure, based on a more detailed diagram presented by Andrew Wiget in *Native American Literature*, has proven useful in creating a visual representation of the varieties of Native narratives.

On the left we have origin stories. These stories explore the beginning of things, such as how humans came to be, the origin of death, the origin of the celestial bodies, the functions of the body, the relationship between men and women, and the nature of spiritual power. The world depicted in the stories is one of creative flux, where the essential nature of things can change. It is usually inhabited by characters who appear to be both animal and human. These characters are not locked into one fixed form or nature but are free to transform at will. They all share a common language and can talk to one another. Stories from this origin era establish the fundamental structures of the world we know today. While referring to this era as the origin era, we should note that many Native oral traditions do not actually describe the creation of the world. Rather, it is assumed that the world exists, and the narrative emphasis falls instead upon subjects such as the nature of the celestial bodies, the creation of humans, and the beginning of procreation and of death. Unnatural creatures and monsters are often eliminated as the world is made safe for human culture. Catherine Attla's tale "Great Raven Who Shaped the World" is an example of a story from this era.

In stories from the transformation era, the basic outlines of human and animal life are already in a fixed and stable form. Animals and humans have consistent natures. They no longer transform at will, and characters act with qualities that are either human or animal. However, the relationships between humans, animals, and the spiritual powers of the world have not been completely formalized. Stories from this era establish a reciprocal relationship between the human and the animal/spiritual worlds. They clarify how humans should behave toward animals and spiritual powers. When humans think and act in appropriate ways, then humans, animals, and spiritual entities exist in harmony. Often the stories tell of the origin of human social institutions such as marriage, hunting, and potlatches. Throughout these narratives, a series of covenants and institutions is initiated that defines a human being's place in the world while delineating the origin of human culture and its values. Stories from this era might fall into a variety of Native genres, depending upon the specific oral tradition. Narratives such as Belle Deacon's "The Man and Wife" or John Dickson's "The Girl Who Lived with Salmon" exemplify this era.

Stories from the historical era are mostly concerned with the actions of named and known people. They may be the narrator's experiences or those of a specific ancestor, relative, or famous person. The narratives may concern hunting, warfare, spiritual activity, or relatives. Their function is to carry on the process of developing and defining the nature of humanity's experience in the world. In the sphere of these narratives, human and animal nature is fixed in forms we recognize today. Transformation is limited to special occasions such as shamanistic healing, and humans must be constantly attentive if they are to experience power. Ritual and personal vision help connect humans to the spiritual world. However, the basic principles and processes that created the world as we perceive it today are still functioning. These stories serve as a contemporary link to the ancient times. In this anthology, we present a number of these narratives, such as Peter John's "I Belong to My Mother's Side" and Fred and Katie John's "When Russians Were Killed at 'Roasted Salmon Place.'"

If considered as a chronological spectrum, clearly the sweep of narratives is movement from flux to fixed natures, from the lack of social institutions and cultural values to their establishment, and from a world hostile to humans and human culture to a world where humans have a place. Some readers might be tempted to categorize the stories from the origin era as myths and the narratives from the historical era as personal reminiscences or perhaps legends, but such Western terms risk suggesting that the former are false and the latter true or possibly true. However, Native American storytelling does not distinguish between truth and falsehood, but rather between distant time and recent time. All the stories are regarded as true to their respective eras, but reality (and thus truth) was of a completely different order during the origin era than it is today. The world was different back then. Different rules governed the interactions between beings, but the processes, values, and truths of that era are as real to that time as contemporary personal experiences are to ours. In a sense, they are even more true and more real to both eras since they are sacred history and explain the unseen, eternal world of spirit. It is also possible that some readers might perceive this chronological presentation as a model of cultural progress from an animal world to human culture or as a fall from an idealized paradise. Neither of these interpretations is accurate. The stories explain the changes in the world in a very nonjudgmental manner, highlighting valuable knowledge. They tell of the natural and foreordained processes of the world without the constrictions of Western definitions of Good and Evil or the concept of evolution.

STORYTELLING AESTHETICS

One might ask why the storytellers here have been chosen and what marks their art as exceptional. Communities often single out accomplished storytellers because they have learned an impressive body of stories or because they have learned the stories from a particularly well respected tradition bearer. However, listening communities also recognize the style and aesthetics of a gifted storyteller as representative of the best of their oral tradition. Certainly, these aesthetic qualities vary from tradition to tradition, but a few general characteristics might be widespread.

First, audiences sanction storytellers who use a variety of techniques to engage the listeners. For instance, Belle Deacon uses questions while speaking in the persona of a character and thus brings the listener closer to the interaction between characters in the story. However, she also adopts the position of an audience member when she asks questions about what will happen next. Thus she is able to move away from her narrative position as a storyteller at the same time that she moves closer to the audience and views the story, as it were, from the outside. Here the aesthetics of engagement create a dynamic relationship between the storyteller and the listener. Mrs. Deacon also masterfully uses well-placed provocative, descriptive detail to create a series of foci of emotion and meaning that engage a listener. Another technique that she and other skilled storytellers rely upon is the use of dialogue. In an exchange between two or more characters, the speakers may not be identified as frequently or as clearly as non-Native listeners and readers might wish, but the storyteller indicates who is speaking, either through changes in voice during an oral performance or through the context of the situation in which the dialogue takes place.

Second, many storytellers like Catherine Attla are able to highlight the structural foundations of a story so as to keep a listener mindful of the framework of the narrative. Reversals, parallelism, journeys away from home and back, doubling, and other structural devices of oral narrative are marked and delineated. Storytellers in this volume who are particularly adept at using these devices include Catherine Attla, John Dickson, Maudie Dick, Kitty Smith, John Billum, and Anna Nelson Harry.

Third, storytellers are keenly aware of their audiences' expectations that, whenever possible, narratives will include the names of places where events have taken place. Topographical references are a feature especially of historical narratives and personal accounts, but they also appear at times in distant-time stories, identifying a place known today whose origin the story explains or otherwise functioning as a link between a story that does not seem to reflect the world we know today and a place that is firmly a part of our world. Athabaskans are great travelers, and in any given audience some listeners themselves are likely to have followed the trail, fished the lake, hunted the mountain range, trapped along the creek that figures in the narrative. Storytellers with geographical knowledge of the territory about which they speak are able to draw these listeners into familiar narrative situations, if not as participants in the actual incidents related, at least as kindred spirits having shared similar experiences. The storytellers usually do not describe the natural features of land and water in detail; the Native place name itself evokes for the listeners a visual image. Writers and oral narrators represented in this book who demonstrate this skill include Katherine Peter, Gertie Tom, Peter Kalifornsky, and Katie and Fred John.

Fourth, the most respected storytellers are able to hold in dynamic confluence all of the culturally moral subjects that the story addresses. Since most of the stories are not simple didactic fables, they can consider a variety of important ideas and subjects and present them on a number of levels of appreciation. Such ability marks the most esteemed storytellers. As they do engage these subjects, they also address specific audiences with specific interests. Each recitation may be crafted to resonate with a particular group of listeners, often addressing social and political matters that may constitute an overriding cultural conversation. As Cruikshank suggests, the storytellers "tell stories that make meaningful connections and provide order and continuity in a rapidly changing world" (*Social* xiii).

We have outlined a few of the aesthetic principles of Northern Athabaskan narratives. Others may yet be defined by Native audiences and by scholarly readers of the texts. We warmly await such inquiry.

HISTORY OF RECORDING AND PUBLISHING

The earliest recorders of Alaska and Yukon Native tales were, of course, the Native people themselves, whose skilled keepers of tradition inscribed the narratives on the tracks of their memories, performed them through voice and gesture, and taught with them the values and practices of their varied cultures. After Caucasian outsiders settled on their lands and navigated their rivers, these newcomers sooner or later tried to collect and preserve some of those tales. Narrative artistry, however, was not their foremost interest, if it was a concern at all. Nor were the personalities and talents of individual storytellers, many of whom were never identified. Nor was English the first foreign language into which the tales were translated.

Westerners who collected and published Native stories included explorers, anthropologists, and missionaries. During the second quarter of the nineteenth century, for example, the Russian Orthodox priest Ivan Veniaminov, stationed first at Unalaska in the central Aleutian Islands and later at Sitka in southeastern Alaska, wrote down — in Russian — both Aleut and Tlingit tales as relevant to his ethnographical studies of the people. He published his work in 1840; no English translation of the entire book was published until 1984.

Through the first quarter of the twentieth century, anthropologists continued to focus upon Aleuts and Indians of the Pacific Northwest Coast, including southeastern Alaska. Waldemar Jochelson phonographically recorded tales in Aleut, translated them into Russian, and published the translations of a few, the Aleut texts of several others with their Russian translations. (English translations, by Jochelson himself and by others, came later; a definitive edition of the entire collection, with complete Aleut texts and English translations, was not published until 1990.) John R. Swanton collected both Tlingit and Haida texts, published many of them with English translations, and presented only English versions for many others. Franz Boas did the same with Tsimshian stories from British Columbia. Given the prevailing view of Alaska from the outside beginning with the first arrival of Caucasians until nearly the end of the nineteenth century, this interest in and emphasis upon the Pacific coastal areas should not be surprising. As Russian America, after all, the land had been divided administratively into five districts: Atka (western Aleutians), Unalaska (eastern Aleutians), Kodiak (Gulf of Alaska), Sitka (southeastern), and Interior or Everything Else, what today is regarded as the greater entity of the state.

Another important focus of attention in the North during the early twentieth century was the culture of the Inuit/Inupiat throughout their Greenlandic, Canadian, and Alaskan homelands and waters. The explorer Knud Rasmussen's ethnographical work is well known in English translation from its Danish original, and it includes many examples of northern Eskimo storytelling. More limited in scope, the published work of Diamond Jenness offers Inupiaq texts of numerous stories together with English translations.

Explorers, anthropologists, and missionaries each had different purposes in eliciting and recording indigenous tales. For explorers, they could sometimes serve as verbal maps, however incomplete, of the new territory. More

often than not ignored or overlooked, though, were the names of topographical features carried by the stories; published cartography tended to
give these places new names commemorating outsiders who frequently had
only tenuous connections with the North. For anthropologists, the antiquity of the stories confirmed or supplemented what Native people were telling them, and what artifacts were showing them, about their traditional
cultures. Imagery of material objects in the stories and situations in the narratives describing how those objects were used often illustrated what might
have been unclear in explanations by informants. Some of the storytellers in
our book, however, suggest that by having listened more attentively to the
stories as such, the ethnologists might have learned more about the psychological points of view of the Native people than they did by analyzing the
cultural facts that they were amassing. For missionaries, the traditional
stories that had been retold over centuries served as introduction to the Native languages in their most conservative grammatical and rhetorical forms.
The missionaries had to learn the languages in order to translate the Bible
and other Christian materials into those languages, the more readily to
teach the people and to convince them to accept the new religion.

Interest in the vast area of interior Alaska and northwestern Canada from
which the narratives in this book have come began early but developed spo-
radically. Although explorers remained active in this region, later years
brought to prominence the linguists who came to study the Native languages for their own inherent values as well as for comparative analyses in
more comprehensive studies of all Native American languages. The collecting and publishing of Athabaskan tales from this area can perhaps be best
traced according to three periods, in each of which the work of a different
profession seemed dominant. The era of the missionary spanned roughly
the half-century from the 1870s to the 1920s. For about the next forty years
emphasis fell upon the work of the anthropologist. The period from the
1960s onward has been that of the linguist.

During the first of these periods, four missionaries stand out as having
made invaluable contributions to the knowledge of Northern Athabaskan
linguistics and oral literature.

In the mid- and late 1860s and into the early 1870s, Father Émile Fortuné
Stanislas Joseph Petitot of the Oblates of Mary Immaculate worked among
several Athabaskan groups of the Northwest Territories of Canada. He collected many traditional tales of four peoples — Chipewyan, Dogrib, Slavey,
and Gwich'in — and according to an anonymous note in a recent English
translation, "wrote the words down in the Dene language" (*Book of Dene*
[vii]). *Dene* is the root word for human being (that is, Athabaskan or Indian

person) in most Athabaskan languages. Petitot learned at least these four languages, and in 1876 he published a substantial Northern Athabaskan–French dictionary. In recording narratives, he identified the storytellers and translated their tales into French. He published first the translations (in 1886) and then the original texts together with the French translations (in 1888). English translations of some of the stories, made from the French but checked against the Athabaskan texts, were not published until 1976.

Petitot moved on farther north to work among the Inuit. A contemporary Anglican missionary, however, the Archdeacon Robert McDonald, was working in the 1870s among the Gwich'in people and with their language in a manner that encouraged literacy among them for generations. Based upon the dialect of the Upper Porcupine River Gwich'in group in the Yukon Territory (and in a northwestern corner of the Northwest Territories), he developed an orthography used to translate the Book of Common Prayer, the Anglican Hymnal, and the entire Bible. These translations were first published in 1873, 1881, and 1898, respectively. The writing system is known as *Dagǫǫ* (in current standardized spelling of Gwich'in; in earlier orthographies *Takudh*, *Tukudh*, and *Tukkuth*, after the name of the Upper Porcupine group). No traditional Gwich'in tales were recorded in this literary dialect, but the religious publications constitute what Michael Krauss of the Alaska Native Language Center has called "the base of a literacy tradition that became by far the strongest of any Alaskan Indian language" (Peter viii).

The naturalist Edward William Nelson is best known for his monumental ethnography of both Yupiit and Inupiat in the region of Bering Strait and Norton Sound. Late in 1880, however, he traveled along the lower and middle Yukon and Innoko Rivers. The notes he kept of this trip remained unpublished for nearly a century. They contain six Athabaskan tales that he took down in English, three from Deg Hit'an and three from Koyukon narrators.

The Reverend Jules Jetté, a Jesuit, and the Reverend John Wight Chapman, an Episcopalian, both used the word *Ten'a* (Petitot's *Dene*) for the Alaskan Athabaskan people among whom they lived, Jetté for a quarter of a century, Chapman for more than forty years. Jetté began his work in Koyukon villages along the middle Yukon and Koyukuk Rivers in 1898; Chapman had worked at the Deg Hit'an village of Anvik since 1887. Without the phonographic recording equipment of their day, each man took down narratives in the respective Native language, which he had learned.

Jetté's situation was particularly difficult. His Koyukon storytellers performed in settings of total darkness, and when the priest tried to light a candle so that he could see to write, both narrator and audience became silent. Jetté explains his recourse: "I had, therefore, to trust to my memory for the main facts of the tale, and by dint of persuasion induce the story-teller to repeat them piecemeal during the following days" (38:299). He then checked his Koyukon-language texts by reading them aloud to groups of local people, but he admits that they "are not quite as rich in detail" as they had been in performance.

Like Jetté, Chapman wrote down stories while he listened to them being told but apparently not in a typical nighttime storytelling situation with an audience present. He later alluded to the difficulty that Jetté had faced and commented on the comparative ease of his own experience: "I have found several excellent story-tellers who were perfectly willing to sit down with me and tell their legends, repeating with the utmost patience, phrases which gave rise to any difficulty" (*Ten'a Texts* 2).

Of the stories he recorded, Jetté published thirteen in 1908 and 1909. Thirteen others remain unpublished among his papers in the Crosby Library, Gonzaga University. Jetté's work is a monument of linguistic and ethnographic scholarship. For each story his Koyukon-language text is accompanied by a literal, interlinear English translation and is followed by a set of notes explaining features of the language and of the culture and by a free English translation in prose. Jetté identified his storytellers by name and by home village.

Of the more than forty stories he recorded, Chapman published English translations of only six in 1903. In 1914, however, he brought out a book containing readable English translations of all the stories, followed by Deg Hit'an texts of seventeen stories (with literal, interlinear English translations of these). Chapman identified most, but not all, of his storytellers, either by name or by relationship with another villager. Ten years later, in 1924, Chapman used a Dictaphone to record another story in Deg Hit'an, told by Charlie Longman, an elder. In statements he made about this recording, Chapman demonstrated his appreciation of oral narrative as dramatic performance and his awareness of how much is lost not just in translation but in transcribing the Native language by hand and, especially, in converting from oral to written form. Stories written from dictation, he wrote, "can never give an adequate idea of the wealth of native idiom employed by a good storyteller, or of the variety of his intonations and the gusto with which he practices his art." Longman, he wrote, "was talking into the Dictaphone with the same gusto that he would have told the story anywhere. At the exciting passages he seemed to forget himself, shouting and gesticulating with one hand while he held the mouthpiece with the other. Once or twice he forgot that he was holding the mouthpiece, and began to wave that too" (*Athabaskan Stories* iv). Longman's story, titled "The Avenger," was not published until 1981, together with fifteen of Chapman's other Deg Hit'an texts, in James Kari's retranscription and retranslation.

During these years of the late nineteenth century through World War I, collection and publication of narratives from other Athabaskan areas of Alaska and the Yukon Territory were taking place but not in the Native languages. In 1900 Frank Russell published English versions of three Gwich'in and two Slavey tales, and in 1915 C. M. Barbeau published thirteen Gwich'in stories that had been told in English to Charles Camsell of the Geological Survey of Canada. In 1910 the Smithsonian Institution published as a pamphlet sixteen Han stories collected in English by Captain Ferdinand Schmitter, a United States Army physician stationed at Fort Egbert, near Eagle, Alaska.

The summer of 1923 marked a significant event in the history of collecting and recording Northern Athabaskan narratives. At a summer camp in Pennsylvania the renowned linguist Edward Sapir, a specialist in American Indian languages, sought out and worked with John Fredson, a remarkable young Gwich'in man employed as a counselor there between college years. As a youth Fredson had accompanied the Episcopal Archdeacon Hudson Stuck on his missionary travels by dogsled and by boat; at age sixteen he had maintained the base camp for Stuck and his mountaineering companions while they climbed Denali (Mount McKinley). Through the interest of Stuck and his teachers at Fort Yukon, Fredson had attended a private high school in Massachusetts and then the University of the South in Tennessee. For Sapir's study of the language, Fredson told nineteen stories in Gwich'in (eleven traditional, eight historical and autobiographical). Sapir took some of them down by hand and recorded others on phonodiscs. Then he transcribed them and made very literal, word-by-word English translations of them. Not until the mid-1970s were these narratives published, as retranscribed in the new standard orthography by Katherine Peter for the Alaska Native Language Center. A second edition in 1982 contained free English translations.

The stage in the preservation of Northern Athabaskan narratives in which anthropologists became dominant may be thought of as starting with the ethnologist James A. Teit's publication in 1917 of twenty-five Kaska stories in English versions. But sustained activity by anthropologists became noteworthy in the late 1920s and throughout the next three decades.

Two whose ethnographical fieldwork in the 1930s included some collecting of stories were Robert A. McKennan and Cornelius Osgood. Both relied upon English-speaking narrators or upon interpreters who would orally translate narratives told by others in the Native languages. Both ethnographers stenographically recorded the English versions or in unfavorable circumstances took notes. Later they prepared readable English texts for publication.

McKennan worked among the Upper Tanana people during the summers of 1929 and 1930 and among the *Neets'ąįį* (Chandalar River) Gwich'in group in the summer of 1933. He was unable to publish his Upper Tanana study until 1959 and his Gwich'in work until 1965. In each book, however, he devotes a substantial section to the stories and identifies all his narrators by name.

Osgood spent summer seasons among the Dena'ina (1931, 1932), the Han (1932), both Canadian and Alaskan Gwich'in (his principal focus in 1932), and the Deg Hit'an (1934, 1937) peoples. His book on Gwich'in culture, published in 1936, contains a section of six stories, all by Richard Marten of the *Teetł'it* (Peel River) Gwich'in group in the Yukon Territory. Osgood uses one story by *Vantee* (Crow River) Gwich'in narrator Charlie Crow to illustrate a brief discussion of shamanism. He published his book on Dena'ina culture in 1937, and in like manner, it contains a brief section of fifteen stories with narrators identified. Osgood acknowledges that these stories are "for the most part fragmentary," included "to give some taste of the myths of the people in so far as that can be done with free translations." The stories in all of Osgood's publications are generally regarded as abridgments rather than as complete renderings. Osgood published three volumes on Deg Hit'an ethnography, in 1940 (their material culture), 1958 (social culture), and 1959 (intellectual culture). The third volume contains a section of twelve stories without identification of narrators. This section is followed by a list of forty-five stories "interpolated in the descriptive text" of the second and third volumes, that is, to support or illustrate points in the ethnographical discussion. Osgood did not publish his work on the Han people for nearly forty years. When he did so, in 1971, he reprinted, as a section on storytelling, all but one of the narratives that Captain Schmitter had collected more than sixty years earlier.

Two other anthropologists whose work among Canadian Athabaskans resulted in major ethnographical works also published some narratives. John J. Honigmann spent the summer of 1943 in Slavey territory and the summer of 1944 and five months of 1945 among the Kaska people. He included five autobiographical accounts in English, with narrators identified, in his study of contemporary Kaska life, which he published in 1949. Douglas Leechman spent the summer of 1946 with the *Vantee* Gwich'in group and in 1950 published five of their tales. Effie Linklater had written four of these and told one, all in English, and she provided eleven additional stories in English to Charles J. Keim, a professor of English and journalism, who published them in 1964.

An anthropologist whose fieldwork, research, writing, and publications on northern peoples span seven decades is Frederica de Laguna. Although her studies focused initially upon the archeology of Cook Inlet and the ethnology of the Coastal Tlingits, she also worked among the Ahtna and several other Athabaskan cultures. She and Kaj Birket-Smith of the Danish National Museum, working together, first demonstrated that the Eyaks were a unique group, different in culture and in language from all their neighbors — the Eskimos of Prince William Sound, the Tlingits of southeastern Alaska, and the Ahtna Athabaskans of the Copper River Valley. In 1938 she and Birket-Smith published in English the first recorded Eyak stories. In 1995 she published, also in English, stories that she had recorded among the Koyukon and Lower Tanana Athabaskans in 1935.

A student, and later a colleague in the field, of Dr. de Laguna's is the anthropologist Catharine McClellan. Some of McClellan's work was with Coastal Tlingits and Gulf of Alaska Eskimos, and she and de Laguna together spent some time among the Ahtna and Tanacross Athabaskans. The principal focus of McClellan's work for the past half-century, however, has been the cultures of the southern Yukon Territory and northern British Columbia. In 1975 she published a major work on Southern Tutchone, Inland Tlingit, and Tagish ethnography, which incorporates stories or portions of stories to illustrate points in the ethnographic exposition (in the manner of Osgood). Her interest in the artistic values of narratives is especially strong: in 1970 she had published an exemplary study of eleven versions of a single tale as told by narrators from all three groups. It is to be hoped that the large number of stories that she collected while engaged in archeological and ethnological fieldwork will soon be published.

Ethnologist Richard Slobodin worked among Canadian Gwich'in groups, in particular the *Nangwachoo* (Mackenzie Flats) and *Teetl'it* (Peel River), from the late 1930s to the 1960s. In addition to his ethnographical works, he, like McClellan, demonstrated his appreciation of oral narrative as art by publishing in 1971 a valuable critical study of a single Gwich'in tale.

Marie-Françoise Guédon, in her study of a single Upper Tanana community (Tetlin, Alaska) published in 1974, included some narratives in English as supporting material for her ethnographical discussion.

Emphasis on linguistics in the collecting and recording of Northern Athabaskan narratives may be said to have started in 1960. It was then that linguist Michael E. Krauss joined the faculty of the University of Alaska. By the middle of the decade he was deeply engaged in study and documentation of the Eyak language; his work resulted in the private publication of an Eyak dictionary and a large volume of Eyak tales told by three of the four remaining speakers of the nearly extinct language, an older relative of the Athabaskan family. Krauss spearheaded the effort to persuade the Alaska state legislature to establish the Alaska Native Language Center in 1972. The center, a part of the University of Alaska Fairbanks, works to fulfill several related functions: studying and documenting Alaska's Native languages (there are twenty, eleven of which are Athabaskan); transcribing and translating texts; fostering Native literature; developing literacy materials for use in schools; and helping to train speakers of Alaska Native languages for employment as bilingual teachers and aides. Although the emphasis in Native-language studies at the University of Alaska during the 1960s and early 1970s had been on Eskimo languages, with the establishment of ANLC, Alaskan Athabaskan languages received equal attention. Joining Krauss in work with Athabaskan were two Native linguists, Eliza Jones and Katherine Peter, together with James Kari and Ron Scollon, among others. Their work has resulted in many publications of traditional (and some contemporary) narratives and is represented extensively in this volume.

Also active during these years were linguists associated with the Wycliffe Bible Translators and Summer Institute of Linguistics. Like the earlier missionaries, some of these linguists recorded and studied distant-time stories as documentation of the languages into which they proposed to translate Christian scripture and related materials. These linguists included Richard Mueller (who worked with Gwich'in), Paul G. Milanowski (Upper Tanana and Ahtna), and Raymond L. Collins (Upper Kuskokwim). Several of the Native linguists who joined ANLC had worked previously for these groups.

The major, and most significant, effort at collecting and recording Alaska Native stories during the early 1970s was the oral-literature project of the Alaska Library Association supported by the Alaska Federation of Natives and the Tanana Chiefs Conference. In 1972 and 1973 workers were sent with reel-to-reel tapes and recording equipment to thirty villages representing ten Native languages, six of them Athabaskan (Deg Hit'an, Holikachuk, Koyukon, Gwich'in, Han, and Lower Tanana). The field workers, some of them Natives themselves, sought out elders skilled at storytelling and elicited from them both traditional tales and historical and autobiographical accounts. The result was a bank of about seven hundred narratives, most in the Native languages, some in English. The original tapes are housed in the Alaska and Polar Regions Department of the Elmer E. Rasmuson Library,

University of Alaska Fairbanks. Copies on audiocassettes are available through the Alaska State Library system. A few of the stories have been published as broadsides by the Alaska Library Association, and certain individual narrators have had their stories published in other ways (for example, Belle Deacon's stories in this volume, initially published by the Alaska Native Language Center and the Iditarod Area School District). Not all of the material has been translated into English.

In the early 1970s some Koyukon and Gwich'in stories, in Native-language texts and English translations, were published in small booklets by Alaska State-Operated Schools; in an unusual venture, two stories that had been written in Koyukon and two that had been narrated orally in that language were translated into Upper Kuskokwim and published in individual booklets.

Also in the early 1970s, English adaptations of certain Deg Hit'an, Koyukon, and Gwich'in stories were published in somewhat lengthier books by the Adult Literacy Laboratory of Anchorage Community College.

Throughout the first half of the 1970s, the Alaska Methodist University Press, under the editorship of O. W. Frost, brought out a Native Alaskana series of traditional stories written in English by Natives and contemporary studies of Native peoples, some by Natives, some by non-Natives. Although most of these publications dealt with Eskimo storytelling and issues, one was a collection of Tanacross tales; after the series was discontinued, Frost privately published a long cycle of Koyukon tales by Arthur R. Wright, another protégé of Archdeacon Hudson Stuck whom the churchman had sent, as he was to send John Fredson a decade later, to the private high school in Massachusetts. (Wright's stories were first published in installments, from 1926 to 1930, in the Episcopal *Alaska Churchman*.)

During the late 1970s and early 1980s, the National Bilingual Materials Development Center operated as a unit of Rural Education, University of Alaska Anchorage. It published a number of small collections of stories from Athabaskan areas of south central Alaska and from southeastern Alaska. Like the publications of ANLC, these collections include Native-language texts and English translations but with less attention to linguistic concerns.

Following the transfer of jurisdiction and responsibility for public education in bush villages from the state to regional school districts in the 1970s, two Athabaskan districts in particular became active in publishing Native stories. Throughout the 1980s the Iditarod Area School District brought out traditional Deg Hit'an and Holikachuk narratives in small individual booklets, had them translated into Upper Kuskokwim, and published these in similar fashion, all with English translations. During the same period the Yukon-Koyukuk School District copublished, with ANLC, the works of Catherine Attla. It also sponsored and published a series of autobiographies told in English by elders from Koyukon, Lower Tanana, and Upper Tanana villages and edited by Yvonne Yarber and Curt Madison.

A number of independent scholars have collected and studied Alaskan Athabaskan stories. In 1966, Swedish folklorist Anna Birgitta Rooth recorded (and later published) narratives about the creation of the world as told in English by Lower Tanana, Tanacross, Upper Tanana, and Han individuals. Beginning in the 1970s and continuing yet today, Alaskan folklorist Craig Mishler has done extensive fieldwork, especially among Gwich'in speakers, recording many narratives in Gwich'in and publishing some of them with English translations, as well as writing critical studies of Gwich'in storytelling and music. In 1984, Jane McGary, while working as editor at ANLC, completed a master of arts thesis that critically analyzed the Gwich'in oral tradition and included Gwich'in texts and English translations of many narratives from the Alaska Library Association's collection together with some that Mishler had recorded. During the last two decades of the twentieth century, Alaskan educator Bill Pfisterer recorded and published two book-length autobiographical narratives, each by a remarkable Gwich'in elder, one of whom had lived for more than a century.

In Canada linguistic work with the Native languages of the Yukon Territory flourished in the late 1970s and early 1980s with the establishment of the Yukon Native Languages Project. Methods of documenting the Athabaskan languages of the Yukon — and Tlingit, spoken by many in the southern Yukon — included the recording of place names, traditional tales, and oral history, but the primary objective of the project was to develop programs and provide training for persons who wanted to become literate in the Native languages and to teach them in the schools of the territory. In 1985 the project became the Yukon Native Language Centre (YNLC), affiliated with Yukon College at Whitehorse. Its major emphasis continues to be the training of teachers and the development of curricula for teaching the Native languages in the schools. The Centre houses a large amount of textual material, but most of it remains unpublished. Linguist John Ritter directs YNLC, and its staff of Native linguists has included Gertie Tom, whose work is represented here. Linguist Pat Moore and anthropologist Julie Cruikshank have also been staff members of YNLC, and their work too appears in this anthology.

Other publishers of Yukon Native narratives have been the Council of Yukon First Nations (previously the Council for Yukon Indians), the Kaska

Tribal Council, the Lower Post First Nation, and the National Museum of Man of the National Museums of Canada.

TRANSCRIPTION, TRANSLATION, AND FORMAT

The history of the publication of Northern Athabaskan narratives shows that until twenty years ago they almost invariably appeared in print as paragraphs of prose. Texts recorded in the Native languages, translations into English, and versions narrated in English all appeared in this format, which had become standard for the publication of tales from aboriginal languages around the world. The paragraph divisions often seemed arbitrary, even by principles of composition in Western languages, and explanations were not offered of how the paragraphs might reflect structural components of the Native story, if such components were even recognized or acknowledged by the collectors and translators. This format, used almost exclusively over many years, resulted in readers of the narratives associating them with European "fairy tales" or folktales, as they had come to be known in published prose versions, and even with short prose fiction written in long-literate Western cultures. The format obscured the oral origins of the narratives and their similarities to the earliest, recited poetry and dramatic performances of Western and other civilizations.

It is true that, beginning in the mid–nineteenth century, songs of Native American peoples in the contiguous United States were being translated and published as verse, at worst in English accentual-syllabic verse with rhyme, at best in what later became known as unrhymed free verse. These translations sometimes encompassed other American Indian compositions in language, probably including some narratives. As recently as 1951, however, A. Grove Day, an otherwise astute scholar of Native American songs and art in language, could maintain that "the Indian customarily told his tales and legends in prose, and reserved the poetic style for non-prosaic purposes" (8).

The issue of format is inextricably entwined with two others. The first is that of translating from one language to another when the two differ vastly in structure and represent widely divergent world-views. The second is that of converting words spoken or recited in performance to words printed on a page. Our attention has been called to the Italian expression *traduttore traditore* (translator traitor), two nouns in apposition. The close similarity between their terms for the two agents perhaps gives Italians greater perception of the problems under consideration here than others may have. They might more readily have questioned the work of a nineteenth-century American poet, an admirer of Dante and of Native American poetry, than did his contemporaries in the United States. Henry Wadsworth Longfellow translated the *Divina Commedia*, and he converted Ojibwa oral traditions into his own written "Song of Hiawatha," one of his most popular and most famous poems.

The basic theory of translation in Longfellow's time was not substantially different from what it is today. Indeed, the scholar George Steiner maintains that "over some two thousand years of argument and precept, the beliefs and disagreements voiced about the nature of translation have been almost the same. Identical theses, familiar moves and refutations in debate recur, nearly without exception, from Cicero and Quintilian to the present day" (251). Since the seventeenth century, Steiner finds, theory has focused on three kinds of translation: "strict literalism"; "restatement," which, while reproducing the original as closely as possible, results in a new text "natural" to the new language; and "imitation, recreation, variation, interpretative parallel," all of which significantly adapt or modify the original (266). In the translation of the Native narratives of Alaska and the Yukon, literalism seems from the beginning to have been important, certainly as an initial method, and restatement has been a desired objective, more and more successfully attained in recent years. Imitation has generally met with hostility, probably because in addition to the collections already discussed, numerous other "retellings" of Native tales that were published earlier in the twentieth century drastically misrepresented the cultures they purported to depict.

"Strict literalism" is illustrated by the word-for-word translations of Alaska Native texts made by linguist Sapir and by missionaries Jetté and Chapman. The latter two used these literal translations as a base for composing "restatements" or free translations in which they attempted to retain the sense and spirit of the original while changing sentence structure, word order, and ways of expressing ideas. Their method has generally been followed by most of the translators who have worked with Alaska and Yukon Native texts from their time to the present. Practices have been conservative. If the "restatement" of an expression strikes the translator as too free, he or she often places the literal translation immediately after it in brackets, or the literal translation may be given prominence and the free version placed in brackets. Notes are frequently used to explain the literal translation of an expression or to justify the free rendering. This approach may be attributed to the continuing participation of religion-oriented linguists and the increasing involvement of academic linguists in translating the narratives of Alaska and Yukon Natives.

Steiner has postulated that "all theories of translation ... are only variants of a single, inescapable question. In what ways can or ought fidelity to be achieved? What is the optimal correlation between the A text in the source-language and the B text in the receptor-language?" The answer, he believes, remains that which Saint Jerome gave in the fourth century: partially in his own words, partially in Steiner's restatement, "*verbum e verbo*, word by word in the case of the mysteries, but meaning by meaning, *sed sensum exprimere de sensu*, everywhere else" (275). The spiritual mysteries of Christianity needed to be translated literally from Hebrew and Greek to Latin (for Saint Jerome), to Dagǫǫ (for Archdeacon McDonald), to Koyukon (for Jetté), and to Deg Hit'an (for Chapman); restatement could be used for the rest of the scriptures.

Alaska and Yukon Native narratives transmitted the ancient wisdom, the spiritual mysteries, of their cultures down through the ages. As attested by some of the stories included here, the words by which this oral transmission took place were valuable. It was of paramount importance to get them right and to tell the stories correctly, even by rote, according to some pronouncements. All this applied while the story still knew only its Native language. Thus translating it into French, Russian, English made extraordinary demands, more so than translating secular literature from one European language to another, a formidable enough task. Many of the academic linguists who have translated Alaska and Yukon Native narratives are themselves Natives fluent in the languages and bred in the cultures from which the stories come (and some of them did their first linguistic work with missionaries). Their non-Native colleagues have developed deep understanding of and keen sensitivity to the Native cultures. These translators, Native and non-Native alike, are at home both with literalism and with the restatement or transformation of an expression whose meaning cannot be translated literally into a judicious, often artful phrase or sentence in English — yet one that accurately conveys the sense and spirit of the original.

For the past twenty years the ideas and methods of Dell Hymes and Dennis Tedlock have strongly influenced the ways in which Native American texts and translations have appeared in print. Both Hymes and Tedlock are linguists, educators, and scholars; each has worked extensively with certain American Indian languages, Hymes with Chinook in particular, Tedlock with Zuni and Quiché. In their work of translation and transcription, Hymes dealt primarily with Native-language texts published in earlier years from hand-recorded transcripts, whereas Tedlock studied recent tape recordings of performed narration. Although the format devised by one for the presentation of narratives on the printed page resembles that devised by the other, each format represents a different theory of verse structure and a different method for perceiving it.

Stated in oversimplified summary, Hymes looks for recurrent patterns of structural particles in the Native-language text and treats them as markers signifying distinct segments of the narrative, which he sets up as separate lines and, where warranted by the structural features, separate stanzas. In the introduction to *"In vain I tried to tell you": Essays in Native American Ethnopoetics*, Hymes describes his work in this way: "The work is structural in method, poetic in purpose. The structural method is no more than an application of the elementary principle of structural linguistics: look for co-variation in form and meaning. The poetic purpose is to come as close as possible to the intended shape of the text in order to grasp as much as possible of the meanings embodied in this shape. Much will still escape. The gestures, voices, tunes, pauses of the original performances cannot be recovered for most of the materials dealt with here. Still, much of structure persists and can be perceived" (7). Many linguists working with Native materials have been influenced by Hymes's structural approach. For instance, Chad Thompson and Eliza Jones both comment on a four-part structure discernible in Koyukon distant-time narratives. Pat Moore has also identified a four-part structure in Kaska narratives and has labeled the sections acts in keeping with their presentation as dramatic performances. Hymes believes that such insight into the composition and the organization of narratives can reveal features of meaning not readily apparent.

Tedlock, with taped recordings to analyze, can recover the "voices, tunes, pauses of the original performances," if not the gestures, and for him it is the length of the pause that indicates where lines and stanzas should end. Tedlock discusses his theory and method in the introduction to *The Spoken Word and the Work of Interpretation*:

> Once the audible text is in hand, there is the question of how to make a *visible* record of its sounds. . . . the visible notation of sound . . . can make it possible for the reader to restore the temporal dimension . . . the flowing of long and short strings of sounds amid long and short silences in *measurable* time, which can be made visible through spacing. . . . What we have done so far, if we have punctuated our visible text according to the rising and falling contours of oratorical periods and shaped its lines and stanzas according to the stops and starts of dramatic timing, is to begin to free ourselves from the inertia, from the established trajectory, of the whole dictation era, an era that stretches (in the West) all the way back to the making of the Homeric texts. (5, 7)

Besides the pauses that he shows as line endings and, for longer pauses, additional vertical spacing between lines, Tedlock uses certain typographical devices to signify other aspects of the spoken narrative. For example, words and phrases in capital letters indicate greater volume, modifying words in italics and enclosed in parentheses describe tone of voice (for instance, *softly*), and extended repetition of a letter (six or eight *es* in a row) reflects the long, drawn-out pronunciation of the sound.

Over the past two decades, transcribers, translators, editors, and publishers of Northern Athabaskan narratives have generally adopted the basic Hymes/Tedlock template for most oral texts, whether spoken in the Native language or in English. Researchers such as Cruikshank and Ridington have extended and refined the basic approach. And most have followed Tedlock's method for determining lines and stanzas. Although the result may be called a verse format (as opposed to the traditional prose format), we shall call it a *line/pause format*, a more precise term that avoids confusion with the conventional forms of verse in Western cultures (Greco-Roman quantitative verse, Anglo-Saxon accentual verse, French syllabic verse, and English-American accentual-syllabic verse).

Through physical format on the page, in medium of composition (speech or writing), and with language of narration, the narratives in this anthology illustrate the diversity of contemporary Alaskan and Yukon Native literature. They are the work of seventeen oral storytellers and three writers. Most of these narratives were published for the first time within the past twenty years; two of them are published here for the first time. In some instances, the oral recordings and first transcriptions were made more than twenty years ago, but for the most part the work represented here is recent. Yet eleven of the narrators — more than half — are no longer living.

Four of the oral narrators chose to tell their stories in English: Peter John (whose Native language is Lower Tanana), the late Annie Ned and the late Kitty Smith (Southern Tutchone), and the late Angela Sidney (Tagish). For the Yukon women, Tlingit was a second Native language, and for them and Mr. John so was English. Considering the young people of their cultures to be their primary audience and recognizing that for most of the youth English had become the first language, indeed, the Native language, they chose to transmit their own life experiences and their knowledge of their cultural past in the language that those young learners would understand best.

English-language narrations by Alaska Native elders are altogether warranted and appropriate, according to linguist Ron Scollon in his prefatory note to each volume in the series of biographies published by the Yukon-Koyukuk School District of Alaska, from which we have made our selections from Peter John. And in the editing of those narratives, Scollon goes on to say, retaining the speaker's individual English diction is preferable to changing it to a more standard style (5). Anthropologist Julie Cruikshank, who recorded, transcribed, and edited the narratives of the three women, regards their English renderings as translations made by the storytellers themselves from their Yukon Native-language thought processes, and she summarizes the advantages as well as the disadvantages of these mental translations: "Their English is lively, colorful, and highly metaphorical. Although there is undoubtedly loss in form and style, the narrators are at least able to retain their own rhythm and idiom, their own expressions, the nuances of their unique narrative performances" (17). Cruikshank cast the distant-time narratives of her three storytellers in the line/pause format, their personal accounts in prose paragraphs. Curt Madison and Yvonne Yarber, editors of the school district series, published the biographies, including Peter John's, in prose.

Thirteen of our storytellers narrated orally in their Native languages. Eight of these have had their work published by the Alaska Native Language Center (in some instances cooperatively with a joint publisher). There is a preponderance of material from ANLC because more authentic narrations of these tales in Alaska Native languages are no longer likely to be found anywhere; the transcriptions and translations have been rendered carefully by linguists who are specialists in the respective languages and who, in most instances, have worked with the narrators themselves; the translations are faithful to the meaning and spirit of the Native-language texts; and the translations stand on their own artistic merit.

In addition to moving from prose paragraphs in their earliest publications to the line/pause format in their more recent ones, linguists at ANLC have used the space of the page in other ways in an effort always to keep the Native-language text prominent as a reminder to the reader that it is the source of and the authority for the English translation. By reproducing only the English translations, we have unavoidably but unfortunately omitted this important feature of the original presentation. In recompense, we can only describe that presentation here.

The Deg Hit'an stories told by the late Belle Deacon, the Koyukon stories by Catherine Attla, and the Tanacross stories by Gaither Paul were published with the Native-language text on one page (left or verso) and its English translation on the facing page (right or recto), both in line/pause format. This placement allows smooth reading in either language with, for the reader literate only in English, the constant equivalent display of the source language. The Eyak narratives of the late Anna Nelson Harry were published in double columns, that is, with the Eyak text in the left-hand column and the English translation in the right-hand column of the same page. This presentation keeps the Eyak original even closer to the eye of the reader of the English rendering. A free English translation in prose paragraphs follows the line/pause format of the dual columns, not page by page but story by story. The Upper Tanana stories told by Mary Tyone and the Ahtna narratives by Katie and Fred John and the late Huston Sanford, all in line/pause format, are printed in yet a third manner, each line of Native-language text followed immediately by its line of English translation. This method binds the translation tightly to the original. For the editors of this anthology, pulling out the lines of English for reprinting here is a humbling if not mortifying experience. One feels that one is undoing the strands of a beautiful cord and discarding the stronger, more basic one to present the weaker, less authentic counterpart.

The Alaska Native Language Center also published the work of two of the three writers represented in our book. The late Peter Kalifornsky wrote his narratives in Dena'ina and was actively involved in translating them into English. As written composition they were printed in prose paragraphs on facing pages, that is, Dena'ina text on the left and English translation on the right. Katherine Peter wrote her narratives in Gwich'in and made her own translations. They too were printed in prose paragraphs on facing pages. The work of our third writer, Gertie Tom, was published by the Yukon Native Language Centre. Mrs. Tom wrote her narratives in Northern Tutchone and, like Mr. Kalifornsky, was actively engaged in translating them. They were printed in prose paragraphs but in dual columns with Northern Tutchone text at left, English at right.

To account for our remaining five oral narrators, two were first published by the National Bilingual Materials Development Center. The Ahtna stories of the late John Billum and the Upper Kuskokwim stories of the late Miska Deaphon were printed as prose paragraphs, with each story complete in its Native-language original preceding the complete English translation.

The oral narratives of two others, the late Maudie Dick and the late John Dickson, were initially published by the Kaska Tribal Council. Mrs. Dick told her story in Kaska. Mr. Dickson, in an unusual narrative act explained in greater detail in the headnote, told his story partly in English, partly in Kaska. Each story was printed in Kaska with interlinear English translation, accompanied by a Kaska text in prose paragraphs, then a freer English translation, also in prose paragraphs.

Our anthology introduces one hitherto unpublished oral narrator. Lena Petruska told her stories in Upper Kuskokwim; their English translations are printed here in prose paragraphs. We are privileged to bring her stories before the reading public for the first time.

EDITORIAL PROCEDURES

For most previously published material, our copy text for the English translation or English version is that of the original publication. In two instances in which a revised edition has been published, we have followed it. In two other instances, the translators of the stories as originally published have given us revised translations for use here. And in one other instance the translator has modified the format of his translations (from prose paragraphs to line/pause format stanzas) for this volume.

Our goal has been to present these stories to new readers in the manner in which they have previously appeared in print or in the way they have more recently been prepared for us. In following our copy texts, we have remained faithful to the sentence structure, syntax, and punctuation chosen by the authors, translators, and/or earlier editors. We believe that their choices have been deliberate and are related either to meaning in the narratives or to usage in spoken language in Alaska and the Yukon. In the original publications, some of the translators/editors have explained in some detail their practices with regard to style and punctuation. We have made no attempt to conform these features of the texts with conventional standards of English composition, nor have we tried to edit such features of the texts for consistency with one another.

When meaning and Native narrative style are not at issue, we have modified the typography and mechanics of our sources in the interests of consistency in the overall presentation of the stories on the printed page.

The typeface in most of our copy texts is roman, with italic used for Native-language words and expressions retained in the English translation or English version. In the few instances in which the original editors have reversed this procedure (that is, using italic for the basic text, roman for Native-language words and expressions), we have reverted to the more common standard. One exception to our practice is noted and explained in the relevant headnote. In a few instances in which the original editor has not differentiated by typeface between English and Native-language words, we have used italic for the latter.

For personal names in the Native languages, we have used roman type in keeping with the standard practice of most current manuals of style. We have extended this practice to include the Native names for the people themselves and for their languages (usually the same term for both); if referred to as a word, however, such a name appears in italic type.

In reproducing the line/pause format, we have followed the most frequent practice of original editors in handling lines that are too long for the width of the page: the single long line is carried over into an indented second line (sometimes even into a third or fourth line, likewise indented). The lines that start at the left-hand margin (even when they do not begin with capital letters) are the structural lines; indented lines are continuations of preceding lines. However, songs and other interpolations within narratives are usually set as indented blocks in keeping with the format of copy texts.

To achieve consistency in presentation of dialogue, we have used only double quotation marks. Doing so has necessitated our changing to double quotation marks the single quotation marks used by some translators or original editors (and in one instance, double hyphens used to enclose segments of direct speech). Dialogue within dialogue (as when one character within his or her own speech quotes another) is enclosed within single quotation marks in keeping with standard practice.

Square brackets in the narratives as we reprint them are those used by the translators or original editors, in many instances to add words that have not been literally translated from the Native-language texts but that are needed to clarify meaning in English, in other instances to add editorial explanation. In like manner, all ellipses are those used by the translators or original editors to show omissions or lapses of one kind or another. None of the ellipses or bracketed material in the narratives is ours. Where translators or editors have used parentheses instead of square brackets around their own interpolations, we have changed the parentheses to brackets in the interests of consistency throughout our anthology (and in deference to standard practice). Parentheses that remain set off parenthetical elements in the Native-language texts and reproduce parentheses used by the translators and original editors both in those texts and in the translations.

Most of the narratives were accompanied in their original publications by translators' or editors' annotation, sometimes placed at the foot of a page, sometimes at the end of a story, sometimes all together near the end of a book. We have presented all such annotation as endnotes to individual stories. Other notes that we have added are labeled " — Eds." (Deviations from this practice are explained in comments introducing the notes in question.) Where the notes of translators or original editors have contained technical information that does not seem relevant to our presentation of the narratives, we have omitted notes or parts of notes; where notes have been keyed to the Native-language text rather than to the English translation, we have sometimes altered the way the note begins or other phrasing. Thus square brackets and ellipses in the notes do indicate our editorial comments and omissions, unlike those in the narratives themselves.

We have silently corrected obvious typographical and certain other clear errors, and we have standardardized the spelling of a number of common words (for example, using *toward* rather than *towards*).

The titles of two stories are enclosed in brackets. "To Build a Fire" is a title we have given to an otherwise untitled passage from a longer narrative by Kitty Smith. "The Girl and the Dog" is the title given by Birket-Smith and de Laguna to an untitled story told to them by Galushia Nelson; they used parentheses to enclose this title in their book on the Eyaks.

WORKS CITED

Athabaskan Stories from Anvik. Texts collected by John W. Chapman. Retranscribed and edited by James Kari. Fairbanks: Alaska Native Language Center, 1981.

Barbeau, C. M., ed. "Loucheux Myths." *Journal of American Folk-Lore* 28 (1915): 249–57.

Bergsland, Knut, and Moses L. Dirks, eds. *Unangam Ungiikangin kayux Tunusangin / Unangam Uniikangis ama Tunuzangis (Aleut Tales and Narratives).* Collected 1909–1910 by Waldemar Jochelson. Fairbanks: Alaska Native Language Center, 1990.

Birket-Smith, Kaj, and Frederica de Laguna. *The Eyak Indians of the Copper River Delta, Alaska.* Copenhagen: Levin & Munksgaard, 1938.

Boas, Franz. *Tsimshian Mythology.* Thirty-first Annual Report of the Bureau of American Ethnology for the Years 1909–10. Washington DC: Government Printing Office, 1916.

———. *Tsimshian Texts.* Bulletin 27 of the Bureau of American Ethnology, Smithsonian Institution. Washington DC: Government Printing Office, 1902.

———. *Tsimshian Texts* (New Series). Publications of the American Ethnological Society 3. Leiden: E. J. Brill, 1912.

Brean, Alice. *Athabascan Stories.* Anchorage: AMU Press, 1975.

Chapman, John W. "Athapascan Traditions from the Lower Yukon." *Journal of American Folk-Lore* 16 (1903): 180–85.

———. *Ten'a Texts and Tales from Anvik, Alaska.* Publications of the American Ethnological Society 6. Leiden: E. J. Brill, 1914.

Cruikshank, Julie. *The Social Life of Stories: Narrative and Knowledge in the Yukon Territory.* Lincoln: University of Nebraska Press, 1998.

Cruikshank, Julie, with Angela Sidney, Kitty Smith, and Annie Ned. *Life Lived Like a Story: Life Stories of Three Yukon Native Elders.* Lincoln: University of Nebraska Press, 1990.

Day, A. Grove. *The Sky Clears: Poetry of the American Indians*. 1951. Reprint, Lincoln: University of Nebraska Press, 1964.

de Laguna, Frederica, ed. *Tales from the Dena: Indian Stories from the Tanana, Koyukuk, and Yukon Rivers*. Seattle: University of Washington Press, 1995.

Eliade, Mircea. *Myth and Reality*. New York: Harper, 1963.

Guédon, Marie-Françoise. *People of Tetlin, Why are You Singing?* Mercury Series 9, Ethnology Division. Ottawa: National Museums of Canada, 1974.

Honigmann, John J. *Culture and Ethos of Kaska Society*. Yale University Publications in Anthropology 40. New Haven: Yale University Press; London: Oxford University Press, 1949.

Hymes, Dell. *"In vain I tried to tell you": Essays in Native American Ethnopoetics*. Studies in Native American Literature 1. Philadelphia: University of Pennsylvania Press, 1981.

Jenness, Diamond. *Myths and Traditions from Northern Alaska, the Mackenzie Delta and Coronation Gulf*. Vol. 13, part A of the Report of the Canadian Arctic Expedition 1913–1918. Ottawa: F. A. Acland, 1924.

Jetté, Jules. "On Ten'a Folk-lore." *Journal of the Royal Anthropological Institute of Great Britain and Ireland* 38 (1908): 298–367; 39 (1909): 460–505.

Jochelson, Waldemar. *Materialy po izucheniyu aleutskogo yazyka i fol'klora* (Materials for the study of the Aleut language and folklore). St. Petersburg: Rossiyskaya Akademiya Nauk, 1923.

———. "Obraztsy materialov po aleutskoy zhivoy starine" (Samples of living Aleut antiquity). *Zhivaya Starina* 24 (1915): 293–308.

John Fredson Edward Sapir Hàa Googwandak (Stories Told by John Fredson to Edward Sapir). Retranscribed by Katherine Peter. 1974–1976. Edited and translated by Jane McGary. With biographical sketch by Craig Mishler. Fairbanks: Alaska Native Language Center, 1982.

Keim, Charles J., ed. "Kutchin Legends from Old Crow, Yukon Territory." *Anthropological Papers of the University of Alaska* 11 (1964): 97–108.

Leechman, Douglas, ed. "Loucheux Tales." *Journal of American Folklore* 63 (1950): 158–62.

Madison, Curt, and Yvonne Yarber, eds. Yukon-Koyukuk School District of Alaska Biography Series. North Vancouver BC: Hancock House Publishers (for nos. 1–9); Fairbanks: Spirit Mountain Press (for subsequent numbers), 1979–present.

Mannheim, Bruce, and Dennis Tedlock. "Introduction." In *The Dialogic Emergence of Culture*, edited by D. Tedlock and B. Mannheim, 1–32. Urbana: University of Illinois Press, 1995.

McClellan, Catharine. *The Girl Who Married the Bear: A Masterpiece of Indian Oral Tradition*. Publications in Ethnology 2. Ottawa: National Museums of Canada, 1970.

———. *My Old People Say: An Ethnographic Survey of Southern Yukon Territory* (parts 1 and 2). Publications in Ethnology 6. Ottawa: National Museums of Canada, 1975.

McGary, Mary Jane. "Gwich'in Gwandak: Edition and Translation of Alaskan Athabaskan Narratives." Master's thesis, University of Alaska Fairbanks, 1984.

McDonald, Robert, trans. *Chilig Takudh Tshah Zit (Hymns in Takudh Language)*. London: Society for Promoting Christian Knowledge, 1881.

———. *Ettunetle Rsotitinyoo, Thlukwinadhun Sheg Akǫ Ketchid Kwitugwatsuị: Takudh Ttshah Zit Thleteteitazya* (Takudh Bible). London: British and Foreign Bible Society, 1898.

———. *Ettunetle Tutthug Enjit Gichinchik Akǫ Sakrament Rsikotitinyoo Akǫ Chizi Thlelchil Nutinde Akǫ Kindi Kwunttlutritili Ingland Thlelchil Tungittiyin Kwikit (Book of Common Prayer and Administration of the Sacraments and other Rites and Ceremonies of the Church according to the use of The Church of England)*. London: Society for Promoting Christian Knowledge, 1899.

———. *A Selection from the Book of Common Prayer, according to the use of the United Church of England and Ireland*. Translated into Tukudh. London: Society for Promoting Christian Knowledge, 1873.

McKennan, Robert A. *The Chandalar Kutchin*. Technical Paper 17. Montreal: Arctic Institute of North America, 1965.

———. *The Upper Tanana Indians*. Yale University Publications in Anthropology 55. New Haven: Yale University Press, 1959.

Osgood, Cornelius. *Contributions to the Ethnography of the Kutchin*. Yale University Publications in Anthropology 14. New Haven: Yale University Press, 1936.

———. *The Ethnography of the Tanaina*. Yale University Publications in Anthropology 16. New Haven: Yale University Press, 1937.

———. *The Han Indians: A Compilation of Ethnographic and Historical Data on the Alaska-Yukon Boundary Area*. Yale University Publications in Anthropology 74. New Haven: Yale University Press, 1971.

———. *Ingalik Material Culture*. Yale University Publications in Anthropology 22. New Haven: Yale University Press, 1940.

———. *Ingalik Mental Culture*. Yale University Publications in Anthropology 56. New Haven: Yale University Press, 1959.

———. *Ingalik Social Culture*. Yale University Publications in Anthropology 53. New Haven: Yale University Press, 1958.

Peter, Katherine. *Neets'ǫįį Gwiindaii (Living in the Chandalar Country)*. 2nd ed. Retranslated by Adeline Raboff. With an introduction by Michael Krauss. Fairbanks: Alaska Native Language Center, 1992.

Petitot, Émile. *The Book of Dene*. Yellowknife, NWT: Government of the Northwest Territories, 1976.

————. *Dictionnaire de la Langue Dènè-Dindjie, Dialectes Montagnais ou Chippe-wayan, Peaux de Lièvre et Loucheux.* Paris: E. Leroux, 1876.

————. *Traditions Indiennes du Canada Nord-ouest.* Paris: G.-P. Maisonneuve et C. Leclerc, 1886.

————. *Traditions Indiennes du Canada Nord-ouest: Textes Originaux & Traduction Litterale.* Alencon: E. Renaut-de Broise, 1888.

Report of the Fifth Thule Expedition, 1921–1924: The Danish Expedition to Arctic North America in charge of Knud Rasmussen. 10 vols. Copenhagen: Gyldendalske Boghandel, 1927–1988.

Ridington, Robin. "Voice, Representation, and Dialogue: The Poetics of Native American Spiritual Traditions." *American Indian Quarterly* 20, 4 (1996): 467–88.

Rooth, Anna Birgitta. *The Alaska Expedition 1966: Myths, Customs and Beliefs among the Athabascan Indians and the Eskimos of Northern Alaska.* Acta Univ. Lundensis, Section 1, Theologica Juridica Humaniora 14. Lund, Sweden: Gleerup, 1971.

————. *The Importance of Storytelling: A Study Based on Field Work in Northern Alaska.* Studia Ethnologica Upsaliensia 1. Uppsala: Acta Universitatis Upsaliensis, 1976.

Russell, Frank, ed. "Athabaskan Myths." *Journal of American Folk-Lore* 13 (1900): 11–17.

Schmitter, Ferdinand. *Upper Yukon Native Customs and Folk-Lore.* Vol. 56, no. 4 in Smithsonian Miscellaneous Collections. Washington DC: Smithsonian Institution, 1910.

Slobodin, Richard. "Without Fire: A Kutchin Tale of Warfare, Survival, and Vengeance." *Proceedings: Northern Athapaskan Conference, 1971.* Edited by A. McFadyen Clark, 259–301. Ottawa: National Museums of Canada, 1971.

Songs and Legends: Alaska Library Network Audio Cassette Catalog #2. Rev. ed. Juneau: Alaska State Library, 1979.

Steiner, George. *After Babel: Aspects of Language and Translation.* 2nd ed. Oxford: Oxford University Press, 1992.

Stories of Native Alaskans. Fairbanks: University of Alaska Press, 1977.

Swanton, John R. *Haida Texts — Masset Dialect.* Vol. 10, part 2 of *The Jesup North Pacific Expedition.* Memoir of the American Museum of Natural History. Edited by Franz Boas. Leiden: E. J. Brill; New York: G. E. Stechert, 1908.

————. *Haida Texts and Myths — Skidegate Dialect.* Bulletin 29 of the Bureau of American Ethnology, Smithsonian Institution. Washington DC: Government Printing Office, 1905.

————. *Tlingit Myths and Texts.* Bulletin 39 of the Bureau of American Ethnology, Smithsonian Institution. Washington DC: Government Printing Office, 1909.

Tedlock, Dennis. "Interpretation, Participation, and the Role of Narrative in Dialogical Anthropology." In *The Dialogic Emergence of Culture*, edited by D. Tedlock and B. Mannheim, 253–87. Urbana: University of Illinois Press, 1995.

———. *The Spoken Word and the Work of Interpretation*. Philadelphia: University of Pennsylvania Press, 1983.

Teit, James A. "Kaska Tales." *Journal of American Folk-Lore* 30 (1917): 427–73.

Thompson, Chad. *Athabaskan Languages and the Schools: A Handbook for Teachers*. Edited by Jane McGary. Juneau: Alaska Department of Education, 1984.

Toelken, Barre, and Tacheeni Scott. "Poetic Retranslation and the 'Pretty Languages' of Yellowman." In *Traditional American Indian Literatures: Texts and Interpretations*, edited by Karl Kroeber, 65–116. Lincoln: University of Nebraska Press, 1981.

VanStone, James W., ed. *E. W. Nelson's Notes on the Indians of the Yukon and Innoko Rivers, Alaska*. Vol. 70 of *Fieldiana: Anthropology*. Chicago: Field Museum of Natural History, 1978.

Veniaminov, Ivan. *Notes on the Islands of the Unalashka District*. Translated by Lydia T. Black and R. H. Geoghegan. Edited with an introduction by Richard A. Pierce. Alaska History 27. Fairbanks: University of Alaska; Kingston, Ontario: Limestone Press, 1984.

———. *Zapiski ob ostrovakh Unalashkinskago otdiela* (Notes on the islands of the Unalaska District). St. Petersburg: Imperial Academy of Science, 1840.

Wiget, Andrew. *Native American Literature*. Boston: Twayne, 1985.

Wright, Arthur R. *First Medicine Man: The Tale of Yobaghu-Talyonunh*. Anchorage: O. W. Frost, 1977.

Deg Hit'an

Deg Hit'an means "people from here" or, as linguist James Kari translates it, "people of the local area." That area comprises a section of the lower Yukon River, the lower Innoko River (a tributary of the Yukon), and the middle Kuskokwim River. *Deg Hit'an* refers to both the people and their language, and it is their preferred term for both. Until fairly recently, they and their language had been labeled "Ingalik."

Chapman classified Deg Hit'an stories as creation stories, Raven stories, and vapid children's tales. He also thought that the Deg Hit'an seemed to have little sense of history in their oral traditions. In his assessment, Chapman may have been influenced by Jetté, whose published collection of Koyukon tales he knew, and who also discerned three categories ("inane" stories, myths "intimately connected with what may be considered as their historical records," and stories "analogous to our works of fiction"). Despite Chapman's views, it appears that Deg Hit'an oral tradition does establish two distinct genres: historical and distant-time narratives. In both Deg Hit'an and its neighboring Athabaskan language Holikachuk, *xudhoyh* is the word for the distant-time genre. Osgood reports that such stories were often told in the kashim (community house) and that they were accompanied by audience comments. He also notes that it was unwise to tell a story twice in the same year because it might lengthen the winter (*Social* 37, *Mental* 137).

Belle Deacon was born September 23, 1905, and died November 7, 1995. The daughter of John and Ellen Young, she spent most of her life in the vicinity of the lower Yukon River. At fourteen she received her first formal education at the Anvik Mission school. Chapman had been at the mission a little over thirty years and was to stay a little over ten more. Ironically, the sixty-year-old missionary was engaged in his studies of Deg Hit'an storytelling at the same time that the teenage girl, hearing Bible stories at his mission, was also learning *xudhoyh* as part of the oral tradition from her maternal grandmother, Marcia. All through her formative years, Mrs. Deacon spent much time with her grandmother and from her learned not only storytelling but also craftwork.

After her first husband died, Mrs. Deacon began to support herself by making baskets. Later she married John Deacon, whose native language was Holikachuk. The couple lived together for forty-one years, first at the village of Holikachuk on the upper Innoko River and eventually at Grayling on the Yukon, after all the people of the Holikachuk village moved there. Mrs. Deacon was the mother of ten children and was honored frequently for her exceptional basket making, often being asked to demonstrate or participate in museum shows. In 1992 she was named a National Heritage fellow and honored in Washington.

A number of the stories that Mrs. Deacon recorded were told in both Deg Hit'an and English to Karen McPherson as part of the Alaska Library Association's Native Oral Literature Project. A selection of these stories is presented in *Engithidong Xugixudhoy (Their Stories of Long Ago)*. The tapes are archived in the Oral History Department of the University of Alaska Fairbanks Rasmuson Library. James Kari transcribed the tapes, and Mrs. Deacon and Kari did the translations. In 1981, 1985, and 1992, Kari recorded more stories. Those we have chosen are English translations of Deg Hit'an transcriptions.

Mrs. Deacon suggests that the story titled "Polar Bear" takes place in Yup'ik Eskimo country. Deg Hit'an territory borders the lands of Yup'ik-speaking people. The history of cross-cultural borrowing includes narratives as well as elements of material and social culture. While the story deals with the personal actions of jealousy and abandonment, it also explores the nature of social roles and the communal effects of violating implicit and explicit prohibitions. The final transformations express the basic assumption that the animal and the human worlds are not so far apart when spiritual power comes into play.

"The Man and Wife" is a richly textured narrative that casts Raven in the role of beneficent spirit guardian. Guilt and loss start the action moving, but the story quickly extends its scope to address attitudes toward the accumulation of possessions and personal happiness. While the marital roles of husband and wife ground the listeners' concerns, the nature of the interaction between spiritual beings and humans is also being defined. The story, which starts in imbalance, is brought back into balance with the restoration of the wife and the dispersal of goods.

SUGGESTIONS FOR FURTHER READING

Chapman, John W. *Athabaskan Stories from Anvik*. Retranscribed and edited by James Kari. Fairbanks: Alaska Native Language Center, 1981.

Deacon, Belle. *Engithidong Xugixudhoy (Their Stories of Long Ago)*. Fairbanks: Alaska Native Language Center and Iditarod Area School District, 1987.

de Laguna, Frederica, ed. *Tales from the Dena: Indian Stories from the Tanana, Koyukuk, and Yukon Rivers*. Seattle: University of Washington Press, 1995.

Osgood, Cornelius. *Ingalik Mental Culture*. Yale University Publications in Anthropology 56. New Haven: Yale University Press, 1959.

———. *Ingalik Social Culture*. Yale University Publications in Anthropology 53. New Haven: Yale University Press, 1958.

Ruppert, James. "A Bright Light Ahead of Us: Belle Deacon's Stories in English and Deg Hit'an." In *When Our Words Return: Writing, Hearing, and Remembering Oral Traditions of Alaska and the Yukon*. Edited by Phyllis Morrow and William Schneider, 123–35, 227–39. Logan UT: Utah State University Press, 1995.

Deg Hit'an Gixudhoy

The People's Stories

They said this about the way my stories go.
In the time of long ago [they would tell us this]:
"If you don't fall asleep, you can obtain the old wisdom"
that was being told to us when I was a child.
"Even if you are sleepy, you should try to stay awake.
And you shouldn't fidget.
You should just think about everything.
Then you'll get the old wisdom that was told to us in the past."
After we'd thought about it a little,
"Tell it to us," they would say to us.
When we start to tell it, [a story] is like a bright light ahead of us,
just as though it were written as we speak.

Taxghozr
Polar Bear

That's the one that came over from that other village. It's a brown bear woman. And this [one], on other side, it's a polar bear woman. So he tore up this brown bear woman, tore up his own wife. It's a really good story.

There was a village, they say, on the coast.[1]
It was a big village.
And a husband and wife lived in the middle of this village.
At the downriver end of the village,
a poor, dear grandmother and her granddaughter lived.
From time to time, the old woman would go up to the village.
She would go to find out what was happening in the village, and then she
    would go back home.
As for this young hunter,
a very powerful woman was married to him.
She was tough and very strong.
Whenever he looked around outside
she would suddenly attack him and beat him up.
"You looked outside at other women.
Why are you looking at the women walking around?" she said to him.

Then he paddled up to shore.
He didn't even look about, but he was really getting tired of her.
So at last he thought,
"It would be better if she left me alone.
Why, if I so much as look out at women, she always fights with me,"
he said, thinking.
He went back down into his kashim.
He towed seals to shore.

In his big boat he went hunting on the sea.
I don't know where he paddled, but he hunted seals and towed them back.
Then this woman, his wife, would go down to the end of the village
and give food to that poor, dear old woman all the time.
With that food, she raised her granddaughter.
They lived there a long time.
Everyone liked them and spoke kindly of them.
As for him, he had a good reputation.
He never looked around, because she was jealous.
So, then, things were all right.

Then one time he paddled back out [to sea].
He was gone a whole day, and
in the evening, far out on the ocean,
they looked for him, and far out on the ocean there was a kind of black
    spot.
It was him, paddling back in.
He paddled back to shore.
All the people came out to the bank and looked at him.
The women too.
He towed a great many sealskins to shore.
They were impressed when they saw them.
"He gets so many!" they thought.
At that, that wife of his got angry again!
I-i-y!
She started fighting with her husband right there on shore.
Meanwhile, all the people up there said,
"Why does she do that, that one?
She ought to just leave him alone.
She's just jealous, doing that again to the one she lives with," they said.

So then he went to his kashim.
In there she gave him a black eye.
She punched him in the face.
And then when she brought food in to him, he didn't eat.
He was very, very angry.
That was that.
He thought to himself,
"I should paddle away
somewhere far across the water to where my bones will lie.

It's better that I should paddle away, for I'm really tired of her.
Well, for a long time now,
even though I don't speak with women,
she has been beating me with no reason," he thought.
She brought food to him, but he didn't eat.
"Well, eat," she said, but he didn't; he just looked down all the time.

Meanwhile, down at the end of the village,
the poor, dear orphan girl was growing up.
She reached puberty, and
her dear grandmother raised her.
She didn't let her go out.
She went out only early in the morning.
"Don't look from shore out to sea.
Just keep looking down at your feet and come back in," she told her.
"That is how we [behave] whenever we menstruate," she told her.
So she did just that.
Early one morning the young hunter got up.
There on the beach was his big boat, with his big paddle in it.
He went down to it there.
He launched it in the water.
He started to load it.
He stuffed it full with all his blankets and all the furs from his cache.
As it was just starting to get light, he paddled away from shore.
Meanwhile, in the village, everyone lay sleeping.
The one who was menstruating went out.
She looked out on the ocean and saw a black spot on the horizon,
so she quickly averted her eyes.
But then she did not tell her grandmother.
Then out onto the ocean, outward
he moved, on water so calm it seemed frozen.
Then he paddled out to sea all day,
until at last the sun started to set in the west.
At last, being hungry, he ate some food,
and after that he rested, and then he started paddling again.
He paddled all night.
All night it was as calm as if it were frozen.
The next day he paddled all day again.
For two days and one night he paddled.
Once again, it started to get dark.

Poor thing, he paddled this way for two more nights and two days.
Then on the third day, at last, far across the water, he saw
signs of the shore appearing.
"I-i-y," he thought. "How tired I am!
Thanks! Land is visible," he thought.
He kept paddling quickly until
very soon there he was, paddling right up to the shore.
Meanwhile, all around him seals and whales were swimming about.
He didn't look at them or pay any attention to them,
he just kept paddling; what else could he do?
He paddled to shore and landed on a nice beach.
He paddled on upstream [on a river there].
And just then, there, back from the shore, there was a slough.
He paddled to its mouth.
He stood still there.
After a while he thought to himself,
"I ought to paddle up [the slough]; it seems good up there.
Up there I'll look for a suitable spot for my bones to lie," he thought.
So he just started paddling up [the slough].
He hadn't paddled very far
when he saw a house standing back from the river.
And a cache was standing up there too.
"E-e-ey," he thought.
"I wonder who lives there?
I hope it's a man's place," he thought.
"I hope it's not a woman's place," he thought.
He paddled to shore, and up on the bank
a big woman came slowly out of the house.
He looked at her.
Iy, she spoke to him in the other [Eskimo] language.
Then he said to her,
"I'm trying to go to where there are men.
I am doing this to find a place for my bones to lie.
I don't want a place where there are no people," he said.
"Don't say that; come up here and rest.
Why ever are you saying that?
Come, spend the night," she said to him.
So he walked up [the bank].
A big fish camp was there.
I-i-y, all around outside a lot of sealskins

were hanging up; nothing was lacking.
King salmon and plenty of everything was there.
It was after spring breakup.
Then she cooked and she fed him,
and he went to the bench across the room.
She handed the dish toward him over the fire.
"Come, have a little something to eat.
Then you can go to bed; you seem tired," she said to him.
"That's true —,
While I paddled for three nights and three days,
fortunately it was calm for me."
"Come on," she said to him.
"Go to bed, go on," she told him.
She went to bed on one side [of the fire] and he on the other.

Meanwhile, during all this time, across the water — in his absence across
    there —
his wife, i-i-y, got furious.
She went out in the village, wrecking things.
"Where is my husband? You hid my husband!" she was saying angrily.
She rushed down to the end of the village, and she knocked down the cache
    there.
"Why, we didn't hide him. What are you doing anyway?" they said, but it
    was no use.
She rushed down to the end of the village, and
she went to that old woman, that poor, dear old woman.
"Now my husband is missing.
Now they've hidden my husband," she said.
"Now I'll kill you all unless you tell me something.
Now he will never [be able to] stay away from me," she said.

"What are you saying anyway? Why, they didn't hide that one.
Here is a corner girl, in puberty seclusion.[2]
Well, she stayed there several nights.
Having gone out, although I told her not to look out to sea,
even so, she glanced out to sea," [the old woman] said.
E-e-y,
"She looked out and she saw someone paddling out to sea,"
she told her.
"Aha . . . well, I've wanted to know this.

I've been wrecking the village;
I should have spoken to you first," she told her.
"Tomorrow I'll just get a canoe, and I'll go in the canoe.
Then I'll paddle after him," she said.
"And as for this corner girl, I'll take her along in the canoe too."

"Oh no," said the poor, dear old woman.
"You really mustn't do that.
Why, one who is having her period doesn't go in a canoe."

"Well, I'll just take her in it anyway, that one," she told her [laughing
    meanly].
Then she loaded the canoe, and
putting that corner girl in the canoe in front of her,
she paddled out to sea.
How could they stop her?
"I'll kill you guys," she told them.
Terrified, they just put [the corner girl] into the canoe.
All the way across [the sea], then, it seemed calm to them.
Far across, she paddled over to shore.
I don't know how long she spent in doing this.
She was so angry that she paddled along very fast.
She paddled to the beach and on up [to the shore].
There was a slough.

And as for the others [the husband and his new wife], this is
what was happening with them:
"Well, okay," [the new wife] said.
"Your wife, your wife has gotten smart.
Your wife has paddled after you.
You mustn't go outside now.
You go here under the blanket, while I go to meet her alone."

"What will we do with one another?
I already married her, but I married you too.
I already took her [as my wife], so I better not [hide];
I've already stayed with her a long while.
I still love her very much,
in spite of her always fighting with me,
but finally I got tired of it and I came here," he said.

Here, it seems, that woman [the new wife] made a noise [making
    medicine]
while she [the other wife] paddled there.
"She's paddling along near here.
That's why I'm saying this," she said.
"Wait! Don't go outside," she told him.
Meanwhile, she ran back in.
"She's paddled into the slough, and
her boat is coming out there," she told him.
Mmm.
"A big boat is starting to appear," she told him.
"Get underneath this mat here,
for I don't know what we'll do to each other,
but if she attacks me first, I'll fight her," she said.

Then, down in the water, a boat was approaching shore, while
someone said "Yey . . . ," from out on the water.
"Adey', you have stolen my husband from me.
Can you keep living when you've stolen my husband from me?" she asked.

Meanwhile, [the new wife] stood up on the bank.
She began to descend toward the shore, walking along very slowly.
"Yey," [the first wife] said, and suddenly she charged up the bank at her.
Charging up the bank at her, she grabbed her and they started fighting.
Meanwhile, down below, that corner girl
hid down in the canoe, while
out by the shore
the ground started to shake.
The place was shaking and shaking and
there was not another sound except the shaking.
After a long time it quieted down, and
[the new wife] came back inside.
The woman of this place,
"It's all right now," she said to him.
"Well, she did it to me first.
Don't feel sorry or be sad.
Whatever I did, she did to me first;
she wronged me.
Don't be sorrowful," she told him.
"Come on now, get up from under that blanket," she told him.

"Go back outside," she told him.
Yey, outside everything was destroyed!
His wife was out there,
and she was in pieces; she had torn her to pieces.
She had torn her up.
He went back inside and started crying.
Saying, "My wife," he started crying.
But she went back to him.
"Don't cry anymore," she told him.
"For a long time she has mistreated you.
I will be your wife.
I am a woman too," she told him.
Thereupon he stopped crying.
Her hands and her fingers were nothing but blood.
For she had torn her entirely apart.
Having gathered all the pieces together and having piled them up,
they took the things down there in the boat,
and they piled them onto it, taking everything, and then they set it on fire.

And all of a sudden, as they were unloading the canoe,
there was a woman sitting in it, that young girl.
"Have pity . . ." she said to [the new wife].
"Have pity . . ." she said.
"Have pity on this poor little orphan," she said to her.
She was crouching down there in terror.
So the woman picked her up and brought her up the bank.
"Don't worry about it,
you can stay up there and we'll adopt you," she told her.
Meanwhile, she put all those things into the fire.
The big paddle and the big boat were also out there.

They started living there.
The young man worked and started to do well.
He started hunting for her a lot.
He started hauling caribou back from the uplands.
He brought back a lot of caribou.
One day he woke up and his voice was gone.
"What's wrong with you?" she said.
"I just remembered my village; that's why I'm this way.
This girl she brought with her

was being raised by a poor person back over there.
Maybe her grandmother wants her," he told her.
"Hey, we're living here quite well;
why are you saying that, anyway?" she said to him.

"We ought to go across there to get the news," he told her.
So they loaded the boat; there was a big paddle in it.
"Let's use the paddle that I paddled over here with;
let's use that one," he said to her.
"Oh no . . . ," she told him.
"We will be safe only if I use my paddle."
"Your paddle is too big," he told her.
So they got into the canoe and left.
When they got out onto open water, a storm overtook them.
I — y, it got so cold;
the waves were as big as mountains and
the boat pitched and tossed.
With the fourth wave he paddled through,
the paddle shattered.
They capsized.
Up on the waves the child came to the surface, that little girl.
Half of her was woman and half of her was fish.
And her hair streamed ahead of her, floating on the surface of the water.
Out in the ocean she came up to the surface:
"Grandchild! Grandchild!" she said.
At the same time, that man and his wife came to the surface.
One of them, the wife, suddenly had become a big, white bear, a polar bear.
Her husband also surfaced as a polar bear.
All right then, it is finished.

NOTES

1. Belle thinks the story takes place in the Norton Sound area.

2. The term "corner girl" refers to a menstruating woman. It comes from the
practice of sequestering menstruating women in corners of houses.

Nił'oqay Ni'idaxin
The Man and Wife

This story came from Anvik when I was around maybe twelve years old.[1] . . . One named Old Jackson told this story to four of us girls. And he told us to listen to it good, because if you don't get the stories [now], even if you never even think about it [again], you don't [ever] get the story. He told us to really think about it. It comes from way [back] generation[s], from the story beginning. They pass it on to one another. That's what he told us.

A man and wife, they say, lived at the mouth of a side stream.
They lived there year in and year out.
They didn't know how they got there.
They didn't know where they came from.

One time, when it was becoming fall, [the man] put traps out.
He did a lot of trapping,
and every evening he came back with marten piled over his shoulders.
His pack was completely stuffed full of skins, too.
His wife worked outdoors.
As she worked outdoors, she made a big pile of firewood.
She had all the wood piled up by the door.
She also built a fire every evening.
Having finished all that work, she sewed.
She made beautiful parkas, boots, mittens, caps, and blankets,
which she packed away in big storage bags.
What great big storage bags they were, so big.
She filled them up.
Then she put them in the cache.
She never told her husband what she was doing.

Whenever her husband came home, she would just be twisting thread.
He never asked her, "What are you doing?"
This made her very happy.
She cooked for him.
After that, always, "I really want some ice cream,[2] that's all.
I'm so accustomed to that fat ice cream," he said.
So she always took the ice cream to him.
After he ate that, then he skinned what he trapped.
He skinned all the marten and he left some in a big pile there.
There were many of them.
Early in the morning, before dawn, he would wake up.
He would skin the rest.
He put them on stretchers and hung them up outside.
After that he'd go hunting again.
"Why don't you stay home a day sometimes;
what will you do with all those skins you're getting, anyway?" she said to
     him.
"How many days will I be alone?" she asked him.
"I get very lonesome here."
"I do it because I enjoy being out," he said.
"Ah, keep yourself busy," he said to her.

Soon after that, he left again.
As soon as he left, she started sewing again,
putting her belt around her waist.
This young woman was just very neat, very clean and orderly.
She was dressed in very pretty clothes.
The young woman was very pretty.
She was just like a doll.
And her husband thought a lot of her;
whenever he came home, he always put her on his knees, holding her.
After he did that, they would eat and then go to bed.

Whenever he went out, she would make him fish ice cream.
Once in a while, too, she would make snow ice cream.
With all that, and the half-dried fish, they had plenty to eat.
I don't know how many years went by while they went on this way,
doing the same things every day, nothing else.
They would leave the ice cream outside to keep it cool.

In the summer, when it was not very cool outside, she made only enough
    ice cream for one meal
because she didn't want it to get sour.

Fall came again.
Soon it got cold again, and he started setting traps again.
I — y.
One day, I don't know what happened, but she didn't feel well.
And so then
"I don't feel like making ice cream," she thought.
"If he goes one night without ice cream, what will happen?" she thought to
    herself.
Soon evening fell as she was sewing,
and she didn't get any firewood because she just didn't feel well.
In the evening he came back.
He lowered his pack and she took it.
Then she gave him what was cooked,
and, when the time came,
"Where is the ice cream?" he said to her.
"Well, I didn't make ice cream.
I haven't felt well
all day," she said.
"No, I couldn't [make it]."
"Well, I really want it; you should still make it;
I won't get full [without it].
Whenever I eat that, I sleep well all night," he told her.

"Well, why don't I make a little ice cream for you?" she said to him.
"If you want to," he told her.
So she went outside.
She took a little bowl and she took a wooden spoon too.
Then she went outside for snow.
"I'll make it with snow," she said to him.
She went outside and was gone a long time.
She never came back in.
She was gone a long time.
Finally, he started worrying about her.
"Where is my wife, what's happened to her?
It isn't like her to be gone so long; when she goes out,
she usually comes right back," he thought.

Then he put on his boots and went out after her.
He went out to search for her.
He called for her, but where was she?
He looked for her up in the cache.
It was quiet.
She wasn't there.
Then he went into the house and lit a piece of birch bark.
He walked around outside with it, but he could not find any tracks.
Then he went down the path, and there was her bowl.
There it was, lying beside the trail.
Farther down [the trail] lay the wooden spoon.
The tracks went only as far as the water hole, and there were no other tracks
     around.
"Iiy, what has happened to her?" he thought.
"What could have happened?" he thought.
He went back in and started crying.
"It's all my fault.
Why did I ever tell her to make ice cream?
I should have gone without it," he thought.
He started crying and he just kept on crying.
Early the next morning he went out again, searching for her.
But there were no tracks anywhere.
Where he had his traps there were only his own tracks.
Out where she gathered wood were only her own tracks.
He searched all around the village for human tracks,
but there were no others.
He went inside.
He started to cry.
He cried all day.
He didn't eat.
He started getting thin
without realizing it.
He would eat a tiny bit, a little dried fish
for the chest pains when he became very hungry.
When he looked down at his fingers, they were all bony.
He felt his body with his hands.
When he felt his face with his hands, his cheekbones felt as if they were
     protruding.
"That's fine," he thought.
"Because of me, she's gone," he thought.

"So it must be that [I'm destined to] cry in this house and my bones will
     drop here.
I'll starve to death here.
It will be fine," he thought.
"What happened to her was my fault," he thought.
Finally, he went outside to get a little of the wood
that his wife had stacked by the door.
His strength was failing.
He was so weak, he could barely go outside.
He bound something around his belly.[3]
He tied it around his stomach and bound up his clothes.
He went outside; he was getting so thin.

All fall this happened.
Then it came to be midwinter.
It had become dark outside.
Outside the door there came the sound of someone knocking the snow off
     his boots.[4]
The man just did not know what to do.
"Maybe my wife came back," he thought.
He stayed still there, barely breathing.
"Who could it be?" he was thinking.
"Who could it be at this place where my bones are about to drop?" he
     thought.
Then he pushed the door curtain aside.
Who was this?
A poor, dear old man was there;
a nice, little, very white person[5] was there, and he came inside.
"Ne — ," he said to him.
"Someone is there," he said to him.
"Grandchild," [the old man] said to him.
"Whenever I look down on this earth[6]
and see you, I'm very sorry for you.
You are crying in the palm of my hand.
I knew your bones would drop very soon; that is why I've come here.
I wouldn't do this for anyone else, but I think very highly of you.
You were so good to each other, and now your wife is gone from you.
That is why I've done this.
You are lamenting right in the palm of my hand," he said to [the husband].

"Well?" the man said to him.
"I hope what you say is true;
I won't forget what you are saying," he said.
Then he just girded himself tightly, and then he went outside.

There were some caribou skins rolled into a bundle.
There was a marten-skin blanket
that had a caribou fawn skin sewn to one side.
He brought it inside for [the old man].
"Here, you'll sleep on these while you stay with me.
I'm really thankful to you," he told him.
"I feel as if my bones will drop soon.
My time is coming.
I'm so lonely; still, with my wife it was nice.
It was just as if many people were here.
Now that she is gone from me, I don't know what to do," he said to him.
Then, "Come on," the old man said to him.
"She is not anywhere on this earth," he told him.
"She was taken to a land deep down in the water.
Down below is an invincible one.
A giant did it.
He willed her not to make ice cream that day.
He thought that
your pretty wife was the only woman up above [his world].
So he stole her," he told him.
"He is the one who did it, but [you] can't do anything about it," he told
     him.

"Is there some way [I] might get her back?" he said.
"No," he told him. "Only with my help will you get her back.
You can get her back with my help, and we'll all be well."

"Well, I hope that my bones won't fall without her [in her absence].
I really want her back," he told him.

"All right, everything is in my palm.
She is down there crying, too," he said.
"And you are constantly crying here on earth," he told him.
"Meanwhile, up there in the sky,

far, far up in the sky, I am a Raven person.
There is another place up above there, above the place I come from," he told
    him.
"Yes!" he said to him.
"Come on," he told him.
"Come, get a good sleep and eat a little,
because we have a lot of work to do,
and you have no flesh on you," he told him.
So at that, he took a little to eat,
as is good for a person who has fasted.
Then he lay down, and having eaten a little, he went to sleep.
I don't know how long he had slept
when the old man said to him, "Grandchild,
how are you?"[7] he said to him.
He woke up at once.
"I already woke up," he said.
"Come on," he said to him.
"Down below here I saw something standing.
There's a very big spruce tree that we'll work on all day," he said to him.
"We'll cut it down," he told him.
Then they took a wedge down [to the tree].
They pounded it in with an axe,
and they chipped away at the tree.
That was a stone axe.
They kept chipping at it with a little stone axe all day.
There were only stone axes then, because there was no iron.
They chipped all day until dark,
like beavers eating a tree.
They knocked it down that way,
right there on the bank, and it fell nicely.
And then they went to it and limbed it.
They limbed it and then,
e — y,
they limbed it some more and cut the top off, too.
So then he made it about twelve arm spans long.
The next day he started peeling the bark from it.
They went back.
The man realized that the old man had not eaten at all.
"Why aren't you eating?" he asked him.
"Well, I don't eat that food of yours;

I can't eat your food, grandchild," he told him.

"I don't eat the food of this world.

From up there [in my world] is the only food [I can eat]; I brought some of
    it with me," he told him.

"Ah," he said. "All right," he said.

The man started to eat and gave some of it to the old man, who was very
    grateful.

"Make a fire down on the bank tomorrow,

and put this food on the fire; it will burn," he told him.

"It will go up into the sky that way," he told him.

"E — y."

The next day they peeled all the bark off the tree.

Then they started to carve a head.

The head was made in the shape of a fish.

Then he carved its head into the shape of a big pike's head.

He shaped it with his hands until finally he had completed the whole head.

Down below

they carved out its insides, its stomach, and its mouth.

An entire month passed without their realizing it.

They worked at it for an entire month.

They thought they were just starting on it.

"Hey, this is too much," he thought.

[Raven] looked up now and then;

the sun was going back to the warm side.

So then, "That's it," he told him.

"It's finished," he told him.

What a big fish; he had made it in the shape of a big pike.

Its tail was big too.

"Come on," he told him.

"Grandchild," he said to him,

"we will tie a rope to it and

drag it over there," he said to him.

Then they tied a rope to it and tried to drag it.

I — y, they could barely drag it, but they dragged it there.

They left it down at the water hole.

"Come on," he told him.

"Do you have anything to paint it with?" he said to him.

"Yes," he said.

"What color?" he asked.

"Grayish and dark black," he told him.

"That's all I have to paint it with," he told him.

"Okay, go on up to get it," he said.

He went up into the cache to search for it.

He found a certain rock, used as paint [when crushed into] a powder, and he brought it down.

Then they put it in a little dish and mixed it with some water.

He started stirring it.

After that they started to paint.

They painted the back side all gray,

and they painted white spots [like those of a pike] on it.

E — y, it was such a beautiful fish.

"All right," he said to him.

"Go up [to the cache] again," he told him.

"You people have everything here.

You are the richest people in all of the world that I see.

Your wife is so skillful," he told him.

He went back up into the cache.

In it were eyes like large beads.

He brought down those things [beads] that were like eyes.

"Is this all right, I wonder; I hope it's what you want," he said.

"That's it," he said,

"That's just it," he said.

Then he used a medicine song on those things in some way and then immediately put them into place.

The eyes started moving.

The eyes wiggled around.

The eyes moved this way and that.

The young hunter was very surprised.

"I — y, what is he doing?"

"All right, go back up [to where you are staying]," he told him.

"Go back up and fetch an ice chisel," he told him.

So they walked the length of [the fish] and measured it.

It was twelve arm spans long.

"All right," he said.

"Chop a hole in the ice big enough for it," he told him.

They chopped out a hole the right size beside it.

Then, "That's it, it's finished," he said.

"Go back up [to camp] again," he said.

"Go and fetch a clay lamp about this big," he said.

"Pour some oil into it," he said.
"Then put a wick into it so it can be lit," he said.
"It will be your light," he told him.
Then he went back up for it.

He brought back down a little clay lamp.
He filled it with oil and then got it ready to burn down there.
E — y, what was he going to do?
He was so surprised.
[Raven] had done so much.
"How can he do this?" he thought.
[The man] did as he was told.
"All right," [Raven] said to him.
"In your wife's sewing bags
are two least weasel skins," [Raven] told him.
I wonder how he knew that.
"All right," he said.
"I already know what is in there," [Raven] told him.
He untied her bag.
He untied it and reached inside,
and felt a weasel about so big with a short tail.
The weasel skins in there were from up in the sky.
"Okay," he said.
"Go up and get some food for your lunch," he said.
"They won't discover you away from the village;
[the fish] will stop traveling with you," he said.
"When it lands, you will come out of its mouth," he said.
"This lamp will keep burning," he said.
He gave him the weasel skin.
Afterward, "Go back up again," [Raven] said.
"Bring back some black birch punk," he said.
"You will go to another village with it," he said.
"Hold these weasel skins in your hands.
Hold them well.
In one hand you will also hold the birch punk.
You will stop when you get behind the village," he said.
"There is a lot of grass piled in the forks of trees
in which you will hide [behind the village]," he said.
"That birch punk is going to talk to them," he said.
That Raven said this.

"Yes," [the man] said.
"I will do only what you have said," he said.
He went into the fish,
and Raven blew with his hands and made medicine with a song.
He hit the fish on the back and it sank to the bottom [of the river].
Down on the bottom, a humming noise came out of the fish, shaking the
    man.
He didn't know how the noise was made.
It was like electricity to him.

He fell asleep.
He woke up and ate.
He ate a little bit now and then.
The noise continued.
He fell asleep again.
How long the fish kept doing this!
He woke up suddenly, and it had stopped.
He got up and it had landed on shore.
Just as Raven had told him,
the fish's head was on the shore, and [the man] ran out from it.
It was a nice beach.
He came out from it to a village
where they were hollering and playing ball.
At that village was the man, a powerful giant.
He brought a crying woman out into view.
They were shouting that they were going to have a mask dance.
Then [the man from the fish] went up[stream] in the brush; he went
    upstream.
Up there
was a big kashim and many winter houses.
He stopped there.
He went upland from there to where grass was piled in forks of trees.
He hid behind [the grass].
Meanwhile, none of the people saw him.
He still held the weasel skins.
He held onto them, as [Raven] had told him.
Then [the people] were starting to have a mask dance and singing.
"In the morning there will be a mask dance," someone said.
Then two women came, holding a woman by the arms;

it was his wife!
Such a pretty woman!
She was thin from crying;
tears fell from her eyes.
She cried.
They brought her to the kashim.
"I need to relieve myself.
I'll go behind the grass," [she said].
"Okay, we will take you."
"You wait for me here.
You hold me all the time, taking me around.
That's why I cry.
Leave me alone and I won't cry.
I'm already your sister-in-law.
Why do you do this to me all the time?
You always hold my arms and carry me around," she said.

Up there [in the tree], meanwhile, he was holding the punk.
He put it down out there, as Raven had said.
She went there, and all of a sudden her husband was standing there!
He handed a least weasel skin to her.
They each swallowed one.
Then they turned into little weasels and ran downstream.
They ran back into the brush.

"Ready?" [one of] the other women asked.
"I'm not ready," [the birch punk] said.
"How can I go so quickly?
Just a moment," it said.
"Just a moment."
Meanwhile, [the man and his wife] went downstream,
pulled the skins off, and became human again.

They entered the mouth of the fish, whose head was [still] on the shore.
[The other women] were looking for her.
The two women started going inland.
Below was the birch punk.
It was talking!
"Our sister-in-law disappeared!" they shouted.

"She disappeared?"
There was a noise in the kashim.
They started to shout for her.

"You won't live; you won't take her back.
I am powerful.
I'll kill them all," [the giant said].
There was a boat by the shore.
Because there was water,
it was summer,
they put arrows and big spears into the boat.
Downstream there, the big fish still had its head on shore.
They went to it.
They started to shoot arrows at it down there,
and it started to back away from the shore.
I — y.
[The wife] didn't say anything to [her husband].
[The fish] started to back away as [the villagers] approached.
As they were about to shoot arrows, it shook.
[The villagers] all got into a canoe,
and it tipped over with them in it.
As they came back up to the surface, the fish started to swim around.
Blood went everywhere.
Yi — y, what will happen?
The fish swam up to where the village was.
It swam around below the village and swamped the village with waves.
The village disappeared.
Only the remains of the village floated around.
Afterward, the fish straightened itself,
and it began making that humming noise again.
Then the man and woman in the fish noticed that it had stopped.

Raven was standing there [on shore] waiting for them.
"Very quickly, my grandchildren, quickly," he said.
"I [had] told the fish not to do anything wrong," [Raven said].
"The fish ruined the whole village.
You should have told it not to do it like that," [the man said].
"It happened when you were in danger.
Come quickly," [Raven] told them.
They ran inside [the house].

"Quickly, go to the cache," he said.
"Urinate on a rag
and bring it down," he said.
"That fish is too dangerous," he said.
Its entire face
and its teeth were covered with blood.
[Raven] washed its head and teeth [with the rag].
He cleaned its teeth and made them white.
Then he put teethlike bones into its mouth.
Its eyes were moving.
"Okay," [Raven] said.
"From now on, stay in a place where there are lakes, where no one will go,"
he said to the fish.
"For people who step there on the ice of the lake,
you will shake your little tail," [Raven] said.[8]
[The fish] went to the bottom.
They went back up the bank.
The fish went to the bottom, but they didn't know where.

They went up the bank.
"Okay," he told them.
The woman started to work.
All day long she made ice cream with fat in it.
She washed her face
and changed the clothes she was wearing.
They got dressed up in new clothes.
They got cleaned up and she started to work.
She made a lot of grease ice cream for him.
She was going to give the frozen fat and cooked game to Raven.
"This is the last time I'll come with you for a long time.
I was here in your world, and your wife has returned.
So I'll stay with you just one more night.
I've been in the world of humans for a long time.
I am Raven from the upper world.
I don't eat this food.
I live only on food that is placed in fire," he said.
"I'm wearing this worn-out marten parka," he said.
"I'm wearing wolverine boots.
They are too old, too.
I've worn them a long time.

If you dress me anew, I'll be very grateful to you," he told them.
"I'll camp in that marten blanket and fawn skin blanket and sleep,
and I am thankful to him [the husband].
But you won't dress me in that," he said.
"In the morning, as it gets light,
I'll leave you," he said.

"We love you and what you say," they said.
"Well, just go outside with me," he told them.
"After you do everything,
you will build a fire out there on the bank," he told them.
"You will put my bedding on the fire.
Afterward you will put the new clothes on it.
Put the food on the fire first," he told them.
"First put the food on the fire, then put on the other nice food.
Then it will all burn.
You'll make me disappear afterward," he said.
Then they went outdoors.
"Well, now," he said to them, "Goodbye, my grandchildren.
I brought her back for you,
so now you'll live well again," he said to them.
"I did that for you because you would have died in my presence," he said.
Then he floated upward.
It was white beneath him.
He disappeared behind the clouds up in the other world.
That is as far as the story goes.

NOTES

1. When Belle tells this story in English, she calls it "The Old Man Who Came Down from Above the Second Layer of This World."

2. In Northern Athabaskan cultures ice cream is a combination of animal fat or oil, dried meat or fish that has been pounded to crumbs or powder, and berries, all whipped together and kept cold or frozen. — Eds.

3. Belle says that this was done in times of starvation. He was so skinny that his clothes were loose and he needed binding to keep them on him.

4. Two of Catherine Attla's Koyukon stories (not included here) explain that this is a sign of friendly intentions on the part of the person about to enter the house. See *Sitsiy Yugh Noholnik Ts'in' (As My Grandfather Told It)*, pp. 119, 121, 215. — Eds.

5. Later in the story we learn that this man is Raven.

6. Osgood understood the people to have believed in a universe of four levels

(*Mental* 106). Besides "the apparent world of normal living things," three other levels either above or below the surface of the earth were occupied by various supernatural creatures and by the temporarily or permanently departed spirits of human beings. One of these levels, according to Osgood, was called "up on top of the sky." — Eds.

7. Concerning the Deg Hit'an expression *Q'ithe li*?, which he translates as "how are you?," Kari notes that "Belle comments that these are high words." — Eds.

8. The fish will thus indicate someone's impending death.

2

Koyukon

The name Koyukon derives from the Koyukuk and middle Yukon Rivers where the villages of these Athabaskan people are situated. Their rich oral tradition has been noted for generations. Structuring this tradition is a broad distinction between *kk'edonts'ednee* and *yooghe done*. The first genre consists of stories of the distant time when humans and animals could talk to each other and when they shared a common nature. While many actions in *kk'edonts'ednee* set precedent for actions today, the expectations and codes of behavior were different in the distant-time world. *Yooghe done* embody narratives set in the recent past, often personal narratives. Sometimes they emphasize the mistakes people can make or the successes they achieve by overcoming obstacles. They might transmit knowledge vital for success in hunting or for prosperous living in a complex world. While they entertain, they also instruct in a practical manner.

Traditionally, *kk'edonts'ednee* were told in "high language." This style used many metaphors and archaic words. The narratives were told in the dark during the winter, often in a slow and deliberate manner. The audience was expected to make some response at appropriate times, and many people have commented on the active conversations that could accompany the telling.

Catherine Attla of Huslia was born in 1927. She speaks of being lucky to be raised by her grandparents Francis and Christine Olin. Both were excellent storytellers, and they taught her the many stories that she knows. Mrs. Attla did not speak English until she was fourteen. Later, as she continued subsistence activities, she learned to read and write. She worked a number of jobs and in Huslia started her own sewing business. She has worked in the schools and on many state and local committees and boards. For years she has been known in the interior of Alaska not only for her craftwork and storytelling but also for her many efforts to perpetuate and foster Koyukon culture. She has published three books of *kk'edonts'ednee*, from the first two of which we have taken our selections: *Sitsiy Yʉgh Noholnik Ts'in'* (*As My Grandfather Told It*), *Bekk'aatʉgh Ts'ʉhʉney* (*Stories We Live By*), and *K'ete-taalkkaanee* (*The One Who Paddled Among the People and Animals*): *The Story of an Ancient Traveler*.

These narratives were recorded in 1976 in Denaakk'e (the Koyukon Athabaskan language) and transcribed between 1978 and 1980 by Eliza Jones, noted Koyukon linguist. The tapes are archived in the Alaska Native Language Center. Jones, with the help of Melissa Axelrod, Chad Thompson, and Bob Maguire, translated the narratives. Jones, herself a Koyukon Athabaskan, recalled storytelling sessions from her youth and translated with a special sensitivity. Her goal was to create English translations that are as close to the Koyukon as possible without presenting awkward English. When that goal proved difficult, she opted for accurate reproduction of the style of the Koyukon. Eliza Jones's achievements in working with her native language were recognized by the University of Alaska Fairbanks, which granted her an honorary doctor of letters degree in 1990. The *Koyukon Athabaskan Dictionary*, published by the Alaska Native Language Center in 2000, is the monumental result of work begun by Jetté one century ago and continued by Eliza Jones since 1974. The publication recognizes Jetté and Jones as coauthors.

The introduction to *Stories We Live By* presents Catherine Attla's statement about the concluding formula used by Koyukon storytellers: "It is said that if we do not say the phrase, 'I thought the winter had just begun and now I've chewed off part of it,' the winter will be very long. When it was like that in the old days, times were very difficult. Each time we tell a story, we always repeat this phrase: 'I thought the winter had just begun and now I've chewed off part of it.' That was the way they prayed, by saying that. They prayed to the spirits for a better life. Praying to the spirits is the same as praying in the Christian sense." Often Mrs. Attla has likened the function of these stories to the function of the Bible for Christianity. As sacred history, the stories present the wisdom of the past, while they reveal insights necessary for living in the world today.

In these selections we are introduced to the elusive trickster/transformer Raven. He is the powerful and humorous character central to many *kk'edonts'ednee*. Motivated by his desires, especially for food, he transforms the world, kills monsters, establishes precedents and social institutions like the potlatch. Paradoxically he can mold the positive nature of the world while teaching by negative demonstration.

In "K'etl'enbaalots'ek," the reader learns something of the appropriate and inappropriate interactions between the world of the dead and the world of the living. We also discover the nature of the afterlife world. In "The Woodpecker Who Starved His Wife," the reader will recognize jealousy, loyalty, and revenge as themes common to many narratives about love and marriage. Here each event leads to a more extreme response. One small deception eventually brings ruin to a whole village. "Wind Man" illustrates the conviction that initiative and self-reliance combined with respect for the spirit world can change the conditions of man's life. While these stories are exciting and entertaining, they are structured more by the exploration of culturally moral subjects than by plot concerns.

SUGGESTIONS FOR FURTHER READING

Attla, Catherine. *Bekk'aatugh Ts'uhuney (Stories We Live By): Traditional Koyukon Athabaskan Stories.* Rev. ed. Transcribed by Eliza Jones. Translated by Eliza Jones and Chad Thompson. Fairbanks: Yukon Koyukuk School District and Alaska Native Language Center, 1996.

———. *K'etetaalkkaanee (The One Who Paddled among the People and Animals): The Story of an Ancient Traveler.* Transcribed and translated by Eliza Jones. Fairbanks: Yukon Koyukuk School District and Alaska Native Language Center, 1990.

———. *Sitsiy Yugh Noholnik Ts'in' (As My Grandfather Told It): Traditional Stories from the Koyukuk.* Transcribed by Eliza Jones. Translated by Eliza Jones and Melissa Axelrod. Fairbanks: Yukon Koyukuk School District and Alaska Native Language Center, 1983.

de Laguna, Frederica, ed. *Tales from the Dena: Indian Stories from the Tanana, Koyukuk, and Yukon Rivers.* Seattle: University of Washington Press, 1995.

Jetté, Jules. "On Ten'a Folk-lore." *Journal of the Royal Anthropological Institute of Great Britain and Ireland* 38 (1908): 298–367; 39 (1909): 460–505.

Nelson, Richard K. *Make Prayers to the Raven: A Koyukon View of the Northern Forest.* Chicago: University of Chicago Press, 1983.

Doz K'ikaal Yee Nogheełt'uyhdlee

The One Who Used to Put His Nephew into a Fishtail

In the time very long ago
an uncle and his nephew were living together in summertime.
Apparently it was Mink and the Raven, who was always Mink's uncle [in
    stories].
Some of their relatives must have died.
"We're going to have a potlatch this coming winter," they said.
This is the reason people have memorial potlatches today.
When people don't have potlatches for their relatives,
it's said that their spirits stay around for a long time.
People say that otherwise the spirits will linger on in a place
and that's the reason for having a potlatch.

"Well, we'll make a potlatch this winter and we'll send a messenger to
    announce it," they said —
it must have been Raven who said this, since he was the one who was always
    in charge.
So now they put up a lot of fish.
Their wives helped them put up a lot of fish.
And late in the summer [Raven said],
"Are we going to have only dry fish —
how about some meat?" he asked.

This is the reason that the one with a black hide [the black bear][1]
is so important at potlatches, it's said.
Planning on making a potlatch,
they now took off by boat,
paddling up the creek where the dog salmon had gone.

"Nephew, I'm going to cut a dog salmon's tail and put you in it
but you'll have your knife as a weapon," he told him.[2]
"Okay," he said to him.
"There is no other way to catch one," he [Raven] told him.
There was no way for them to catch the black bear,
because it was summer.[3]

So now he cut a dog salmon tail and put his nephew into it.
He left it on a bear's trail.
"Uncle, if it looks like I won't survive this thing, be sure and kill the bear,"
    he [Mink] told him,[4]
[meanwhile thinking to himself] "I'm going to kill him [if I don't survive
    this]."[5]

The tail was sitting on the bear's trail while Mink waited inside it.
All of a sudden, he heard a thumping noise approaching.
Something [the bear] swallowed him.
And he cut the inside of its belly until he had cut all the way through, and it
    dropped.
Then he jumped out from inside its belly.
And there was no one around.
Where was the one who was supposed to help?
"I was cooking[6] inside the belly and where was he?" he said,
he said this to his uncle.[7]
"*Ha!* Nephew, I got stuck among the trees when I was trying to get to you,"
    he replied,
as he held a spear crossways between two trees and pretended to jerk on it.
Actually, he had just been scared.

So they had caught a bear
and, after that, only his nephew would catch bears now and then;
he [Raven] never caught a thing.
They were also putting up grease in birch-bark baskets for the coming
    winter
so they were putting up grease from very fat bears.[8]
"Nephew, running a line over the portage
and letting the grease run through it and into the dish, is the best way," he
    told him.
"How are we going to do that?" he [Mink] asked.

"What's wrong with just pouring it into the container?" he [Mink] asked.
"*Ha*! Nephew, what does he[9] mean [trying to make shortcuts],
the correct way to do it is to run a line over the portage," he told him.

They were also drying intestines.
So they put some intestines end to end and ran them over the portage.
(They were making it like a pipeline.)
Now, "I'm going to stay down at the lower end of the portage
and I'll be pouring it [into the dish] there," he [Raven] told him.

He left then, taking a dish with him.
And so he [Mink] was pouring a little more oil into the line than would fit
    in the dish he [Raven] had taken with him
and he kept pouring more and more into it.
Apparently, he [Raven] wanted to drink it but it was too hot.
So by running it over the portage in a line, he could drink what came
    through at the end after it had cooled.
He [Mink] figured this out but [didn't say anything because he] knew he
    [Raven] was the boss.[10]
He kept pouring more and more into it.

Now he was pouring much more than should have filled up the dish that he
    had taken.
So after pouring in a little more, he ran down over the portage.
And he found him down there with his mouth on the end of it.
Apparently, he was drinking it.

"*Haa*! I thought it sounded like a trick when he suggested it," he [Mink]
    shouted at him.
"*Ha*! Nephew, Nephew, a gosling blocked up the line," he told him.
Apparently, he told him that a gosling had bitten it and blocked it up.
He got very angry at his uncle once again
but there was nothing he could do because of Raven's power over him.[11]

So now, every once in a while, he [Raven] would cut a fish tail and put him
    into it.
They had lots of meat now,
but he told him, "Uncle, it looks like we're running out of tails."
"There's no fish left," he told him.
"*EEE*'! Okay, Nephew, are you the only one who will have food?[12]

Why don't you cut a fish tail and put me into it?" he said to him.
"*Haa*! I don't think what he's suggesting is possible," he answered him.
"*Ha*! Nephew, it'll be all right,
you'll be watching me," he told him.

He started cutting the fish tail so that he could put his uncle into it
and then, as his uncle usually did for him, he started blocking off the
    opening,
he started blocking off the opening with fish meat.
"*Ha*! Nephew, let my beak stick out," he told him,
"How am I going to breathe?" he started repeating.
"How is that going to work?" he [Mink] asked him, but to no avail,
so he let his beak stick out a little.

And now he had put his uncle into a fish tail
and left it on a bear trail.
Because he was suspicious of him,
he hid right nearby with the spear.
He hid there, ready with the spear.
And then they heard a thumping noise approaching.
He was all ready.
He didn't think Raven would go through with it.
He was keeping a close eye on him because he didn't trust him.
Now, it [a bear] walked right up to him [Raven] over there.
And it had just begun to open its mouth to eat him when he screeched,
    "*Ggaakk*!" and flew away.
In the meantime, that Mink just rushed at it and thrust the spear through it
    from below.
It really tried to kill him.
He was just barely able to kill it.
Doo', he [Raven] almost caused his nephew to die.
So he was really angry then,
"Why did he suggest it,
doesn't he know what he's like [what a coward he is]?" he started scolding
    him.
"It was to be expected that you'd get scared,"
and this was so true that there was nothing he [Raven] could say.
So now they cut that one up too.
They were staying there now, spending all their time drying meat.
There weren't any fish left so they were drying only some bear meat.

Then he [Raven] went back, saying, "I'll bring some wood home."
So he [Mink] was staying there and he [Raven] was gone.
"I wonder what he's up to," he was thinking.
He was really suspicious of him.
"I suppose he's up to something," he thought.
He was sitting there worrying.
Then, all of a sudden, a black bear rushed toward the fire.
It rushed right toward him.
As soon as he realized that it didn't really sound like a black bear,
he grabbed some partly burned wood,
and with that he slammed it right across the bridge of the nose,
right across the face.
He hit it really hard in the face.
It rushed back into the woods.
He was sitting around,
and here he [Raven] came, walking out of the woods, holding the bridge of
    his nose.
And he [Mink] was sitting there wanting to laugh
but he knew that would make him [Raven] angry so he didn't.
Because he [Raven] could do magic [Mink didn't want to make him angry].
So he was sitting there trying to keep a straight face.
"*Ha*! You should know that I worked so hard,
it was bound to happen[13] that I finally almost killed myself," he [Raven] said.
"*Ha*!" he said.
"Not realizing that the tree was rotten way up at the top, I began [pushing]
thinking that it would fall over.
It broke way up at the top
and it fell down and hit me on the bridge of the nose," he said.
And sure enough, the bridge of his nose was bruised and swollen.
He knew that he had hit him really hard in the face.
Apparently he'd taken the skin from what they'd been catching
and made himself into a bear.[14]
But he [Mink] knew [that it was] him.

So they were staying there.
They also made a lot of the grease which he told him they should run over
    the portage.

It was now late fall and they would travel now and then.
Now it was winter.

"Be a messenger, go for people," he [Raven] told him [Mink].
Following that custom, there was a *geebakk*[15] in 1930, it's said.
Maybe in the '20s, I don't know when, a long time ago.
It's said that the *geebakk* used to go over to the Kobuk.
He [Raven] was apparently starting that custom.
The custom has carried on from that time.
"Please go for people," he said.
"When you come to people,
tell them I said, 'Only the fat people should come,'" he told him.[16]
"When they get back to a certain place from over that way . . .
then they should start racing," he said.

Now he [Mink] started out to find people
and he traveled down to where there were a lot of people.
He traveled around among many people.

"When you come to where there are people
don't approach them openly.[17]
When you come to where there are people, hide
while saying, 'A ptarmigan landed in the tree out here,'" he must also have
    told him.

Now he came to where there were people;
he sneaked into the village.
To a man there, a young man,
he said, "I came to get people and I'm not supposed to show myself."
"Oh, come on then," he told him.
He brought him up the bank with him.
And then he hid him in the house
while he went back out and [said],
"Ptarmigan . . . ."

Some people say *aaggozyaakk*[18] and I don't know what that is
and some people say *tʉkkʉghʉldaal* and that's a ptarmigan.
It must be the way they used to say ptarmigan in story time.

"A ptarmigan landed in the tree out here," he started shouting.
People didn't know what this meant and they started rushing all around.
People really began running around . . .
I don't know what it was.

And he must have come out that evening.
And he said, "We're starting to have a potlatch."
"We are starting to have a potlatch,"
they must have been starting the custom of having potlatches.
They never said whom they were having a potlatch for
but they were having a potlatch.
So then they all started back with him.
Lots of people.
They say [they were] really looking forward to eating because it was said
    that a lot of food was put up.
So they made a rush to this place where they said there would be a feast.

So then when they got there,
he said that they would start running to find out who traveled the fastest.
And that was a race.
Now all the people began running
and there was a wolverine that started outdistancing the rest.
But then each time he saw a little spruce tree
he went to rub his butt on it, he rubbed his butt on it.
Apparently his mother had bound a small spruce tree around his baby
    carrier.
Doo', he would have won but he never passed a spruce tree [without
    stopping to rub his butt on it].

Because of that, people say that they never used spruce to work on baby
    carriers,
because it makes them [the children] travel slowly.

So I don't know who won, maybe it was the wolf,
it's said that the wolf also travels very fast.
Even though the wolverine was traveling really fast, he kept stopping and
    rubbing his butt
and so he kept getting left behind,
he got left behind.
Now he [Raven] had also established the custom of racing.
They play all kinds of games now [in addition to racing, at potlatches].

Now, also in the evenings, in the hall
they wrestled, maybe within the potlatch fence.

The swan was really beating everybody.
Now he was out there and everyone was challenging him, but without
    success — he was beating everybody.

And now it was the teal's turn.
The teal walked out there now
and, gee, he didn't even reach the top of his [the swan's] legs.
And then he [the teal] rushed at him [the swan].
Now he started wrestling around with the big person [the swan].
And to everyone's surprise, he slammed the big person down.
Doo, that swan was really surprised,
he'd thought that no one would throw him down.

And that's the reason that the other name of the teal is "he threw down the
    swan."
They always used to call him only "he threw down the swan."

Now the big wrestling match was finished.
And the teal had knocked down the one who was beating everybody.

And now there was a big potlatch,
almost every evening there was a potlatch.
Now they were starting to make the final potlatch.
And now they were going to bring in the baskets of grease.
They were starting to bring out all the food now.

Then he [Raven] also brought in some grease.
They were out there making speeches now.
And the Great Raven walked out to the grease
and also the meat,
and said of it, "My nephew didn't spear this with me."
Meaning, "My nephew didn't help me catch this."
[He said this] after he almost got his nephew killed!
He [Mink] said something to him but I've forgotten that part.
He said something like, "Why did he even say that."
He said something like, "He should be ashamed of himself."

Then it started getting dark,
apparently he [Raven] got angry [and so was making it dark].

Everyone hollered, saying, "Take back what you said, take back what you
    said."

"Oh, [all right] he must have caught them by himself then, the worthless
    old thing,"
he apologized to him.
It's said that it started becoming daylight again then.

Now he was out there starting to chip up the fat, as it had solidified in the
    birch-bark baskets.
Now he really stabbed it with a knife.
And to everyone's surprise, the grease caved in.
Darn, apparently only the top part had solidified!
And meanwhile early last fall, he had stuck in his beak
and drunk up the rest.

"*Eee*! You would think that women would be careful how they handle
    dishes,"
he [Raven] started saying about his wives.
"Here they bumped the bottom of the basket on something again," he said.

He was accusing them of having punched a hole through it.
It's said that he [Raven] apparently drank it up earlier in the fall.

There were also all kinds of carnival activities now.
And now they were going to go their separate ways.
I don't know how quickly —
he [Raven] must have gotten some pitch
and had apparently stirred it up.

Now into the hall, now for the last time [for the final activity],
now they went into the hall,
now, just before they all left.
It is said that it was midwinter.
The hall was really crowded
and they must have been eating again.
Then, "Close your eyes.
Now you will see something else really unusual happen," he [Raven] said.
"*Hee*! I wonder what he's talking about," they said.
They had seen many things going on that they had never seen before.[19]

This [happened] while they were there.
They were all very excited in anticipation [of what would happen next].
They all closed their eyes while he [Raven] was walking around among
  them.
Now they kept their eyes closed
and meanwhile he [Raven] brushed their eyes as he walked around.
So, in the hall where there were really a lot of people,
he went around doing that.
And now, down by the doorway,
there was an orphan by the door.

There's always an orphan [in this kind of story],
  it's said that he sits by the door at potlatches because that's the least
    important place.

Now he [Raven] only touched him [the orphan] on one side [only on one
  eye],
and told him, "Ask, 'Ha! What's that he put on your eyes?' "

He [the orphan] opened his eyes but he could see on only one side.
One of his eyes was stuck shut.
"Hʉdeeyh! What did he put on your eyes?" he asked.

They began opening their eyes
and realized that all their eyes were stuck shut.
Then they all began killing one another.

Even though he was establishing events that were to become traditional,
he [Raven] persisted in making trouble.
He must have done this figuring he would have food to eat [if they all killed
  each other].

And now they all stabbed each other
because they really couldn't see.

Apparently, he had been planning this
when he said to let only the fat people come.[70]

Now, that's as far as I know the story.
I thought that the winter had just begun and now I've chewed off part of it.

NOTES

[The *Denaakk'e* (Koyukon language) words in this story and in its notes contain several orthographical features that have been superseded since *Sitsiy Yugh Noholnik Ts'in'* was published. To avoid confusion on the part of those consulting this source and to follow customary scholarly practice, we have not altered the spelling of these words to conform to the current standard orthography, in which single *a* and single *i* are replaced by single *e* and *tł* is replaced by *tl*. Reprinting the story without these changes is also the preference of translator-linguist Eliza Jones.]

1. It is taboo for women to say the name of the black bear so they use circumlocutions like *bilił daałitł'idzee*, "the one with a black hide."

2. Raven wants to clean the meat out of a dog salmon tail and hide his nephew, Mink, inside the cavity. The fish tail will then be used as bait to catch a black bear. When the bear eats the fish tail, Mink can use his knife to kill the bear and then escape.

3. Bears are usually hunted in fall or winter while they are in hibernation. It is much more difficult and dangerous to hunt a bear while it is foraging in the summer. Raven and Mink didn't have a gun, and arrows or spears were often ineffective against such a large animal.

4. Mink's death must be avenged or his soul won't be able to rest.

5. Mink is thinking that if Raven doesn't avenge Mink's death, his spirit will return to annoy the Raven and make his life miserable.

6. Mink says he was cooking because it was so hot inside the bear's belly.

7. Mink is speaking indirectly to his uncle so that he may complain and criticize him without being disrespectful.

8. The bears they were catching were especially fat because it was late summer, just before the bears were to go into hibernation for the winter.

9. Raven is speaking indirectly to his nephew here.

10. He knew that Raven had magical power.

11. The Raven has very strong magical powers and Mink is afraid of angering him.

12. Each person brings a dish of his best food to a potlatch and then makes a speech. Raven is thinking about what he will have to bring to the potlatch.

13. When one works very hard, there is more opportunity for an accident to happen.

14. Raven did this so that he could scare Mink away and then eat the meat they had been drying.

15. A *geebakk* is a messenger who announces an upcoming festival or trade fair. The *geebakk* is sent to another village to present the invitation and describe the festivities being prepared.

16. Raven wants only the fat people to come because he's planning to eat them.

17. As Jetté says of the *geebakk*, "They approach the end of their voyage stealthily,

and must time their traveling to arrive at night, unexpectedly, that their coming may be a surprise to all."

18. From Yupik *aqesgiq* "ptarmigan."

19. The wrestling and racing were new to them.

20. Raven had been planning to kill and eat his guests.

Dotson' Sa Ninin"atłtseen

Great Raven Who Shaped the World

In the time very long ago
there were people
and there was a village.
And then there were big animals . . .
Before our time
it's said that there were giant animals in the world.

(In story time there were big animals around here
of all different kinds, it's said.)

Those will go into the water.
They informed a man of this.
If you don't kill them all, it will flood.
That's as long as the world will last, they said.
And there was a man, a very strong person, [to whom they said],
"These big animals will go into the water.
If you don't kill them all and they go into the water, it will flood," they said.
So, "All right, I'll kill them
and then the world will remain as it is," he said.

Those are their big bones that they find every now and then.
It's said that they existed in story time.

And the Great Raven said, "Make a raft."
He [Raven] began building a raft.
They built a BIG raft.
It wasn't something built right away.
And meanwhile the world was about to be taken back.[1]
It was coming to that time.

It really took a long time [to build the raft].
How long they worked on it!
Then they finished it.

Now the water began to rise, it began to rise.
Meanwhile he arranged all the different kinds of animals in pairs,
all the animals that exist now, all of those,
he began putting on the raft.
They all went on the raft with him.
They put food on it.
Meanwhile, the whole world was now being flooded.
So all these animals, and also the water mammals,
all of the flying things,
he crowded them all onto the raft in pairs.
In the future, when the world is remade,
all these good animals will exist [and that's why he put them on the raft].

Now the raft began floating around with them [on it].
It began floating around with them.
The food that they had put on board was being used sparingly now.
I don't know how long that raft was floating along with them.
Then [they decided to] go looking for land in every direction.

When the Great Raven was building the raft,
the seagulls and the robins were the biggest helpers in building the raft,
it used to be said, they say.

Now a seagull and the Raven
said, "Let's fly around the sky in opposite directions.
We're going to fly around in opposite directions in search of land," they said.
They took off in opposite directions now.
They were gone a lo——ng time.
They met each other at the end of the earth.
They had flown in a complete circle [around the world].
There was no land.
There was really nothing.
There was ONLY water,
all over the world.

They were running out of food now.
Then, "How about [you] water animals,

those that can go under water and stay a long time,
how about going under water in search of land," he [Raven] said.
Now they began searching downward.
They kept diving.
But water kept pushing and pushing all of them back up and out.
Then, to everyone's surprise, a muskrat was gone for a long, long time.
Bubbles kept coming up and coming up.
Then finally he came up from below,
with just a li——ttle mud,
he came swimming back up holding it to himself.
The beaver and he began helping each other.
Then they all began doing that again and again.
Then they began making the raft into land [by piling mud on it].

During story time, they really used to perform a lot of magic [transforming
    objects into other things].
They also used to bring people back to life
by closing their eyes.
Things happened just the way they wished
[because they wished] using medicine power.
The medicine power then was very strong.
And it's said that when it flooded, the *sinh taala'* [2] apparently floated to a
    faraway land.
For that reason they used to say there would come a time when there would
    be no more medicine people in our country.

Now the land came back into existence
all over the world.
Now plants were growing.
Also berries.
There were also fish now.
Now the plants were growing.
And on that thing they had made back into land,
the Great Raven now began making rivers.
He drew lines on the world.
(It must be our land.)

Now he made the rivers so that the current ran both ways.
One side flowed inland.
The other side flowed downstream.
So the current [in the same river] flowed in opposite directions.

So they almost didn't need to paddle
when they were traveling around.
That's how it's said he made it at first.
Then, "Oh, this is too much,
it's just like giving people a free ride," he said.
So, using a paddle, he made the current on one side of the river flow back
    downstream again.
Then the current flowed only down.
The current only flowed one way.

So now meanwhile, there were no people.
There were no people with them.
There were only animals.
"Now humans — we're going to remake humans.
Humans will be remade," he said.
So then he made a man out of rock.
Then he realized that they [men made of rock] would live forever.
They would live forever.
They would never die.
This man, then, wouldn't die.
And in addition, his mind would not be right
because he was a rock.
So, it's said that that's what he made the first time,
a rock man.
But it didn't work.

So now clay — this time he shaped clay into a human form.
He shaped it.
He made it into a human shape.
And this one had a mind, it could think.
It could also reproduce
continuously,
over and over,
he made it that way too.
Now he had it all figured out, it is said.

Now he had made a man.
Meanwhile, all the animals were in pairs.
And they were quickly multiplying.
So now he started making a woman.
He had made a woman now, it's said.

And now there were people.
There began to be a lot of people,
both women and men.
They started having children,
one after the other.
So I guess they would die and then come back to life again,
that was how he had made them, but [then he changed his mind].
But then, "How many ways are we giving them a free ride?"
So he fixed it so that they would live only once.

He got ready to marry one of the women.
Then some other men started to take her from him.
And he got angry.
So he walked into the woods.
And he got some dry, rotten willow.
He crumbled it up.
And he filled up a BIG bag.
And now he started home with it.

And he came back to where they were staying.
And he got back there
and broke it [the bag of crumbled wood].
And it was just like dust.
While doing that he said, "I hope it turns into mosquitoes and really eats
    them up."
That was his way of making them miserable.
So that's how he made mosquitoes.

Now he'd made everything,
since there were people now.
And the animals started being animals.
They were all people during story time,
and now they became animals, it is said.

That's as far as I know the story.
I thought that the winter had just begun and now I've chewed off part of it.

NOTES
[The *Denaakk'e* (Koyukon language) words in this story and in its notes contain several orthographical features that have been superseded since *Sitsiy Yʉgh Noholnik*

Ts'in' was published. To avoid confusion on the part of those consulting this source and to follow customary scholarly practice, we have not altered the spelling of these words to conform to the current standard orthography, in which single *a* and single *i* are replaced by single *e* and *ł* is replaced by *tl*. Reprinting the story without these changes is also the preference of translator-linguist Eliza Jones.]

1. The world was about to be destroyed by a flood.

2. The *sinh taala'* is the object with which medicine people make medicine.

K'etl'enbaalots'ek

In the time very long ago
there was a village.
A girl had reached puberty.
Her mother went from the village with her, over a hill.
Her mother built her a house and left her there.
Her mother would often bring her food.
She stayed there.
She stayed there and sewed.
It is said that that is what girls in puberty seclusion used to do.

She was staying there.
Then she heard people come to her door.
"What are you doing here? What are you doing here?" they asked her, but
    they got no answer.[1]
They kept asking her.

Then she said, "Oh, I'm staying hidden."

"Come home with us," they started telling her.

"No, my mother always comes to see me here," she said, but they would not
    listen.
They continued to urge her.
Then they took her.
She said, "No," but in vain.
She left for their home with them.
They left so fast it was as if they were flying.

Apparently they were the spirits of dead people.
People who have died are the ones we call "*naaghedeneełne.*"
The *naaghedeneełne* took her.
They were so fast they traveled as if they were flying.
They traveled a great distance.
Then they came to what looked like a mountain of ice with a slick surface.
It looked like a mountain that no one could climb.
They had come to something, the entire surface of which appeared to be
    slick ice.

One of the men had taken the girl to be his wife.
They went up the mountain,
but she kept slipping and slipping with him.
He couldn't do anything for her.
She couldn't climb up.
He tried wetting the bottoms of her feet with water and with saliva,
hoping that her feet would freeze to the side of the mountain.
They couldn't do anything for her.
She could not climb up.
Apparently it was because she had not died yet.

Way down at the bottom of the mountain,
the man built a house.
He started living there with her.
The spirits who had gone up the mountain would come often to visit.
They would travel as if they were flying around.
When they would start going back up, they would go up the mountain very
    fast.
They would go up the thing with the icelike surface
as if they were flying.
She was living there with that man, her husband; he provided for her.
They all loved her.

One day, she heard people crying off in the distance.
She heard people crying.
She asked one of her friends, "Friend, what is that noise?"

"Well, there is a woman there who's going to have a child. She's going to
    give birth,

but they deliver only by cutting the stomach," she said.[2]
"They're saying that she's not going to live."

"O——h! Bring her to me.
In the place they took me from, we help each other give birth," she said.

Then they said, "Bring her to her. She might be able to help."
Then they brought the woman in labor to her,
and she made a place for the woman to give birth.
She put up a pole.
Every time she felt a contraction, she would lift the woman up.
She kept doing that to her,
and then a baby was born.
Nothing was wrong with the woman who had given birth.

After that, they were very happy that she was there.
They loved K'etl'enbaalots'ek even more than before.
They took very good care of her.
They also gave her many things.
Apparently she hadn't died yet, but she was living among the dead.

She was living there,
but she was thinking about her mother.
Then she said, "Oh dear! You know I have parents."
She cried, saying she was lonesome for her parents.
Then her husband took pity on her.

"What are you going to do?" he said to her.

"I want my mother and father," she said.

"If that's what you want to do, I'll build a canoe for you
so that you can go home in it," he said to her.

She had been sewing, as was her habit.
She was sewing.
She was making a lot of clothing,
mittens and boots.
Then she put everything into the canoe.
Her husband cried very hard for her as she was leaving.

Then she paddled and paddled back downriver.
She was paddling along.
She stayed overnight here and there.
She spent the night here and there.
She would see people along the way.
She had been paddling a great distance.
She set up camp again.

Then, all of a sudden, she saw someone paddling out from down around a
   bend.
She heard him saying something.
She was listening to him.
Then it sounded as if he were singing.
"My daughter, I shun you. My daughter, I shun you."[3]
The one saying this was paddling upstream very quickly.[4]
She said in vain, "Father, it's me, K'etl'enbaalots'ek."
He kept right on going upriver.
He was in a canoe that looked as if it had been burned, using a paddle that
   also looked as if it had been burned.[5]
That is why people burn food for someone who has died.
Because whatever we burn,
the *kk'ʉnkk'ʉbedze* or *naaghedeneełne* live on.[6]

Realizing that her father had died, she threw into the fire the boots and
   mittens that she had sewn.
She could see him putting on the clothing, and as he was putting on the
   clothing, he said, "These sure look like the handiwork of my child,
   K'etl'enbaalots'ek."
She had found out that her father had died.
She kept paddling downriver toward home.
She cried for her father and for the husband she had left behind.

Then she paddled back to where she was from.
She had decided to sneak into the place.
She sneaked back
and heard her mother crying
for her child and her husband.
Her mother was back in the woods searching for firewood.
There she saw her mother.
"Mother, is that you?" she said to her.

"My dear child!"
There was her child, K'etl'enbaalots'ek.
She embraced her tightly
and said to her, "My dear child."

Great Raven was living there among the people.
"I suppose your grandfather will want to marry you," her mother said to
    her.
Her mother hid her.
The poor woman kept her hidden back there where she lived.
K'etl'enbaalots'ek had a younger sister.

Then they started eating.
Great Raven was with them.
Her little younger sister saw her older sister
and shouted, "Hey! Mom, my older sister K'etl'enbaa . . ."
Her mother grabbed her and threw her back against the wall.
She started crying.

Great Raven began asking, "What did she say? What did she say?"

"As if it's the first time she's seen the things K'etl'enbaalots'ek has sewn,
she said, 'My older sister K'etl'enbaalots'ek sewed this,'
saying that these are what K'etl'enbaalots'ek worked on.
That is why she said her late older sister's name," the mother replied.[7]
Raven found out about K'etl'enbaalots'ek anyway.
He found out that she was staying there
and began asking for her.
I don't know what happened to her.
He must have married her.

Then she died
sometime after that.
It wasn't very long after K'etl'enbaalots'ek had returned that she died.
Then she, too, took off upriver as if she were flying.
She flew up there to where she hadn't been able to climb before, to that
    place where she had kept slipping.
This time, she went flying up the mountain with her husband.
Then she went to the land of the dead.

She was very happy.
I thought the winter had just begun and now I've chewed off part of it.

That's the reason it is said that when people die they go to a good place.
That is what has been said ever since Distant Time.
They also say this in the Bible,
but this was said even by people who did not know Christian clergymen.

NOTES

1. Girls in seclusion were not supposed to talk to anyone other than family members or close friends, so the girl was reluctant to answer the people at her door.

2. They delivered only by Cesarean section.

3. Her father was dead and was, therefore, wary of the living. He could not go over to her because she was alive.

4. It is believed that people's spirits travel upstream after they die. Her father paddled quickly because traveling upriver is easy for spirits.

5. Her father was going upriver to join the *naaghedeneełne*. His belongings had been burned so that they could be taken along to the spirit land.

6. *Kk'unkk'ubedze* and *naaghedeneełne* both refer to the spirits of the deceased. *Kk'unkk'ubedze* means "eye spirit," and *naaghedeneełne* means "those who are being healed." The Jesuit Jules Jetté wrote in his unpublished dictionary of Koyukon, circa 1905: "The kk'unk'ubidza is the living spirit which animates the body, or the soul as we conceive it; it is immortal and, after death, migrates to the naaghadincełna ta, where it lives for a time in disembodied form."

7. One is not supposed to say a person's name soon after his or her death. K'etl'enbaalots'ek's mother used this as an explanation for silencing K'etl'enbaalots'ek's younger sister by throwing her against the wall.

Dekeltlaal De'ot Etldleeyee

The Woodpecker Who Starved His Wife

In the time very long ago,
people had stayed at their individual spring camps during breakup.
That spring they all gathered together and were traveling together.
They must have been traveling downstream to the mouth of the river.

The people all gathered together and celebrated.
A man had given a woman a wooden comb as a memento, without her
    husband's knowledge.

The summer passed.
People had stayed in fish camps,
and they put away a lot of fish.

At that time a man looked through his wife's things.
To his surprise he found a *tlughulee'oye*, a wooden comb that had been
    given to her.
The comb was made of wood;
that is what he found.
Apparently this husband was very jealous.
He asked her, "Where did this come from?"
"I don't know," she kept saying,
but he had discovered her secret.
Evidently it had been given to her during the previous spring, when people
    were gathered together,
and she had kept it hidden.

All during the fall and winter
he scolded her over and over again.

It was now late winter.
He scolded her the entire winter because of that wooden comb.

They went on a nomadic hunt, traveling around.
He did not feed her anymore, not since the beginning of their nomadic
    hunt.
They did not have any children,
only a dog.
The dog pulled a sled with her.
It pulled the sled for this woman.
The man walked ahead of his wife.

They camped here and there.
The dog was fed by its master.[1]
It would hide some of its food.
It had found out that its mistress was not eating
and began to give her food that it hid.

When they camped, their sleeping places were made on both sides of the
    campfire; a fire burned in the center.
He did not keep her by his side
because he was afraid she would steal some food.
She stayed on the other side of the fire, where there was nothing.
The dog often gave its mistress food.
The man found out about it
and began feeding the dog very little as well.

He would cook a whole skewer of spruce grouse over the fire.
She would watch him.

Again and again he would say, "Mother of Seey'e, bite off a piece of your
    wooden comb. How can you be hungry when you have that?"
It was the dog that was called Seey'e.[2]
So he called her only "Mother of Seey'e."

Apparently he resented the fact that she had been given a memento.
He said this again and again to taunt her.

It got to the point where the dog could not give its mistress any more food.
The winter was ending.

The man was pulling around a big load of food on the sled,
but there was no way she could touch it.

One time the dog was pulling the sled for her.
She was walking behind, following her husband.
While traveling across a lake, the dog began to sniff its way back toward the
  woods.
It kept going to the edge of the lake.
"Why is it doing that?" she wondered.
While the dog stayed at the sled,
she went to the shore
and walked into the brush.
To her surprise, a bear's den was there.
Apparently a bear was in it.
She went back out onto the lake.
I don't think she blocked the entrance to the den.
She went back down the bank to the dog.
She resumed following her husband.

Then her husband prepared camp again.
As usual, he prepared a place for her across the campfire from himself.
There she sat, facing the fire.
He had a whole skewer of spruce hens
roasting over the fire.
Really! He was eating all those broiled spruce hens.
He said, "Mother of Seey'e, what do you lack that makes you hungry?
Why should you be hungry?
Take a bite of the wooden comb."

She was looking at the dog,
and it kept nodding its head with sleep.
It must have been hungry itself.

Then she said, "Hey! Is that the same one that kept dragging me off the trail
  today that is nodding its head with sleep?"

"What? What are you saying, Mother of Seey'e? What are you saying?" he
  started asking.

"Oh, I meant that dog," she replied.
"I was saying that I wonder why it is nodding its head now. Today it was so
    strong that it kept dragging me off the trail," she said.[3]

"Mother of Seey'e, eat these and tell me about it.
What are you talking about?" he began asking.
He threw her spruce hen wings with part of the breast meat on them.

My! When was the last time she ate?
She began to eat.
Then she was full.
She fell asleep.
The whole night passed.

In the morning he said, "Mother of Seey'e, let's go to that place you were
    talking about."
Then they went back upriver to the area where they had been.
They came back to the place where the dog had kept going off the trail.
The man went back up into the woods.
There was a bear in its den.
The man killed it.
Then they started to spend the night there.
"Mother of Seey'e, we're going to bind each other's back to a tree.
We're going to feed each other until we're full," he started telling her.
How was she going to refuse him?
They took turns tying each other's back to a tree.
She began to feed a lot of bear meat to her husband.
Then the man fed his wife the food that they were carrying on the sled.
As it turned out, that was the only time she was to eat.
They started carrying the bear meat around on the sled too.
She was very hungry.
He only fed her a little bit once in a while.
I don't know how she was able to keep walking.

They camped here and there.
He chopped beaver houses now and then
and pulled out beaver after beaver.

Eventually she was barely walking along, barely keeping up.
Then they came to a place and camped.

She could not get up anymore.
She was barely able to go out now and then.
At each place, he made a little shelter of small spruce trees.
He was still chopping beaver houses.
He continued taunting her, saying, "Mother of Seey'e, bite off a piece of
    your comb," over and over again.

One night she had a dream.
She dreamt that she saw her older brothers coming into the shelter.

In the morning her husband said, "Bite off a piece of your comb."

"I didn't know that I had any older brothers while I was in this condition,
and here I dreamt that my older brothers were coming into the shelter," she
    said.

"Hey! Her older brothers are going to feed her. They are going to come to
    her," he began to say, mockingly.

She was lying down, unable to get up.
He went down the riverbank to a beaver house.
He kept looking up and checking on her as usual.
He kept looking up at the sled.
The sled was in front of the shelter, still full of food.

Suddenly, she heard a noise and raised her head.
There stood her two big, older brothers.

"What is wrong with you?" they asked her.

"He stopped feeding me long ago.
That is why I am in this condition," she replied.

"What is that out on the sled?" they asked her.

"Oh, that's food," she said.

"If what you say is true, go outside
and untie the lashings," they told her.
The food was all lashed down.

She barely managed to get out of her bed. She was close to death.
She stumbled out the door
and somehow managed to make it out to the sled.

Her husband was looking up now and then.
He was looking up from the beaver house and checking on her.
That is why the woodpecker always looks up from its pecking
and looks around.
It is because of that.
He checked again and noticed that she was by the sled, doing something.
"Hey, Mother of Seey'e, you've finally done it."
She finally decided to risk her life.
He rushed up the bank, carrying his ice chisel.
She shuffled back to the shelter.

"You've finally done it," he said,
rushing back into the shelter.

He was startled; there stood two big men.
He said, "Mother of Seey'e, go ahead and help yourself."

Since someone else had come, she could now talk back to him.
Before, she would have been killed.
She said, "Since when do I touch the things on the sled?"
She began talking back, now that she had the chance.

"Oh! She means that there is a yellow path of grease leading away from her
      entryway,
I feed your little sister so well,"[4]
he said in fear.

She shuffled back outside, so happy to be able to get food again.
She untied the bindings of the sled.
She barely managed to bring the food back in to her brothers.
Then she ate with her brothers.

At last, she ate again!
Apparently it had been his intention to let her starve.
He had stopped feeding her altogether.

At first he gave her food now and then,
but then he stopped doing even that.

Then he said, "I don't know what is wrong. Usually beavers are easy for me
   to catch, but I just can't get this one out."
This was foreshadowing his death, because he was going to die.

"Let's go down to it," the brothers said.

They went down the bank to it
and cut a hole in the beaver's lodge.
They took the beavers out
and brought them up the bank.

In the evening they decided, "Let's cook them."
They had brought up only some of the beavers.
"You know, when our ancestors had a hard time catching a beaver, they
   would put around the fire the sticks it has chewed.
Then they would have an easy time catching it in the future," the brothers
   said.
They brought some of those chewed sticks up the bank
and put them around the fire.
They put the food over the fire.
It had come to a boil.
They took it off the fire while it was still boiling.

They told their brother-in-law, "Friend, only when we pass our faces over
   the top of it does it get grease on the surface.
Let's pass our faces over it," they said.
Then they started to pass their faces over it.
Just as their brother-in-law was passing his face back over it,
one of the brothers grabbed a stick chewed by the beaver and hit him over
   the head with it, knocking him into the pot.
Doo', he swallowed the boiling broth
and died.
He flew away as a woodpecker with grease on its head.

They say that is why the woodpecker has yellow markings on its head,
and why, when you cook beaver, it has no grease on top.

No matter how much fat is on the beaver, when you boil it, the fat does not
   appear on the surface.
They say that is the reason for this.
When you boil moose or bear meat, there will be grease on the top, and you
   scoop it off.
They say this story explains why that it is not true for beaver meat.

Doo'! They killed their brother-in-law.
They started taking their little sister back home on a sled.
How could she walk? She did not walk.
They took her back to their village on the sled.
They said, "Our brother-in-law starved to death, and we barely found our
   sister in time."
The woodpecker's older brother was the flicker.
"Hey! They're telling me my younger brother starved to death.
My younger brother?
My younger brother used to stay out two nights on just one spruce grouse
   gizzard.
How can they tell me, 'Your younger brother has starved'?" he said.

Right away, the flicker married his sister-in-law
and began taking the dog out hunting with him.
When they camped, he would not let the dog sleep.
"Seey'e, was your father killed?" he asked it.
How is it that a dog can speak?
Again and again it said, "My dad starved."

Again, it was in the springtime after breakup.
The flicker began to go out hunting in his canoe while he was married to
   his former sister-in-law.
He began to keep the dog from sleeping.
He stayed in camp with it and never let it sleep.
Each time it started to nod, he would jerk up its head.
"Seey'e, how did your father die?" he would ask it.
"Was your father killed?" he would ask it.

"My dad starved; my dad starved."

He was really wearing it down.
Soon it became very sleepy.

Then, just as it was beginning to fall asleep,
he jerked it up by the head.
He held a knife to it
and demanded, "Seey'e, was your father killed?"

"My dad was thrown into the darkness like a bone."
That was its way of saying that its owner had been murdered.
Right there, he stabbed the dog and killed it.

He started to paddle home.
He arrived back home.
Then he began pounding on something.
I don't know what he was pounding with, maybe a rock.

Someone said, "Oh no! It's going to happen again."
Evidently the flicker acted like this when he was angry and was going to
    make trouble.
They all knew this.
Everyone began to run away.
Why did he not just kill the woman and her family?
He began to kill everyone in the village.
He speared the ones who ran into the caches.
He killed everyone.
I don't know what happened then. This is as far as my late Grandpa used to
    tell the story.
I thought the winter had just begun and now I've chewed off part of it.

NOTES

1. The Koyukon words for a dog's owner literally mean "his grandmother" or
"his grandfather."

2. Seey'e means "my son" if a man says it, or "my brother's son" if a woman says it.

3. It would have been improper for her to specifically say the word *bear*, so she
spoke it indirectly. Her husband knew immediately what she was talking about.

4. He is claiming to have brought his wife so much nice, greasy food that their entryway is yellow from the grease that dripped from the food as he brought it in.

Ełts'eeyh Denaa

Wind Man

In the time very long ago
there lived a man.
He lived alone in a camp where he had a house.
One day the wind began to blow, and it blew for days.
It blew as if it were never going to stop,
blowing and blowing with big gusts of snow.
It looked as if it would never stop,
and he was beginning to use up the small amount of food he had stored.

"Well, what am I waiting for? I should do something.
Where is that wind coming from?" he wondered.

Gusts of wind and snow were blowing down from the mountains.
Then he started to walk uphill.
The wind became so strong that it almost blew him away.
He was bucking the wind, barely managing to climb.
The wind would pick him up and blow him off balance
when it blew. He kept on walking through the storm.
Suddenly, he came upon a man.
Every time the man would swing his axe,
the wind would blow and blow.
He sneaked up behind him
and snatched his axe away.

"Hey! Why is he doing this,
as if he's the only one who needs to make a living?[1]
Doesn't he think that other people would like to eat too?
Doesn't the one who's doing this think of that?" he said to Wind Man.

Suddenly, the wind stopped.
It was not blowing anymore.

"Don't! Just give my axe back to me gently," Wind Man told him.

"I will not give it back to you.
I'm hungry too.
I want to go out and try to get something to eat
but I can't even manage to go outside.
Do you think that you're the only one who wants to live, and is that the
    reason you want your axe back?" he asked Wind Man.

"Give it to me. Give me my axe," Wind Man told him,
but Wind Man could not persuade him.
"If what you say is true,
go back to wherever you're from.
When you have returned home, if you have a canoe,
tie it to the entrance of your house
and go to bed.
You just might wake up to find the world very different," Wind Man said to
    him.

He did not believe Wind Man
but did it anyway.
He began chopping a rock with the axe,
chipping the blade of the axe until it was rounded.
Then he threw it back to Wind Man.
He didn't believe what Wind Man had said, but he prepared to leave
    anyway.

The wind man took back his axe
and looked at it.
He ran his tongue over the edge
and then said, "Oh, he almost ruined it."
It was magically returned to its original condition.

Then the man started walking back down.
He returned to his house below
and went to bed just as he had been told.
He also tied his canoe to the entrance of his house.

He went to bed and woke up thinking that only one night had passed.
To his surprise, he heard water coming into his entryway.
"Hey! What's that noise? What's happened?" he wondered.
He jumped up.
He rushed out the door.
The water was high and up to the willows,
and from all directions he could hear the noise of red-necked grebes.
Apparently the winter had passed.

For this reason, whenever we tell stories,
at the end of every story,
it is said that we should say, "I thought the winter had just begun and now
    I've chewed off part of it."

Long ago, when times were hard,
people would appeal for mercy
by telling stories.
It was their way of praying.

Furthermore, when we tell stories,
we should not tell only part of a story.
They also used to say
that we should always finish telling it.
If we take a long time to tell a story,
then the winter will be long.
It used to be said that when the winter was long, people would have a hard
    time.

NOTE

1. Someone from Western culture would say, "Hey! Why are *you* doing this, as if
you're the only one who needs to make a living," but Athabaskans consider such direct reference, especially when criticism is implied, very rude.

3

Gwich'in

Like *Hit'an* in *Deg Hit'an*, *Gwich'in* means "dwellers of," or "people of," but a topographical or geographical term often precedes it to identify a particular group. These Athabaskan people inhabit villages along the middle Yukon River and its major tributaries in Alaska and along the upper Porcupine, lower Peel, and lower MacKenzie Rivers in Canada. Indeed, a great many more of those on the Canadian side of the international boundary live in the Northwest Territories than in the Yukon Territory. *Gwich'in* is also the name of their language, and its speakers generally use one term — *gwandak* — for all narratives. Like other Athabaskans, however, they tell stories of two basic kinds. Katherine Peter, whose work is represented here, points out that more specific terms — *deenaadai' gwandak* and *nahgwan dai' gwandak* — can be applied, respectively, to traditional distant-time stories and to modern historical and biographical narratives. She translates *deenaadai'* as "old time" and *nahgwan dai'* as "very recent." Gwich'in narrators also tell stories that appear to have developed as hybrids of the two basic genres — stories grounded in historical time and biographical fact that have taken on some features of distant-time tales, usually in certain superhuman attributes of the protagonist. Such narratives would be called legends in Western literary terminology.

Katherine Peter was born January 27, 1918, in Koyukon-speaking Stevens Village on the middle Yukon River. In the summer of 1926, she traveled by steamboat with her mother, Annie Joseph, to Fort Yukon, the large Gwich'in community upriver. Her mother died there within half a year, but before her death she had arranged for her daughter to be taken into the home of Chief Esias Loola and his wife, Katherine. In this household the eight-year-old child, who had arrived knowing neither Gwich'in nor English, was quickly immersed in traditional Gwich'in culture and in Christian doctrine. Looking back as an elder, she says that she had to learn

Gwich'in in order to communicate in the Fort Yukon of her youth, and she credits her classmates at the Bureau of Indian Affairs school and at Bible school as her best teachers in learning not only Gwich'in but English. She discovered her aptitude for learning language, and the use of the Dagǫǫ Bible in Bible school and at home enabled her to become literate in Gwich'in as well as a fluent speaker.

Married to Steven Peter when she was not quite eighteen, Mrs. Peter lived first at Arctic Village on the East Fork of the Chandalar River, a tributary of the Yukon, and then at Fort Yukon. In both places, she taught school, and in Fort Yukon she raised her family. She became active in Gwich'in-language work in the late 1960s and early 1970s, first as a translator of the Bible for the Summer Institute of Linguistics and Wycliffe Bible Translators, then as a staff member at the Alaska Native Language Center. She quickly learned the new standardized orthography for writing Gwich'in, even though she was accustomed to using the older (Dagǫǫ) system. During her eight years of full-time employment with ANLC, she transcribed and composed what Michael Krauss has called "by far the largest and most important body of Gwich'in writing in this century." She also became a teacher of Gwich'in at the University of Alaska Fairbanks, in courses that, as Krauss has noted, marked "the first time that language was ever taught at a university." Officially retired since 1980, Mrs. Peter has continued to be significantly involved in Gwich'in-language projects of ANLC, and she spends a large part of each week helping to care for patients in a Fairbanks medical/nursing facility. In 1999 the University of Alaska Fairbanks awarded her an honorary doctor of laws degree.

The value of her contribution to Gwich'in literature and linguistics cannot be overstated. In original composition, she has retold traditional *gwandak*, often designing them for youthful readers; she has written many other instructional materials for use in Gwich'in-language programs in schools; and she has created an autobiographical narrative of a crucial decade in her life. In transcription, she has enlarged and enriched the Gwich'in-manuscript corpus of both distant-time stories and historical accounts, by transcribing directly from tapes recorded by more than a score of Gwich'in elders during the past quarter century and by retranscribing (in the modern standard spelling) texts that had been written half to three quarters of a century ago in earlier orthographical systems. In translation, she has been instrumental, either solely or in collaboration with others, in making the English translations of Gwich'in-language publications of ANLC and of other organizations.

Of her work presented here, the first two selections were originally published in 1974 by Alaska State-Operated Schools, in a small book titled *Dinjii Zhuu Gwandak*. Mrs. Peter wrote these stories in Gwich'in and translated them into English prose. Both "The Old Woman" and "K'aiiheenjik" illustrate the devastating effects of human jealousy. The moral force of the first may be missed by readers outside Gwich'in culture, in which, as Osgood has observed, polyandry was practiced and polyandrous women were "greatly admired" (*Contributions* 143, 148, 187). The young woman in this story is doubly virtuous because she is a model wife for two husbands, not just for one. Her mother's vice is doubly wrong because she covets both husbands and commits a gruesome murder to get them. Seldom have sheer horror, ludicrous humor, and heartfelt poignancy been so artfully and economically combined as here. The legend of "K'aiiheenjik" is widely told among the people. Mrs. Peter's version is probably the most concise of those that have been published, compressing the narrative within a shorter span of time, omitting a number of characters, and doing away with the strong man's living as a recluse for many years before his spectacular death. In recompense, Mrs. Peter develops the basic situation by building great tension between the frightened boy and the worried, distrustful K'aiiheenjik. Vengeance comes quickly and forcefully.

Our third and fourth selections are taken from *Neets'ąįį Gwiindaii (Living in the Chandalar Country)*, winner of an American Book Award for 1993. Katherine Peter wrote this autobiographical narrative in Gwich'in prose paragraphs in 1976; it was first published in 1981, with her English translation. A second edition appeared in 1992, in which Mrs. Peter's daughter, Adeline Raboff, made revisions in the Gwich'in text (changes in paragraphing and punctuation) and in the English translation; Mrs. Peter examined the revised versions and made additional changes. The text reprinted here is that of the second edition. The book covers the first dozen years of Mrs. Peter's married life, beginning with her adjustment to a much more rigorous way of life with her husband in and around Arctic Village than she had known with the Loola family in Fort Yukon.

Our first selection from it is the greater part of the fourth chapter, covering a year's cycle of subsistence living, from the fall of 1938 to the fall of 1939. Mrs. Peter focuses here upon her integration within her husband's family and the Arctic Village community as the people travel the mountains, lakes, and streams, hunting, trapping, and fishing. Her brother-in-law Joseph, though gravely ill, chooses to continue this way of life rather than to languish in a Fort Yukon hospital bed. With simple but moving details, Mrs. Peter writes of marriage, of survival, and of the most elemental of human experiences — birth and death.

Our second selection is the seventh chapter complete. In it we come to know Katherine Peter as a resourceful woman who has learned how to take care of herself and her three small children while traveling with a team of "poor dogs" on a winter trail through wilderness terrain. She is no longer the town girl from Fort Yukon or the inexperienced young wife trying to adapt to bush living in Arctic Village. Sickness continues to provide a muted backdrop for this chapter, but survival in a rigorous and demanding, if not hostile, environment is a major theme, and it is an achievement both physical and spiritual ("There were many in *Jalgiitsik* who did not expect that I could do these things").

SUGGESTIONS FOR FURTHER READING

Cruikshank, Moses. *The Life I've Been Living*. Oral Biography Ser. 1. Fairbanks: Alaska & Polar Regions Department, Elmer Rasmuson Library, University of Alaska, 1986.

Frank, Johnny and Sarah. *Neerihiinjik (We Traveled from Place to Place): Johnny Sarah Hàa Googwandak (The Gwich'in Stories of Johnny and Sarah Frank)*. Edited by Craig Mishler. Fairbanks: Alaska Native Language Center, 1995.

Fredson, John. *John Fredson Edward Sapir Hàa Googwandak (Stories Told by John Fredson to Edward Sapir)*. Retranscribed by Katherine Peter. Fairbanks: Alaska Native Language Center, 1982.

Herbert, Belle. *Shandaa (In My Lifetime)*. Transcribed and translated by Katherine Peter. Edited by Bill Pfisterer. Fairbanks: Alaska Native Language Center, 1982.

Martin, Richard. *K'aiiroondak (Behind the Willows)*. Transcribed and translated by Katherine Peter. Edited by Bill Pfisterer. Fairbanks: Center for Cross-Cultural Studies, University of Alaska, 1993.

McKennan, Robert A. *The Chandalar Kutchin*. Technical Paper 17 of Arctic Institute of North America. Montreal, 1965.

Osgood, Cornelius. *Contributions to the Ethnography of the Kutchin*. Yale University Publications in Anthropology 14. New Haven: Yale University Press, 1936.

Peter, Katherine. *Neets'ąįį Gwiindaii (Living in the Chandalar Country)*. 2nd ed. Retranslated by Adeline Raboff. Fairbanks: Alaska Native Language Center, 1992.

Shaaghan

The Old Woman

This story was told long ago. It was told in the land of the Gwich'in.

An old woman lived with her daughter. The daughter was married. She had two handsome husbands.

The daughter was very beautiful. Her husbands loved her very much. The daughter sewed nicely. She sewed beautiful clothes and moccasins out of animal skins. She sewed for her husbands. They were very well dressed, and they were happy.

Every day the husbands went hunting. Every day the wife cooked and sewed. Every evening she watched for her husbands. She ran outside when she saw them. She jumped over a stick. Every night she jumped over a stick when her husbands came home.

The old woman was jealous. She was jealous of her daughter. The old woman wanted the two husbands. She made a plan. She would trick her daughter. She would trick the two husbands.

One day the old woman said, "Come here, daughter. I will pick the lice from your hair."

The daughter came. She put her head in her mother's lap. The old woman had an awl. She had it hidden in her sleeve.

The old woman took out the awl. She quickly poked it in her daughter's ear. The daughter died.

The old woman worked fast. She took the skin from her daughter's head. She put the skin over her own head. She wanted to look like her daughter.

Then the old woman looked at her legs. They were baggy with old age. The old woman wrapped caribou-hide string around her legs. It made her legs look strong.

"Now I look young. I have my daughter's face. I have my daughter's clothes. I will fool the husbands."

The old woman went outside the house. She went to her daughter's stick.

She made the stick lower. She couldn't jump over a high stick. Then she returned to the house. She waited for the husbands.

The husbands came home at dark. The old woman ran outside. She jumped over the stick. The stick fell down. The old woman almost fell down, too.

The husbands looked at their wife's hair. They looked at their wife's face. They looked at their wife's clothes. They were not fooled. They knew that their wife was gone.

The husbands chased the old woman until they caught her. They beat her until she died.

The husbands felt sad. Their wife was gone. They had no wife to help them. The husbands could not bring their wife back to life.

K'aiiheenjik

K'aiiheenjik was as big as a giant. His upper arms were as big around as a baby's stomach. His legs were like tree trunks and just as strong. He was taller than any man. He was taller than any animal. He was so strong he could lift a moose.

K'aiiheenjik was a very gentle man. He never used his strength to harm others. He was also very kind. He helped his friends. He shared the meat he hunted. He was always willing to work.

People were jealous of K'aiiheenjik because he was so strong. They teased him. They wanted to make him angry.

One day K'aiiheenjik's brother went hunting. He went with a group of men. They were hunting for a moose to eat. They did not find a moose and kill it. Instead, they killed K'aiiheenjik's brother. They killed him to make K'aiiheenjik angry.

At the same time, K'aiiheenjik went hunting. He killed a moose. He began to cut it up. The other hunters came to see him. K'aiiheenjik said, "Where is my brother?"

The hunters answered, "He killed a moose. We left him to cut it up."

K'aiiheenjik and the hunters built a fire, and they put the moose head on the fire to cook. It hung from two crossed sticks. The men poked it with a longer stick. The moose head turned around and around. It cooked evenly. It smelled delicious.

K'aiiheenjik was worried. He knew something was wrong. His brother had not returned. A young boy was sitting next to K'aiiheenjik. He was shivering in fear. K'aiiheenjik said, "Why are you afraid? What do you have to hide?"

The boy didn't answer. He couldn't talk. He was too scared. He just sat and shivered.

The moose head was only half cooked. The men sat and watched it. One man sharpened his knife. K'aiiheenjik knew why the man had the sharp knife. The men planned to jump on him. They wanted to kill him.

K'aiiheenjik became very nervous. His brother still didn't come. The boy kept shivering.

K'aiiheenjik went to the fire. He grabbed the moose head. He tore it apart with his hands. He threw the pieces to the men so they could eat. K'aiiheenjik became even more nervous. He knew his brother was dead.

The young boy was still shivering with fear. K'aiiheenjik couldn't stand it any longer. He had a long, sharp bone tied to his arm. He swung his elbow at the boy. The sharp bone hit the boy and killed him.

K'aiiheenjik attacked the other men with the jawbone of the moose. They shot at K'aiiheenjik with arrows. He killed all of them except for one man. Then K'aiiheenjik climbed up a mountain. He stood on a high cliff. He picked the arrows out of his body.

Two great chiefs went to find K'aiiheenjik. They wanted to talk to him. K'aiiheenjik grabbed both chiefs and put them under each of his arms. He called down to the people below. He said, "Don't say that you have killed me. That is not true. You have killed my brother, but you have not killed me!"

When he finished speaking, he jumped off the cliff. K'aiiheenjik fell to the ground below. The two chiefs fell with him.

That was the end of K'aiiheenjik, but the cliff can still be seen. It is up the Porcupine River.

from Gwichyaa Zheh Gwats'à' Tr'ahàajil
We Go to Fort Yukon

That fall we were living at Old John Lakeshore House.[1] They hunted in all directions from this point, and when they killed many caribou we moved camp there. While it was warm we dried it; on the other side of the big lake are three places where they used to dry a lot of meat. And all that dried meat they brought to the house I mentioned and placed it in the cache that was there.

Then in late August when it started getting cold we moved down [to the east] to *Van[Va]ts'an Hahdlaii*.[2] We went there to hunt bull caribou, which they called *khaiints'an*.[3] Joseph Peter and David[4] went with Steven. We lived there close together. Meanwhile, it became obvious that Joseph was sick. [We didn't know it at the time but] he was [terminally] ill with TB. Even so, he worked very hard. Then it was so cold they built a very high open cache and tossed up the quartered caribou [rumps and shoulders].[5] All the while Joseph was very sick and even as he yelled out [in pain] he continued to work. Finally it was David who took him to the hospital. He took him down to Fort Yukon in a skin boat and took him to the hospital.

Meanwhile, we went back to Old John Lakeshore House. Soozun[6] lived in that house. Since Tabitha's husband was in the hospital, she set up her tent beside ours. This we did in the fall of 1938. At the time Joseph's children were Jermi,[7] John, Abraham, and Joel. [Joel] was born that spring and I delivered him! He was born a little ways from Arctic Village.

We set a fishnet across the lake from our Old John Lakeshore House. Myra[8] set out the net and I helped her, and we also put out set lines with hooks. There was no snow on the ice yet and it looked very far to the bottom. We went to it with dogs. I tell you truly that Myra was an expert and thrifty worker.

When David took his older brother down [to Fort Yukon] I don't remember how he returned. But that fall he and Steven trapped around *Gwa-*

k'an Choo.[9] When they had taken enough animals there and Christmas was near, they went to Fort Yukon with dogs. "We're going to spend New Year's Day on the shores of Old John Lake," they said.

Meanwhile, we were living there alone and so Myra and I said, "Let's cut wood." The reason was that we didn't want to do this while it was cold.[10] We really had plenty of food. There was fish, dry meat, and frozen meat. The cache was just full of it. Whatever they ate, I ate with them.[11] Soozun boiled frozen whitefish with all its guts. As for the firewood I mentioned, we cut a lot of it. Meanwhile, it was near Christmas. We piled the wood in front of our dwellings. We brought it home two toboggan loads at a time.

At that time we made cigarettes with Velvet tobacco in a can. Myra was twenty-one years old but she still wouldn't smoke in people's presence. We only smoked in Tabitha's house and also outside when we were working. I guess we were bashful about smoking. Harry Frank came there to visit us and he brought us tobacco. Even what they called "Apple Sam."[12] He was coming from just this side of Arctic Village.

It was almost Christmas when Steven and David came back. After they arrived in Fort Yukon, Joseph asked to leave with them, it seems. They told him no, but even so he clung to them. So at last they made arrangements for him to come by airplane. At that time, whoever got into a hospital bed could not get down and walk around. The *Dinjii Zhuu*[13] knew that men became weak there and so people did not like to stay in the hospital.

They made a mark on the big lake for the plane and Jim Dodson landed with him. He also brought the stuff they had bought [while in Fort Yukon]. There in the log house we spent Christmas and New Year's. New Year's passed and then we moved further down around where there was plenty of firewood. There was still plenty of food.

While we were living there, people quickly came to us from Arctic Village.[14] These people came: Elijah Henry and his family, Moses Sam and his family (Lilly was born then in 1939), Sarah Simon and her children, Gabriel Peter and his family, and Lucy Frank. There was no food and so Soozun distributed a little to all among them of what little dried meat we had. Even so, the food went like nothing. Meanwhile, they hunted, but they killed no game at all. It was no use, and they all left us.

The old lady Lucy Frank lived with us, and my brother-in-law Joseph was in bad shape too so he did not hunt. Only David and Steven did.

Then Soozun went ice fishing. All day she sat at the fishing hole, even though sometimes she only got one little fish. She managed the food for all of us. We were one household and she distributed whatever food was available among us. Even so, Tabitha's children, being little boys, were so hungry.

Finally Steven said to me, "Let's go east to *Ch'at'oonjik*."[15] We went to Johnny Frank's old house [at *Ch'at'oonjik*]. As it turned out, he shot a moose there and we dried it slightly so it would not be so heavy for the dogs to pull. We were in a stand of trees there with a few houses around. [As much as we enjoyed it] we went back quickly with the food.

At that time James Gilbert and his father were living around *Zheh Gwatsal*.[16] Albert Tritt and his family were living at Fort Yukon.

Then in April Steven said, "I'll go to Fort Yukon on foot." With a tiny bit of dried meat, he left. He walked to Fort Yukon in only three days![17] He even got blisters on his toes.

At that time David Wallis was the interpreter at Fort Yukon. A white person raised him and he understood English well. He immediately made arrangements for Jim Dodson to bring enough food to hand out to all the people.

When he had set off to go down there, Steven said, "Do you suppose you folks could make it to the shores of *Salmon Vavàn*?"[18] That's what we did. That night after he left, Tabitha's little child Joel died. He was sick, and we didn't know it.

While this was happening Myra was living with me. She gave her uncle [Steven] a letter to deliver to David Frank,[19] who was working at the N.C. store. At the time she spoke to me in confidence saying, "Now I will really leave my grandmother's family."[20] She made new things decorated with beadwork for herself.[21] She had all these things ready when the plane landed. Even as Jim Dodson was saying, "Who is called Myra," a little white bag was carried forthwith to the plane [by Myra herself]. "David Frank has sent for her," he said. [As there was no previous discussion] only then did they not care for this idea, but it was too late. So Soozun said, "I'll go with her," and she left with her. If Myra hadn't done this, there's no telling when she would have been married. Alexander Alexander really wanted to marry her. But in the spring of 1940 she was married; David Francis, whose wife had died shortly before, married her.

From *Salmon Vavàn* they said, "Let's all go to Arctic Village." There had been no food for a long time and the dogs were in poor condition. Grandmother Lucy even pulled her own blanket, holding her cane as she walked with us. I think we camped two days going down. There at the mouth of Black Gull Creek grayling are abundant in spring and there we camped on the hill.

At the time Gabriel Peter and his family lived at Arctic Village. Meanwhile, my brother-in-law Joseph's health was progressively getting worse, yet he sat all day at the fishing hole. Then just as breakup was making travel conditions bad we arrived in Arctic Village. There too, we went fishing on all the lakes in the area. On one occasion Alice, Steven, and I went fishing one lake over [from where we were living]. We fished the whole night but there were no fish. So we came back and by chance stopped in front of Alice's house. As it were, her husband Gabriel got some fish that had swum into the fishnet and got caught there. He had prepared boiled fish, fried fish, and fried fish guts for us.[22] I tell you that man could make some good tea! When we came into his presence he said, [Don't just stand there, can't you see] "There's plenty of tea!"

My brother-in-law Joseph was now in very poor health, and we stayed only in Arctic Village with him. It came to the point where he urinated only occasionally, and then Steven went to Fort Yukon to get some medication for him. This was in the summer of 1939. I tell you on this occasion when Steven went to Fort Yukon he did it in a hurry considering that a trip like this usually took him one month!

This time his mother, Soozun, came back with him, and also a white man named Jack Kennedy. Then on the other side of *Vatr'agwąągwaii*[23] Mountain she apparently became sick, vomiting bile. However, she came back with them.

Suddenly we saw a tarpaulin flapping in the breeze up on *Dachanlee*.[24] As it turned out, it was them.

Meanwhile, David was constantly hunting in all directions, but he killed no game. Then while he was gone we saw a herd of caribou just above us on the open tundra with scattered trees and willows upon it. As Noah was a small boy at the time, Tabitha ran up to [tell] me. We had set up a tent for my brother-in-law Joseph on a bluff just down a ways from Peter Shajol's grave site. They saw it from there.

Gabriel Peter was the only man, so they told him about it. Thereupon he paddled across [the stream] and was approaching them along the bank. Joseph could see him from where he was and said, "He's going to scare them off." Meanwhile, Noah disappeared up the riverbank. You see, he ran very fast because he was a small man. While Gabriel was sneaking toward the caribou, Joseph, who was in the weakened last stages of his illness, said, "I used to live so well and now I wonder why I am in this state," and all the while he would grab for his gun and yell out in pain. "I knew this would come to pass," he said, "therefore I made every effort to behave properly toward all living beings and now where are they?"[25]

The caribou sensed Gabriel and then they just disappeared. After a short time we heard shooting up that way. It was Noah who ran after them and killed four caribou. It wasn't long before he came running back to get us. "I didn't take a knife," he said incredulously. At the same time now Alice, Tabitha, and I went up with our pack dogs. When we arrived up there, Gabriel was already butchering the caribou.

After all that, Joseph became very ill and said, "Let blood be taken from my arm."[26] He asked Alice to do this to him. Alice started to do it, but his blood would not leave him. It was really very strange. She pricked him with an awl, yet the blood remained as if in a bag. Then because of that, she said the time of his going was near.

That white man, Jack Kennedy, asked if one of the men could go with him east to the *Khiinjik*.[27] So David went up with him, and then only Gabriel and Alice remained with us. Now that Soozun was feeling good, we set up a tent for Joseph down by the riverbank next to where I was living. Four of us took a blanket and carried him there.

Alice, Soozun, Tabitha, and I went right through the Fourth of July and didn't even know it. There was no food and Steven hunted constantly.

One morning he said he was going up to the pointed hill above us. He said, "If anything adverse should happen, then be sure to signal me with a fire."

On July 9, 1939, at midday Tabitha came in to me. "Your brother-in-law over there is now very ill. Why don't you go see him," she said to me. I went over immediately.

In the tent they had set up a big black mosquito net that one could see through. As it was still daylight, we sent a child to fetch Alice. Just as I stepped into the mosquito netting he leaned his head forward and said, "Put my legs out straight." He said, "Put something under my head," and it was I who sat before him and placed a pillow upon my lap and laid his head there. Meanwhile, Tabitha sat beside him.

After he touched her with affection he started to pray. "Lord in heaven, send your messenger to take my breath," he said. At that moment his breath began to expire, and then he was gone. It was very calm. Truly the Lord gave Tabitha strength. For all of one year she took care of her husband, and so we dressed him. On this occasion I put on him a pair of moccasins with beaded bands around the heels which I had made for Steven. Well then, who was there to pray over him? At the time of his death I read the Lord's Prayer and sang Hymn Fifty over him. He died while he was Second Chief. You see there were no men, only us women, so we laid him in the church[28] before rigor mortis set in.

Meanwhile, Noah went down to *Halii Van*[29] where Sarah Simon was living with her children. He went on from there with one of Sarah's sons to the shores of Old John Lake where Christian Choo and his grandson Peter were living.

After we made him ready, we set some small trees afire. Apparently Steven saw this and came back.

That evening Christian Choo and Peter arrived. They took boards out of a log house and with them they made him a coffin. If Christian had not done this, perhaps we women would have dug a grave in the earth.

His remains were in the church just below me, yet it did not afflict me. We felt sorrow, yet our minds were steadfast. He himself had been tired of his suffering, so why should we cry? You see, sometimes we had no food because of his illness.

It was then that I found out what famine meant. When my mother-in-law, Soozun, told stories, she always told about famine, so we knew to be prepared, yet it meant nothing to us. Yet it seemed to me sometimes that there were no other people in the world.

Now that my brother-in-law was gone it was imperative that we go out and get food. We were expecting the fall caribou migration, and after we stayed there for a while we saw them. We set up camp upon *Vatr'agwąą-gwaii*. We stayed there long enough to work on the few caribou Steven shot. We dried that in no time and moved on to Old John Lake. Tabitha brought her children along with us. That summer there were very few caribou. Now and then he shot a few caribou.

Finally we went up into the mountains at the other end of Old John Lake. We were hoping to see Elijah Henry and the preacher Albert around there. Then we saw the cache they had there. While we were living there it snowed during the night, much to our surprise as it seemed that the summer barely passed. It was September already and surely it would not melt now.

Tabitha asked me to bleed her temples and that was the first time I ever made an incision on a person. I was twenty-one years old at the time. At first I told her no, but then she said, "It's really hurting me." As it turned out I made a good incision.

Then it snowed, and we went back to the shore of Old John Lake. We hitched up the dogs and went to Old John Lakeshore House where my mother-in-law, Soozun, was living. This we did in the fall of 1939.[30]

NOTES

[For the revised edition, which we have followed, Adeline Raboff added annotation, and Tom Alton, editor at ANLC, prepared an index of people who figure in the narrative. Because our readers do not have access to this index or to the index of place names carried over from the first edition, we have provided many more notes. Those that identify people and places derive their information from the two indexes. Mrs. Raboff's notes are marked with her initials. All others are ours.]

1. Peter John's house just below Peter John Mountain. — A. R. (Peter John — not to be confused with Chief Peter John, whose Lower Tanana stories appear later in this volume — was Steven Peter's father. Also known as Peter Shajol, he had died at the time of Katherine's marriage to Steven and had just been buried in Arctic Village when the new bride arrived there.)

2. A lake three to four miles from Arctic Village. The name is translated as "where a stream flows from the lake."

3. The name of the bull caribou in August before they go into the full rutting period. During the full rut bull caribou have a powerful odor and flavor. Literally, "faint smell of winter odor." — A. R.

4. David, like Joseph, was a brother of Mrs. Peter's husband, Steven.

5. The wind chill factor is very high in this area. In the winter and sometimes during the fall, men cut the caribou into quarters with all the fur left on. The meat was stored in the open, and the fur helped preserve the meat and ward off predation. Frozen or raw rumps and shoulders are heavy. — A. R.

6. Mrs. Peter's mother-in-law. Earlier in the book, Mrs. Peter has written that "She was certainly an old woman rich in stories" and that she told stories to her new daughter-in-law.

7. Jeremiah. Jermi was a lifelong pet name he bore. — A. R.

8. Myra was a granddaughter of Soozun Peter, a niece of Steven, David, and Joseph (their sister Sarah Jane was Myra's mother).

9. Literally, a "big burned area" east of Christian Village, a Gwich'in community south of Arctic Village, north of Fort Yukon, that is no longer inhabited.

10. Usually there are cold spells during the holidays. Note the division of labor. — A. R.

11. When she first went to Arctic Village, Mrs. Peter had trouble adjusting to the largely caribou diet after the variety of food, including non-Native food, she had become used to in Fort Yukon.

12. A brand of chewing tobacco. Mrs. Peter has explained to the editors that the girls ground it between their hands and then rolled it into cigarettes.

13. Alaska Native people.

14. Of the visitors mentioned here, Elijah Henry and Lucy Frank were two of the Arctic Villagers who in 1933 had told stories to the ethnologist Robert A. McKennan. Johnny Frank, whose house is referred to shortly, also had been one of McKennan's most prolific raconteurs, and one of the Gilberts, probably the father, contributed to

several of the narratives in McKennan's book, *The Chandalar Kutchin*. Craig Mishler has recently published an extensive collection of the stories of Johnny and Sarah Frank, *Neerihiinjik (We Traveled From Place to Place)*.

15. This is the upper part of what is officially known as the Sheenjek River, east of Arctic Village. The name literally means "nest river."

16. Christian Village.

17. Approximately 145 miles. — A. R.

18. Salmon Lake.

19. Myra's stepfather. "N. C." (at end of sentence) is colloquial Alaskan for Northern Commercial Company.

20. Myra was twenty-three years old. At the time girls were married between fourteen and seventeen years of age. — A. R.

21. *K'eekaii* usually means mittens, hats, gloves, and boots sewn and decorated with beadwork. — A. R.

22. *Ch'its'ik*, the fish guts, are cleaned and fried. They are chewy and rich. Formerly it was considered an omission not to serve them, like serving turkey without dressing. — A. R.

23. Literally, "divided mountain," located northwest of Arctic Village.

24. A tarpaulin was hung up for protection against the elements. — A. R. (*Dachanlee*, translated "timberline," refers here to hills southeast of Arctic Village.)

25. The idea, expressed in his frustration at being so ill and unable to hold his gun, is that his proper behavior toward animals should have brought him luck in hunting.

26. Bloodletting was a common practice. — A. R.

27. Sheenjek River.

28. In Arctic Village.

29. A lake near Arctic Village.

30. Nearly fifty-eight years later, in ill health in Fairbanks at age ninety-one, Steven Peter wanted to return to Old John Lake to live his remaining days. Mrs. Peter and Mrs. Raboff took him there by helicopter on May 31, 1997, and he died on June 2. He is buried on top of a small hill overlooking the lake from its south side. He had been born on its north side.

Jalgiitsik, Tł'yahdik Hàa
Chalkyitsik and Tł'yahdik

Later in March 1942,[1] David returned,[2] but Steven said he was sick. "You leave with David," he told me. So then I harnessed up those poor dogs, put the three children in the sled, and followed him by dog team. I mean to say that David's dogs were really good! Every now and then he waited for me on the way up. Finally near *Jalgiitsik* I think he got exasperated and he was gone.

The moon was shining [on the snow] and gave the luster of daylight all around. The wind was blowing when I finally came to a lake that looked like a back channel to a river. I looked up ahead and saw that the trail divided and I had no idea which trail to take. I stopped the dogs and took a good look at the trail and, of course, I took the trail with the freshest dog tracks. It was very windy and I didn't know where I was going. I was never here before. In spite of that I kept going.

Paul, who was seven months old, became tired and began to cry. Hannah was three years old. Bessie was five years and two months old. Finally when I was totally exhausted I came upon an empty erected tent. Perhaps it is a man out trapping, I thought. I was so exhausted that I thought, "Enough already! I'm going to spend the night here."

I went in and there was a little wood to start a fire inside. I lit the fire and put snow on the stove in a bucket, and I told Bessie to stay there with her younger brother and sister. The sun rose just as I was about to look for wood. I had no snowshoes, so I waded around in the snow looking for firewood. The wood was a long way off! All the while I worried about the children. I gathered wood anyway and chopped it up. I fed the dogs and finally came in. I fed the children and they fell asleep right away as they had been running and playing in the warm tent.

I sat by the hot stove and drank hot tea. "I wonder what I'll do tomorrow," I thought. Just then those poor dogs let out a few barks. I stuck my head out of the tent flaps and, as it were, someone was coming up the trail I had used by dog team. I had hot water on the stove. I thought, it's the man who was out on his trap line.

The team came there and he tied up the dogs; he certainly didn't expect me. He came in and turned out to be Ervin John Sr. He swore and said to me, "What are you doing here?" "I'm lost," I told him. "Where is your husband?" he asked. "He's sick at Fort Yukon and I left him there," I replied. "I was going with David Francis, but my dogs couldn't go fast, and I don't know where he is," I said to him. "*Jalgiitsik* is just a little ways to the north," he told me. "Come there with me," he said, but I said no. "The children wore themselves out and will sleep well," I told him. He had a little trail food and, saying that it was for the children, he gave it to me.

After he left, not much time passed before my dogs barked again. And now what was happening? It was David come back to get me, as it were. He said to me, "It's not that far off; come back with me anyway." I was loathe to do it, but even so I dressed the children and put them in his toboggan. The dog team whisked me along after him in an empty toboggan. Now in the light of the moon those dogs were going so fast that every time we came upon a curve on the trail it was all I could do not to be flung off!

We arrived up there, and I don't recall whose house I went into. We camped there at *Jalgiitsik* to rest the dogs. There were many in *Jalgiitsik* who did not expect that I could do these things.

Then the first thing in the morning, with him [David] in the lead, we set off for *Tl'yahdik*. His parents, Francis and Bella, were living there. Myra was there also with her two-month-old child. That was Frankie.

I arrived with the children, and the next month, in April, before traveling conditions got bad, I was expected to go back to Fort Yukon to see about Steven. I packed up the children in the toboggan again. Simon Francis was very young at that time, perhaps seventeen. And it was Simon who went with me to *Jalgiitsik* at his mother's bidding. David Francis was an industrious man who always made a good living. There was no way he could just up and leave, so Simon went with me. He went with me, but not without a great deal of jiving and laughter.

I was going to go on alone from *Jalgiitsik*. I remembered that it was a very long way to Fort Yukon, so I started out very early, about six o'clock in the morning. It was spring and on the way down I shot a few rabbits. I had no snowshoes, but still I shot rabbits and waded through the snow for them. It was warm and my clothing got damp. I arrived in Fort Yukon at nine o'clock in the evening. I was so tired I couldn't even take the harnesses off the dogs. David Frank was at his house, and he brought in the children and fed the dogs.

Meanwhile, Steven, who had told me he was sick, was gone. I cried because of him, and after midnight he came in; well, I had gotten back, apparently, and that was that!

I mean to say, at the time David Frank really boiled up those rabbits fast!

A short time after that we moved back up. We spent the spring thaw with them at *Tł'yahdik*. I tell you that Francis and Bella were very thoughtful and took good care of us! I used to like to hunt for muskrat, but I didn't know that country, so I just took care of the children. The ice went out and then we all went to Fort Yukon by boat. Farther downriver at the place they call Grafy we disembarked. They intended to fish with a fishnet for one week. And then a moose came out by us and they shot that. From there we made only a few short stops to Fort Yukon. Then we arrived at Fort Yukon.

NOTES

[The following notes are by the editors. As with the preceding selection, information about people and places is derived from the indexes of characters and geographical names appended to *Neets'ąįį Gwiindaii (Living in the Chandalar Country)*.]

1. Chalkyitsik is the conventional spelling (found on most maps) for the Gwich'in village located on the Draanjik or Black River, a tributary of the Yukon east and southeast of Fort Yukon. In current standardized Gwich'in orthography, the village is Jalgiitsik. *Tł'yah* is "a black rock used for medicinal purposes," and Tł'yahdik refers to a place on the Porcupine River northeast of Fort Yukon where this rock is quarried. The three places that figure in this account form a triangle lying on one of its long sides with Fort Yukon at its western apex and Tł'yahdik and Jalgiitsik at the eastern ends of its sides. The base of the triangle is the shorter north-south distance between these two places referred to by the men who come upon Mrs. Peter at the trapper's tent.

2. At the end of the preceding chapter, Myra and David Francis have "made haste" to travel to Tł'yahdik. The people of Fort Yukon have just suffered an epidemic of influenza, in the midst of which Myra has given birth to a son. Mrs. Peter herself has just recovered from the flu, and her husband tells David Francis that he and his wife will go with Francis and his wife if they make another trip to Tł'yahdik. As the present chapter begins, David Francis has returned from Tł'yahdik and is ready to make another trip there. Although we learn later in the chapter that his parents live there, the curative properties of the black rock would seem to have something to do with the purpose of these trips to Tł'yahdik during times of illness.

4

Northern Tutchone

As one proceeds upstream on the Yukon River, the Gwich'in word for story, *gwandak*, becomes *hodëk* among the Han Athabaskans, who traditionally inhabited a large area bisected only for the past century by the international boundary. Farther upriver, the word is *hunday* for the Northern Tutchone Athabaskans, in the Yukon Territory of Canada (the name *Tutchone* has the meaning "woods" or "forest"). The Northern Tutchone people apply the term *hunday* to their contemporary historical and biographical accounts and a modified term, *hudę hundāy*, to their traditional tales. Linguist John Ritter translates *hunday* as "story" or "narration" and *hudę hundāy* as "long ago story." In her article "Tutchone," the ethnologist Catharine McClellan discusses speakers of Northern Tutchone and speakers of Southern Tutchone together as one culture. Of their "long ago stories" she regards those about Beaver Man (or Beaver Doctor) as their "major myth cycle" explaining "the present nature of the human world." She sees their cycle about Crow, or Raven, as important but less prominent. Tutchone narrators of these and other ancient tales demonstrate great skill, McClellan finds, in "developing the psychological possibilities of the plots." In their historical accounts of their first contact with white men, she observes, they do not hesitate to make themselves the butt of humor (502).

Mrs. Gertie Tom has done extensive work in recording, transcribing, and translating *hudę hundāy* as told to her by several Northern Tutchone elders, and she has written in Northern Tutchone others that she herself remembered. She has also written what may be regarded as a special genre of *hunday* that presents her geographical knowledge of her Northern Tutchone homeland through accounts of her lifelong experiences in the region. She derived her geography from her family's nomadic life and from elders' identification of topographical features by Northern Tutchone names.

Daughter of Jim and Jessie Shorty, Gertie Tom was born in 1927 at the confluence of the Big Salmon and Yukon Rivers. At that time Northern Tutchone people inhabited the village of Big Salmon there, about halfway between Whitehorse and Dawson. Given the Northern Tutchone name Et'áts'inkhälme, Mrs. Tom belonged to her mother's clan, *Hanjät* (Crow). Growing up along the Big Salmon River meant traveling with her family to fish and hunt and to cut wood, which they sold as fuel to the riverboats. Mrs. Tom has written that during her first twenty years she and her brothers and sisters "hardly spoke English" and that her parents taught her the Northern Tutchone names of "the places we travelled to — lakes, rivers, mountains" (*Èkeyi* 7). She and her family moved to Whitehorse in 1948, as sternwheeler traffic on the upper Yukon River was diminishing. Big Salmon Village has been deserted since the early 1950s, when the boats stopped running altogether.

In Whitehorse over the past fifty years, Mrs. Tom has been engaged in various occupations calling upon her Northern Tutchone and English language skills. She was a translator and broadcaster for CBC Radio from 1961 to 1965. She worked for the Northern Health Service in the late 1960s and early 1970s. In the summer of 1977 she did some translating for the Alaska Highway Pipeline Inquiry. From 1977 to 1992 she served as Northern Tutchone Specialist with the Yukon Native Language Centre, earning a Native Language Instructor Certificate from Yukon College in 1986. Ritter, director of YNLC, has written that she is "the first Northern Tutchone speaker to help devise and learn to use a writing system for her language." As Founding Elder, Mrs. Tom continues to work part-time at YNLC in workshops and training sessions. She sews and does craftwork, some of which has been displayed in museums in Vancouver and Ottawa.

Her published work consists of *hunday* and educational materials: *How to Tan Hides in the Native Way*, a student's noun dictionary, conversational lessons in Northern Tutchone, and *Èkeyi: Gyò Cho Chú (My Country: Big Salmon River)*. *Èkeyi* grew from a place-name project designed at the Yukon Native Language Centre as an exercise for Mrs. Tom while she was learning to write Northern Tutchone. Although her parents had been first to teach her about their home landscape, she sought further topographical information from other elders. Ritter has observed that as Mrs. Tom "became more comfortable with the writing system, her interest shifted to documentation of how and where her family had travelled in her childhood, of stories she had heard, and of Tutchone place names she remembered" (*Èkeyi* 2). Thus the greater part of *Èkeyi* consists of eight *hunday*, which present the places identified by the names as settings for incidents that Gertie Tom experienced in her lifetime. In them Mrs. Tom achieves an artistic blending of natural landscape with human personality.

The selections that follow are from this book. Gertie Tom wrote these narratives in Northern Tutchone. Working together as a team, she, Ritter, and the ethnologist Julie Cruikshank made word-by-word interlinear English translations and from them the free translations reprinted here. For five of the eight *hunday* in *Èkeyi*, Mrs. Tom uses a distinctive opening statement that reminds the reader that the original medium for the transmission of all Athabaskan narratives was the human voice, not the printed page. "I'm going to tell you a story," she begins, and in the last two *hunday*, as if recognizing that more people will probably read her English translations than her Northern Tutchone compositions, she adds, "in the Indian language."

The first and longest *hunday* in *Èkeyi*, reprinted here, does not use this introductory formula. Titled "Living at Big Salmon: 1930s and 1940s," it follows a typical Athabaskan construction for narratives about the traditional way of life. The spatial center for this narrative is Big Salmon Village as it was during Mrs. Tom's childhood and teenage years; the temporal markers for the explanation and description of her family's subsistence during those years are the four seasons. To sustain life in the village in winter and spring, the families who live there must travel outward in various linear and circular movements in summer, autumn, and even into the winter. They fish, hunt, and trap, traveling by water and by land, in hand-built boats of moose skins stretched over a birch frame and on their feet with dogs as pack animals. While emphasizing the traditional activities of the seasonal cycle, Mrs. Tom from the beginning makes felt the presence of the new ways of life — especially the "Whiteman" food, transportation, and economy. Even though she helped her father cut wood to sell to the steamboat, an Athabaskan work ethic motivated them, and in the conclusion of the narrative Mrs. Tom leaves no doubt that she believes true values for living today can be found in that ethic.

Incidents involving human characters may seem few and brief in this narrative, and it contains only one instance of direct speech. Yet Mrs. Tom distinctly sketches the people around her and sometimes even the animals they encounter. Perhaps we are meant to see as the real, lasting, eternal characters in this narrative Big Salmon River, its tributaries, their surrounding hills and trails, the mountain with "sharp rocks sticking out" that marked the farthest point in the family's loop of travel from home — all the places with their Northern Tutchone names that give rise to the plant and animal life in which humans find sustenance.

In the other two *hunday* presented here, Mrs. Tom tells of trips she made to Northern Lake, in a mountainous region north of the Big Bend in the Big Salmon River (well upstream from its confluence with the Yukon). These two narratives form an interesting pair of companion pieces illustrating culture change over a twelve-year span. In the first, Mrs. Tom describes her trip as a seventeen-year-old girl in 1944, traveling by traditional means with extended family and friends, engaged in a wholly subsistence way of life. In the second account, Mrs. Tom returns to Northern Lake in 1956, a woman of twenty-nine, flying there with a few family members and friends, staking claims for a business organization. Against the background of the earlier trip, the second account evokes sadness for lost lives and times.

SUGGESTIONS FOR FURTHER READING

McClellan, Catharine. "Tutchone." In *Subarctic*, vol. 6 of *Handbook of North American Indians*. Washington DC: Smithsonian Institution, 1981.

Tom, Gertie. *Dùts'ūm Edhó Ts'ètsi Yū Dän K'í (How to Tan Hides in the Native Way)*. Whitehorse, Yukon: Council for Yukon Indians, 1981.

————. *Èkeyi: Gyò Cho Chú (My Country: Big Salmon River)*. Whitehorse, Yukon: Yukon Native Language Centre, 1987.

Gyò Cho Chú

Living at Big Salmon, 1930s and 1940s

Long ago when I was young our whole family used to live at Big Salmon —
my dad, my mother, my older sisters, my younger sisters — eight of us lived
there at Big Salmon. Lots of people used to stay there: John Shorty, George
Peters, Pack Charlie, Harry Silverfox lived at Big Salmon too. In summertime we would go to *Tacho*[1] to cut wood in exchange for food. I helped my
dad cut wood and then we always stayed there for summer.

We cut wood quite some distance away [from the camp] and we used to
go up there every day. We would carry a lunch with us each day to eat at
noon. We worked all day long cutting wood for the White Pass steamboat
which traveled back and forth from Whitehorse to Dawson. After we cut
wood, we got food in exchange. We only worked for food; we didn't ever see
any money to speak of. My dad really worked hard to get food for his children. That's how we all learned to work hard. My dad and my mother
brought us up to know how to work. Living in the bush we all learned how
to work hard. We didn't stay in town and travel around in a car.

In the old days people used to like to travel around for their food.

We were staying at *Tacho* when the salmon came up in July. From there
my mother, my young brother, and I went to the place they call Gold Point.[2]
We put up a tent and drying racks and we dried fish. We camped right there
at an old camping spot. My dad took us up there by boat and helped us set up
camp before we went back.[3] We went there for salmon. We set up our tent
and brought in wood [for campfire].

Then I helped my dad set a fishnet for salmon. We tied rocks on it to
weight it down. Then he went back to *Tacho* to cut wood for food. My
mother and I camped there. Then I ran a fishnet and my youngest brother
held the boat rope so it wouldn't drift away. I would check the net. Sometimes in the morning we would catch thirty fish and at night we would catch
thirty. When it turned dark we would light a lantern and then we filleted fish

by that light. We really worked hard, my mother and I, drying lots of fish by ourselves. We had a boat but it didn't have a motor on it.

Then my two sisters came up from *Tacho*. When they got there the salmon was already dry. We were planning to take that dried salmon back to Big Salmon, so we loaded up the boat with salmon and pulled it upriver. One of my sisters sat in the boat, pushing it away from the shore with a pole. We pulled the boat upriver for a whole day. When we got to where we lived we stored the fish in a cache.

Then we got ready to go out for meat. We unloaded the boat and packed it all up to the storage cabin. When we finished putting it all inside we planned to go up Big Salmon River. My dad came up from *Tacho* to go with us. He had been cutting wood in exchange for food and he picked up the food and brought it with him.

Then we headed out for meat. We went up Big Salmon River. We put the food in dog packs and we took what we needed to survive — like a tent and axe and things you need in the bush. The dogs packed food for us and we each carried our own blanket.

Then we went on to the place they call *Chu K'óa* [Little Cold Water]. We camped right there. In the morning we started going again and kept walking and walking.

A foot trail goes up on the hillside from a place they call *Shā* [Fish Trap]. In the old days people used to set a fish trap there for salmon so they named it *Shā* in Indian language. The trail leads to the place they call *Ekín*[4] from there and we went there. It used to be really nice along that trail. The ground was really hard and there was pine and red spruce mixed together, and lots of grouse. We killed grouse while we were walking along.

We stopped close to *Ekín* where there's a big creek running out. The water was too deep for us to cross so we put down our packs and my dad cut down a bunch of trees to make a bridge. So we worked there for a while. We made poles and then built a bridge and then we went across it and camped on the other side.

From there, the men went out hunting. They were hunting over the mountains. My dad and my mother camped there and my dad's sister camped with us too. My oldest sister, Rena, and her husband camped with us there, and also another sister [Mary] and her husband. Altogether there were four camps there.

From there the men went out hunting and they killed a bunch of moose. Then they built a cache and a drying rack to dry the meat.

That's when men packed the meat in and people cooked the guts up for themselves. After they filled up, they went to sleep. In the morning they packed up their supplies and put them in dog packs and then they tied the packs onto the dogs and they went for the meat. Everybody went out — each camp went out for the meat. When they kill one moose they divide it up; whoever kills the moose used to do that, the old-time people. Then people went out to the place where they killed the moose. When a man kills a moose he cuts it up and gets the whole thing ready [that is, cuts it into pieces the right size for packing, before he invites people to come]. When people got up there, they made tea and they cooked the meat on a cooking stick stuck in the ground by the fire. Meat is really delicious when it's cooked that way.

After people cooked themselves a nice lunch — tea and meat — they loaded up the dog packs. They cut up the meat in pieces and took out the bones, and people packed the bones. It's too hard on the dogs to pack the bones. After people loaded up the dogs [and balanced the packs and tied them on] they went back.

Sometimes when they kill a moose too far from the camp, people move the camp there. If it's close by, they bring it back to the camp.

My mother and my aunt were sitting in camp. They unpacked the dogs. They had already cut the willows to put the meat on. They cooked for us before we went back and then we ate too. Then they turned around and started working on the meat. They took the meat out of the dogs' packs and put it on the willows. Then they cut the meat up. My mother cut it up and we put it on the poles to dry it. We stayed at the bottom of *Ddhäla* [Little Mountain][5] for a long time.

When the meat was a little bit dry we went out for porcupine. We took the dogs that go after porcupine smell; when they find porcupine they bark. That's the reason my sister Ida and I always walked around for porcupine; we walked around on the hillside for porcupine and our dogs walked around with us. When our dogs barked we went and killed the porcupine they found, and then we still kept on walking and killed another one the same way.[6] Then we headed back home.

After that we arrived back. When people kill porcupine they always give it to another person and she cooks it. Then he or she divides it into small pieces and gives some to everyone in the camp. That's what my mother did — she gave it to my auntie and she singed it and boiled it and divided it among everyone in the camp.

After we dried all the meat we aimed for *Ttheghrá Ddhäl.*[7] We headed off in a big loop and we kept on camping and traveling. From *Ddhäla* there's another mountain but I don't know its name. We camped up that way. Again, people hunted for moose and they killed lots of moose there. When we had lots of meat they freighted ahead with it and we followed behind moving the camp. [Men freight ahead with dogs, return, then all go again with dogs in the morning.] From that mountain people started to freight ahead toward *Ène Chú* [North Fork].[8]

After that we went there — they call it North Fork in English. People freighted ahead to there. As soon as we got there my dad called a moose by rubbing a shoulder blade against a tree. The moose had started rutting already and he called it by rubbing the shoulder blade right from the camp when we got there. Every time people move the camp and get a new place they set up a cache to dry meat. After that they take the meat out of the dog packs and put it on the cache and they make a really nice camp. After they put all the meat up on the cache, then they cook something for themselves. While they were cooking I walked around by the shore. I walked around and looked across *Ène Chú* — here a bull moose went into the water toward us. I didn't even say a thing. I just took off to the camp. I told my dad a bull moose was swimming across toward us. Just like that all the men who were there jumped up and grabbed their guns. By that time, the bull moose was getting out of the water on this side. They killed it right there too. Then we stayed there for a while until we dried the meat.

They built a raft there to get across *Ène Chú* and we crossed. We reached the place where *Ène Chú* runs into *Gyò Cho Chú* [Big Salmon River]. There people hunted, planning to build a moose-skin boat. When we got to that junction of North Fork and Big Salmon we stopped, we put up the tent and built a cache for meat.

By now it was September and the moose had started rutting. People stayed there and from there they hunted along the river. That's when we built a big boat for two camps. There were two camps to one boat, so they made two boats [for four camps]. They sewed three moose skins together to build each boat. The men also built a raft to carry the dogs [because meat is in the boat].

We also picked berries then: the women would go out for berries and the men go out hunting.

We had already picked lots of cranberries, but we didn't bother with mossberries because we had no way to keep them. After that they started making a really good boat. They looked for a small tree so that they could make the ribs. They brought back a whole bunch of them and then they bent them the way they wanted to make the boat ribs. That's how they made a moose-skin boat in the olden days. While the men go out to get the small trees for the boat ribs, the women sew the skins together using a big three-corner needle.

You twist the sinew [to make it stronger — that is, special sinew for boat] with that strong sinew you sew the skins together overlapping them and sewing it twice. Then they build the ribs and they cover the frame with hide [and tie it onto the ribs]. After that men go out and look for soft pitch [spruce], [pick "beige" color pitch and heat it]. They heat it up and then they glue it where it's sewn so the water won't get through. After that they let it sit to dry.

When the boat is really dry, they go out and look for something you can peel like birch bark. They peel off spruce bark strips and they put it inside the boat to make the floor of the boat. Then they load the meat up and they get ready to go back along *Gyò Cho Chú* [Big Salmon River]. When you make that kind of boat, two camps can put all their meat and supplies in it because it holds quite a bit of weight.

After that they put the dogs in the raft and one person floated down with them to where we live at Big Salmon Village. After we dried enough meat for the winter we went back to where we lived, where Big Salmon River runs into Yukon. We went to *Ttheghrá* to get sheep meat; we would kill lots of moose and sheep for our winter meat.

Then we got back to where we stay at Big Salmon Village. We had a big log house there and we always stayed there. Lots of people have their homes there. We all had high caches there and when we got back, we put the meat inside the high cache.

Now it was starting to be fall and starting to snow but before it got too cold, and everything froze, my dad went out again to get fresh meat for winter. When he went out hunting he took dog team with him so they could pull back the meat when he killed it. People used to get ready for winter before it started to be too cold long ago.

In those days there were no stores. We cut wood at *Tacho* in exchange for food. If there was money left over from cutting wood, we kept it. We got lots of Whiteman's food by the wood we cut. My dad also went out in wintertime to hunt furs and he took the furs to *Hudinlin* [Whitehorse], to buy food. He brought back what we needed and then he bought food ahead to come out on the first boat in spring. (He did the same thing in summer — saved money from wood and ordered food from Whitehorse to come on the last boat in fall).

When we got back there in wintertime, the women made skins from the moose people killed. (I forgot to mention that when people killed moose they would bring all the dry skins back). After that, it's getting to be fall time and the men go out hunting for fur. That's when the women smoke the skin, soak the skin, keep doing that until the skin turns soft. When the skins turn soft, they have the poles already up in the bush to tan the skin. My mother asked me, "Could you come with me so we can tan a skin?" So I went there to the bush and we tanned a skin. Down below where we stayed at the house there was no wood for an open fire so we tanned the skin in the bush.

When we got up there, we stay all day long. While we are tanning the skin we would keep the fire going all the time and keep turning the skin and working it. I was helping her to tan the skin. I kept the fire going for her by putting in wood.

By the time it started to get dark the skin was dry and my mother took it down from the pole and we started back and arrived home. After that she cut around the edge and she sewed it up to get it ready for final smoking. When it's smoked you can make moccasins and mitts for men going out to hunt in wintertime. We never really thought of selling it, we just made it for our own kids.

By now men were hunting lots of fur all winter. When it passed Christmas they went to *Hudinlin* [Whitehorse]. Fur was really expensive [after Christmas] so they sold it and brought back lots of Whiteman food. After that my dad bought food to bring back. When he's ready to go back to Big Salmon he orders ahead the food for the first boat in springtime. He comes back in March. As soon as the ice breaks up and the water rises in June the steamboat comes on its way to Dawson. Inside that boat arrives all the food that my father bought up ahead.

Long ago people really used to think ahead about how to survive. Not like now when people work at steady jobs to buy food. Long ago nothing was hard for them because the head of the family taught kids when they were young how to survive. They would teach them how to make a good home. If a person is lazy he doesn't have anything. Old-time people used to really teach their kids a lot by talking to them.

I'm telling the story about how we used to live long ago. That's what I'm telling.

NOTES

[*Èkeyi: Gyò Cho Chú* does not include annotation of the text. It does, however, contain a catalog of Northern Tutchone names of specific topographical features, a literal English translation of each name, the officially recognized name for the place (if there is one), and its map coordinates. The editors have prepared the following notes, drawing all information about place names from the catalog in *Èkeyi*.]

1. This name is used synonymously with Byer's wood camp, downriver on the Yukon from Big Salmon. To the people, it means three mountains north of the river

and behind the wood camp. There is no official name for the place, and no exact translation for *Tacho*.

2. They have traveled much of the distance back upriver on the Yukon toward Big Salmon.

3. That is, back home to Big Salmon.

4. A hill between Big Salmon River and Walsh Creek. The name is translated as "den," but the place has no official name. The catalog of place names states that "the old people used to say that giant worms lived at the end of this mountain" (see Maudie Dick's story "Dzǫhdié' Kills the Giant Worm" in the Kaska section, which follows).

5. A hill between two creeks that are tributaries of the Big Salmon. It has no official name.

6. The usual method is by clubbing with a large stone or heavy piece of wood.

7. *Ddhā̀l* means "mountain," and *ttheghrá* has the literal meaning of "sharp rocks sticking out." The official name is Mount D'Abbadie. They have now traveled a considerable distance upriver from Big Salmon Village and inland from Big Salmon River. From this point they begin the homeward trek of their loop, moving north to the North Fork of the Big Salmon, then downstream on the North Fork and on the Big Salmon.

8. The official name is North Big Salmon River.

K'ènlū Mǎn

Northern Lake, 1944

I'm going to tell you a story about the time we went up through *K'ènlū*[1] [Northern Lake] pass. I'm telling what I remember about 1944 when my mother, my dad, and my three sisters, who later died, were still living.

We lived along *Gyò Cho Chú* [Big Salmon River] and in wintertime we would take off from there with a dog team.

One time we went by dogsled to the place they call *Shā*[2] [Fish Trap] and we camped overnight. We set out for *Ddhäla* [Little Mountain] and when we arrived there we made a really good camp. From there, people went hunting and killed moose, which they hauled in on a toboggan. Then the women made skins. People kept on killing moose.

Some of the men freighted ahead with dogsled and in that way they kept on moving.

From *Ddhäla* we walked up through the pass which goes through to *K'ènlū*. We went past *Ddhäla*. I was walking with my older sister [Ida]. The snow was really deep. You couldn't walk around without snowshoes or the snow would go right up to your waist. We were just walking around on the mountain looking for porcupine when we saw something walking around over in the distance.

We wondered, "What is it?"

We thought it might be a bear walking around over there. Here it was a moose struggling in the deep snow. He could scarcely climb through the snow because it was so thick. We could hardly see it. We got frightened and took off.

After we got back to the camp we told our mother about it.

"What is it? We saw something big and black walking in the snow," we said to her. Then the men went out after it. They saw by the tracks that it was a moose.

We had figured that it was a bear so we got scared and took off!

After that we camped there for a long time. That's the time I learned to make a skin. They gave me a skin and I made it. They gave my older sister one too and she also made a skin. We fleshed the skin, then we framed it, then we scraped it. When you scrape it that way the skin becomes soft.

From there we kept on moving camp. [Whenever we stopped] we soaked the skin so it would be soft and easy to carry. When it is stiff it is hard to carry on a toboggan.

We kept on camping in the mountains and we kept moving. Finally we all got to Ène Chú [North Fork of Big Salmon River].

There the men went out hunting for moose up K'ènlū pass. They killed lots of them. The moose don't travel around much in wintertime because the snow is so deep. That's the reason that even the bull moose were fat because they were staying one place when we were camped up that way.

From that camping place we set out for K'ènlū. We walked up North Fork for quite a distance. We stopped and made camp at the place where the draw from K'ènlū Mān creek runs into North Fork.

My grandpa, Soo Bill, and Selkirk Billy came over toward us [to this side of the mountain] and met us right there. I guess my mother knew they were coming so we came up through the mountains to meet up with them right there. My grandpa, Soo Bill, his wife [Kitty], their children — the whole family — came over this way from Ross River by dog toboggan. They stayed with us. Selkirk Billy, his wife, and Clifford Billy too because they raised him and he was staying with them, they too stayed with us.

After that, people killed lots of moose up in the pass through to K'ènlū. We all went up there and then men hunted moose.

Just this side of K'ènlū Mān we stopped and made camp and stayed there. Again, the men killed lots of cow moose and bull moose. The moose were really good and fat. After that the women made skins.

By now it must have been April, and before long it was the end of April. When spring arrived we went along K'ènlū and we camped on the shore. From there the men freighted ahead down toward Gyò Cho Chú, to the place they call "Big Bend" in English. Then we all reached the river [Gyò Cho Chú]. By now it was really spring and the ice had already broken up on the river.

When we camped there [at Big Bend], people went out with dogs to round up moose. I don't know exactly how they used to do that. They did it when the snow was deep and a crust formed on top. The dogs walked around on the crust and they rounded up the moose. The dogs were trained to go after moose and to keep them in one place. People would go out on top of the crust early in the morning [while it's still frozen]. The dogs also walked on the crust. They kept the moose in one place while people killed them. People killed lots of moose there.

People staying there were in four camps. They dried lots of meat, they put up a cache and they cut the meat flat for drying. I helped my mother cut up meat. Lots of people were drying meat.

Then the men went hunting beaver. Long ago people used to hunt fur wherever they wanted to. That's the time I'm talking about. Now they have registered trap lines. In the old days people used to go out to get fur wherever they wanted to.

Lots of people stayed there hunting beaver and muskrat and they killed lots of muskrats. We stayed there until the end of May. By now the ice was completely melted.

We stayed right there at the place they call Big Bend along *Gyò Cho Chú.* Then Teslin people came downstream hunting beaver — Louis Fox, Walter Fox, and Peter Fox — three of them named Fox came downstream along Big Salmon River from *Chu Lą*[3] [Quiet Lake] hunting beaver. From there they arrive at our camp. When strangers came it was the custom to cook the best food for them. When those Teslin people came, they cooked the best food for them. They even gave them dry meat.

When we stayed there, people killed moose. After they fleshed the meat out they kept the skin so they could build a moose-skin boat. After that each separate camp made its own boat: the women made the skins and sewed them together — each camp used three skins for a boat. My grandpa's family did that too.

Then the men went out to get materials to build the frame for the moose-skin boat. They shaped the wood and then they covered it over and made the boat. When they were finished with that, it was about June. Now the water was starting to rise. While they waited they went out to hunt beaver. When they finished making the moose-skin boats we went back to *Gyò Cho Chú* where we lived.

After that people went to Carmacks[4] to sell their furs. The men went by themselves with fur. They sold the fur and bought Whiteman food with it and brought it back.

Before they went they put the boat in the water and that's how they traveled to Carmacks to sell the fur. Then they came back and we went down to *Tacho* where we always went for summer. [Every summer we always went there to cut wood at Byer's Wood Camp.]

That's all.

NOTES

[As with the preceding story, the notes here, which have been added by the editors, are based upon information in the catalog of place names in *Èkeyi*.]

1. The word has no literal translation. *Män*, often used with it, means "lake." The official name is Northern Lake.

2. The word identifies a site on the Big Salmon River where fish traps had once been set when salmon were running. The place has no official name, and Mrs. Tom notes that during her lifetime it has not been used for fish traps.

3. Translated literally, *chu* means "water," and *lą* means "end." Quiet Lake is the official name of one lake, but the Northern Tutchone term encompasses the entire system of lakes, including Quiet Lake, at the head of Big Salmon River.

4. Community on the Yukon River between Whitehorse and Dawson, named for George Carmack, who, with his Tagish wife Kate, her brother, and their nephew, discovered the gold that set off the rush to the Klondike.

K'ènlū Măn

Northern Lake, 1956

My dad, my two younger brothers [Norman and Joe], and I traveled over to *K'ènlū*[1] [in 1956]. The time I'm talking about is after I came back from hospital in Edmonton. We went from Whitehorse on a small plane to stake for a company.

We got on the plane and flew along Big Salmon River. There is a small lake by the river under *Tthęl Tadétth'ät*.[2] The plane landed us right there. We took along four dogs with us to do the packing. We put packs on the dogs and left from the place where we landed, and we climbed up *Tthęl Tadétth'ät*. We climbed and we climbed. It was difficult for me because I had just come out of hospital, but I still followed, climbing behind the others. I went so that I could stake for the company.

When we had climbed up, we camped on the mountain near the place where we were going to stake.

Then we went from there up the mountain. When we were almost at the top, we saw sheep walking around. My father and my two brothers sneaked up to the sheep while I waited for them, sitting on the rocks on the mountain ridge. They sneaked up and killed the sheep. Even though there were lots of sheep there, they only killed two of them because there was no way to carry any more.

Three sheep started to come toward me where I was sitting. They were coming straight for me. I knocked on the rocks with my walking stick and then the sheep turned away. After that, I went over to where my dad had killed the sheep. They were cutting up the sheep and taking out the guts. We all started packing some meat back to where we were staying, and when we got back we cooked it up.

Then we packed up the dogs and we went back to the place where we had killed the sheep. The dogs packed some meat and the men carried some back. We packed it over the gully and into the draw and then we stopped and made camp there. Then the men went back and got the rest of the meat from those two sheep they had killed. We went on from there to the mountain where we were going to stake. Field Johnny and John Shorty traveled with us to stake too. That's the point at which we went up on the mountain to stake. We stayed there for a long time until we had finished staking. Then we hung up the meat and dried it and we used that for food while we were traveling. We had no way to carry fresh meat around.

Once my brothers and my dad had finished their staking, my dad helped me. When we were all finished, we headed from there over to where we were camped at *K'ènlū Mǟn*. We went over the mountain, and when we reached the draw we made lunch. There were groundhogs whistling all over the mountains, so they shot lots of them and we cooked them. Then we went down to *K'ènlū* where the plane was going to pick us up. We followed the creek that ran down the draw. While we were walking down the draw we saw a big bull caribou up in the mountains. Even so, we let it go. We didn't bother to kill it because we had no way to carry it. We followed the creek down the draw, but it was really bushy. We kept on heading toward *K'ènlū Mǟn*. We walked and walked, and finally we reached the lake.

A small plane was supposed to pick us up and take us to Whitehorse. I think that we camped there for two nights—I'm not really sure. It was while we were there that we saw a moose standing in the bay. My two brothers sneaked up on it and I went with them. The oldest one shot at the moose, but nothing happened: the moose just stood there!

That's when my youngest brother picked up his gun. "How come the moose's ear isn't even moving around?" he joked with his older brother.

Then he aimed his gun and shot the moose, killing it. It fell down right there. My dad made a cache so we could dry the meat and make it light for the plane. We cut the meat and hung it to dry, but we threw away the skin because the plane was too small to carry it. We hung the meat and started a fire, which we kept going to smoke and partially dry the meat.

We stood on the shore and threw out a hook and pulled it in. We caught a few trout. There are lots of good trout in *K'ènlū*.

Finally, the plane landed on the lake to pick us up and we loaded everything up and went back to Whitehorse. When we got back, the company paid us for the claims we had staked for them.

That's all for this story.

NOTES

[As with the preceding story, the notes here, provided by the editors, are based upon information in the catalog of place names in *Èkeyi*.]

1. See note 1 to preceding narrative.

2. A mountain standing between Teraktu Creek and Big Salmon River, where it is believed that someone lost a stone axe. Translated literally, *tthęl* means "stone axe," and *tadétth'ät* means "got lost." The mountain has no official name.

5

Kaska

Speakers of Kaska may define their territory in relation to the high mountains at the borders of their traditional homeland: Steamboat Mountain in the south, Three Aces in the west, the Mackenzie Mountains in the east, and Keel Peak in the north, the mountains where the animals left their rafts in mythical times after the earth was flooded. Kaska territory also coincides with the drainage of the upper parts of the Pelly and Liard Rivers in the southern Yukon and northern British Columbia. The name that the people use to refer to themselves is *Dene* or *Dane*, a term that means "person" or "people" and is also the self-designation of many groups in the Northwest Territories and Prairie Provinces. The name *Kaska* seems to have originated from the name of a creek in the Cassiar region of Kaska territory. The name came to be used in English for all the speakers of Kaska in the Liard drainage, and eventually for all Kaska speakers in accordance with the European ideology that a people, the "Kaska people," should be identified with a language, with "the people who speak Kaska language." The term *Dene* was not as limited in this way when applied either to groups of people or to languages, but could refer outward to what are now considered other languages or groups of people.

In the Kaska language, nouns and verbs are often related in form and meaning, a characteristic of Athabaskan languages generally. The word for "story," *gudech* or *gudeji*, is the same or nearly the same as the verb for "he/she is telling a story," *gudech*. A Kaska person might ask a storyteller, *"Esdał gundech,"* "Tell me a story." There are two main Kaska genres that may each be used in a single performance. The genre of *gudech*, "story," includes any narrative that is performed by means of spoken language and gesture. It might include a speech, an account of some current event, or oral history, as well as stories about mythical times. The other main genre associated with stories is song, *hin* (*meyiné*, "his/her song"; *ejin*, "he/she is singing"), and in some stories the storyteller becomes a singer.

Although some writers have proposed that Yukon Native people distinguish between stories of actual events and stories of mythical times — the "long ago" stories — this distinction is problematical. Accounts of recent historical events may include elements relating to the supernatural, while storytellers may assert that stories describing mammoths or other extinct animals occurred only recently. Storytellers may provide contradictory clues about whether they believe a story to be an actual historic event or a "long ago" story. Maudie Dick begins her account of "Dzǫhdié' and the Giant Worm" with "Long ago," and concludes with, "It must be getting to be a long time, on this earth," which would seem to place it securely with the "long ago" stories. She provides a contradictory comment, though, when she says the story took place in "recent times, they say."

John Dickson, a well-known Kaska elder and storyteller, was born around the turn of the century. He learned many stories, including "The Girl Who Lived with Salmon," from his grandfather, Siwash Tom, while growing up with his family in the Pelly Banks region of the Yukon. His family followed the Kaska traditional round of activities, fishing in the larger lakes and in the Pelly River for salmon and traveling seasonally to the high mountain country for large game such as caribou. As a young man he worked as a special constable for the Royal Canadian Mounted Police, serving as an interpreter, guide, and cook for the first police officer stationed in the Ross River area, Sergeant Claude Tidd. While working as a special constable and on boat crews, John Dickson practiced speaking English. Although English was his second language, it was also a source of pride and status for him since it opened many job opportunities.

Mr. Dickson used both English and Kaska in telling "The Girl Who Lived with Salmon." It would have been possible for him to tell the story either in Kaska or in English exclusively if he were addressing an audience with limited abilities in either language. On this occasion, however, in May 1990 at his home in Upper Liard, he was addressing Ann Mercier, a fully bilingual Native-language teacher, and Pat Moore, a non-Native linguist with some facility in the Kaska language, so he chose to use both languages and engage in code switching. Whatever he said in English has been recorded verbatim and is printed in italics. The original text in both English and Kaska was transcribed by Mrs. Grady Sterriah and Pat Moore and then translated by them into English. Mr. Dickson recorded many stories before his death in 1996, and several have now been transcribed and translated. "The Girl Who

Lived with Salmon" was first published with another of his stories, in prose paragraphs, by the Kaska Tribal Council in 1999.

"The Girl Who Lived with Salmon" is presented with line breaks at pauses, in what is sometimes called a verse-format translation. Verse-format translations are favored by many translators working with Native American literatures because they believe this format better captures the original structure, manner of presentation, and feel of the actual performance. The use of verse-format translations as opposed to prose translations was discussed extensively at the Kaska literacy sessions in 1997. The participants in this workshop were all Kaska-language teachers and translators, and all of them favored prose translations, both for their own reading and for use with language students. They felt that prose translations were easier to comprehend, and that the verse format with its frequent breaks and more literal style of translation often created the impression that either the storyteller or the translators were unsophisticated and had an imperfect command of English. The verse format has been used for the stories here, however, because that form is favored by many of the prominent scholars working with Native American literatures.

In John Dickson's and Maudie Dick's generation, Kaska women tended to speak Kaska almost exclusively while Kaska men had more experience speaking English and were likely to switch to English when addressing non-Natives. Because of this pattern, English and Kaska are "gendered" when they are used together by a bilingual speaker like Mr. Dickson. In framing the story at the beginning and end, he presents himself as a male storyteller by using English extensively. Throughout the story he uses English to echo statements he has already made in Kaska. This technique of repetition is also used for emphasis in stories told exclusively in Kaska by storytellers like Mrs. Dick. Switching from one language to another provides even more emphasis and also seems to assert the validity of the story from both a Native and a non-Native perspective.

Kaska stories commonly have four major parts, which are based on a simple two-part theme of "going out" and "coming back." Dell Hymes and others have reported that the four-part story based on "going out" and "coming back" is very common for many North American groups including many Athabaskan groups. Because each of the four parts of the story also typically includes a core of quoted dialogue between major characters, these major parts of the story have been labeled as acts. The second act of "Dzǫh-dié' Kills the Giant Worm" has two sections, each occurring in a separate location, so these have been labeled as two parts within a single act.

In "The Girl Who Lived with Salmon" the first half includes the disappearance of the girl and her round trip to the sea and back, while the second half describes her restoration to human form. On this journey the girl becomes a salmon and then turns back into a human being. The core of each section is quoted dialogue, and this dialogue is often presented in Kaska as it would have been actually spoken in a traditional fish camp long ago. Even in this context, however, Mr. Dickson uses echo statements in English to reinforce his points. The medicine man who is restoring the salmon girl also uses English extensively in one key address. Mr. Dickson seems to be equating the status of the medicine man with his own status as storyteller by using this device.

Maudie Dick was also born around the turn of the century. Her mother, Louise Dease, was from the Dease Lake region of British Columbia, and her father, Pelly Smith, lived in the Ross River and Pelly Banks regions of the Yukon Territory. Mrs. Dick's uncle, Albert Dease, worked as an informant with James Teit, an associate of Franz Boas, in preparing a collection of Kaska stories published in 1917.

Maudie Dick told "Dzǫhdié' Kills the Giant Worm" entirely in Kaska to Mrs. Grady Sterriah, a Native-language teacher who is fluent in Kaska, and to Pat Moore. The story was recorded along with several others at Mrs. Dick's home in Ross River in November 1989. Mrs. Dick recorded many stories before her death in 1991, but only one, "Dzǫhdié'," has been published, initially with Mr. Dickson's stories in the anthology by the Kaska Tribal Council in 1999. As with "The Girl Who Lived with Salmon," the earlier prose paragraphs have been rendered here in the verse format by the translator, Pat Moore.

She framed this narrative as a "long ago" story and made references both at the beginning and at the end to the traditions associated with the culture hero, Dzǫhdié'. According to Kaska tradition, Dzǫhdié' was discovered crying in a pile of moose-hair scrapings and was raised by an older woman whom he called his grandmother. The older men of his camp, his "uncles," often made fun of his size and otherwise acted disrespectfully. As part of the background to this story, they have insulted him by refusing to share caribou marrow bones with him because they say he is too small to be worthy of such a delicacy. Dzǫhdié', however, has peculiar abilities to accomplish whatever he wants through his dreams and magical powers.

The story is framed also as a story within a dream, for while Dzǫhdié' is dreaming, his dreams are actually being acted out in the bush. In the narrative, Dzǫhdié' "goes out" to the giant worm in his dreams, and then the giant worm "comes back" to him. With the assistance of his grandmother,

Dzǫhdié' finally succeeds in killing this monster, which seems to represent personified fear. The entire story has the four-part structure typical of Kaska stories, with a centerpiece of quoted dialogue in each section. The story of "Dzǫhdié' and the Giant Worm" demonstrates Maudie Dick's mastery of both the Kaska language and traditional storytelling.

Pat Moore

SUGGESTIONS FOR FURTHER READING

Honigmann, John J. *Culture and Ethos of Kaska Society.* Yale University Publications in Anthropology 40. New Haven: Yale University Press; London: Oxford University Press, 1949.

———. "Kaska." In *Subarctic*, vol. 6 of *Handbook of North American Indians*. Washington DC: Smithsonian Institution, 1981.

Moore, Pat, ed. *Dene Gudeji (Kaska Narratives).* Watson Lake, Yukon: Kaska Tribal Council, 1999.

Teit, James A. "Kaska Tales." *Journal of American Folk-Lore* 30 (1917): 427–73.

Gédéni Gēs Gagáh Nédē

The Girl Who Lived with Salmon

ACT I

Down there,
someplace,
Dawson I think,
this side someplace.[1]
You know that little kid.
Children were playing with small fish about this big.
You make it slough.
That here salmon,
salmon little bigger now.
They dammed it.
They made a dam.
All that three,
four kids.
Yes,
two girls,
two boys.
It must have been that those children went back.
That one girl was gone,
about that big.
He [she][2] *got necklace.*
It was like *that watch chain.*
He [she] got here
necklace
that cross.[3]
Yes,
it must have been that
her mother was gone.

Gee
they went around [looking] for her [the girl] but,
she was really gone.
She's gone.
Children
one-two boys
she played with fish in the water then.
She's gone.
She disappeared.
She disappeared.
They really ran around, but for nothing,
he said.[4]

Her mother really cried.
Her mom cried.
Her father,
all over.
"Grizzly bear must have taken her," he said.
Medicine man,
One medicine man make medicine.
He sang,
he sang,
he sang.
"This
you all eat."
He gave it to them.
"She became this small fish.
She became a salmon.
She was taken far away.
They went with a boat.
For us the fish went with a boat.
They traveled far by boat.
What happened that she disappeared?
Maybe she will come back.
You all make a fish trap
there,
when summer comes again then."

"Yes,"
they all said.

ACT II

Where the child disappeared, there,
really lots of people came there.
The salmon were already arriving.
Fish trap,
fish trap,
they were taking out fish.
The father of the girl,
he packed fish up,
ten.

His wife dried fish,
salmon.
This *last one*
she take, cut its head.
She cuts its head.
Never cut,
"Kats, kats,
kats."
She cut something,
ten.[5]

Well she holler here, medicine man he come.
He came.
"That's it.
That flowing water,
you all bury it across there."
Those feathers,
feathers,
that here swan
feathers[6]
they put over it.
People didn't go across then.
"You all watch it always.
Tomorrow then when it is starting to get light."

ACT III

Gee,
her mother,
she didn't know what she was going to do.
She's got that salmon.
Salmon they took across like that.
They didn't *cut it.*
He [medicine man] always watched it.
Those feathers happened to rise then.
There was foam then. That foam went up and down like that then,

"You got to see it.
Just you tell me then,
me.
People are not to go across to it,"
that medicine man.
"Only me alone, I will go across."
They spread feathers over it [over the salmon].

Her mother always watched across,
her mother.
Her father too.
That he come here,
foam.
Next time like that,
the people they saw it like that.
That salmon was sitting across.
The salmon was sitting there before.
"Tell me about it then," he said, that medicine man.
Suddenly her mother ran to there.
"Feathers are rising with breathing over across."

"Finally she is coming back," he said.

ACT IV

He [the medicine man] went across to her.
It rose more,

those
feathers rose with breathing.
Rhythmically.
He went to her.

He made the sign of the cross like that.
He sat facing her.
He sing.
"Come here, I'm telling you all,"
he said.
"I am going to lift my left arm
then she was your daughter," he said.
Her father too,
just two.
Only those *come.*
Not too many people.
After a long time he lifted up.
They ran up crying.

"Don't cry, all of you,"
he said [the medicine man].
A child was sitting up like this,
little girl.
She saw her mother.
That salmon was gone,
the whole thing *that here* salmon.
She was a person, her daughter.
Medicine man,
he give her a little water,
water, *some warm water.*
He sign the cross before he give it.

"Mom!" *he [she] call 'em.*
She spoke as soon as she swallowed that water.

"Daughter!
Then there was nothing,
we cried about it,"
they said.

"Dad!" she said to her father.

[He said to her,]
"This is your grandfather,
the one that made you come back then.
That one is a doctor."

"My house,
our house,
you all really stink for me, Mother," she [daughter] said.
"They took me downstream on this.
I went downstream with people.
Downstream there were really lots of people.
We paddled with a boat.
They came up with that birch bark boat.
For us they are fish.
Someplace we stop, we sit down, like that we go out again,"
she said.
Finally the people *all come.*

"People really smell," she said.
"You stink."

Then that man, the medicine man
you [he, medicine man] give her something to eat.
you [she, daughter] got that necklace,
you [she, mother] cut it. That here you [she, daughter] got her neck like that.[7]
She's [daughter] got her hair like that.
He [she, mother] give her clothes.
Her mother, *she give her clothes.*
Now she get up,
she talk,
"Don't you play so far.
Your life, that here salmon," she said.
They cried for her continuously.
In *one week* it was over.
She became that big.
A long time ago children got a small fish and played around with it.
"Ah! Ah! Don't!" they said.

That's a true story.
That's grandpa he tell me.
"You got here kids,
you've got kids,
tell them, 'don't play with small fish.'*
Anyone,
little fish, grayling like that.
Don't play.
Don't play with it, that's what you eat."

NOTES

1. Mr. Dickson is saying that this story took place on the Yukon River, downstream from Kaska territory but upstream from Dawson, possibly somewhere in the vicinity of Fort Selkirk in Northern Tutchone territory.

2. Kaska, like other Athabaskan languages, does not differentiate gender in personal pronouns. Narrating these lines in English, Mr. Dickson uses *he* in a generic, not gender-specific, sense. He is referring to the girl who has disappeared. In the next stanza, again narrating a few lines in English, he uses *she*. In the translation of his lines narrated in Kaska, *she* and *her* have been used in all such instances.

3. This cross is pictured as being like a Christian cross that was made of stone. Mr. Dickson believed that many aspects of Christianity, including knowledge of a supreme God, the wearing of a cross, and the custom of crossing oneself when praying, all preceded contact with missionaries and actually reflected traditional Native belief. On the use of *here*, see note 7.

4. The translation for the Kaska expression *éhdī*, "he/she said," is complicated because it makes reference to a whole series of storytellers. The expression indexes the people who originally witnessed these events, the girl and her family, who then became the original storytellers. It also indexes all those who subsequently told the story, including Mr. Dickson's grandfather. It could also be translated as "it is said," since *éhdī* can also be used in an indefinite sense.

5. The word *ten* mirrors its use in the preceding section. The father has taken ten salmon from the fish trap, and the mother scrapes something hard around the neck of the tenth fish as she prepares to cut it open.

6. Swan down was used by medicine men in the context of traveling to heaven and being reborn. It was a sacred substance that was widely used in a number of contexts.

7. Remember that John Dickson is narrating these italicized lines in English. He is using the adverb *here* as an equivalent for a Kaska directional particle. In the prose translation published by the Kaska Tribal Council, this sentence reads "She had it

around her neck like that" (*Dene Gudeji* 46). In personal correspondence dated March 28, 2000, Pat Moore notes that "the fit of Kaska directionals with English deictics isn't very good so there are some uses of *here* and *there* that are a little odd for normal English." — Eds.

Dzǫhdié' Gų̄h Chō Dzéhhīn

Dzǫhdié' Kills the Giant Worm

ACT I

Long ago
Dzǫhdié', I say,
Dzǫhdié'.
People always fought with him, they say.
He lived with his grandmother,
Dzǫhdié', they say.
His uncles lived beside him.
His grandmother and the others were living there.

He said to her, "Grandmother, I dreamed again."

She said, "Grandson, even though you follow your own mind, what did you
    dream?
Tell me about it," she said to him.
Even so he wouldn't reveal it.

"Grandmother, those like that,
make shrubby cinquefoil[1] arrows for me."
He said to her, "Make two of them then."

She sharpened the end.
She sharpened the end.
Then — what do they say then?
They said it was a red willow bow.

He had a bow, they say.
He said, "Grandmother, carve it like that for me."
He packed it around then.

She really made the bow well for him.
She made those shrubby cinquefoil arrows for him,
the points were already made for him.

He sat down.
After a while
he said again, "Grandmother, I dreamed again."

People were living by the edge of a fish lake, they say,
on the other side,
like that,
they were laying trees for lean-tos, living inside that,
depending on fish.

ACT II : PART 1

Across,
that girl
she was packing her little child all bundled.
Her child was making a crying sound.
That girl was running away, they say.
"Something big,
a big worm, was crawling after me.
I ran away from it, my husband was eaten up."

She was packing her child facing the other way.[2]
They say she was going along after her husband.
He said, "I'll go make a camp."
She followed after him, packing her child and pulling her toboggan.
She packed her child facing backward.
She packed it.
That child cried out, "He! He! He!"

"What is happening?" she thought.
She looked back.

People looked through between their legs.
It was taboo.[3]
They say they made a taboo, don't they?

ACT II : PART 2

Then
behind, a big worm,
one this big, not as large in the middle,
was crawling after her.
She pulled out all kinds of beaver fat,[4]
all kinds of fish.
Because then it was hard for her to pull along with it [the food] inside.
She cut it [hide toboggan] up.
She spilled it out. It [the worm] spent time there.
She thought, "It's for him [the worm]."
Like that dried beaver fat, also dried marmot,
also dried gopher.
She put her pack inside, pulled it on the trail, and ran off.

She ran following her husband.
Her husband
was going, going.
Finally,
among lots of dead trees,
by the river there was a slough.
There he was shoveling [snow] near the top of a hill.
He was cutting a lean-to.
She said, "Hey, let's run off."
Behind, a big worm was crawling after them.
She said, "My toboggan was like that, and then I cut it open.
I threw everything away.
Hurry, let's run off!"

"Where is the dried beaver fat?
What are you telling me?
Where is the dried beaver fat?
Maybe I'll go back and get it."
They said he said, "You lie."

"What did you say?
I was pulling my little son on my back when he cried out for something.
I looked behind,
there was a worm this big crawling after me.

It was already getting near.
I cut my hide toboggan open and threw everything away.
There too, marmot too,
gopher too,
beaver fat, whatever.
I was going along," she said.
"It was like that even so."

It [the worm] hadn't arrived yet when it started to get dark.
It must have been eating.
It must have been eating its food.

Then she said to him, "Hurry! Hurry! Let's go."

"Tomorrow maybe I will go back for my food.
I can't just let it go," he said.

"On the other side[5] I became tired.
What are you saying?" she said to him.
They sat across from each other feasting on fried beaver fat.
Those like that,
like that,[6]
she cut two branches in a line.
She put those two beside each other.
Off to the side she made a good trail
and hid its end [the start of the trail].
Her snowshoes and other things she hung up.
Her fire,
her fire, whatever she kept it in,
it was ready.
She was sitting nursing her small child.
They say this: it made her doze off a little bit.
On the other side her husband didn't hear them.
There was a sound of [the worm] eating.
It made a noise, "Slurp, slurp, slurp," they say.
As she turned her head, the huge thing stuck its head in, eating that man.

Quietly then she sneaked away.
Her child was moving a little nursing.
On the side she had hung a small bit of food.

She went there to it.
Then she put her snowshoes on.
She put her child under her small pack of food and ran off.
She remembered there used to be people living far away.
The people were living on fish.
She ran.
She ran,
they say.

ACT III

Then
almost,
almost daylight, just before,
a man started a fire.
As the fire started up, the smoke went all over, just like that.
Across she ran along that person's trail;
she came to him.
"Behind me a huge worm is crawling after me.
I cut open my toboggan to give him its contents.
I said to my husband, 'Let's run away!'
He slept there then.
He was eaten — there was nothing I could do — I ran off,"
she said.

"What are we going to do then?
What are we going to do then?" they said.
The people all cried.
On this side they dug a hole.
On the other side, there they dug a hole in the ice.
"There will be water blocking behind," they thought.[7]
That's what they did, they say.

ACT IV

Then
across later
people spent three days;

three nights passed.
It was crawling,
it was crawling across, they say.
That girl ran away.
She was gone, they say.
She dreamed something.
Things were not right.
She took off, she was gone.

Dzǫhdié' said,
"Grandmother, warm up a shrubby cinquefoil [arrow].
Warm up my bow."

She said, "What is it really for?"

On the other side the hole they dug was visible.
Like that.
Like that.
It was really long, they say.
On the other side it was still visible then;
at this end, on this side they made a hole for that giant worm, they say.
People were crawling into camp like that [paralyzed by the worm].
People were all cramped up and crawling around, they say.
His grandmother and all of them were crawling around.
"Grandson, maybe we will survive.
What do you say that for?" she said to him.

Beside that worm
it happened that he [Dzǫhdié'] flew.
The big worm was raising [its head] for a person,
up to . . .
Its head was already raised near the person.
It was like that then.

From beside its head he shot an arrow,
then flew over to the other side too.
From the other side he shot an arrow.
It went right through like that.
His arrow disappeared.
This big worm made a sudden jerk like that then.

All the ice was broken up, they say.
When it died, only that big head was sticking out.

He also shot its eye with an arrow; he did that.

His grandmother and all,
his uncles and all,
were crawling around like that.
His grandmother was also crawling around.
They could have been eaten up crawling around like that.
"If it wasn't for me, you would all be [eaten].
Hurry and get up, all of you.
Do it with your own strength," he said, they say.

Only his grandmother stood up.
With his mitts,
"Get up!
Get up!"
he told his grandmother
as he whipped her [with his mitts].
His grandmother got back up.

Then his uncles were crawling around too.
"They were really acting smart to me," [he thought].
"Hurry and get up on your own strength," he said.

They gave him arrows,
whatever they were eating.
They gave him mountain sheep meat with fat on it.

He said, "My uncles will get up.
My uncles will get up."
He used his mitts,
he blew on them,
"fu, fu," he said then [blowing].
They say they got up, all of them.
His uncle's wife's mother,
they say he left her like that,
crawling around.

He said, "Hurry, urinate on me still.[8]
You underestimated me.
Hurry and get up, all of you."

They gave him hide too, they say.
Axe case like that,
they also gave him blankets,
they rewarded him with a sheepskin blanket.
His grandmother collected them.
He whipped people with his mitts;
all of them got up, they say.

They moved to another place.
That girl ran off again, she disappeared.[9]
From then on,
From then on they never saw her again;
they turned back.
She had come back for the people, they say.
They were walking above on the hillside.
Their fire was showing.
"What's that black thing[10] coming?" they said.

"I really have no food," she said.
That's why she went to another place
where people were catching fish.
People were living there, they say.

Recent times, they say.
Where was it from?
Desk'eshe Tu, "Grayling Water," they say.
Out near Frances Lake, they say.
Through there, they say.
They say it is.
The giant worm came behind people.
It must be getting to be a long time,
on this earth.
There must have been an animal that big,
coming, following, crawling, through, he said,[11] they say.
That small person killed it, they say.
He said, they say.

NOTES

1. A small bush with yellow flowers.

2. She was packing her child on her back so he was facing backward as she walked along the trail.

3. It was prohibited to turn around to look at something, so they would look back between their legs instead.

4. The insulating layer of fat on a beaver was carefully taken off the carcass and often smoked and dried for later consumption. It is considered to be a delicacy.

5. Back down the trail where she came from, which is now on the other side of the fire from them as they speak.

6. Mrs. Dick repeats "like that" because each of two branches is cut and placed in the snow to conceal the trail.

7. The first hole was dug on this side of the lake, the side on which they were originally camped when the young woman arrived. A second hole was dug on the other side of the lake, where their trail across the lake neared shore.

8. Meaning "show me disrespect."

9. The young woman who was first pursued by the giant worm ran off.

10. A reference to the earlier approach of the giant worm.

11. *Éhdī*, "he/she said," can refer to any of the storytellers, from those who witnessed the events to those who told the story to Mrs. Dick.

6

Tagish

In *den k'e* (as the people call their language), *Tāgizi* was once the name of a place. Literally translated, *Tāgizi* means "it is breaking up," and "it" refers to the spring ice. The people inhabiting that place along the headwaters of the Yukon River in the southern Yukon Territory and northern British Columbia were Tāgizi Dene, Tagish Indians. Through their increasing contact with both Alaskan Coastal and Canadian Inland Tlingits during the nineteenth century, the place name became Tlingitized to *Tāgish* and was used to identify both a lake and a town (McClellan, "Tagish" 481, 490).

Catharine McClellan notes that prior to the 1940s little was known about Tagish culture. Yet of all Northern Athabaskan people, probably the three most famous individuals at the end of the nineteenth century and well into the twentieth were Tagish: Kate Carmack, her brother Skookum Jim, and their nephew Dawson Charlie. With Kate's white husband, they were the party that found gold on Bonanza Creek, off the Yukon downriver from Tagish territory, and thus started the Klondike gold rush. Construction of the White Pass and Yukon Railway at the turn of the century and the forging through of the Alaska Highway during World War II further disrupted Tagish culture. According to figures cited by McClellan, the number of Tagish at any one time between 1885 and 1980 has been estimated from 50 to 115.

Heavily influencing Tagish storytelling are Tlingit traditions and Tagish experiences of contact with white miners and other migrants. Carcross, center of Tagish population since 1900, had been named for the caribou that once crossed the river there annually. Caribou and other southern Yukon land animals live on in the storytelling, and sea creatures are prominent in many tales too, those that Tagish narrators learned through generations of intermarriage with and descent from Tlingits.

As in Tlingit, the Tagish term for distant-time narratives is *tlaagú*. These include the Crow (Raven) cycle; stories about humans who violate taboos regarding an animal, are taken into the world of that animal, and learn respect for the animal's way of life; and clan stories that explain how a clan acquired a certain animal as its crest and gained the right to tell certain stories. Tagish also tell historical and biographical accounts, often about the gold-rush and highway-construction eras. McClellan singles out as "uniquely Tagish" the story of Skookum Jim's having a Frog spirit helper and meeting Wealth Woman, an unusual combination of biographical figure with distant-time characters (490).

Angela Sidney told stories of all these kinds and more. She was born near Carcross on January 4, 1902, daughter of Tagish John and his wife Maria, a Tlingit woman. Through her mother the child belonged to the *Deisheetaan* (Crow) clan, and in addition to her English name, she had both a Tlingit name, Stóow, and a Tagish name, Ch'óonehte' Má. The girl learned all three languages, and when she died on July 17, 1991, she was one of the last known speakers of Tagish. Between the ages of seven and ten, Mrs. Sidney had sporadic formal education in the Anglican mission school at Carcross, but she was learning traditional ways of life as her family traveled the territory and she observed her father and male relatives hunting in fall and fishing in summer.

At age fourteen she married George Sidney, an Inland Tlingit man twice her age. She bore him seven children, four of whom died in infancy or childhood. They continued to hunt, fish, and trap, but her husband gradually began working for wages. He became chief at Carcross. After his death in 1971, Mrs. Sidney began to travel to Southeastern Alaska, home of her Tlingit ancestors, where she developed an even stronger sense of her identity and her heritage than she had grown up with. She began teaching young people by telling her stories in schools, helping to inspire what has become the Yukon International Storytelling Festival. In 1984 she participated in the Toronto Storytelling Festival, and in 1986 the governor general awarded her the Order of Canada for her accomplishments in linguistics and ethnography.

Mrs. Sidney worked with linguists Victor Golla and Jeff Leer, as well as with John Ritter, and she was one of McClellan's principal authorities on Tagish culture. During the last seventeen years of her life, she and anthropologist Julie Cruikshank worked together on a number of projects in oral history and literature, which resulted in several local publications: *Place Names of the Tagish Region, Southern Yukon; Tagish Tlaagú*; and *Haa Shagóon (Our Family History)*. Four other books contain many of Mrs. Sidney's stories, together with many by other Yukon Athabaskan women and extensive commentary by Cruikshank: *My Stories Are My Wealth, Athapaskan Women, The Stolen Women*, and *Life Lived Like a Story*.

Mrs. Sidney chose to narrate in English. Cruikshank tape-recorded the storytelling sessions and kept handwritten notes that she used to ask questions about each story immediately after Mrs. Sidney had finished telling it. Before their next meeting, Cruikshank made typewritten transcripts of the stories. The two women then reviewed each transcript, and Cruikshank made all corrections and changes that Mrs. Sidney called for (*My Stories Are My Wealth* iii). Cruikshank recorded about ninety hours of material with Mrs. Sidney. Copies of the tapes are held by the Yukon Native Language Centre and the Yukon Archives.

Cruikshank's presentation of Mrs. Sidney's *tlaagú* in *Life Lived Like a Story* represents the achievement of the storyteller/teacher's goal: to preserve the distant-time stories in writing for others and to use them as a framework for her autobiographical/historical accounts. Each even-numbered chapter includes one or more *tlaagú* that provide cultural context for the autobiographical account in the immediately preceding odd-numbered chapter. This organizational pattern, Cruikshank acknowledges, is the result of her having edited the transcripts of Mrs. Sidney's storytelling "to bring together materials recorded in many different sessions and over many years as one continuous narrative." She adds that in arranging the chapters she followed a chronology that accorded with Mrs. Sidney's instructions regarding "the 'correct' way to tell her life story" (*Life* 18). When they were first published in the earlier books, Mrs. Sidney's distant-time stories appeared in prose paragraphs. For *Life Lived Like a Story*, Cruikshank chose the line/pause format for them but used prose paragraphs for the autobiographical sections.

"Getting Married" (section 13 of the book) is Mrs. Sidney's account of the circumstances and negotiations leading to her marriage and of the early years of her life with George Sidney, her "Old Man." These were the final years of World War I. Emblematic of the clash between cultures in the southern Yukon at that time is her depiction of the two wedding "ceremonies": her mother's sending her, in a traditional Athabaskan way, to sleep in a tent with the man chosen by her relatives to be her husband, followed by her former teacher's insisting upon her and George Sidney, in their best clothes, having their union formally sanctioned in the Anglican Church.

"The Stolen Woman" is one of three stories in section 14, two of which have to do with women who are abducted from their husbands. Stories about stolen women are prominent in Tagish and neighboring Athabaskan cultures. They are sometimes historical accounts in which the theft of a woman precipitates war between two groups. Among the features that mark Mrs. Sidney's story as a distant-time narrative is the "point of land in the lake," which in summertime "lifts up" to allow the woman's abductor to take her "under it" to a place of winter, but which blocks her pursuing husband from following there until later, after he has made certain preparations. More than in other stories of this kind that she tells, Mrs. Sidney here seems to be muting the distant-time elements in order to focus upon the psychological state of the woman. The story thus reflects the adjustments that she herself had to make in her own youthful marriage.

SUGGESTIONS FOR FURTHER READING

Cruikshank, Julie. *Athapaskan Women: Lives and Legends.* Canadian Ethnology Service Paper 57. Ottawa: National Museums of Canada, 1979.

———. *The Stolen Women: Female Journeys in Tagish and Tutchone.* Canadian Ethnology Service Paper 87. Ottawa: National Museums of Canada, 1983.

Cruikshank, Julie, with Angela Sidney. "'Pete's Song': Establishing Meanings through Story and Song." In *When Our Words Return: Writing, Hearing, and Remembering Oral Traditions of Alaska and the Yukon.* Edited by Phyllis Morrow and William Schneider. Logan: Utah State University Press, 1995. 53–75.

Cruikshank, Julie, with Angela Sidney, Kitty Smith, and Annie Ned. *Life Lived Like a Story: Life Stories of Three Yukon Native Elders.* Lincoln: University of Nebraska Press, 1990.

McClellan, Catharine. "Tagish." In *Subarctic*, vol. 6 of *Handbook of North American Indians.* Washington DC: Smithsonian Institution, 1981.

Sidney, Angela. *Tagish Tlaagú (Tagish Stories).* Whitehorse, Yukon: Council for Yukon Indians and the Government of Yukon, 1982.

Sidney, Angela, Kitty Smith, and Rachel Dawson. *My Stories Are My Wealth.* Whitehorse, Yukon: Council for Yukon Indians, 1977.

Getting Married

I stayed with Old Man year 1916.
Well, I was still a kid yet.

After I came out from under the bonnet,[1] I went to Atlin with my aunt, Mrs. Austin, Sadusgé. They [Sadusgé and her white husband, Shorty Austin] were going prospecting, head of the lake. Her boys were going to stay in Carcross with her mother, and she took me to Atlin with her, year 1915. Here she got sick, so we stayed in Atlin.

My aunt used to talk to me about George Sidney: "If I see my nephew, George Sidney, I'm going to throw you at him!" And I used to think, "You marry him yourself!" but I never said it aloud, though. George's father was her cousin, too, so she called him "my nephew."[2]

I was shy to George when I first saw him. I used to talk respectfully to him: I used to say, "my nephew," "*Eshidaa.*"[3] They taught me to talk that way to show respect to people. My old man [husband] used to call me "*A̱xaat*": that means "my auntie [on the side of] my father's people" in Tlingit. Here, he used to say that even among white people! Gee, I don't like that! I get shamed. It's old-fashioned! I used to say, "Why do you say that in front of people? You know they're going to think she married her own nephew. White people don't understand!"

"Well, you are *A̱xaat*, Indian way," he tells me. His father, Jim Sidney, was *Deisheetaan* — that's why I'm *eshembe'e'* to him Tagish way; *a̱xaat*, Tlingit way.

The Sidneys are Teslin people — they were at Johnson's Crossing that year, 1916. George was staying with his cousin, Jimmy Jackson. My father sent word to him and told him, "If you're going to Teslin, you better come this way. I want to see you." He was working longshoreman in Whitehorse. Whitehorse Billy called him up, "Come on for supper. I've got moose ribs."

So after he got off at five o'clock, he went there. Whitehorse Billy was staying in Whitehorse, in tent frame — and so George went up there for supper. Whitehorse Billy had campfire outside, moose ribs boiling and cooking, I guess.

After they finished eating, that's the time my father's niece, my aunt, Mrs. Whitehorse Billy[4] — Gunaaták's daughter — said, "My uncle, Tagish John, sent word to you. He said for you to go back to Teslin now, by Marsh Lake. That's the word my uncle sent to you."

"Okay, well, how am I to go to Marsh Lake?"

And her husband, Whitehorse Billy, tells him, "Well, there's Pelly Jim: he's going back to get some grub tomorrow. Get in touch with him."

So he did. Early in the morning, he got sugar, flour, everything. He's got little tent, too, five by seven [feet]. And here he saw Pelly Jim. "Can I go back with you to Marsh Lake?"

"Okay, I'm going back to Teslin — I'm going to work my way back that way."

"I want to see Tagish John — that's how come I want to go back with you." And that's how he got to Marsh Lake.

When he saw his father and his mother and his aunt, he told them Tagish John wants to see him. And his father told him after a while, after he thinks about it, "What does Tagish John want to see you for? Maybe he wants to give you his daughter or something like that." Before George leaves, his father tells him, "Go. Whatever he wants you to do, just do it. It's okay." That's how come he came directly to us. This is fall, 1916 — that's how come he stayed with us.

Well, I kind of didn't like it — he's a stranger to me, you know. But when my father and mother told me to give him a cup of tea, to feed him, stuff like that, I had to do what my mother and father said. I never ran around like kids nowadays! As long as he's Wolf, I'm supposed to be his aunt; I'm Crow. He calls me "Auntie." And me, I have to call him "my nephew" when I feed him. "Eat, *Eshidaa*." I have to talk respectable, not crazy, like nowadays. That's Indian law — as long as I'm Crow and they're Wolf, they have to call me "auntie." So I gave him tea. He came nighttime with Pelly Jim and that bunch.

When he first came to us, he talked to my mother. He said, "My father sent me to you people to help you out with things." Well, the old people — they understand right away what he meant. I wasn't surprised. They had talked to me about him, long time ago. That's when I told you Mrs. Austin — Sadusgé — used to tell me about him. "You marry him yourself,"

I used to think, but I never said it out, though. "You marry him yourself!" I used to think that way.

When Old Man came to us, first year he stayed with us, he put up meat behind that *Chookanshaa*, behind Jake's Corner. He put up a cache there, way up high. We dried meat there, and he packed it all up. That's when he started to go with us. Well, my father and mother let me stay with him right away as soon as we came back to the main camp. He didn't want to make him work too hard for nothing.[5] "You might as well stay with him. He wants you. That's why he came to us."

They made a big feast for us: just us — my father and my mother and the baby Dora[6] and me. Oh, they talked things over with my aunt Sadusgé already, I guess. "Let them stay together." They made a nice big dinner. Up on the mountain and back of Jake's Corner — *Tlo'ó K'aa' Dzéłe*, they call that mountain. That's when we got through drying meat, I guess. We were going to put meat in the cache, next day.

That's the time my father talked to him — made a big supper for us and talked to both of us. He talked to George and told him, "I don't want you fellows to have a hard time. Maybe you came to us for your aunt, so you fellows stay together. Don't be too old-fashioned: I'm not old-fashioned. A long time ago, people work for their wife for a long time. But I'm not like that. I don't believe in it." And he made me sit by him where he's going to eat. That's the way they made me stay with him.

That night — he's got a little tent outside he's sleeping in it — us, we just stay in a brush camp, pull fly tent over it. I was sleeping with my mother. Instead of going to my bed, they told me to go to the tent. "Go with him. Go in the tent." So I took my blanket and I started to make my bed in there.

"What are you doing?" George asked.

"Well, my mother told me to sleep in this tent . . . sure looks like it's going to rain . . ."

"Yeah?" he said.

After I fixed my blanket, he pulled my blankets. "Come sleep with me." And we started fighting and laughing over that blanket. And pretty soon I forgot about sleeping alone!

Now. You know it all. Everything!

But one of the school women, W.A. women[7] — her name was Mrs. Watson — she used to be my teacher in the school. She heard about me being married. So one day I had a visitor. Here it was Mrs. Watson — her maiden name was Thompson — "Miss Thompson," we used to call her. Oh, she was so kind, she loved me up and everything. And then she told me, "I understand that you are married."

I said, "Yes."

"Did he give you a ring?"

"Yes, he gave me one — his own ring — one time when we went to cache."

"Are you married in church?"

I said, "No."

"Well, you know what?" she said. "You're not supposed to be like that. You've got to get married in church!" Well, I told her I didn't mind, but my husband wouldn't want it — not to get married in church.

"Why?" she asked me.

"Well, I don't know . . . he's pretty shy, I guess."

"Where is he?" she tells me.

"He's working on the section."[8] Sure enough, she watched for George when the section crew came home.

"I understand you're married," she told George.

"Yes, Angela Johns."

"Well, you know you've got to get married."

"We are already married, Indian way. It's just as good, isn't it?"

"That's not good enough," she told him. "You've got to marry her white-man way. I raised that kid!" she told him.[9]

My Old Man said, "Why? What's the difference?"

She said, "You see that Church of England?" That church was sitting on skids already, ready to pull across. It was too far for the kids to cross from Chooutla school, so they moved it across to where it is now. Mrs. Watson said to my husband, "You see that Church of England sitting on skids? It's not going to be moved unless you get married. You've got to get married first."

George just gave up. Gee. "Okay," he said.

Then she came over one night and asked me what I'm going to wear. I had a Sunday dress — it was kind of blue. Well, blue was good, I thought — but no. Here the W.A. gave me a cream-colored linen suit. She brought it down. She asked me what kind of shoes I've got. I've got nice white canvas shoes and a cream-colored hat with a black band. All that! And she gave me pearls to wear on my neck. She told me everything I should wear.

She asked George if he had a suit. He had a nice gray suit — when he first came to Carcross, he spent the winter in Whitehorse cutting wood, and when he sold the wood he bought a suit for himself — bought it for a celebration. He left that suit in Whitehorse with the Second Hand man, and that spring after we came he wrote to that man about it. And the Second

Hand man, he sent it up by train. So she told George, "You wear that." That was 1917.

My mother and dad couldn't come to that wedding — just me and George and Sophie, my cousin. Then there were the white ladies — Mrs. Watson and Mrs. Johnson and the others. So Mrs. Watson gave me away. We got married in Carcross. We were married twice. I was glad about it in the end.

After I started staying with Old Man, he got a job on section. My father and mother had to leave me then to be with my husband in Carcross. There was hardly anybody in Carcross that fall — just me and my husband, and my aunt Kate Carmack, and old Hunxu.aat — Tagish Jim's mother — and my uncle Billy Atlin, and Jimmy Scotty. They used to call me "Carcross Chief" because I stayed in Carcross. I used to give them lunch anytime, give them lunch or supper.

My father and brother sold meat to Chooutla school that time. Mr. Johnson was principal of that school that time. He said, "The kids eat meat at home. Why shouldn't they eat meat at school, too?"

George was supposed to go back to Teslin that fall — he wanted to send word to Teslin people. But here that fall he started going into the mountains, killed moose for us — for my parents, too — started going round with us instead of going back. And he never did go back to Teslin till later on, maybe two years. I stayed with him all that fall.

All winter we lived together with my mother in one big tent, twelve by fourteen. We had our own little tent — we got stove in it. But wintertime when it gets cold, we just wanted to cut wood for one place, so we stayed with my father and mother that winter in that twelve-by-fourteen tent.

Us kids, we cut wood. Well . . . I still felt like a kid even though I was living with Old Man — I was just like a child then! When he was gone during the day, I played. Oh, I was still a kid yet, played around, rustled around. One time when he's gone, my little brother Peter was with me, and we set gopher traps on that *Chílih Dzéłe'*, that Carcross mountain. We caught some gophers and cooked them for supper. When Old Man came back he said, "Where did you get that from?" he asked me.

"What do you think I did?" I told him. "We went out gopher hunting!" Oh, he was surprised. He was proud of me!

George and my brother Johnny would go out trapping, sell meat once in a while. And they started buying everything half-and-half — partners. My father didn't have to think about anything! In the fall time, they've got a big pile of grub. When grub comes, they're the boss.[10] The first year we stayed together, my old man killed twenty-two lynx and my brother killed eighteen lynx. Old Man bought a bottle of whiskey, to show respect, and gave it to my father — *and* all the grub. They're the boss of it! Nowadays people don't do that anymore.

Christmastime, my brother and my Old Man came to Skwan Lake — *Skwáan Taasłéyi*. They killed some moose and roasted moose head by the campfire. We caught a great big fish, and my father cooked that for Christmas dinner. He invited Grandma Hammond — Aandaax'w — and our cousins Isabel and Willy and my daddy's cousin Susie and her family. Mrs. Dyea John — she stayed with Hammonds when she was getting old — they're the ones that started calling her "Grandma Hammond." But her real name is Aandaax'w, Mary John, Dyea John's wife.

Of course, we didn't know much about Christmas. But that's the time he taught us peace songs: he taught us this song and told us stories, and that's our Christmas fun . . .

And then they went out to get moose, and my uncle went out with them to get meat. Here they got up in the morning and my uncle said, "It's snowing hard, and gee, the stars are out!" So my brother looked up, and here the tent was on fire! That's how come they could see that — the snow and the stars.

NOTES

1. The headgear worn by a girl while she was secluded from her community during puberty. McClellan describes it as "a large hood stretched over a willow frame so that she could neither see out nor be seen" ("Tagish" 488). In section 11 of her autobiography, titled "Becoming a Woman," Mrs. Sidney describes the bonnet she wore as "a fancy flannel blanket" and tells in detail the circumstances and disappointments of her own seclusion at age thirteen. The concluding lines of her story "The Stolen Woman," which follows, illustrate the dire consequences believed to result from a girl's looking at someone or something, or from someone's meeting her eyes, when she is in this condition. — Eds.

2. George Sidney's father and Angela's aunt Sadusgé were both *Deisheetaan* and were classificatory brother and sister; consequently, Sadusgé would use the nephew term meaning "my brother's son" when she spoke to George, and when he spoke to her he would address her by the aunt term meaning "my father's sister." (The other nephew and aunt reciprocal terms, "sister's son" and "mother's sister," are entirely different because they refer to individuals of one's own moiety.) Because the system of kinship reckoning merges generations on the male side, Angela would use the same nephew term to address her future husband as would Sadusgé, and he in turn would refer to his future wife as "my aunt."

3. She is using Tagish kinship terms here when she explains how she addressed

him, and using the Tlingit terms by which he addressed her (because his language was Inland Tlingit).

4. This aunt was the adopted daughter of G̲unaaták̲, the Marsh Lake Chief, and his wife, Tashooch Tláa — Angela's father's sister. In other words, she had the same sociological relationship to Angela — a cousin Angela called "father's sister" — that Sadusgé had to George. An opposite-moiety aunt in the relationship of "father's sister" had a privileged role in marriage negotiations.

5. In earlier days a prospective husband would be expected to work for his parents-in-law for at least a year before marriage. Her father considered himself a progressive man, "not old-fashioned," as he states in his speech further along.

6. Her sister Alice Dora. In section 5 ("Childhood") Mrs. Sidney identifies another Dora among siblings who had died in infancy or childhood. Because she was especially fond of that sister, she, and then others, began calling the new baby by her middle name. — Eds.

7. "W.A." refers to the Woman's Auxiliary of the Anglican Church.

8. George Sidney worked for the White Pass and Yukon Route on a regular seasonal basis for years, on their railway between Skagway and Carcross; during these periods, he and Angela based themselves in Carcross.

9. Mrs. Watson taught at the Chooutla residential school when Angela was in first grade.

10. Ideally, brothers-in-law worked together as "partners" in this way. Her comment "they're the boss" refers to her parents: her husband and brother gave them food, which was then her parents' to redistribute.

ANGELA SIDNEY

The Stolen Woman

One time there was a man who was camping with his wife close to a lake.
He went out hunting, but she stayed home.
You know how when they become a woman they wear a bonnet?
She was wearing her bonnet yet.

All of a sudden, somebody came.
He started asking her questions, how come she's staying there.

"My husband went out hunting," she told him.

"Your husband shouldn't leave you," he said.
"Come with me."

"No, I don't want to do that.
I love my husband — I want to stay."

They argued for a while.
Finally, he grabbed her and started to drag her away —
He threw her bonnet away,[1] and dragged her.
There was a little trail going down to the water —
That's how her husband found her — by following this little trail.
All the time that man is dragging her, she grabs at little branches and breaks
    them.
By the time they get through, it's just like there's a big road down to the
    water.

He put her in his boat, then floated around until her husband came back.

Finally, her husband came back.
He came to the water, and here she was in the boat.

That man who took her took an arrowhead.
He tied a little strip of gopher and loon's head to it with babiche
And he threw it to her husband.
"Here, this is for your wife. I pay you."

"No," that man said,
"I want my wife. You can't pay for her!"

That man started to go, started to row.
The husband started to follow, too.
Paddle, paddle . . . keeps going, going . . . don't know how far they go.

Finally, they came to a place where they say a point of land in the lake lifts
        up.
And that man went under it, to the other side.
Well, that husband can't go under it —
On the other side was winter. Snow.

From there, where that point lifts up, that husband had to turn back.

It took him two or three days to get back to camp.
He dried up some meat and then he went to look for his brothers-in-law.
He had told that man [who stole her],
"She's got lots of friends.
Don't think we won't come after her!
Don't think you're going to get away with it!"

Ah, that man laughed at her husband.
"You won't come after us. You can't!"

When that guy who took that woman got past that point, he put up his
        boat.
He followed a trail with that woman and caught up with his people.

Meantime, her husband gathered up her brothers and his brothers.
They're going to follow.
They go to the cache and get dry meat for their food.
They travel along the shore.
When they come to that point, here it lifts up and they go under it.
On the other side, here it was really deep snow.
There was an old trail there, so they started to follow it.

Here, there were two little old ladies camping there.
They've got a little trail to the water and they've got a fishhook, fish for ling
     cod.
Every day, they catch two or three.
They cook them all.
They had enough to supply people who went by.

Just the husband went up to them.
"Did you see my wife walk by with someone?"

"Yes, we heard there was a girl from a different country going by with a
     bunch."

"How long ago?"

"Quite a while ago, but you can follow this old trail," they tell him.
"Every evening late in the evening,
Your wife always goes back along the trail to get wood."

He went back to his gang.
One of them went back just to listen to those two old women, in case they
     say anything.

One said, "My son used to go out to hunt early in the morning, just before
     daylight breaks."
The other one said, "My son used to go out a little while after when the
     daylight really breaks."

Both those women wished their sons would get away before anything
     happens:
They know these men are going to make war on people.

Then those men followed the trail.
Sure enough, they start to catch up to people one evening, don't know how
     many days after that.
They just hear somebody chopping wood up ahead of them.
Just that man, that husband, went to where they hear that chopping.
Sure enough, it's her.
Just when she lifts the wood she is going to pack home, he grabs it.
She pulls, she turns around — here it's her husband!

He starts to ask her questions.
"Your uncles and your brothers are all with me and so are my uncles and
    my brothers.
We have run out of food.
Can you get some for us?
We're going to make war, but your uncles, your brothers, we are all hungry.
We've run out of grub."

"Okay, I'll see what I can do.
I've got food in my skin toboggan, too."

"Well, try to get some."

She had a stone ax, like old time.
And he cut the string that holds the ax on the handle — cut it off.
"Tell your mother-in-law you broke that string, ax string.
Then you can take the string off the toboggan."

She went home without the wood.
She told her mother-in-law, "My ax string broke."

"Well," her mother-in-law said,
"Take the string off your skin toboggan and fix it."

"Okay," she pretended to fix it.
Then she stuffed that dry meat under her arms.
She stuffed willow branches into that toboggan to make it look full.
Then she went out to her husband to give him that food.

Again, they pretended that babiche broke off that ax.
She came home again, told that mother-in-law,
"That string is broken again.
Maybe mine is not strong. Maybe yours is stronger."

"Go ahead and help yourself," her mother-in-law said.
So she helped herself to her mother-in-law's toboggan.
She took lots of meat under her arm, under her blanket —
They used blankets in those days.
Again she breaks willow branches, stuffs her mother-in-law's toboggan.
Then she went to her husband again.

"What do they do?" her husband asked.

"Well, when the hunters come back,
Everybody always goes to bed early," she tells him.

"Where is your husband now?" he asks.

"They're both out hunting."
She's got two brothers for husbands.

"When they come back tonight, play with them.
Make them tired out so they will go to sleep."

"Okay." She brings that wood back.
Her husbands come home.
After they eat, she starts playing with them, playing with them.

The oldest one said,
"Don't bother me; I'm tired."

So she started playing with the youngest one.
He said the same thing:
"I'm tired. What's wrong? You never did that before.
How come you're doing that?"

"Oh, I just feel like playing."
Then she went out for a little while.
She listened for what her mother-in-law is going to say.

Her mother-in-law comes in and says,
"My sons, I love you, boys, used to be.
My sons, I don't know what is wrong with your wife.
Your wife is acting very strange.
Her ax string broke . . .
She came and took a string from her toboggan
And when she went out, she looked big to me.
And then she came back and told me her ax string broke again.
So she took some off my toboggan.
And the same way, she looked very big when she went.
Be careful, you boys. Sleep light!"

"What do you expect, Mother?
It's a long way to where that woman comes from.
Nothing but lynx droppings around here —
That's all there is, lynx."

"Well, just the same, you look after yourselves good," she tells them.

And finally, they went to bed.
The woman's husband had told her,
"Sleep with your clothes, and don't tie up your blanket."
See how smart he is?
"So you can jump out if they grab you;
They're going to try to grab your blankets."

When that young wife heard them, she just jumped up.
They just grabbed her, just grabbed her blanket.

She jumped up, went outside.
In the meantime, they both got killed — the whole camp, everybody got
    killed.
And that old lady who said, "My son goes out before daybreak,"
Sure enough, he was gone.

When they do that, it's bad luck to start to eat right away.
They have to take scalps first — then they wash their hands — they tend to
    the dead.
They did that all during the day.
Then one or two followed the trail to get that boy who went hunting.
When he came back, he was dragging white caribou, they say — must have
    been reindeer —
They killed him, too.
Then they had fresh meat, that caribou.

Finally, they're through everything and they start to go home.
So they have lots to eat.

On the way home, they came by those two old ladies' camp again.
Those old ladies dig a tunnel in the snow.
That husband took a walking stick, and shoved it in the snow.

Then, when he took it out, there's blood on it.
Those two old ladies made nosebleed and make it look like they are killed.

So they let them go — they left them some meat — then they went on.
Those two old ladies could tell when they are gone.

They came to their boat, paddled to the place where the point lifts up.
It was summer on the other side.
They came back to their own camp.
From there, they are home.

They say that point doesn't lift up anymore.
When a woman first becomes a woman one time, she looked at that point.
That's why it doesn't lift anymore.

NOTE

1. This outrageous violation of a taboo in the human society foreshadows the revelation later in the story that the abductor and his people are not humans. — Eds.

7

Southern Tutchone

Like the Tagish, the Southern Tutchone people live in a region of the Yukon Territory that encompasses headwaters of the Yukon River, but in addition their homeland includes the upper reaches of the Alsek River before it descends through the coastal range of mountains to the Pacific Ocean. In their language, *kwädą̄y kwändür* and *kwändür* are the terms, respectively, for "long ago story" and for "story" or "history" (the spellings are Ritter's, the definitions McClellan's). McClellan notes that within both categories stories generally perform two major functions, instruction and entertainment ("Indian Stories" 118–19).

The instructional purpose covers explanations of cosmological and natural phenomena (for the most part in *kwädą̄y kwändür*), guidance in morality (both categories), demonstrations of how individuals should face and deal with psychological and social stresses (both categories), and information about significant events in the lives of contemporary Southern Tutchone individuals or of their ancestors (in *kwändür*). The last of these teaching functions is paramount in the narratives about first contact between Southern Tutchone people and whites.

The entertainment purpose includes the prompting of laughter through the depiction of ridiculous occurrences, the eliciting of admiration through the unfolding of great exploits, and the stimulating of amusement in Southern Tutchone audiences "by poking fun at themselves," as McClellan puts it. These aspects of entertainment characterize both major categories, although the poking of fun for amusement is especially prevalent, McClellan has found, in contact narratives; in fact, she suggests that the storytelling of the Southern Tutchone people might be said to include "a comic genre of contact literature in which they themselves play the dupes" (in contrast to the Coastal Tlingits' self-portrayal "in a somewhat heroic manner" in their narratives about their first encounters with whites) ("Indian Stories" 128).

Just as this possible "comic contact" category falls within *kwändür*, so the Crow cycle and the *Äsùya* (Smart Man or Beaver) cycle belong to *kwädąy kwändür*. Another category, important among the southernmost Southern Tutchone bands, who have adopted Tlingit social organization, is that of sib traditions: for example, stories about how certain clans acquired their crests. McClellan has observed that some of these narratives are *kwädąy kwändür*, others *kwändür* (*Old People* 67).

Winter was the season when most Southern Tutchone storytelling traditionally took place, but McClellan observes that the *Äsùya* cycle "could not be told during the cold season because stormy weather would follow." Elderly men were the principal storytellers, and they rendered such narratives as the Beaver Man and Crow cycles in a formal style and at great length. McClellan writes that the men of highest rank and greatest age "had a fairly formalized responsibility for handing on the most important knowledge" through storytelling. She adds that "the older women, who are often busier than the men, also tell stories to the younger people, but they usually do it in a less formal way." Formal storytelling by a male elder to a sizable group of young people is no longer common. Instead, a young person might cut wood or carry in water for an old lady and be paid with a story or two (*Old People* 66–67).

Ntthenada is the Southern Tutchone name given to the female child born more than a century ago who became Mrs. Annie Ned. She was born and spent her early childhood near Hutshi (no longer inhabited), about halfway between Whitehorse and Haines Junction. Her grandmothers, one Tlingit and one Southern Tutchone, strongly influenced her upbringing, instilling in her the traditional beliefs of both coastal and interior Indians. Her paternal grandfather, called Hutshi Chief, was influential in the trade that had developed between the Tlingits and the Athabaskans. Her first husband, Paddy Smith, who was some years older than she, hunted to feed their family of five sons and three daughters. After his death, and in keeping with Athabaskan custom that a widow should marry a close male relative of her late husband, she married Johnny Ned, some years younger than she, a "kid" whom she and her first husband had raised after Johnny's mother had died. Johnny Ned became a shaman and a leader of the people in his southern Yukon homeland. Following his death, Mrs. Ned took a third husband. She lived through the two events that most greatly disrupted traditional Southern Tutchone culture: the Klondike gold rush (1896–1898) of her youth and the construction of the Alaska Highway (1942–1943) in her middle age. Mrs. Ned died on September 23, 1995.

Annie Ned's views on the importance of storytelling in the Southern Tutchone culture are reflected in two titles: *Old People in Those Days, They Told Their Story All the Time* (a booklet of her stories published by the Yukon Native Languages Project) and "Old-Style Words Are Just Like School" (her section of Cruikshank's *Life Lived Like a Story*). Having first met Mrs. Ned in 1970, Cruikshank began working with her ten years later on an oral-history project that she already had in progress with other elderly Southern Tutchone women. Knowing that among young people English had replaced Southern Tutchone as the language of education (as well as of entertainment and of ordinary usage), Mrs. Ned chose to narrate in English. In doing so, her primary objective was to teach Southern Tutchone youth the traditions of their ancestors and the experiences of her life. Cruikshank tape-recorded thirty hours of her narratives and edited them more than those of the other women, "not by changing her words, but by rearranging them to meet the grammatical demands of English where such reorganization seems to make her meaning clearer." The overriding editorial hand, however, is that of Annie Ned herself, "deciding what should remain and what should be eliminated," as Cruikshank puts it (*Life* 268–69).

Like Annie Ned, Kitty Smith was trilingual in Tlingit, Southern Tutchone, and English. She had three Native-language names: K'ałgwách, Kàdùhikh, and K'odetéena. Her paternal grandmother was one of four Tlingit sisters who had married interior Indian men. In addition to having bicultural ancestry, her father went to school in Juneau, Alaska, and married a Tagish woman, Kitty's mother. Kitty was born about 1890 at a fish camp near the mouth of the Alsek River, southeast of Yakutat, Alaska, on the Pacific coast. Her father died when she was an infant, her mother when she was still a child. Through childhood and young womanhood, she lived with her father's people at Dalton Post, a center of Tlingit-Athabaskan trade located east of the coastal mountains within Southern Tutchone territory. Her grandmother trained her in traditional Tlingit ways, and her Athabaskan grandfather became a constable with the Northwest Mounted Police. Upon separating from her first husband, however, Kitty joined her mother's relatives in the Marsh Lake region of Tagish territory, considerably farther inland. There she married her second husband, Billy Smith. The influence of her maternal grandmother was as strong as that of her father's family had been. Each of her marriages had been arranged by one of the grandmothers with other relatives, and the Tagish grandmother lived with Billy and Kitty Smith.

Although these family influences were traditional and conservative, throughout her life Mrs. Smith exercised considerable economic independence for a woman of her time in her culture. Early in life she made a name for herself as a successful trapper, and she developed a keen sense of the commercial value of Native-made garments. Yet she also raised a family. She greatly enjoyed her own role as grandmother until she died in June 1989 at the age of about one hundred years.

In several emphatic statements Kitty Smith expressed what may be her major observation on the importance of storytelling in Southern Tutchone culture. These statements, either preceding or occurring within stories that Mrs. Smith and Cruikshank regard as *kwädąy kwändür*, insist upon the truth of these tales from the distant time. Mrs. Smith believed further that storytelling is important "as a critical way of acquiring knowledge," as Cruikshank has observed (*Life* 161). One particular — and complex — kind of knowledge that Mrs. Smith explored in her narratives, Cruikshank has written, is "the nature of the ethnic boundary distinguishing Tlingits from Athapaskans and the implications of bicultural ancestry" (*Life* 163). Thus Kitty Smith is like Annie Ned in giving prominence to the educational purpose of storytelling.

Cruikshank has identified three specific narrative techniques characteristic of Mrs. Smith's storytelling: "her masterful use of dialogue," her presentation of both a woman's and an elder's point of view, and her use of "events from her own experience as the framework for presenting the relevance of her *stories*" (that is, her *kwädąy kwändür*) (*Life* 164, 165, 172, 174).

Cruikshank met Kitty Smith in 1974, and over the ensuing decade taperecorded forty hours of her stories narrated in English. Besides a booklet of family history designed for her descendants and other relatives, Mrs. Smith's narratives appear in five other publications: *My Stories Are My Wealth, Athapaskan Women, Nindal Kwädindür (I'm Going to Tell You a Story), The Stolen Women,* and *Life Lived Like a Story.*

Cruikshank's methods of working with Annie Ned and Kitty Smith were generally the same as those she used with Angela Sidney. Copies of the tapes that she transcribed and edited are located at the Yukon Native Language Centre and in the Yukon Archives. She explains her editorial procedures in detail in *Life Lived Like a Story* (18–19). In presenting the stories of Mrs. Ned and Mrs. Smith in that book, Cruikshank followed the same organizational pattern and format as for Mrs. Sidney's Tagish stories, that is, oddnumbered sections of life history *(kwändür)* and even-numbered sections of distant-time narratives *(kwädąy kwändür)*. The autobiographical sections are arranged in a generally chronological order, with each section related thematically to the section of long-ago stories that immediately follows it. The *kwändür* are printed as prose paragraphs, the *kwädąy kwändür* in the line/pause format (in earlier publications, Mrs. Smith's stories of the second kind had appeared in prose paragraphs).

Annie Ned's stories reprinted here are the first two as they appear in *Life Lived Like a Story*, the initial pair of personal account and traditional tale. We have omitted several passages from the traditional tale, as indicated in notes. Brackets and ellipses, however, are Cruikshank's, used to clarify meaning and to indicate long pauses or incomplete thoughts in Mrs. Ned's narration.

In the first selection Mrs. Ned achieves three interrelated aims: she establishes her ancestry, she insists upon the storytelling authority of elders who either have experienced or have learned from their elders the events of which they speak, and she teaches her readers what life for the Southern Tutchone people was like before white men came to the Southern Yukon but after the Tlingits (who already had contact with whites) had discovered the rich natural resources of the interior.

In the second selection Mrs. Ned tells a sequence of related stories that help to illuminate the traditional Southern Tutchone ways of life and help to explain how some of those ways came to be. Among Athabaskan groups of the Yukon and Alaska, the stories about Crow (or Raven) are usually told as a separate cycle from those about the Traveler, who, in Northern and Southern Tutchone and in Upper Tanana, is called Smart Man, Smart Beaver, or Beaver Man. Crow often has a companion in his adventures, and so does Beaver Man (usually his brother, especially in his early travels). Mrs. Ned's narrative brings Crow and Beaver Man together as partners in the quest to make the world a place where human beings can benefit from game and fur-bearing animals instead of being killed and eaten by them.

The first of Kitty Smith's stories presented here is a masterpiece of irony with four masterful characterizations. It complements the autobiographical section with which it is linked ("My Husband's People") in that the wife in the *kwädąy kwändür*, as Cruikshank has pointed out, is forced to choose between loyalty to her husband or to her brothers (*Life* 168). Only from the title and from one early clue do we know that the boatman who rescues a man from death is an octopus; later he assumes his "devilfish" form to exact vengeance on the man's brothers-in-law. Mrs. Smith artfully uses the dual nature of this character, together with the less-than-human nature of the brothers-in-law, to develop the story's theme: that human beings should treat one another humanely.

Our second and third selections from Kitty Smith's work are taken from the last pair of sections, "Life at Robinson" and "Grandmothers and Grandsons." Robinson is a community between Carcross and Whitehorse where Mrs. Smith spent her middle years. Her encounter with the commissioner of the Yukon Territory over the building of a fire at a hunting camp is probably the greatest put-down in all Northern Athabaskan literature. As a final, posthumous, ironic triumph for Mrs. Smith, one of her granddaughters, Judy Gingell, holds the post of commissioner at the time of this writing. Approaching the end of her life, Mrs. Smith mourns for all her friends who have died but believes in the power of continuity among the generations of a family. In telling "The First Time They Knew *K'och'èn*, White Man," she artfully blends references to herself and her grandson Kenneth into this narrative about another grandmother whose grandson heard a voice in a rainbow foretelling the coming of white people and introducing the boy to white men's food but also providing traditional Indian food for Grandma for the rest of her life.

SUGGESTIONS FOR FURTHER READING

Cruikshank, Julie. *Athapaskan Women: Lives and Legends.* Canadian Ethnology Service Paper 57. Ottawa: National Museums of Canada, 1979.

―――. *The Stolen Women: Female Journeys in Tagish and Tutchone.* Canadian Ethnology Service Paper 87. Ottawa: National Museums of Canada, 1983.

Cruikshank, Julie, with Angela Sidney, Kitty Smith, and Annie Ned. *Life Lived Like a Story: Life Stories of Three Yukon Native Elders.* Lincoln: University of Nebraska Press, 1990.

McClellan, Catharine. "Indian Stories about the First Whites in Northwestern America." In *Ethnohistory in Southwestern Alaska and the Southern Yukon: Method and Content,* edited by Margaret Lantis, 103–33. Studies in Anthropology 7. Lexington: University Press of Kentucky, 1970.

―――. *My Old People Say: An Ethnographic Survey of Southern Yukon Territory* (Parts 1 and 2). Publications in Ethnology 6. Ottawa: National Museums of Canada, 1975.

Sidney, Angela, Kitty Smith, and Rachel Dawson. *My Stories Are My Wealth.* Whitehorse, Yukon: Council for Yukon Indians, 1977.

Our Shagóon, Our Family History

Since I was ten, that's when I got smart.
I started to know some things.

I'm going to put it down who we are. This is our *Shagóon* — our history. Lots of people in those days, they told their story all the time. This story comes from old people, not just from one person — from my grandpa, Hutshi Chief; from Laberge Chief; from Dalton Post Chief. Well, they told the story of how first this Yukon came to be.

You don't put it yourself, one story. You don't put it yourself and then tell a little more. You put what they tell you, older people. You've got to tell it right. Not *you* are telling it: it's the person who told you that's telling that story.

My grandpa, one man, was Hutshi Chief. He's got two wives: one from Selkirk, one from Carcross; his name is <u>K</u>aajoolaaxí: that's Tlingit. Oh, call him a different one: Kàkhah — that's *dän k'è* [Southern Tutchone] — that's an easy one. His Coast Indian name comes from a long time ago: it was from trading they call him that way. You see, long-time Coast Indians, they go through that way to Selkirk, all over.[1]

We'll start off with Hutshi Chief first. We'll do the women next time. He married first my grandma from Carcross: Däk'äläma. His Selkirk wife was K'edäma: she's the one they call Mrs. Hutshi Chief.

My daddy's name was Hutshi Jim: my daddy, Hutshi Jim, is the oldest. Another brother is Chief Joe — Hutshi Joe — he had the same mother. One grandpa we've got, and I've got lots of cousins up at 1016[2] from this lady, Däk'äläma. Jimmy Kane was her grandchild, too: Jimmy Kane's mother, Mrs. Joe Kane, is her daughter.

These kids are all born around Hutshi. Hutshi is a Coast name: Coast Indians call it *Hóoch'i Áayi* — means "Last Time Lake." That's when they go back. Then after white man came, they didn't come back [to Hutshi]. The *dän k'è* name is *Chùinagha*. Lots of people used to live at Hutshi. My grandpa had a big house at Hutshi . . . all rotten now. Oh, it used to be good fishing spot! King salmon came that way, too. Everybody came there together. *Kajìt* [Crow] owns that place, but they're not stingy with it.

Dalton Post, too — just free come fish![3] But this time [it's] no good, they say.

Wintertime, people hunted fur, used dog team. After they came [back] from Dalton Post, they hunted dry meat, put up food, berries. They put them in birch bark, they freeze them and put them away. They put stoneberries in moose grease — that's just like cheese. And roots are like potatoes: they clean them up and cut them and put them in grease, for the kids. There's no hard times. There used to be caribou there all the time. I remember big herds of caribou. But now no more.[4]

My daddy, my uncles, they all stayed around Hutshi Lake. But when they got married, the woman maybe wants to go someplace [with her family]. That's the way.[5] Now Indian woman when she marries white man, he takes *her* home . . .

My grandpa's house is there yet, though, all fallen down, rotten. Lots of houses there, used to be. But at Hutshi, nobody is there yet. You see [the cemetery] where there's lots of dead people there? My grandpa died at Hutshi, and his two wives are buried there with him.

My mother's name is *Tùtałmạ* and she was from Hutshi. Her daddy was Big Jim. There's another Coast Indian man from Dalton Post they call Big Jim, but that one's different — this one is Big Jim from Hutshi. I don't know his dad, though. My grandpa was too old [to tell me] by the time I got smart.

Big Jim's Indian name is *Kàkhnokh*. He married *Dakwa'äl*, and they had a daughter, *Tùtałmạ*. That woman was my mother. My grandfather, Big Jim, has an old house at Jojo Lake — it's an old house that fell down already.

Long-time people, anyplace they go round. [People] come from Dalton Post — go see everybody from the next country when you've got time. They see them. They talk. Then they go back in time to put up groceries for themselves in winter. They're trapping, and they hunt for fur.

This is our *Shagóon*. *Kajìt*, me — that's Crow: *Ts'ürk'i*. Wolf people they call *Ägunda*; wolf [the animal] is *ägay*. Hutshi Chief was *Kajìt*, and Big Jim was *Ägunda*. That Big Jim from Dalton Post was Crow.

My mamma's people are Crow — *Gaanax̱teidí*. My daddy is different; they're Wolf, *Ägunda*. That Crow started with our side. Crow claims Frog. All Crows, we claim it, used to be. But this time, nothing [people don't know about this].

Now I'm going to tell a story about long time ago. This is my two grand-pas' story, Big Jim's and Hutshi Chief's. I'm telling this story not from my-self, but because everybody [old] knows this story. This is not just my story — lots of old people tell it! Just like now they go to school, old time we come to our grandpa. Whoever is old tells it the same way. That's why we put this on paper. I tell what I know.

This time people talk way under me, not my age. They say they know! What I see, I tell it, me. This story is my grandpa's, Hutshi Chief.

Well, Coast Indians came in here a long time before white people. People had fur, and they used it for everything themselves. Nobody knows alcohol, nobody knows sugar before those Coast Indians came. They brought guns, too. No white man here, nothing.

At Noogaayík, Tlingit people first saw chips coming down from upriver.[6] People making rafts, I guess, and the chips floated down.

"Where did this one come from?" they asked. So that time Coast Indians wintertime to Dalton Post. That's the way they met these Yukon Indians. Yukon people are hunting, and they've got nice skin clothes — Oh, gee, por-cupine quills, moose skins, moccasins! Everything nice.

Coast Indians saw those clothes and they wanted them! That's the way they found out about these Yukon people. Right then, they found where we hunted. Coast Indians traded them knives, axes, and they got clothes, ba-biche, fish skin from the Yukon. They've got *nothing*, those Tlingit people, just cloth clothes, groundhog clothes. Nothing! Goat and groundhog, that's all.

But people here had lots of fur and they used it in everything them-selves — ready-made moccasins, buckskin parky, silver fox, red fox, caribou-skin parky sewed up with porcupine quills. You can't see it, this time [any-more], that kind. I saw it, that time. My grandma got it . . . so pretty . . .

So that's how they got it! Coast Indians got snowshoes and moose-skin clothes — all warm — parky, caribou parky, caribou blanket, caribou mat-tress. Anything like that they want to use. Those people wanted clothes from here in Yukon . . . Skin clothes, sheepskin, warm mitts . . . So they traded. They did it for a purpose. Our grandpas make different snowshoes [from Tlingit style] in this Yukon. They fixed them with caribou-skin babiche, nice snowshoes. Coast Indians traded for snowshoes, traded for clothes. They traded for snowshoe string, for babiche, for sinew, for tanned skin — all soft.

I don't know the time Coast Indians came to this Yukon. My grand-mother, my grandpa, *they* told me that's the way.

These Yukon people told Coast Indians to come back in summertime. So they did, next summer. Yukon people had lots of furs. That time they don't know money—they don't know where to sell them. So Coast Indians brought in guns. Well, they're surprised about that, Yukon people! They've been using bow and arrow! So they traded.

Coast Indians got guns, knives, axes. They came on snowshoes. They packed sugar, tea, tobacco, cloth to sew. Rich people would have eight packers each! They brought shells, they brought anything to trade. They traded for clothes. Coast Indians brought sugar, tea. At first these Yukon people didn't want it. But pretty soon, they went to Klukwan. They took their fur. They knew where to sell it now. They would go down wintertime with toboggan, Dalton Post way or by Lake Arkell.

But people here got crazy for it [trade goods]. They traded for knives, they traded for anything, they say—shells, guns, needles. When you buy that gun, you've got to pile up furs how long is that gun, same as that gun, how tall! Then you get that gun.[7]

I don't know those guns—that's before me. I don't see it. But my grandpa had that kind at Hutshi. I saw what they've been buying, though—blankets, not so thick, you know, quite light. You could pack maybe fifty blankets, I guess, from the coast. They would bring all that. Everybody bought their grandpa, their grandma a knife that time!

My grandpa, Hutshi Chief, had a trading partner, Gasłeeni. We fixed up his grave, my brother and myself. Old people were satisfied with Coast Indians, what they used to bring—cloth, guns, and matches. They used flint before, and birch bark. Coast Indians taught people to chew [tobacco]—I never used it, me. I never used to use sugar, either.

Well, Coast Indians would rest there and then they could go anyplace, see? They go hunting; then they go back. Then these people would go down to see them.

Dalton Post people are all our people, and Burwash people—all ours. Some from Carcross, too. This time just where they stay, they stay; that's what it looks like to me.[8] It was my grandpa, my grandma who told me about that, about before.

I never saw *those* ones—I know lots of Coast Indians, but they didn't bring anything in my time: I didn't see Coast Indians packing. It was before me, I guess, when my grandma was young—about one thousand years ago, about two thousand years ago, now!

When Skookum Jim found gold, that's the time everything changed. This time we can't do it now, can't travel around. People stay where they stay.

NOTES

1. Fort Selkirk on the Yukon River was another longstanding center for Tlingit/Athabaskan trade. In 1848 the Hudson's Bay Company tried to build its own post there, but Tlingits were unwilling to tolerate the competition and destroyed it.

2. Haines Junction. Until Canada underwent metric conversion, numbered mileposts marked the full fifteen-hundred-mile length of the Alaska Highway from its beginning in Fort St. John, British Columbia, to its terminus in Fairbanks, Alaska. "1016" is the old milepost number marking the location of the community of Haines Junction and is still used as a place name by older people.

3. King salmon arriving at Hutshi would have made the long journey from the Bering Sea up the Yukon River, then up the Nordenskiold River to Hutshi. People living near Dalton Post occupied a different river drainage and had access to the richer sockeye salmon coming from the Pacific via the shorter Alsek and Tatshenshini route. . . . Mrs Ned's comment about Dalton Post's being "no good" now refers to recent government restrictions placed on Indian fishing there.

4. There is evidence that moose and caribou habitats have shifted during the last 150 years. Biologists are still not sure of the reasons for their disappearance and reappearance.

5. Ideally, in the "old way" a couple stayed with the wife's family for at least a year after marriage, though it is unclear to me how often this actually occurred. By custom, a man then contributed to his wife's parents' household for the rest of their lives. A common reference to this tradition comes in the way a woman may still refer to a new son-in-law: "he's working for me, now."

6. According to McClellan (*Old People* 28), Noogaayík was an important fishing village on the Tatshenshini River in the nineteenth century. The village was established by Tlingits who had moved into the interior, probably from the Chilkat area, after striking up a trade in furs with people farther inland. From Noogaayík a trail led directly to Klukwan, a Chilkat Tlingit headquarters close to the coast.

7. Tlingit traders reputedly used this practice in their trade with interior Athabaskans, relying on their middleman position to charge high prices and to maintain a trade monopoly with their inland neighbors.

8. By naming communities that are now widely dispersed, Mrs. Ned is contrasting present-day, permanent villages with settlement patterns in former times, when mobility was essential to a sense of community.

How First This Yukon Came to Be

Some people tell stories Coast Indian way. Me, I tell it Yukon way.

Crow and Beaverman

    Well, I know lots of people, old people, long time.[1]
    They tell the same stories, old people
    That's the ones I know,
    [About] first when this land comes,
    When this ground was fixed.

One time, lots of people camped at one place.
People go one way [in one direction], one way they go.
Other people don't know which way they went.
They don't come back, don't come back, don't come back home.
They just go.

Crow and Beaver — they call Beaver Äsùya — that means Smart Man,
The two of them [go together], that's all.
They figure they want to go the way those people go.
Somebody tells them to go because people don't come back.
They go . . . they follow — they follow the track.
They go . . . go . . . go.

Pretty soon they come to a mountain, a mountain.
They climb to the top of the mountain:
It goes downhill, bad place.
From here they slide down, those people [who disappeared].
Then, Wolverine stays down there:

He's got something to kill people when they slide down —
Dry something — little dry tree, you know;
They slide down,
And it's just like they're poked inside [impaled] with that one,
Get killed.
In those days that Wolverine, he's big, big!
Long time ago, they're big, they say, Wolverines.
They eat those people.
His wife, too, is big.
As soon as they get people there, they eat them.

   I said that old people tell me this story.
   Not one man told me, but ten people, old people.
   My grandpa and my grandmother,
   They're all with me when they died.
   Other old people, too, they told me.

So Crow and Äsùya killed him.
They come to that Wolverine place, to the slides.
They know that down there something is killing the people.
Those Wolverines put water down there to [make a] slide down.
Then it froze, and you can slide down fast.
Just then, they're poked inside.

Crow and Beaver take off their shirt.
They put the branches inside and make it [look] like a leg, too.
Then they push it down.
Pretty soon, a man is down there on the bottom
And he pokes at the branches they put in the shirt, filled up like a person.
They see him.
Then he pulls it — it's light, that one.
He's got a camp there.
His wife is there, his family is there.
He comes down.
He started poking a stick into them.
So Crow and Äsùya think about it theirself, and they killed him with bow
   and arrow.

They've got a sharp rock, I guess, a long time ago — a bone.
And when it hits him, it comes out.
It goes right through and kills him.

"That was not a person, that one, Wolverine."

Oh, big. They're big!
So they kill him.
They ran down one side [of the slide] and they killed that Wolverine. Big
    one.
They poked him with that bow and arrow.

His wife stays there, too; she's big, too, that one.
Fat.
They eat lots of people, I guess.

Then they come to his wife.
"What for you eat people?
What for your husband eats people, you too?" they tell her.
"I suppose you got to be game, you."

Just like they lesson people, teach people, that Crow and Beaver.

Well, they talk.
"We got to kill her."

"Yes, we got to kill her, too."

That one's got pups, that woman.
They kill her, kill with bow and arrow, same.
After that, they cut her open.

Those pups climb up trees like this. Wolverine.
They're alive then,
As soon as they kill her, Crow and Beaver run to the tree.

"What are we going to do [with them]?"

"Well, when they grow how big they are now [that's enough]."

They don't want [them to be] big.
It's just like they hit them.

"So, we've got to kill them.
Save two, one female and one man."
They saved two; the rest they want to kill them.

That Beaver wants to climb up to where they got in the tree.
But they pee on him!
He comes back.

Then Crow does that: he flies there and kills them.
He asks each, "Are you a girl?"

"Yes."

"And you?"

"Yes, a boy."

That's all. Two only, they save.

Then he tells them,
"You've got to be the same big. Don't eat anybody!
It's no good!"

See? Lots of people, I guess, they eat.

   Long time, first this land is mud, I guess, that time.
   Then from there, this story comes . . .
   They tell next man, next man, next man.
   Now it comes to the last.
   But these schoolkids don't know, this time, this story, see?

Then they say,
"We're going to give you feed, what you're going to eat."

They give them ptarmigan.
They kill ptarmigan with bow and arrow, bring a bunch over there.

"You could get it yourself, after.
Don't eat persons again.
You're going to be game, you," they tell him.

When the people went from home
All the far side they go.[2]
All got eaten by Wolverine.
That's what the old people tell. That's lots of people.

From there, they give feed.

Then they tell them, "You eat dried meat cache."

What for they say that!!![3]

"Somebody's cache, and gopher, too, you've got to eat it.
You kill for yourself."
Then they tell them:
"Same big as Wolverine," they tell them.
[That is, wolverines must never grow larger than these pups.]

Then they go from there.

II

They walk around . . . walk around.
Then they camp someplace like this. Snow.

They've got to eat something, I guess, themselves.
They came to a camp.

So they camp.
Pretty soon, one man comes.
Around this land, this ground, first they see him.
First everybody they bring it on this land.[4]
He looks the same as a person.

Then they give this: moose nose they cooked.
They cut it for him:
"Right there, that's what we eat."
That man picks it up; he smells it, puts it back.
Now they found out! That's no good.[5]

They tried to give him something to eat.
If he eats that now, he will turn to person.
Yeah! That man could turn to person like them.
That's why they showed him that one.

He won't take it, what people eat.
He knows it.
He leaves it.

[This is how] they know how true is person:
They got it, that one — they fix up that ptarmigan and they cook it,
That one, too, they give it.
He smells it. He leaves it.

"How come you're not hungry?" they tell him.

Already they know.
Both of them know what he eats: he eats person!
It's for that reason they go round this ocean, I guess,[6]
But this is Yukon story, this one.

Then Äsùya said,
"That thing's no good," he said.
"Which way did he come [from]?"
He follows; he's going to watch it here.

   You know Crow . . . he flies around.

Äsùya follows his tracks and finds his sack —
Moose-skin packsack, used to be, they say, long time —
He opens it.
Here it's kids' feet there! Indians!

   He looks same as a man, too, [like an] Indian.
   They call him Kojel. Yeah. Long time.

He opens that. Crow. Hangs it up again.
He brings moose meat to his partner.
They got moose meat, too; cook moose meat.
They try to show people, too.

Then they camp.
"We've got big place here. You sleep right here, my friend."
They call him *shą'ür*, "my friend," long time.

Now people are coming. Lots of them.
And they camp this side, other side of the fire!

Then they want to dry their moccasins;
They put up pole, those people.
That's why they do that, I guess.
And they fixed it there; they dry moccasins on the fire.

So he sleeps.
They sleep. Two men [Crow and Beaver].
And they bring this along: green club from a tree.
They cut it there, put it there.
They've got bow and arrow, too.

   I don't know who put it [caused it],
   That Smart Man to go round,
   To clean up that kind of people.
   Just like somebody tells him who's no good.
   That's why Äsùya, they call him.
   Ts'ürk'i [Crow] helps, too.

They went to sleep.

Pretty soon, he gets up, that man. He gets up.
Those moccasins, which one is pretty, he moved it in place of his moccasin.
He thought he's going to kill those two.

They know it.
They watch it.

One sleeps one way, one sleeps this [the other] way.
Their feet reach like this [touching].
Soon as that man gets up [they kick each other].
That's why they sleep that way.

Pretty soon he gets up.
How he thinks he's going to kill two men?

They snore.
"Get up, get up!"
They jumped on that man. One of them hit him.
The other one got up and he hit the back.
And they killed him: they clubbed him down!

In the morning, his shoes were there.
He thought he was going to kill those people,
So he's got good mukluks;[7] he put them in place of his moccasins.

So they picked the moccasins up again;
They put them on.
They leave his mukluks there.
They go.
Then they know where he comes from.

Got to go that way, they say.

IV

Then, they go from there.[8]
People got smoke there, under the mountain.
There's a lake there.

[Crow and Beaver discuss]:
"He's a person, all right, that man."

"No, it's just like that Wolverine."

They went to where an old man stays with his wife.
They've got a young girl.

"Ho," the old man says, "I can't climb up to that sheep up there.
You see him?
I can't climb up there anymore.
My leg is no good.
You're going to be my son-in-law [if you kill him]."

He said that to that young man, Beaver.
He'd like that Beaver for his son-in-law.

Well, fourteen years old, she's got a hat, that girl,[9]
Stays a long time away when that happens.
Then he says that, that old man [to Äsùya].

[Beaverman says,] "Oh, my moccasins are no good, all torn."

"Well, I'm going to give it to my daughter quick [to sew].
You take it off."

That, his daughter, he put on [dressed up] like sheep.
Right there, walking around there, that's his daughter.

Äsùya wants to kill those two.

So that old man said,
"I've come this way, and I'll kill him from here."

"All right. All right."

Now he [the old man] sewed it up himself [pretending his daughter did the
    work].
Then he said, "All right, we go. I'll go, too," that old man said.

Äsùya has got sharp bow and arrow under his hair.
They go there.

[The old man tells Äsùya to push the sheep down the mountain but really
    intends to push Äsùya.]

[Äsùya] pushed him down.
That old man's wife was there, has that *shęshęl.*
They see her: Crow, he can see that [by flying around overhead].

Äsùya asks, "Where from? Show me where to step."

That mountain is hard. It's wintertime.
He does that, then. Crow pushes him over.
Here, his own wife kills him at the bottom.

Yeah!

Then Crow, he flies and Äsùya goes down again.
That's his wife, there.

"What does your daddy do? [they ask the daughter].
Are you a person?
What are you?
You want to be saved?"

That Crow comes back.

"Go home."
She's just fourteen years old.
They brought her back to the house.

"What are you?" [they ask her].

"Bear. Bear we are."

"Well, what do you want to do, killing people?
If you're going to keep on, we're going to kill you."

She said, "No more."

They give her food and she eats it, so they let her go.
They let her go.

V–VI

Then after that, they came to a regular bear.
Must be springtime now.
They go around yet, that bear family.
Regular bear. Big bear. They come.

Bear says, "Yeah! We want to get that Äsùya — Beaver there."
They want to kill that beaver, bear.[10]
They want to eat him.

Well, beaver is his people:
[Äsùya asks bear,] "What you been doing?"
[That is, How have you been trying to catch beaver?]

"Well, we tried to kill him.
He goes right in the middle of that place, open place.
We set out fishnet."
Beaver wears a row of teeth around his neck.

Then Ts'ürk'i said, "I think they're no good, these people."
He goes around, he flies.
Sometimes when they get stuck he flies around to find out what it is.

Those bears really want to kill beaver.
Then they caught him.
That's beaver there. Oh, he knows now, Beaver.

He says, "Right close to there, they set a fishnet for me.
They're going to eat people, *shär*, bear.
They eat people. How about you?"

"Oh, bad one, that people.
I've got no place to go, wintertime.
They pretty near got me," [the beaver said].

Well, they killed bear.
They set a beaver net and he chews that one, that beaver.
That's why they don't get him, see?
Then they kill that bear.

One beaver, he goes on the water.
Just Crow alone.
"You've got enough food?" he tells beaver.

"Yeah. Got a little bit now."

So they bring poplar tree, throw in there.

Well, that beaver says,
"We want fur. People are going to get fur."
That's why people now get skin, fur, from beaver.

And that's why bear, he can't kill people.

Grizzly bear, though, he kills people this time, see?
They don't get after him. He passes [escapes] them.

Then they [Crow and Beaver] go from there.
They do everything in springtime there.
Go round, round,
Which way bad people stay.

"Don't kill nobody. Don't bother people.
That's game, you, for people to eat you. Don't do that."

And they go on . . . got boat now . . . float down . . . float down . . . [11]

From there, they split.
Ts'ürk'i goes to Coast Indian side.
Beaver goes to Yukon side.
They're going to straighten up this world.
No more danger, they say.

"So I'm going to be Yukon" [Beaver said].

"Well, I'll come back [Crow said].
I'm going to saltwater side."

That's what I know of this story.

VII

That's why that Crow don't want fish to come from salt water, this way,
    see?[12]
Must be that's why.

That time he put his hand [wing] like that at Klukshu, [pointing toward
    the coast].
At Klukshu, they've got saltwater fish.

He should leave it alone!
Then those fish would come up there, Champagne.

You see that Dezadeash Lake?
About three miles [separates the two drainages].
But he makes Dezadeash come out other side [flowing north].
King salmon, the other side; silver salmon.
He did it there, too.
His hand he put up like that.
That's what they say, old people, see?

Then he did that to this place, too, Kusawa Lake.
Other side water ran down to Klukwan,
Fish came there, too.
What for Crow do that that way?
Glacier on top there, that's what he did!

He *could* have made fish go this way!
Just to Haines summit, fish go.
That Lake Arkell, a mountain goes like that.
From the other side, big river goes down to Klukwan.

NOTES

1. As Mrs. Ned tells this story, she sometimes adds her own commentary, and I have set these reflections off from the narrative by indenting them.

2. Her comment refers to the time at the beginning of the world when the sky came down to the earth at the horizon and it was possible for people to be stolen away to the "far side," where everything was perpetual darkness and winter.

3. Wolverines are notorious for robbing meat from caches. Mrs. Ned's comment expresses the displeasure of her people with Crow and Beaver for this feature of their reformation of Wolverine. — Eds.

4. The line is obscure. In the context of the two preceding lines and the one that follows, it may mean that the being who looks like a man is appearing in the Yukon for the first time. — Eds.

5. Äsùya recognizes two indicators that this individual is not human. First, he will not eat human food. Second, beings who disguise themselves as humans characteristically sleep on the opposite side of the fire from people.

6. According to McClellan (*Old People* 72), Beaver and his companion (his brother in the versions of many storytellers) "planned to circle the world by each going in opposite directions." She adds that the Southern Tutchone people seem to imply "a round disc of some sort" as the shape of the world. The purpose of their travels is to continue reforming evil creatures and animals who eat people. — Eds.

7. In personal correspondence (June 17, 1999), Julie Cruikshank points out that

in the Yukon Territory *mukluk* "is the commonly used term for Athapaskan footwear with the longer cuff tied around the lower calf." In Alaska the term more often refers to the footgear made of seal hide worn by Eskimos (see Russell Tabbert, *Dictionary of Alaskan English* [Juneau AK: Denali Press, 1991] 95). Mrs. Ned appears to use the detail only to indicate one way in which the stranger has disguised himself as a human being, an Athabaskan. The episode of the switched footgear or, more usually, switched trousers over the campfire at night is common to the cycle of stories about the Traveler in many Northern Athabaskan languages, and the stranger is ordinarily Wolverine. — Eds.

8. Section III is obscure in several ways and consequently has been omitted. In it Crow and Beaver defeat two unidentified nonhuman antagonists. — Eds.

9. She is secluded at puberty, under the conventional "long hat."

10. "Beaver" (capitalized) refers to Äsùya; "beaver" (lower case) refers to the animal. There is some interplay here between concerns that beavers and humans share in the following dialogue.

11. The second part of section V has been omitted; in it Crow and Beaver meet harmless ghosts and let them go. Section VI has to do with the reformation of deer, who have been killing people. It has a number of obscurities, and all but the last nine lines have been omitted. — Eds.

12. After Crow went to the coast, he established drainage patterns so that Klukshu drains to the nearby Pacific coast, while Dezadeash and Kusawa lakes drain north to the Yukon and ultimately to the Bering Sea.

Naak̲w: Devilfish, or Octopus, Helper

Some Coast Indians, brothers, were going to an island one time.
They told their brother-in-law there are lots of eggs there —
He's married to their sister.

"I want to go.
I'll go with you.
Your sister wants to eat some eggs," he told them.

"All right. Come on."
They took him.

There are four brothers and this one, that lady's husband.
They keep going, keep going.
Pretty soon, now, island.
Gee! He sees island now — ducks, everything. Lots of eggs.
He picks them up.

They got wood. They cooked them.
He ate eggs, too.
That time, he put some aside for his wife in a net basket.
He filled it up, put it in the boat.

Just when they finished eating, those four boys ran off,
Jumped in the boat —
They let that brother-in-law go.

"Ah, they're just playing with me," he thought.
"I'll sit down here. It's all right.
I'm going to eat eggs."

My goodness, they left him. Don't come back!
It gets dark now.
When they get home, his wife asks them,
"Where is your brother-in-law?"

"Down on shore. He saw something.
We let him go — he'll come back.
He wants to look for porcupine."
That's what they said.
They lied: they put him on that island.

Well, he stayed there.
He lived on eggs, he cooked eggs.
He put out snares for seagull.
I don't know how long he was there.

His wife asked her brothers,
"What's the matter? He doesn't come back."

"I don't know."

He stayed there.
One time he saw a boat.
He lay down.
He should have stayed down until they landed,
But they saw him.
His brothers-in-law came back.
As soon as they saw him, they took off. They went back.
Bad people!

But he's living there — he snares seagulls.
He's got fire all that time — lots of drift logs there.
He stayed there . . . stayed there . . .

He got up one morning.
Boat was there!
Nobody in it, though.
He went to see it. He didn't go close, though.
That man is coming his way.

"Gee, what are you doing here? How long you stay here?"

"Well, my brothers-in-law came here to get eggs.
We've got eggs, and they let me go here.
Pretty near two months I stay here," he told that man.
"But those birds that lay eggs are all gone now.
They fly away.
No eggs there no more."

But he's living, though.
Those seagulls are coming there — that's what he lives on.

He talks to him nice,
"Where's your place?"

"My place is up there."

"Oh, my!"

That man went to his boat. He had dry fish.
"You like this kind?"

"Yes!" He's happy now.

"Get in the boat.
I'm not going to take you right to your city, just close."

Right here is the city . . . right here is a point.
Right there, he let him go: he landed at that point.

"You know your place?"

"Yes, I'm going to walk there."
He sat down there until it got dark.
It's pretty near August now.
When it gets dark, when people are sleeping, that's the time he wants
    to get home now.

He goes home.
They closed that door: his wife's room is behind that door.

"Who's that?" she asked him.

"Me!" Gee, it's a long time since he got lost.
She got up. She came out to him.
Some people were sleeping there.
They go to her room.
She asked him, "What did they do to you?"

"They let me go on that island."

"But they said you went on shore,
That you went to get porcupine on shore.
You don't come back,
So I guessed grizzly bear killed you.
They tried to look around for you on that shore.
People looked around."

"No, they left me on that island."

"Which way did you come back?"

"Oh, some way I got help."
He doesn't tell her, though, that somebody brought him.
"Some way I came back."

He slept there.
In the morning, that lady got up, started cooking.
Her husband slept.
She cooked something and took it to him.
One week, they stayed that way.
He's getting better now, you know — he was pretty thin, I guess.
He's getting stronger.

That's the time his brother-in-law came, the youngest one.

"We're going to look around that way.
If bear killed him, we can find his bones," he told his sister.
"He got off at that point:
'Sometime I'm going to kill porcupine on that shore,' he said.
'I'm going to walk back.'

Something must have killed him, I guess."
That's what he told his sister.

His sister didn't answer back, just kept quiet.

"You want me to go with you?" she asked.

"We're going to take a boat."
They think he's dead on that island, I guess.
"You can't walk that far."

"All right."

She hides her husband.
They're gone.
All four she sees them — gone.

Well, nothing there.
They look all over for the bones — nothing.
"Well, I guess something ate him.
Should be bones here."
Nothing.
He had a knife with a string on — he forgot it there.
Just that one they find — I don't know what kind of knife —
And they came back.

Everyone was down on the shore trying to get clams when they came back.
The youngest brother sat down beside his sister.

"No, we didn't find him.
If something killed him, we should have found his bones.
But nothing there."
He said that.

That time her husband came out!

"What place did I get off?" he asked them.
Gee, he ran outdoors, that boy.
He told his brothers, I guess.

"That man came back!
I was talking with my sister and he came out!"

They get scared now.

That husband and wife were going to sleep when that man [who helped him] came
    to the door.
He told his wife,
"This man brought me."

"What are you going to do with those people?" that Naa<u>k</u>w asked.

They asked the sister,
"What should happen to them?"

That sister said,
"If you go to that island, keep away from them.
They're going to stay there.
You take their boat," she told that helper man.

"All right."

When they hunt, they go to that island, too.
Those boys go again to that island again sometime.
"I don't know which way he came back . . ."
They talked about it, sat down.
"You see . . . he slept right here . . .
He had a pile of wood here . . .
I don't know which way he came back."

They start to go back.
No boat!

"Where's that boat gone? Did you tie it up?
No wind.
Where has that boat gone?"

"You fellows are crazy," that youngest one said.
"I told you, 'Don't let him go.'

You let my brother-in-law go right there.
There's no wind: what would take this boat?
Something is wrong now. We're going to stay here.
That's you people's fault.
Where's that boat now?
You tied it up, you said. No wind.
How quick is gone that boat!
Should be that boat floats around," he tells them.
"You see it now?"

Well, they camp.
They don't know what they're going to do.
Nobody knows that place, I guess.
And, they sleep.

That youngest one hears something — grunt, grunt.
Just like dog chewing, you know.
He wakes up — gee, they're all gone, his brothers . . .
Big thing chewing.
What's he going to do? He sat down there, watched him.

"You leave me alone, me."

"Huh," it said. "Why did you fellows let people go here?
That's why I'm going to eat you people."
He's got six legs, that one, some kind of saltwater thing.
Naakw they call him, coast language —
They say he catches everything.
All he cleaned them.
Just one man he left there.

"You're going to stay here, you," he told him.
He's living there until the end.

People knew they got lost.
They talked about it, I guess.
That man and his wife went to the island.
He's just pretty near bone now, that brother.
Just about fell down.
They found him there.

"Where's your brothers?"

"Something ate them up."

"How come he didn't eat you?"

"Well, I guess because I faced him, that's why I guess he didn't eat me.
Naa<u>k</u>w came here." That's what he said.
"He's the one who ate us."

"You threw me away.
That's why it happened."

I guess that's the kind of thing that took him back home, Naa<u>k</u>w.

His sister and her husband put him in the boat.
They brought him back.

That's because that brother's wife told them,
"Why don't you look around that place where they used to get eggs?"
That's where they found him starving on top.
They brought him back.
His wife went down to see him —
He's just like a little baby, just bone.
They brought him inside.

That man said,
"I told them not to,
Just the same they let my brother-in-law go."
He said that, that man.
That's what happened. We got it, that story.

Should be they didn't do that!
There's a government island now, they say, way out on the ocean.
Seal Island — right full of seals there.
When Paddy Duncan[1] told me that story,
Even then he told me, "It's Seal Island now."

NOTE

1. Mrs. Smith's second stepfather. Her natural father died when she was just an
infant, and her first stepfather died when she was two years old. – Eds.

[To Build a Fire]

I went out to Little Atlin, one time, with my grandson Richard, his wife, my little grandchild. We go hunting out there, you know. That's the time of year moose are running, Little Atlin.

A big truck pulled up . . . stopped — it had its house on top. It's bigshot government man. My grandson Richard knows him.[1] I don't know him, me, but Richard knows that car with its house on. That man comes to me. "Got to take care of that, your fire," he tells me. I don't say nothing. I don't know he's bigshot, that man.

After he finished talking, I tell him, "Look, you fellows spoil Yukon," I tell him. "Yeah! That time my grandpa burned tree when he hunts moose. He makes fire. He don't burn anything. What do you fellows do? This time you throw away cigarette stumps. Big fire. You spoil Yukon, all. Should be where your grandpa country, you stay in. Where's your grandpa's country? Your grandma? Where?" I tell him.

"Well, outside, long way," he said.

"How the hell you're coming here, then? Nobody called you to come here."

"Well, you're right, Missus," he tell me.

"Me, my grandpa's country, here. My grandma's. My roots grow in jack-pine roots all. That's why I stay here. I don't go to your grandpa's country and make fire. No. My grandma's country I make fire. Don't burn. If I be near your grandma's country, it's all right you tell me."

"Oh, you beat me!" he said. He walks away.

After, my grandson came back. "What you tell him, that man. You know that man is bigshot?"

"Well, that's all right," I tell him. "I'm bigshot, too. I belong to Yukon. I never go to his country. I'm born here. I branch here! The government got all this country, how big it is. He don't pay five cents, he got him all. Nobody kicks me out. No, sir! My roots grow in jackpine roots."

He laughs, my grandson. "You're a bad woman, Grandma."

Billy was sick for six years before he died. He was blind then, so I hunted. I looked after him. When he was sick, before he died, he told me, "Should be you find someone to look after you. When I'm gone, you should find a new husband. If one of them asks you, go with him, my nephew."[2]

I tell him, no. "I can't take men no more. I can make my own living." Should be you're on your own. Nobody can boss you around then. You do what you want. My grandchild can look after me. Before, I wanted a husband, wanted kids. I lost six of those kids — six of mine. After I'm past that, though, I don't want to be bothered with men. One *Dakl'aweidí*[3] man used to bring me meat and fish after Billy died — we raised him when he's a kid. One time I asked him to stay with me, but he said no. "Too much it's like you're my mother."

When Billy died, he told me, "I'm going to come back. If I'm still around after I die, I'm going to come back. I'll knock at the window so my grandchild can let me in."

One time we were sitting here: we heard three knocks at door — but that time it was just a dog. I dreamed about it, though. I talked with Susie [Fred], too. She says, "Your old man can't come back that way. He's going to turn into baby. He's going to be *nedlin*."[4] I know it's true.

I miss all my sisters-in-law:[5] Mrs. Whitehorse Billy ... Mrs. Charlie Burns ... Jessie Burns ... Jessie Walker ... Jenny McKenzie ... Jenny Laberge ... Kitty Walker ... Susie Sam ... Might be I'm going to catch them yet. I don't know which way they're gone. All Wolf ladies I talk about — I don't know which way they're gone. I sure loved them all, used to be. Best friend of mine, Jessie Walker, used to be. All Wolf women, all. They don't think about me anymore, when they're gone.

I made song for them [she sings and then translates]:

Where are they gone?
How tough to sing alone.
They all left me.
Where are they gone now, all?
How much power do you people think I have?
You left me.
You don't think about me, back this way.

All my friends, where are they gone?
I'm going to be there someday.

When I go, I'm going to say goodbye. I'm not going to look back. Just one way I'm going to go.

NOTES

1. Here Mrs. Smith is referring to a former commissioner of the Yukon Territory.

2. The appropriate person to marry her when her husband died would be some-one of his own clan, *Dakl'aweidí*, preferably his nephew, his sister's son, or someone in a socially equivalent relationship to him.

3. A clan of the Wolf moiety. — Eds.

4. *Nedlin* refers to a deceased person's rebirth as a new baby. Such a child will give a sign at an early age to an appropriate person that he or she remembers incidents from his or her former life. Often the details the child reveals could be known only by the deceased and the person the child tells. The child is always someone of the same moiety or clan as the deceased person. As the child grows older, he or she for-gets this former life.

5. Mrs. Smith is naming women of the Wolf clan or moiety, who can all be classi-fied as "sister-in-law." As one of the oldest living people in the Yukon, she sometimes finds it sad that all her friends have gone before her.

The First Time They Knew K'och'èn, White Man

You know my grandson, Kenneth?
He looks after me, takes care of me.
They're that way, Indians, long time ago, I guess.

Where they get meat, long time ago,
One Indian boy got meat for his grandma.
All the time he does that, that boy.
No white man that time — they don't know white man.

I'm going to tell you a story about this one, that boy.
He looked after his grandma — he took care.
Where they kill meat, he goes, that boy.
He gets meat. They've got two dogs —
No dogs long time ago, they say; just a little while ago, that dog.

They kill two caribou.
His uncle killed them.
"You get meat: your uncle killed caribou.
Are you going to go?"

He says, "Yes."

They say,
"You take your dog."
He took his dog. Goes.
He told his grandma,
"Don't get wood, Grandma.

I'll come back. I'm going to get wood.
My uncle killed caribou."

People go to get meat.
Everybody packed him: everybody went to that meat place.
That boy, he looked for bones someplace, after people go —
Looks around to see if he finds something: he takes them.
He's got two dogs to pack them, too.

People are gone already.
He goes back. He's the same big as my grandchild Kenneth.
This is a *story*, you know, not "story." It's *true* story.[1]

He sees a rainbow, about same big as this tent.
He stood up about this far from it, and somebody talked to him.

"Go through." He doesn't see who said that.
"Go through."

He comes, his dogs behind. Goes through.
Other side, little bit long way, he stands back.
Big sack falls down there.

"Don't eat that meat anymore!
You're going to eat this grub.
This one in the sack.
Don't drink water from this ground for one week!
That many days, don't take water from this ground.
You're going to use this one, from inside your grub here,
Or else we're going to come, going to get you."

He took that sack.
Put it on top of his pack.
He doesn't see that man who talks to him, but he sees that rainbow.
But he talked to him.

His grandma cooked already —
That's what I do with Kenneth here — cook soup, everything.
So when he comes back, he runs here,
"What you cooking, Grandma, soup?"

"Yes."

Last night he cooked, him. Fed me here.

"I cook some gopher. I kill two, grandchild," she said, that old lady.
"I cook that one."

"No, Grandma, I'm not going to eat.
I've got something to eat," he said.

She looked.
Something's wrong, she thinks.

"I'm not going to eat anymore, Grandma.
I've got my grub here, my sack."

That one who talked to him told him,
"Tell those people to fix some things for you."

He told his grandma,
"Tell those boys they got to come,
Their uncle, too, has got to come here."

Grandma goes to tell them,
"He wants you . . . Don't know what's the matter.
He said it."

They come there and the boys sit down.

"I want you to fix that high bed for me," he said.
"I want to lay down on top."
Just quick they fix him.
"And two bridges, I want you to fix this way."
Bridge goes right there, right here, that far.
"Well, thank you," he said.
"Somebody talked to me; that's why I say that.
You come tonight before you eat: you come to this bridge.
Then I'm going to tell you.
You hold your wife's hand when you come on that bridge.
I'm going to tell you."

His grandma got scared, you know.

"Don't think about it, Grandma. Eat. You eat good."

They fix already that bed for him. On top.
He opens his sack — he doesn't know this kind of grub.
He eats something from there.
Water in there, too. He drinks water.

And he said,
"They're coming now."
He sings some kind of song,
   "Come on, come on, my friends."

"You hold your wife's hand.
Go down, turn that way."
He tells them, "I'm going to be white man."
Nobody knows *K'och'èn* that time. That boy called them *K'och'èn*.
Right today they use it.
He said, "*K'och'èn* you, *K'och'èn* that one."
Turn that way, turn that way.
All that camp.

"You fellows are going to be white." That's what he said.
They don't know what he means.

"I'm not going to eat anymore for seven days," he said.
"One day, this ground going to be full of *K'och'èn*.
You're going to be *K'och'èn*, you people."
Nobody knows.
"Going to turn white man."
How many white-man grandchild have I got now?
That time, look!
I talk white-man way, too, now.
He's honest, that boy, isn't he?

Seven days he stayed there.
And he told his grandma.
He gave her a big sack, that big one — don't know where it came from —
Anything, Indian grub, dried fish, everything is in that sack.

"Right here your grub is going to stay, Grandma.
Anything you want stays there.
It's not gone till you're gone.
That sack is all full of grease, everything.
No more you're going to look for grub.
Anything — fresh meat, you want it —
It's going to stay there — inside.

"You want ribs? It's there.
What you wish for before you open, you say you want that one —
Right there it is.
Until you're gone, I leave this sack for you.
I'm going to stay here two days more, Grandma," he told her.
"Then gone.
Don't be sorry, nothing."

Him, he called them *K'och'èn*.
That's why this time Indians, nothing.
Right today, everybody calls them *K'och'èn*.

That time he gave them bread, nobody knows that.
"This kind of grub you fellows are going to eat."

It's true, this one.
That boy, he's gone — nobody knows where.
Now I sit down on top of that bed,
You sit on bed.
Before that, bed was on ground.

"You're going to be that way and you're going to turn to white man."
What white man?
That time nobody knows it.

NOTE
1. She is emphasizing the distinction between *kwädąy kwändūr* (story in italics) and *kwändür* ("story" in quotation marks) but insisting upon the truth of the distant-time narrative *(kwädąy kwändūr)*. The truth of a historical account *(kwändür)* is normally taken for granted. — Eds.

8

Upper Tanana

The Upper Tanana Athabaskan people live along the Tanana River above Tok, Alaska, and along the many creeks and streams that flow into it, especially those creeks on the border between Alaska and the Yukon Territory. In some earlier studies, they were merged with the Tanana Athabaskans, but recent inquiries have focused on their distinct linguistic heritage and cultural achievement. Unfortunately, little has been written by and about the Upper Tanana people. Consequently, inadequate resources exist for an extensive discussion of Upper Tanana storytelling and oral tradition. Recently Mrs. Mary Tyone and James Kari published the first collection of stories in the Upper Tanana language.

Mrs. Tyone, known in Upper Tanana as Ts'ą' Yahnik, was born to Bell and Laura John on November 15, 1935. She is the only living child of nine siblings. Growing up in the village of Scottie Creek, she was instructed by the old people after she did chores for them, such as cutting wood. In the dark of winter, candles would be lit, and the stories would continue for many hours. Winter was the appropriate time for storytelling because the animals migrated, hibernated, or ranged away from humans. At this time, Mrs. Tyone maintains, one could tell stories and not fear offending the animals.

Listeners were encouraged to think about the stories and to ask questions. She remembers asking about those beings in the distant time, and the old people answered that the sky was not as high then as it is now. They told her about how these beings all spoke the same language and were really all parts of one another. While many of the stories portray animals common to interior Alaska and explore their natures, ultimately they offer wisdom about the human condition, for the distance between animal and human is not far in the distant-time stories.

Mrs. Tyone lived in Fairbanks, Gulkana, and Northway before settling again in Fairbanks. She is noted for her ability to speak four other Athabaskan languages that are spoken by people of regions bordering her own: Ahtna, Tanacross, and both Northern and Southern Tutchone. Through recording and publishing these narratives, Mrs. Tyone hopes that future generations will read her stories and appreciate some of the wisdom of the old times.

McKennan observed that the Upper Tanana people, like most Athabaskans, make a clear distinction between historical and distant-time narratives. Kari points out that the Upper Tanana terms for these two genres are *neenaatthehdą'* and *yaaniidą'*, respectively. Among those narratives in the distant-time genre, McKennan grouped stories as Ancient Traveler stories, Raven stories, and miscellaneous stories. He also noted that traditionally the Ancient Traveler stories were to be told only during the December moon.

In "My Old Grandmother: The Little Man Standing in the Moon," Mrs. Tyone skillfully weaves together many story elements common to interior Athabaskan oral narrative. With humor and precision, the narrative refers to the importance of respect for all people, especially the elderly, the use of indirect language, the importance of spirit power in hunting, and the hazards of taking illusion for reality. "When the Tree Squirrels Cut Fish" is a cautionary tale emphasizing the attitude of respect that beings should have for one another, especially for those beings who give themselves as food. The story "When Horsefly Was Living in a Stump" pits the trickster/transformer Raven against the irritating Horsefly. Raven pretends to be Horsefly's kin. He tricks Horsefly by appealing to the most important social bond in Athabaskan life. Raven then challenges Horsefly to a race. Although he rids the people of a dangerous enemy, in the process he creates a first-class pest. In Raven's world the desirable and the undesirable are always mixed. "Raven and Muskrat Story" shows the powerful Raven receiving help from Frog and Muskrat in order to get his wife back. Raven's actions establish the nature and environment of these two animals, indeed of the whole world around us.

Kari has worked with Mrs. Tyone intermittently since 1988. He records her storytelling and then transcribes the narratives. Later Mrs. Tyone reviews the transcriptions and Kari's draft translations. He confers with her on corrections, explaining changes in thorough review sessions.

SUGGESTIONS FOR FURTHER READING

McKennan, Robert A. *The Upper Tanana Indians.* Yale University Publications in Anthropology 55. New Haven: Yale University Press, 1959.

Tyone, Mary. *Ttheek'ädn Ut'iin Yaaniidą' Qǫnign' (Old-time Stories of the Scottie*

Creek People): Stories told in Upper Tanana Athabaskan by Mary Tyone, Tsʼ ̈ạ' Yah-nik. Transcribed and edited by James Kari. Fairbanks: Alaska Native Language Center, 1996.

Stsǫǫ Shyaan Qǫnign'
Ch'aldzeek Shyii Dineh Gaay Na'ithädn

My Old Grandmother

The Little Man Standing in the Moon

When we look at the moon, we see on it, on the right side, that he is holding
a caribou's ovaries, and on the left side he is holding caribou stomach
sausage.

An object fell out from the top of a spruce [carrying the Man in the Moon's
spirit],
and then popped up among the spruce roots.[1]
And a baby was crying in the timber, and there was an old lady with her
grandchildren.[2]
The woman was raising two girls.
As those girls went for it [that baby], it quieted down.
He was not crying.
Then they went inside again, but the baby was still crying out in the timber.
They heard him and went for him again, but there was nothing.
And then the old lady told them, "I will go for him, you stay inside here."
The old lady went after him, and just as it cried, she stopped by him, and
the baby was sticking up between the roots.
She took him back and brought him in, and she raised him up.
Those women went away.
They were staying with their uncle.

After that time she named him "My Old Grandmother."
So that was his name, "My Old Grandmother."
He is growing, and he grew up and the little man looked bigger and,
"You drag[3] [take] the dog up the mountainside in order to look for a
porcupine," they told him.
He took that dog out with him, and as he went around on the
mountainside for porcupine he was dragging that dog around.
He thought, "Grandmother told me, 'you drag around the dog.'"

He dragged the dog around all day long.

As the sun was setting, he stopped by the doorway.

"My grandmother! My grandmother, I dragged the dog all day."

The old lady ran out proudly, thinking, "He has dragged in a porcupine for
     me."

But the dog had snow frozen in its mouth.

"Hey! How come you strangled the dog?" she said to him.

And he said to her, "My Grandmother, why did you tell me to drag the dog
     around?"

After the dog incident, he grew some more and they [she] told him, "Set a
     snare for rabbits out there under the branches."

He started to set snares for rabbits but instead he set the snares on the side
     of a spruce tree [among the branches], and

a camprobber and a great gray owl got snared.

And his grandmother said to him, "Hey, you are supposed to chop some
     material for a snare fence; then we set the snares," she told him.

"But, Grandmother, why did you tell me to set snares *under* the branches?"
     he said.

So he set some snares for rabbits and he brought back rabbits.

There was a rack up there.

He froze lots of rabbits up on the rack.

Rabbits were all piled up.

Later he tells her, "My grandmother, let's move to the end of the snare line."

They moved out to the end of the line of snares.

Under the rack the old lady [the grandmother] was thawing out rabbits,

and after she weaved a rabbit skin blanket from them, she weaved some
     pants for him, rabbit-skin pants.

She weaved a coat for him, rabbit pants and a rabbit coat.

Later he grew up, and he lived next door to the old lady's younger brother
     [his uncle].

He made a request to him.[4]

"You see that I am about to starve of an empty stomach! [his uncle says].

You make a dream-wish[5] for me."

"Your uncle says you should make a dream-wish for him," his grandmother
     says.

"Yes, my uncle told me to make a dream-wish for him."

Then he laughed and told her, "Grandma, tell my uncle to give me one of
     his arrows."

She brought a large game arrow to him.

He turned it around, and after he turned it around, he threw it in the fire.
"Oh, my grandmother, out there my uncle's arrow is about to burn up!
Oh, my grandmother, my uncle's arrow just burned up!"
All the arrows got burned up.
Afterward he went to sleep, and in the morning he woke up.
"My grandmother, tell my uncle to go up in the mountains."
His grandmother told him [the uncle], "As you are walking along up ahead
    there, if you notice that an arrow has slid down below somewhere, then
    tell him to go there after it."
She went in seeking his uncle and told him that.

So he [his uncle] was going around out there, and he saw some tracks by a
    den.
He followed him, and he followed his tracks to the front of it [the den].
His arrow was lying by the entrance of an occupied bear den.[6]
He took the bear out [killed it] and then butchered it and packed the bear
    back.
So then My Old Grandmother's uncle packed back that bear and then he
    made a feast.
He cooked everything, and the people were eating.
"My Old Grandmother" was lying stretched out by the doorway where they
    go out.
They told him, "move over," but he says, "nope."
As they stepped over him, "Ahaha, I see between your legs," he tells them.
Some of the people, the nice ones, started to walk around him.
As some of them stepped over him, he laughed at them.[7]

He went back into his own home where his grandmother and the family
    are staying.
The caribou were returning.
"My grandmother, you tell my uncle that the caribou are returning," he
    tells her.
The caribou herd had come back.
All the caribou stopped.
In the morning he chopped down a spruce.
He chopped down a big spruce across the way.
Then his grandmother's rabbit coat, the rabbit coat that she had made for
    him along with his boots,
was lying there by him, and he fell forward into the fire.
"My Grandmother! You should say 'My Old Grandmother got burned
    up,'" he said to his grandmother.

He got burned up in the fire, and the old lady was crying.

"My Old Grandmother got burned up!" [the grandmother says].

Later there were tracks leading out to the woods from the tip of the tree that had been chopped down.

The caribou had stopped out across from there.

He killed some caribou, and then he propped up a jawbone, making it appear like a group of sleeping caribou.

He had killed them all.

They were coming to the caribou, and as they were coming, My Old Grandmother already had killed them all.

"You be quiet, they are sleeping, don't make noise," he tells them.

He had already killed the caribou.

Later he said to his uncle, "I say that I already killed the caribou. You tell them to butcher them."

They butchered all the caribou.

When he killed the caribou, he had said to them, "Your blue heart! your black heart!" and then for no obvious reason they all fell over and died.[8]

Later they made trips for the caribou.

They brought back all the caribou and were making sausage out of the small intestine.

Due to that caribou sausage [not giving it to him], he made a curse.

My Old Grandmother said, "Give me the sausage of the lead caribou or of the second one."

All the people were mad over this, and they did not give any [sausage] to him.[9]

So due to that he put a curse on them.

Where his grandmother was staying, there had been a wet snowfall.

It snowed until it covered them up, and

where his grandmother was staying was a bare clearing in the snow that looked like a skin [like a wall of snow].

In here [in the clearing] his grandmother was staying.

Later he got dressed in the rabbit coat that she had made for him.

He came out in snowshoes there on the snow above his grandmother.

"My grandmother, my grandmother, you are still alive!"

"Yes," she told him.

"Hurry, make a request about the snow" [he said].

"Let the snow melt," she told him.

They prayed about the snow, and all the snow started to melt.

All the snow melted and

after that he left his grandmother and went up into the sky and into the
moon.

So that is that poor little boy that stands inside the moon.

That's his name, My Old Grandmother.

That's all.

NOTES

1. The power of the moon as a religious symbol is explained with subtle word play
and humor, as with the silly name for the boy *Stsǫǫ Shyaan*, "My Old Grandmother,"
or with the use of *ch'ǫǫsi'*, magic words of the hunting religion. In the opening episode, the spear falling from a tree refers to the Little Boy in the Moon standing up
and then coming down to earth.

2. In reviewing the transcription and translation, Mrs. Tyone added this comment at this point in the narrative: "The spirit turned into the baby." Similar interpolations in the rest of her stories will be given in notes marked with her initials. —
Eds.

3. The humor here is based upon the pun in the usage of the verb theme *O+ɫio*,
"to drag an object." As an idiom, this verb can be used for an older person without
much strength bringing something along. Here, however, the boy interprets her
command literally, and he literally drags the dog.

4. This line translates a single Upper Tanana word, *Dayuudetkänh*. — Eds. This
word is used for a direct request to a medicine person for success in hunting.

5. The Upper Tanana word translated as "dream-wish" is *nitįįthiit*. — Eds. This
word is used for a good wish. It is not used for hexes.

6. This is the arrow that had burned up.

7. He is observing the people to see who treated him decently.

8. These are the magic words he used to kill the caribou.

9. This is the caribou sausage that The Little Boy in the Moon is holding in his
left hand.

Dlign Mba' Hehk'aayh Ts'ą̈'

When the Tree Squirrels Cut Fish

This is why today we watch what we say about our food.

The Tree Squirrel People were up above slicing fish.
They cut salmon and
they dried lots of dry fish.
They dried fish all summer.
When they dried all the fish, they went out in the country [to hunt], and
    they made fish caches and
they packed the dry fish to the caches.

Down below [on the trail] the backbone of a dry fish had fallen down after
    they had filled the caches all full of fish.
And a Tree Squirrel was packing back a fish, walking behind the others.
A fish backbone was lying on the trail down below.
"Where are we going to put this one?" he said.
He kicked it across and out of the way with his foot.

So they stored the fish and it snowed heavily on them, and
they opened up all of their caches.
They started to starve.
When they opened the caches, there was only tree bark in there.
All of the dry fish had turned into tree bark, and
they all died of starvation.

That one Tree Squirrel that had spoken previously is the only one that lived.
He was eating on shiny spruce pitch and spruce cones for food.
He [that Squirrel] was walking around in a snowstorm.
He went far away and was subsisting on shiny spruce pitch.

All of a sudden in an open bare spot in the snow he walked into the
summer.

He blurted out, "*Dlik, dlik, dlik*," and scampered up a spruce.

And then the people said to him, "How did you survive?"

"Out there I ate the 'spruce's grease' [pitch], and I survived on that."

And this is as far as it goes.

Ch'ǫǫt'üüdn Ch'aachin' Shyiit Eedah
When Horsefly Was Living in a Stump

I am going to tell about the Horsefly.[1]
The Horsefly sat inside a tree stump that was standing by the beach, in an
    "egg stump."[2]
The people were eating, and they went out for eggs
but they would disappear.
He had an axe handle inside the stump with him, and
when the people would climb the tree for the eggs, he would chop them
    with the axe, and then he would eat them.
They kept on doing that; the people went for eggs but they would
    disappear.
And so Raven said, "Let me go for the eggs."
He pretended to go for the eggs.
He climbed way up the "egg stump" [the tree with the nest holes].
And there was Horsefly with the stone axe, "Oh, my father's nephew!"[3]
"So, that's the one my father told about long ago" [Horsefly said].
"You must really be the one that is my father's nephew" [Raven said].
"How come you say that I am your father's nephew?" Horsefly said to him.
"Oooh, he says that he has no one to tell him stories" [Raven said].
"You are my father's nephew," Raven tells him.
He lied to him and [Raven said], "Come on down here to me.
Let's sit together," and
so Horsefly came to him and sat with him.
They told each other stories, and Raven made for Horsefly a birch-bark
    canoe made out of sand.
"Let's go out on the lake in canoes to see who can paddle the fastest," he
    [Raven] tells him.
So Horsefly paddled way out in the middle in the canoe and

[Raven says] "Let the canoe turn back into sand."
And his whole canoe dissolved on the surface and went down into the lake.

Later [Raven says], "Oh! Let me take you to shore."
Raven paddled up to him.
At the prow of the boat he cut his [Horsefly's] head off.
He [Horsefly] sank into the water, and he [Raven] brought his head back to
    the people.
"This is what you have cried tears for until your eyes are red."[4]
He threw the Horsefly's head in to them.
And so that is why now the Horsefly has no head, but just has eyes inside its
    body.
So after that time they named him Ch'ǫǫt'üüdn, "the one that cuts."[5]

NOTES

1. This is a funny story about the bothersome horsefly Ch'ǫǫt'üüdn, "the one
that cuts."

2. "A dry tree with bird nest holes in it." — M. T.

3. "Raven talks in Ahtna here." — M. T.

4. "You know how people cry many times, that Ch'ǫǫt'üüdn makes people cry
lots." — M. T.

5. "And that is why when he bites you he cuts you really bad." — M. T.

Taatsaan' Dzänh eh Q̧o̧nign'

Raven and Muskrat Story

Raven left a spruce by the shore in order to catch some fish, and he [Raven]
    was bringing his wife over to that fish.[1]
He says to him, "Fish, your wife is sure pretty."
Fish jumped out from the water and struck him in his heart, and then he
    slipped back down into the water.
He did that.
"Fish, I wish your wife were as pretty as mine," he [Raven] says to him.
Fish jumped out once again. It struck him in his heart and then he went
    down as he had before.
Finally, finally, Fish jumped way up and struck his heart.
Then he [Raven] fell over backward, and he blacked out.
There was a stick of wood on the beach that was blocking off the Fish.
Then he [Raven] got back up, and he clubbed him [the Fish].
He was about to tell his wife, "Here, I killed the Fish."
He looked for her, but she was gone.

He looked down below for her and across the way, but under the water
    those Fish People were carrying off his [Raven's] wife.
What should he do?
He goes around the beach there, "What is this?"
"How can I go under water?" he thinks.
He goes to the edge of the water, to the lakeshore and
the Frog also is sitting down below.
He went up to the Frog.
"How do you go under the water?" he says to him.
He [Frog] took a cane and he lifted up the water for him [Raven].
The water raised up a little and,
"A little higher, let me look back underneath there," he says.

Across and out in the middle the Fish People were staying with his wife,
    and he asked the Frog,
"How do you go around during the winter?"
"I go inside the ground when it gets winter on me," he tells Raven.
Later outside he picked some fluff on top of the fireweed for him, and
after he made his [Frog's] nest in the ground, he said, "I made you a house,
    so lift up the water for me."
Saying this, he lifted up the water for him.
The spruce and the willow would become the plants that grow in water.
And he [Frog] gave them to him [Raven]:
"water leaf," "underwater spruce," "round foot limb," "cut-out foot
    pattern," and "muskrat candy."

He lifted up the water for him, and he went under the water again.
And he went back upland where his wife is staying, and they [the Fish
    People] are keeping the Muskrat as a slave.
Those Fish People had hid his wife away, and the Muskrat was chopping
    wood in order to cook.
So he hexed the handle of the stone axe, and the axe handle broke in two.
Due to this the Muskrat cried.
So he went up to him, that Raven.
"How come you are crying?" he [Raven] said to him.
"I broke the handle of this axe [Muskrat said].
Due to this they will treat me really badly.
They may try to kill me for what happened," he says.
"Well, I'll fix it. I'll repair the axe handle for you" [Raven said].
He [Raven] said to him, "Do you see someone else with them?"
"Someone different is staying with them" [Muskrat said].
"What did they do?" [Raven asks].
[Muskrat said] "When I started to cook something, the soup would spill on
    the fire, and they would run outside there and then
the water evaporated away, and they [the Fish] came back in, and a while
    later the one who was staying with them [Raven's wife] came back in
    after them."
So he says to Muskrat, "I'll bring you back.
You will come back with me; they took my wife.
You can look after me and I will get back my wife.
After you cook you should first pour a little soup on the fire, and then after
    they come back in, you should pour really a lot of soup on the fire," he
    [Raven] said to him.

He [Raven] is hiding beside the house, by the side of the Fish's house.
And he [Muskrat] spilled a little soup on the fire.
They ran out and then they went back in.
And then Muskrat spilled a lot of soup on the fire and
they all went out and ran away.
"When I get my wife back, you should go out ahead of me," he says to the
     Muskrat.
The Muskrat spilled soup on the fire and they all ran out.
As they came back in, she was coming behind them, his wife.

Raven took back his wife in front of Muskrat.
They [Raven and his wife] ran way out ahead.
"Grow into 'water spruce' to block the way," he [Raven] says to it.
The moose food ["water leaf"] grew fast and meanwhile they [Fish] got
     tangled up in it.
Meanwhile he stopped a long way away.
He also blocked the way with some "water fireweed."
Then he stopped at the beach again, and he says to him [Frog], "Way up
     there."[2]
Frog lifted up the water with a stick and he [Raven] brought out his own
     wife and Muskrat too.

Afterward he [Raven] talks this way to Muskrat:
"In winter when you will do this, you [Muskrat] can trample around for
     the 'muskrat food.'"
Above the shore here he [Muskrat] makes his trails and
up there he [Raven] buried the compacted "muskrat food" for him.
"You will do this and you will live on it," he [Raven] tells him.
So he [Raven] made the lodges way out in the lake for Muskrat and trails
     too.
"Whenever you do this, you can eat [Raven says].
Don't go back down in the water or they [Fish] will kill you," he [Raven]
     says to him.
Later on he [Raven] also made the Muskrat's den on the lakeshore.
"You will eat upon this," he [Raven] tells him.
And so that's why Muskrat makes his houses out on the ice.
And that's how Raven made a place for him up on land, and cached away
     the "muskrat food," just as it is now.[3]
That's all.

NOTES

1. This is an especially entertaining story, telling of the importance of several water plants to the Upper Tanana people.

2. "Raven is speaking in Ahtna here." — M. T.

3. "That's his summer table." — M. T.

9

Tanacross

The word *Tanacross* is a compound of "Tanana River" and "crossing." The language spoken at that crossing in the great river is quite distinct from what has been called Upper Tanana, the language spoken just up the river at its headwaters. Before the Alaska Highway was built, this region was among the most remote in Alaska, and perhaps as a consequence, there is very little recorded oral literature in this language. Based on just the five stories I recorded, I would not want to plunge into generalizations. Still, there is much in the Tanacross storytelling tradition that resonates with other Athabaskan storytelling from Holy Cross, Alaska, to Fort Chipewyan, Alberta. I cannot say for certain, but I would expect that these stories would be much like the *yaaniidą'* ("distant-time" stories) of the Upper Tanana neighbors. Gaither Paul, who told the stories here, was concerned that he be understood. Like other Athabaskan storytellers I have learned from, that was the main concern — that I listen, understand, and learn. Thus I would say that the primary expected behavior of the audience was not just to show attention but to indicate comprehension in some way.

Gaither Paul was fifty-six years of age when these stories were recorded. He was born March 18, 1923, at a caribou hunting camp between Dot Lake and the Robertson River, Alaska. Over the years he lived at Mansfield, Tanacross, and Anchorage. His father was David Paul, the first ordained Athabaskan in the Episcopal Church, and his mother was Laura Luke. His father's father was Old Paul, and his father's mother was Julia Paul; his mother's father was John Luke, and his mother's mother was Laura Luke. Gaither Paul has eight adopted children, fourteen grandchildren, and one great-grandchild. This adoring grandfather is not only a skilled traditional hunter but has also worked as a truck driver, a Cat operator, a gold-dredge operator, and a custodian. He is a self-taught fiddle player, reads two newspapers daily, and is a contributor to the *Anchorage Daily News.*

Gaither Paul is a storyteller, not a social analyst; he is a teacher, not a critic; he is a tradition bearer, not a researcher. When we met in both Fairbanks and Tanacross, we worked together to try to accomplish three purposes. I wanted texts for linguistic analysis, and from that point of view, the rhetorical or educational purposes of the texts were not my main interest. Gaither Paul and his wife, Beatrice, wanted to have his stories recorded in a form that could be passed on to their grandchildren. More powerful than either of these motives, however, was his concern to teach me through the telling of these stories.

When I approached Mr. Paul through his wife, I recall that I asked, in a way that I hoped was polite enough, how he would evaluate himself as a storyteller. He did not directly answer my question. I was to learn that this response was most characteristic of his deep humility. He asked if I was ready to record. I said I was, and he told me the story of Nesdzeegh, "Smear Face," the man who disguised his great handsomeness and strength by distorting his face with pitch and affecting physical disability. Then as the story unfolds, we learn that those who learn from Smear Face's actions of his underlying character are rewarded with his protection. Thus, like Smear Face, Mr. Paul told me that I should look to his stories for my evaluation, not to his own comments about them. This guidance is consistent with his own great concern for others; over the years he and his wife have cared for more than three hundred foster children.

Gaither Paul told me five stories in my office in Fairbanks and in his home in Tanacross during several visits that we made to each other. The original tapes have been stored in the library of the Alaska Native Language Center at the University of Alaska Fairbanks. This center also published both Tanacross texts and English translations of the stories in a collection titled *Stories for My Grandchildren*.

When he told the stories, Mr. Paul was very concerned that I understand his meaning just then in that situation, not only later on after I had had time to digest the Tanacross versions. So each story was told to me in two versions, first in Tanacross and then again in English, the Tanacross for posterity, as it were, and the English for my personal learning. It took me several weeks of listening to the audiotapes, close phonetic transcription, linguistic analysis, and comparison with his English version to arrive at a translation with which I was provisionally satisfied. I then drove back up to Tanacross to show Mr. Paul my transcription and translation and to talk to him about the story.

When I presented my work to Mr. Paul to ask for his comments, his response was much like that of other Athabaskan storytellers I have known or of whom I have known, from François Mandeville, who told stories to Li Fang Kuei in 1928 at Fort Chipewyan, to Ben Marcel, who told me stories there in 1976. Mr. Paul's response was to tell me the next story. This is not the place to discuss my own education. I mention these details here because I believe it was always important to him to focus on what can be taught and what can be learned whenever several people are gathered together. He himself commented that he was continuing to learn new stories — he phrased his deep, broad education as "stories" — from the older people.

Four of the stories were about Brush Indians, two of which are included here. I believe Mr. Paul's stories are particularly poignant in showing the degree of human empathy that could be achieved even between such fearful characters as these superhuman creatures and ordinary people. I am not sure he was trying to symbolize the empathy that could be achieved between indigenous Alaska Natives and newcomers to the land, but both his own life and his choice of these particular stories to tell suggest a lifelong concern with empathy and cooperation between parties who in other cases and in the stories of others are arrayed in fearing and hostile camps.

In each case I took the Tanacross-language story to be the definitive version and that story with its translation to be what Mr. Paul wanted published. I believe he had two motives in this. One was to preserve in print these gems of the Tanacross language. He was acutely conscious of how few young people there were even in the 1970s with any significant competence in the language. But also I believe his second motive was that he was aware of his own sharply honed narrative and descriptive skill. As he told me the story of the man standing on a lookout point watching for moose, he was careful to observe that the very hill we sat upon at the University of Alaska campus in Fairbanks was such a lookout point, or had been at an earlier time. His narrative at this point in the story is masterful, and I can no longer think of either that hill in Fairbanks nor read this story without seeing the broad Tanana River valley spread out toward the distant Alaska Range to the south.

Ron Scollon

SUGGESTIONS FOR FURTHER READING

Lohr, Amy Linda, comp. *Athabascan Story-Teaching.* Alaska Historical Commission Studies in History 183, 1985.

McKennan, Robert A. "Tanana." In *Subarctic*, vol. 6 of *Handbook of North American Indians*. Washington DC: Smithsonian Institution, 1981.

Paul, Gaither. *Stories for My Grandchildren.* Fairbanks: Alaska Native Language Center, 1980.

Rooth, Anna Birgitta. *The Alaska Expedition 1966: Myths, Customs and Beliefs among the Athabascan Indians and the Eskimos of Northern Alaska.* Acta Univ. Lundensis, Section 1, Theologica Juridica Humaniora 14. Lund, Sweden: Gleerup, 1971.

The Child Who Was Stolen by a Brush Indian

There used to be Brush Indians
who stole children
and that's why they came here.

And
here
I'll tell you now
how a child that had been stolen by a Brush Indian
was saved.
I'll tell you about that.

A man
was out hunting.

On a ridge above where a hill sloped down,
on the ridge,
toward his home,
as he went along toward his home
way down in a draw,
down in that draw,
he heard a child crying.

As he listened
he heard that it was a child crying.

He knew there was no child down there,
not from his home,
the girls

were not
there. He knew that and so
he thought right away that Brush Indians
steal children.

So down there
he ran and got ready for him.

And in a while
the Brush Indian
came walking along toward that man.

The man hid from him
with his arrow ready.

As he
came up to that
man who was hiding
the Brush Indian
was holding the child by his hands
and walking along saying
    "mḿ', mḿ', mḿ'."

He was saying that so that the child would sleep
he found out.

Then as he got to where the man was he jumped up
and holding his arrow
on him, "put down
    that child,"
he told the Brush Indian.

The Brush Indian
was surprised and
holding the child
he began to walk
backward.

He carefully stepped backward.

And so that man kept
holding his arrow on him and

"Put that child down.
Go away," he told him.

Even so the Brush Indian
didn't do it and
as he still held the child
then
quickly he swung the child to his chest
and put it there.

So that the man
would not shoot he put the child on his chest.

Then he walked backward.

So the man
  "I'll kill you right through that child.
  So put the child down," he told him.

Even so the Brush Indian walked backward away from him and
then in a moment
the Brush Indian swung the child around
onto his back
and with the child there he started to run.

The man
was strong
and kept right up with him.

Even though the Brush Indian
ran very fast, the man also
ran right behind him and
  "I'll kill you right through that child," he told him.

So then
the Brush Indian
realized that he could not run away from the man and so
putting the child down
he ran away from there.

So the man let him go and,
thinking the child
was from his home,
he picked up the child.

That's all he wanted and so
he let the Brush Indian go.

Then, picking up the child,
he was not from his home.
He was from somewhere else.

Even though he knew that the child was stolen from somewhere else he
took it back.[1]

After that
a long time passed and
the man
sent a message to the people in other places
and since there were none missing there,
to other places
they sent the message
to where there was a missing child.
They kept passing on the message and
long afterward,
when much time had passed,
they found
where the child had been stolen.

Then they sent the child
back to where he had been stolen.

NOTE
1. That is, he took it home with him. — Eds.

How Dentalium Necklaces Came to the Country

After that
there's a different story
they tell
about how those dentalium necklaces
came to the country around here.[1]
The people used to tell the story.

A man was out hunting.

From way up
he was looking out.

He was looking out over the flats and
he was waiting for moose.

And
way over, way over on the flats
on the side of a hill that sloped down
a great big grizzly bear was going along.

Even so he just let it go.

He was only looking for moose so
he just let it go.

He thought he wouldn't kill it.

He just waited for moose.

And then
below

that bear
toward that bear
he noticed
there was a man walking along.

And
so
he was going to yell to him in the distance.

He was going to yell to him
but he thought it was too far for him to hear
and so he just watched him.

He thought maybe it was someone from among the people staying with
him.

So he just kept watching where he was going.

He was walking right toward the bear.

It was
too far and there was no way that he could yell so
he just watched him.

And then that bear
saw the man and
he set himself to attack him.

And then the man
realized that
the bear was going to attack the man and
he got ready.

He thought he would run to him and,

and so he watched where the man was walking.

Just as the man got up to the bear
the bear jumped him and
started to fight him.

That's all the man saw and
what they call a horn club
he had that and
he grabbed his arrows too and started across.

He started running toward him.
Being a fast runner he ran and
there
the bear had grabbed the man
and when he got there
the man was still alive.

That man must really have been strong because
as they rolled around he was holding the bear away.

He really must have been strong because
that bear
was a big one and he was holding it off.

He was still alive and he was still not being hurt.

This was still going on when he got there to him.

So then with his horn club
he hit the bear right on the head and
knocked him off to one side of the man.

The bear fell down and
he kept on hitting him
until he smashed in his head and killed him.

The man that this happened to
started to turn to him and
the man was not from his village.

It was a Brush Indian
who had had the bear on him.

Now the Brush Indian's heart was beating hard and
he was breathing heavily and

as he turned
to the man he told him,
    "Don't look at me. Don't look at me.

    Don't run away.

    Don't run away.

    Wait until I talk to you."

The Brush Indian told the man.

The man
looked at the Brush Indian
and found out that he was a Brush Indian.

He was not an Indian but
he found out that he was a Brush Indian.

Even so he understood him.

He understood what he was saying to him.

So he just stood there.

So the Brush Indian
with his heart beating hard and breathing heavily
waited to catch his breath.

When he was well rested up
and had gotten his breath back,
getting up and coming to
the man's back
he patted him lightly on the back,
    "Don't run away.

    I'm telling you not to look at me.

    If you looked at me you would be afraid and
    you might run away
    so I told you not to look at me.

I am not one of you.

You call us *gųų*.

I am a *gųų*.

I am not one of you.

Even so don't be afraid of me.

You saved me
and I want to give you something"

He told the man.

So then he stood in front of the man.

Now that he had gotten his breath back
he spoke to the man.

> "Don't look at me. That tree
> standing in front of you,
> climb it.
>
> With that little axe under your belt
> climb up
> and from the top you trim it down.
>
> Then
> leave the sticks of the boughs sticking out all over.
>
> From the top all the way down," he told him.

The Brush Indian having told him that, the man
climbed up and
from the top he trimmed it all down,
he trimmed it all.

Then
only its limbs were sticking out.

Then
after that
the Brush Indian came to him and
    "After summer and then winter have passed
    and summer has come again
    as the middle of summer approaches and
    the leaves
    have grown
    you come to this tree here
    and whatever is hanging on it
    is there as something I brought here for you.

    Take all of it and
    take it home. It's yours.

    You saved me and
    that's why I'm paying you back.
    Here
    you'll get it time after time."

All this he told the man.

    "Look around at the country and
    don't lose track of this tree.

    Don't get lost.

    Don't lose track of this tree.

    If you lose track of it
    whatever is on it will be lost.

    Don't lose track of it."

He told that man.

The Brush Indian went away and
that man
when winter had passed
and summer

had come and the middle of summer
had come
those dentalium necklaces were hanging on it.

He gathered them all
and took them home.

Every summer he came back and took what was on it.

And all that,
that Brush Indian
that Brush Indian he had saved,
the Brush Indian
whom he had saved from the bear,
that Brush Indian was paying him back.

And from that he became chief.

That is how this story was told.

That is how
dentalium necklaces came to this country, people say.

NOTE

1. The title of this story as originally published was "Another Story of Dentalium Necklaces." That title and the opening stanza link the story to the one immediately preceding it in *Stories for My Grandchildren*, a story titled "How Dentalium Necklaces Came to the People." In that story a man and a Brush Indian are the only survivors of a battle between hunters and Brush Indians. The two take care of each other's wounds and become friends. The Brush Indian spends the summer hunting with the man and then rewards him for his friendship and hospitality in the same manner as in this story. Dentalium is a marine mollusk whose shells are highly prized, especially by peoples of the interior who cannot get them readily. In telling the first story, Mr. Paul includes a stanza describing the view of the Brush Indian as commonly held by interior peoples:

Brush Indians
came here from a country far away and
would sneak around so that people could not see them,
just sneaking around avoiding people.

All the kids
were what they wanted to steal, people thought, so that's why
they would sneak around where people could not see them.

The stories imply that the "country far away" was on a seacoast, possibly as near (by today's measure of distance) as the Copper River delta. The new title of the present story was chosen by Ron Scollon. — Eds.

Lower Tanana

The Athabaskan people who live in the drainage of the Tanana River as it approaches the Yukon River have been referred to as Tanana Indians. However, they are more precisely designated Lower Tanana, in clear contrast to the Upper Tanana people. Between these two groups, along the middle stretches of the river, live the Tanacross people.

While McKennan and de Laguna have written about the area, little has been published that separates Lower Tanana oral traditions from Upper Tanana, Tanacross, and Koyukon traditions. Much that we have said about storytelling and narrative genres of the other groups applies equally to Lower Tanana stories. De Laguna even consolidates her comments on the Deg Hit'an, the Koyukon, and the Lower Tanana peoples by referring to them all as *Dena*, the Athabaskan word for "the People." Based on her work in Minto, Rooth reports that traditionally Lower Tanana stories were told only in the winter. Some prohibitions existed against disrupting the telling of a story or stopping in the middle. Often a second storyteller would assist the primary storyteller, and Lower Tanana storytellers had a formulaic closing for distant-time stories similar to that of Koyukon narratives.

Peter John was born in the fall of 1900 in Rampart on the Yukon River. He lived in Nenana, on the Tanana River, for five years and attended St. Mark's School, going as far as the second grade. Yet he taught himself much about the world outside interior Alaska by persistent reading. For most of his life, he lived in Old Minto, until the village was moved in 1971 to its present site. During the negotiations leading up to land-claims legislation, Mr. John played an important role as an advocate of Native rights. Throughout his lifetime, he has been deeply involved with subsistence living, but he also worked on a steamship and served as Minto village chief. In 1925, Mr. John married his wife, Elsie. In 1994 the University of Alaska Fairbanks awarded him an honorary doctorate of humane letters to commemorate his service to Interior Athabaskan culture. Today he is a noted proponent of traditional Athabaskan values and is acknowledged as the Traditional Chief for Interior Alaskan Athabaskans.

The selections included here are from Mr. John's autobiography, *Peter John: Minto.* Mr. John was interviewed by Yvonne Yarber and Curt Madison in September 1981 and May 1982. He narrated in English, and they then edited the tapes to create the published autobiography. Their goal was to be faithful to his oral storytelling style, so they made few grammatical changes.

These selections are excellent examples of Athabaskan personal narratives. Loosely placed in the historical genre, their goal was not to aggrandize the ego of the individual; rather, they tried to teach important lessons and to express the worth of traditional values. Sometimes people even told of their mistakes and failures to make their points clearly. Here Mr. John presents a variety of culturally moral subjects having to do with how to learn, the nature of courage, the importance of being steadfast, the necessity of having respect for the natural world, the central role of clan relationships, and the timeless presence of the spiritual realm.

SUGGESTIONS FOR FURTHER READING

de Laguna, Frederica, ed. *Tales from the Dena: Indian Stories from the Tanana, Koyukuk, and Yukon Rivers.* Seattle: University of Washington Press, 1995.

John, Peter. *The Gospel according to Peter John.* Edited by David J. Krupa. Fairbanks: Alaska Native Knowledge Network, 1996.

———. *Peter John: Minto.* Fairbanks: Spirit Mountain Press, 1986.

Luke, Howard. *My Own Trail.* Edited by Jan Steinbright Jackson. Fairbanks: Alaska Native Knowledge Network, 1998.

McKennan, Robert A. "Tanana." In *Subarctic,* vol. 6 of *Handbook of North American Indians.* Washington DC: Smithsonian Institution, 1981.

Rooth, Anna Birgitta. *The Importance of Storytelling: A Study Based on Field Work in Northern Alaska.* Studia Ethnologica Upsaliensia 1. Uppsala: Acta Universitatis Upsaliensis, 1976.

from "Stand for What Is Right"
I Learned the Indian Way

The thing is this, I really don't know when my mother was born. And I don't even know when my father was born. Me and my sister are the only ones that are living. My mother died when I was about two years old. My father raised me.

I don't mind talking to the tape about the things that concern the young people. I give the young people lot of chance to learn what I know and yet nobody take it up. Free for the asking. Nobody wants it. So that's the reason why I let everything drop. Everything is going to die with me when I die. All that I know is going to go with me because nobody don't want to pick it up. Stories, all the old-time stories I know about war going on between different tribes. All that I know myself.

Long time ago people live by these things because that's the only way people can get along. By looking at the things the right way. We live close together. We think about what we say. I can't go down the street and say, "You kill this person over here." Accuse them. I can't say that. The thing is this, we try to do what is right for one another. And we're Indians, Athabaskan Indians. The way I was brought up has got nothing to do with no Whiteman way. Absolutely. What I learned is the Indian way.

These old people that I seen never swear, nothing. Never steal from each other. And you see chiefs up there [Tanana Chiefs in 1915].[1] They're not voted in to be chief. They're the kind of person that's hard to get. Hard to find. These people you see up there, chief. They stand for what is right. They feel sorry for everybody. I don't care who it is. That's the kind of people they call chief. They got to understand. They got to know about people. Any poor people. Any sick person, they never let go. He's going to help that person whether that person is rich or poor. Doesn't make any difference.

People used to move around. Go from place to place. Move. That way people never stayed in one place. But everything change. Whiteman way right now. Everything is changed. You got to stay put otherwise your kids don't learn nothing. The old people used to just stay one place for one week, then move to another place for another week. They keep on doing that. They change the spruce boughs on their floor every time. They move. That way there was no germs. Nobody get sick. I see old people that live over one hundred years old. That's the kind of people I see. Right now the Whiteman way you have to stay put. You see this house. We stay in here for pretty near four years. People come in, go out. Germs everywhere maybe. We don't know. Maybe that's how people get sick so much.

We can't compare ourselves to the people that lived long time ago. No way. These people were really husky, strong. They don't get into nobody's way. They don't go over and pick a fight with anybody. They have respect for one another. That's the kind of people I seen. You never find that kind of people no more.

NOTE

1. He is indicating by gesture or nod his print, displayed on wall or shelf, of a famous photograph of six chiefs of Athabaskan tribes of interior Alaska, together with their interpreter, taken in 1915. Today the Tanana Chiefs Conference, headquartered in Fairbanks, provides medical, educational, employment, and other social services to members of these groups. — Eds.

from "Stand for What Is Right"
Strong People

It's hard to explain the real true way about life a long time ago. The way we see it today is altogether different. I'm going to talk in my Native tongue.

Men-tee nonokhukholtseeyh. Łook'a oononokhukhugheełtseeyh. Dasr khedeltutl, tr'eyeet. Łook'a dekhegheeł'anh. Nodot Noocheloghoyet nenokho-dedek, tr'eyeet. ("They would make weirs on the creeks between the lakes. They would make weirs for fish. They would push boats by poling along the sandbar. They would get fish. They would go to Tanana in canoes.")

From Minto here we pack canoe clean over them hills to Wickersham Dome. Over into Beaver Creek. Go down the Beaver Creek, down the Yukon River, and up the Tanana River. That's the kind of people I'm talking about. I'm not talking about these young people open their door and look out down the street and say, "No, I'm not going to go out. Too cold." I'm talking about people that didn't care if it's cold, rain or snow. It didn't make any difference. They're going to go. The young people today, that live right now, don't compare to the people I've seen. Nobody.

These old people really understand life. How would you like to stand up against a grizzly bear with just a spear? How would you feel? Just with bow and arrow. Brown bear charging you — what you got? Nothing. These people never run away. These people just stand there. That's the kind of people I seen. Right now today, it's just too easy.

It's something we can't understand. I just talk about people that pack canoe over that Wickersham Dome over there. Went into Beaver Creek and come up the Tanana River. It doesn't make any difference how far it was or how long it's going to take them. They're going to go through with it. People that live. Moose snares. Caribou snares. Nobody is equal to these people. You got a spear, you catch fish with spear. You catch fish with bow and arrow. That's nothing new to them. You kill beaver with bow and arrow. Right now it's pretty hard for the young people to do.

About thirty years ago is the last time I see people use bow and arrow. Although my grandson use bow and arrow, but he never try to catch anything with it. Birch is okay for arrows, but it get wet easy. So we get dry spruce. And for the bow we get dry willow. That you can't break and it never get wet.

I never did use the snow machine. I walked and used dogs and covered just as much ground as anybody. The going might be a little slow, but I got there. My boy used snow machine trapping and did all right. The thing is you got to understand the animals. You got to know whether he's going to come back the same way. You got to know how the animals travel.

We stay with trapping from November till February, then we switch to muskrats. Springtime we go to fish camp, make a wheel and fish all summer. We stay there almost until freeze-up and then get ready to trap. Get the sled and everything ready. We never did take it easy. Never. Me and my wife was busy all the time.

I guess if you want to take a trip to Fairbanks, fool around, go down to Second Avenue.[1] If that's the kind of vacation you want, I guess nobody can't stop you. No, everyday life is what we do everyday. It doesn't make any difference if it's vacation or not. It's all the same.

The reason why I never did write my life story before is because who's going to believe what I write even though it's true? That's the reason I don't like to talk about things that nobody's seen. One time we made a fish wheel in sixteen hours from start to finish. Just one day for me, my wife, and my boy. Put raft, basket and everything together in just sixteen hours. If nobody seen me do it, I'll just keep it to myself.

I'll give anybody a chance to learn what I know, these things I learned through the old people. How to look after myself if I was going to get anything. But nobody don't want to learn. My boy would learn, but he isn't around any more.

I was really after animals, game. That's the only way I know how to make a living. I don't work for wages. I call fox. I caught a hundred and ten muskrat one night. Ninety-two another night with my wife. No way absolutely you could understand that.

During the war I sold nine-dollar gumboots for one box of .22 shells, fifty in a box. Shells were hard to get at that time. I went up on the lake, just one box of shells and come back with thirty-eight muskrats and fifteen shells left. Sometimes I catch two with one shot, because I try to save that shell. Now who's going to believe that? I was in the brush all my life and I try to save that shell. If I see two muskrats I try to get them together so I can make one shot out of it. Right now today you get any one of the young people, he'll never do that. They can get another box of shells, why is he going to try to save it? But I was raised when it was really hard time. People had a hard time to get shells and everything.

NOTE

1. He is referring to a two-block area of the main east-west street in downtown Fairbanks, once the home of many bars and in summer the scene of much rowdy nightlife. During construction of the Trans-Alaska Pipeline, its year-round notoriety increased with crime. In recent years most of the bars have been closed, and attempts have been made to develop businesses that can appeal to out-of-state visitors in a safer and more attractive setting. — Eds.

from "Old Ways"
I Belong to My Mother's Side

In our Native way we go by tribes. *Ch'echalyoo, Bedzey-te khut'ana, Toneedze gheltseełna, Tsey-yoo.* That's the tribes we go by. Don't ask me why. We've got that many tribes right here in Minto down the street. I'm Caribou, *Bedzey-te khut'ana.* I belong to my mother's side not my father's. Because that's the right way. If we don't go by tribe, we'll be mixed marriage all together.

My wife is *Toneedze gheltseełna.* She's not my side. There's a difference. My kids are all on their mother's side. That's the Indian way. These things we have to understand. Long time ago people used to fight against different tribes. Therefore you got to know which side you belong to all the time. I don't care where you go. If you don't know, you're going to fall into something you got no business to fall into. Some tribes might be fighting someplace and that fight could come right here. Some people will be safe and the other ones they try to kill. As an Indian we have to understand which tribe is fighting.

People don't have to fight all the time, just when somebody makes a bad mistake. Like what Hitler did over in Europe. Same thing. He try to be too smart for himself and he got the whole world fighting. Same thing can happen if we let a person go. Person that gossip too much or make false statements against his friends. That's the kind that start trouble. That's what people used to be careful for.

It was many years ago there was a war on the Yukon River at the Rapids. People was going down in the springtime and run into it. But they knew about it before and they didn't fight. From what I hear it started way up in Canada. People called *Deeseneena* came down.

There used to be a lot of wars in Alaska. People of the different tribes fight among themselves. I'm Caribou. My wife is *Toneedze gheltseełna.* Chief Charlie from here was *Ch'echalyoo.* And Chief Ivan down at Crossjacket was *Toneedze gheltseełna.* They're the ones that fight among themselves.

These people that fight are not right. They try to do something wrong against their fellow human being and start it off that way. I know a lot of stories about the war, what went on, but I wouldn't talk about it because a lot of people might say I was wrong altogether. And I don't like that because I heard it from other people myself.

We're all together in Minto now. When we go out hunting, six or seven boats go together. We do things together. Fishing and everything. Picking berries. We don't leave nobody home. If somebody want to go, sure, okay, we let them go. 'Cause that's the way we live. Not because we're scared, but the thing is this, we want to try to take care of one another. Now we just went down on Tanana Slough a couple days ago. We drive rabbits. Six or seven boats went down there all hunting rabbits for two days. My wife and I got twelve. That's the way we live.

from "Old Ways"
Try to Make Things

Another time, I wanted to go out. Out walking to hunt, but there was too much snow. I had no snowshoes. So I walked down the street and I saw snowshoes hanging on the wall of somebody's house. I take those snowshoes, went out and got birch. Then I put the snowshoes back and make my own. I started out right there with new snowshoes.

You got to try to make things. If you can't do it on your own, you just have to see how the other people are doing it. By looking and listening. It's the way we understand.

It's hard to learn. Sure it's hard. Anything is hard. I couldn't tell you how to sew with beads or porcupine quills. The only way you're going to learn is by looking at other people. We all have a long way to go. I don't care if you're ninety years old, you're still learning. Don't think you know it all. Never.

I made snowshoes, sled, poling boat, and canoe. But I'm not a carpenter. Some of these young people say they're carpenters. Well, I don't know. They have to be able to make everything. I hewed all the crosspieces for that canoe with an ax. I didn't use a plane or saw or anything. I split all the boards out of a tree. Split them a quarter of an inch thick. It wouldn't take me two hours to get enough for a whole canoe.

You can't do anything unless you're willing to do it. If you're not willing, then you might as well forget about the whole thing. If a person is ambitious to do things, he's going to do it no matter how hard it is.

If a fellow goes out hunting and breaks his paddle, he can just stop there and make paddle. There's certain kind of trees you got to have. You got to understand how to get it. All the trees look the same but they are not. There's hard wood in there. Sometimes you get birch for a sled and hard wood in there will make it twist up. You have to choose it right. You can't tell just by looking at a birch if it's good. Working on sleds is just like working on a car. You got to have parts for it.

One old man told me, "Don't use a crippled sled. It's no good. When you try to fix a sled, try to make a new sled altogether. A wounded sled is not good."

Same for canoe we have to use all the time. And snowshoes. You don't have to buy snowshoes up there in Fairbanks sixty or one hundred dollars. If you know how you could just make one yourself. And it'll be way better snowshoes than what they're selling.

Chief Charlie used to be chief right here in Minto. I seen him. My wife seen him. He was a person that understand. People have respect for him. He give me lot of advice. A lot of things I understand through these people. What to do in an emergency and hunting. All these things. And about other people.

If you go down the street and somebody pat you on the back, you don't say he's a nice guy. You don't say this person is okay. I don't go along that line. I got to know the person. I got to understand them before I can say he is a nice guy. You can't say everybody is okay. I can't. That's a mistake we make once in a while. We think we'll get away with it, but we never do. These chiefs, these old people, really had something that we can't put a finger on. They got a special gift to help other people. And that's what they use.

from "Set Your Mind"
Never Get Scared

When I was a kid I learned by looking at other people. Whatever I'm interested in, if a person do it, well, I go and watch them. That way I learn. I live in the brush all my life. Everything I learn is what I went by. I learn how to hunt, call moose. I track anything if I have to. I hunt with bow and arrow. In fact I kill caribou with bow and arrow, ducks, fish. I see how old people do it and okay, I do it. I catch them. It's something that's a lot of fun. The arrow know to go to the fish. Once you hit them they take off and then that rod just float up and you pull them in.

The people that I seen, they hit a moose with bow and arrow and just shoot right through. Arrow and all. They get grizzly, hit them with bow and arrow, just go right through. They're not weak people that I seen. Real husky people. When he sees a bear he just grabs him by the head and kills him with a knife. That's the kind of people I seen.

We've been taught that once you get scared, that's the end of your life. Never get scared. If you want to tackle something. Okay. You just make up your mind that you're going to get 'em and you'll get 'em. That's what we been taught.

When I was twenty-five nothing's going to stop me. Because I can handle myself and I can take care of myself. Anything going to try to tackle me, he's got to come right up to me. I ain't going to run away from it. My wife was a witness one time I shot three bears with .22. I looked down in that den and there was bear there. I shot him with .22. There was another one and I shot him with .22. I give her my gun and went down there. I tell her you watch to see if another bear come out. I grabbed the one that I shot and I pull him, drag him out of the den. Another dead one, I grab him and pull him out. That one, too. And I look in there and there was another one in there. I shot them all with .22 right in the head. Where else? You can't hit them in the butt.

I live in the brush all my life. It's just no use to get scared. I killed moose, I don't know how many times with .22. See my wife, how small she is. Bull moose come up ten feet from her and she never even get scared. All she do is holler to me that she got no shells. I run across an open place and shot him as he was turning around.

The thing is this, that I never get nervous. I kill bear lot of times close to me as that table. Once when bear was charging me, and there were some other boys with me, I tell them, "Let him come. Let him come." When he got five feet away I shot him and he drop right there. I very seldom missed. That's the reason I never get scared. Now if you think your gun's going to jam or anything, you'll get scared. That's the reason why when you're going to get 'em, you're going to get 'em. That's all you got to think of.

Kids have to start young training for that. My boys, and grandchildren, I try to teach them how to stand up and face things when it come to them. The main thing is to make sure shot. Just once is good enough. The old people tell me, you shoot once. If you wound that one you're after, you're going to have hard time. They say don't miss. When I shoot moose with .22 it drop just like this, because I know where to get 'em.

from "Out on Our Own"
Love Woods Life

If you was in the brush as long as I was, you would understand life. Just like going to school, you'll understand. Because that's the way I learned. I didn't learn it like you, going to school. I learn the outdoor life the way people learned it long before my time. Because it means something on the table for them.

If you're going out hunting rabbits and you got no .22, but you got a snare in your pocket you can still get a rabbit. When you see a rabbit sitting down, you throw sticks over his head and he'll dive for that hole. You run over there and set snare in front of the hole. Then you poke down in the snow with a stick. Chase him out and catch him right there. That's what I know because I've been in the woods all my life.

Right now, everybody depend on money. And why not? How would you like to live the way I was brought up? I don't think you'll like it. It's such a hard life.

I've done some things that even my own people would think couldn't happen. One time I was hunting with four or five boys. I was walking ahead on snowshoes and I see a willow bent forward. On top of the willow was a piece of grass. One piece right on top. I stopped. When those boys caught up I tell them, "Well, I caught a bear."

They all look at me. "Caught a bear? How did you catch a bear?"

"See that willow, bent down? See that grass on top of it? It wouldn't be there unless a bear did it," I tell them. "You boys just look down that way."

They turn off and sure enough there was a bear in his den. You see these things I understand through living in the brush. When that bear tried to get grass for his bedding, it got caught on the willow. You see you got to have your little brain up here. Just like if you're doing mathematics, you got to figure the problem. You have to think pretty hard to get the right number. Same way with that grass. How did it get there? That grass wouldn't be there unless a bear pushed grass by and left one there. See, like a mathematics problem the number's got to be there somewhere. The bear was in his den fifty feet away.

Even if there wasn't much game around, I never felt like quitting the woods life and living in town. If I'm not going to get anything that day, then there is another day coming. I'm going to stick it out. That's the way I felt.

I worked on a steamboat for one summer when I was eighteen. Two-and-a-half a day. Seventy-five dollars a month. All the way down to the mouth of the Yukon, all the way up to Bettles on the Koyukuk, and all the way back up the Tanana River. That's the only time I worked for wages. I said to heck with it. The work didn't like me and I didn't like the work. They wouldn't put me no other place besides deck hand, because I couldn't read or write.

from "Out on Our Own"
I Don't Go Around

It's altogether different kind of person you're talking to. I don't go around and pet my relations. I never go around my sister Lena and I never see her. So that's the kind of person I am. Why should I go around her? She got her own life to worry about. She don't have to worry about me. So I just lay it out the way it is. I see other people from the windows. I see them from out the door, that's good enough.

All I had to worry about was my kids, my family. You hang around people too much you get too many complaints and that's no good. So you going to worry about yourself and just keep away from everybody. Sure, I'm willing to help anybody. I'm willing to help my sister anytime she want help, but she never did ask. So that's the way it is. That's the way it is with human being. I think all of us is like that.

I don't like to travel to new places. For a person like me and my wife, we got to have somebody that knows how to read and write with us. To go to the store we have to ask a lot of questions. We don't like to do it, because that's not the way we live, by bothering people. I don't think it's nice to bother people. I know for sure that me and my wife never did bother nobody. We're not going to go around and ask questions of everybody we see. That's not the way for us. That's not the way to respect people. If you want to respect people you got to be yourself and do what you know only. That's the way we are.

11

Upper Kuskokwim

The Upper Kuskokwim Athabaskan people occupy the headwaters of the Kuskokwim and its tributaries upriver from the Selatna River. This area includes the modern communities of Nikolai and Telida, which were established by Athabaskans, and McGrath and Takotna, which are mixed communities established for trade and commerce.

Linguistically, Upper Kuskokwim is closest to the Lower Tanana language of Minto and Nenana, but the two languages were historically separated by Koyukon speakers who moved into the Lake Minchumina area at the head of the Kuskokwim. The population probably never exceeded three hundred residents. This made it necessary to maintain ties with surrounding Athabaskan people for purposes of trade and marriage. But in spite of these ties with speakers of Dena'ina, Holikachuk, and Koyukon, the Upper Kuskokwim language developed and remained a separate and unique form of Athabaskan. There are now only about fifty fluent speakers left.

Because of their relative isolation, the ceremonial life of the people, including the potlatch, was not as elaborate as that of some of their neighbors. The resource base was not as rich as in some other areas in Alaska, and the people had to rely on a variety of fish and game. They moved with the seasons to fish camps and to hunting and trapping camps. The villages were historically quite small and only seasonally occupied. As late as 1964, my family were the only ones left in Nikolai when everyone else moved to fish camps for the summer. This situation has changed, with most of the Athabaskan residents of the area now living in the settled communities year round.

In spite of the dispersed nature of traditional life or perhaps because of it, the *Dina'ena* (as they call themselves) of the Upper Kuskokwim maintained a rich storytelling tradition. Many elders spent their winter evenings in the isolated camps and small communities entertaining their family and neighbors with traditional stories. The most important of these were the *hwzosh*, or stories of the "distant time" when the traditional world was being formed and shaped by Raven and others. Most adults could share stories of personal or family history and were familiar with the *hwzosh* from a lifetime of listening, but only a select few were able to memorize these stories so they could tell them with the accuracy required of the storyteller. They were usually told during the winter, beginning in the late fall, as the hunting activity slowed and the days became shorter. In the evening as the stories were told, someone in the audience was expected to give traditional responses at appropriate points in the story. The stories might continue late into the night as long as there was an audience. The storyteller stopped when no more responses were heard.

Children were strongly encouraged to remain awake and alert as long as the stories continued, as it was felt the stories would assure a long and successful life. Those who did not listen or quickly fell asleep would pay the price later when they were confronted by situations in their lives that required the wisdom provided by the stories. Listening was considered a more important skill for children to master than was speaking. With age and experience speaking would come, but if they did not learn to listen they would suffer all their lives. In the following story by Lena Petruska about a talking head, this point is made a number of times. The traveler finds her sister living in squalor and poverty because she did not listen when she was growing up.

Upper Kuskokwim Athabaskan was an unwritten language until the mid-1960s. In 1963 Ray and Sally Collins of the Summer Institute of Linguistics moved to Nikolai to begin the first study of the language. Prior to this, Michael Krauss had conducted a brief dialect study and recognized that the language was related to Lower Tanana but was distinct and was not closely related to Deg Hit'an (as some anthropologists, such as Osgood, had thought). Edward Hosley had conducted ethnographic fieldwork in the early 1960s and at first called the people the McGrath Ingalik, but in 1966 he concluded that they were a distinct cultural group and proposed the name *Kolchan*.

By the late 1960s an orthography had been developed, and some initial literacy materials and a noun dictionary were available. In the early 1970s with the growing interest in bilingual education, Ray Collins in cooperation with the Alaska State-Operated Schools held a literacy training session in Nikolai for bilingual instructors. Betty Petruska, one of the individuals trained, went on to become a fluent writer of the language as well as a bilingual instructor in the school. The school program created a need for written materials, and this led to the printing of literacy materials, a junior dictionary, and some traditional stories.

Of the limited number of people who spoke Upper Kuskokwim, at that time only slightly over one hundred, only a few were traditional storytellers. Miska Deaphon was one of the first storytellers to make a contribution. Born November 8, 1905, he was the grandson of Chief Nikolai, for whom the village is named. His father was simply called Deaphon, following the tradition of having only one name, and this was taken as Miska's last name. He followed the traditional ways of hunting, fishing, and trapping all his life. As a child he took part in the nomadic hunts, in which, after early summer fishing, the people would walk out to the Alaska Range and stay until early fall, when they would build a skin boat with moose hides and float back down to the winter village sites at old Nikolai.

In the late 1970s Mr. Deaphon was experiencing bouts of sickness and felt he wanted to leave a legacy, so he made a number of tape recordings of his stories. The National Bilingual Materials Development Center in Anchorage, under the direction of Tupou Pulu, provided him with tapes and a recorder so that he could tape the stories at his discretion. Thus he was able to control what material he wanted to share. Betty Petruska transcribed and translated the narratives, and Collins edited nine of them for publication by the center. Mr. Deaphon lived to see this book, *Nikolai Hwch'ihwzoya*, published in 1980, and he passed away on March 3, 1982, knowing that he had left a valuable gift for the Upper Kuskokwim people. The remaining stories that he recorded, although transcribed and translated, have yet to be published.

Lena Petruska was born August 20, 1920, at Crooked Creek, a Yup'ik-speaking village on the mid-to-lower Kuskokwim River. Her mother died when she was still an infant, and she was raised by her grandmother, who was the sister of Chief Nikolai (Miska Deaphon's grandfather). Originally the family had come from the Innoko River, but Lena's grandmother, with Holikachuk Athabaskan as her first language, had grown up in the Upper Kuskokwim–speaking McGrath area. Living with her grandmother, Lena learned the Upper Kuskokwim language and the stories her grandmother told. She said her grandmother had many stories, and she would often ask her to tell them. She would often fall asleep, however, before they were finished, so she learned only a few complete stories.

While she was still quite young, Lena and her grandmother moved farther up the Kuskokwim River and lived with Lena's older sister. The grandmother died when the girl was still in her preteen years, but she stayed on with her older sister. Fortunately, she was old enough to still remember some of her grandmother's stories. Lena's sister was married to a white trapper named Jack Stewart. From him Lena began to learn English, and by the time she became an adult, she spoke three languages — Upper Kuskokwim, Yup'ik, and English — and could understand her grandmother's Holikachuk language.

While still a teenager, she married Serge Petruska and moved further up the Kuskokwim to the Slow Fork, where his family lived at an old roadhouse. A picture of the Petruska family before her time can be found in Hudson Stuck's *10,000 Miles by Dog Team*, as he stopped at their roadhouse in 1911. Eventually the family moved to Nikolai village, where Serge Petruska died about 1958. By this time Mrs. Petruska had a family of eight, three daughters and five sons. Most of her children were able to go to school in Nikolai and mastered the English language, but their first language was Upper Kuskokwim. She raised her family following a traditional life of summers in fish camp along the Kuskokwim or at Salmon River and winters spent in Nikolai. Mrs. Petruska is well known for her beadwork and has recorded several stories for the Nikolai bilingual program, two of which are published here for the first time.

Her daughter-in-law, Betty Petruska, and Ray Collins followed the same procedure with her stories as they had earlier with Mr. Deaphon's. Betty Petruska worked directly with the tapes made by Mr. Deaphon and Mrs. Petruska, transcribing them in the original Upper Kuskokwim in which the stories had been told. She also did the initial English translations, and then Collins worked with her in editing them and completing more fluent English translations. A thorough study of Upper Kuskokwim style and syntax has not been made, nor have any formal policies been established for its transcription and translation. Betty Petruska had to make use of natural pauses and rely upon her intuition as a Native speaker to create paragraph breaks. Collins attempted to follow these and the Upper Kuskokwim meaning as closely as possible and chose to use English prose paragraphs since the English translations are aimed at an English-speaking audience and do not always accompany the Upper Kuskokwim texts (as they did in Mr. Deaphon's *Nikolai Hwch'ihwzoya'*). For publication in this anthology, Collins has added endnotes to supply information that would have been common knowledge to the Upper Kuskokwim listeners, raised in the culture, but is likely to be unclear to others.

Mr. Deaphon's two stories included here were first published in *Nikolai Hwch'ihwzoya'*, but Collins and Betty Petruska have made some revisions in the translations. Both narratives are episodes in the traditional cycle of Raven stories. In the "Lost Eyes" episode, we learn how laziness can lead to trouble and the danger of crying "wolf." Raven uses his perseverance, knowledge of the country, and medicine power to overcome his blindness. In "Raven Fixes Marten's Arm," Raven uses cunning and power to overcome the physically more powerful Wolves and Bears. We learn the origin of Marten's characteristic gait that leaves tracks with one foot out of alignment with the others.

Lena Petruska's story *"Jezra"* / "Camp Robbers" tells of the origin of these birds and how they acquired their habit of storing away food. As with many other animals, they lived in human form in "distant time." The story of *"Ch'itsets'ina'"* / "The Skull" might better be thought of as "the talking head." This elaborate story is best understood when one looks at how most Athabaskans trained their young women. When a girl experienced her first menses, she went into seclusion for a period of time. During this time her aunts or other related women would bring her beadwork and skins for sewing and instruct her in her new responsibilities as a young woman. The time of seclusion varied from a few weeks to up to a year for some Athabaskans. At the end of this time, the young woman was ready for marriage. The girl in the story is turning down proposals, so she should have gone through this experience; but she is reluctant to grow up, enter a real marriage, and accept adult responsibility, so she must repeat the training and be trained while on her journey. She had hoped to assume a platonic relationship with the talking head. The modern equivalent might be a phone romance with daily conversations but no physical contact.

Ray Collins

SUGGESTIONS FOR FURTHER READING

Deaphon, Miska. *Nikolai Hwch'ihwzoya'.* Translated by Betty Petruska. Anchorage: National Bilingual Materials Development Center, 1980.

Hosley, Edward H. "Kolchan." In *Subarctic*, vol. 6 of *Handbook of North American Indians*. Washington DC: Smithsonian Institution, 1981.

———. "The McGrath Ingalik." *Anthropological Papers of the University of Alaska* 9 (1961): 93–113.

Dotron' Minagha' Sritonedak Di

Raven Lost His Eyes

Here is a story of Raven and what he did. Raven was sitting on the edge of the bank. He looked up and down the river, but he did not see anyone. He was getting tired, so he took out his eyes and left them on the bank. "I will sleep. If someone comes, you will tell me," he said and hung up his eyes on a tree.

Raven went back inside and went to bed. It was not long after he went to bed that his eyes, which he left on the bank, started telling him that someone was coming. His eyes kept saying that someone was coming, so he got up and went out. He put his eyes back on himself and looked up the river. All he saw was a tree root drifting down, and he told his eyes, "You did not look very good. It is only a drift log. There is no one on the river." That was what he said, and he hung his eyes on the tree again and went back inside.

He went back to bed, and after a long time, his eyes started telling him again that someone was coming down the river. This time he thought to himself, "They are lying to me again." His eyes said that someone was coming closer. After a while, his eyes did not say anything anymore.

Raven was blind, so he felt his way back out to the bank. He felt for his eyes where he thought he had left them hanging. He kept searching for his eyes. He really lost the place, and as he felt the ground, he found a deep trail. Up there a little ways, there was a ridge coming down from a mountain. He knew of this place where there were no trees. He thought, "Maybe if I put a berry in my eye, I will see again." So he started for that place.

He had a hard time. He even crawled. When he finally got there, he found a blueberry, which he put in place of his eyes. When he put the berries in, he could not see with them. They were too dark. He knew there was another ridge coming down the mountains and a trail went across there, so he crawled over there.

He found something like cranberries and tried those for his eyes. But when he put them in, everything looked red to him. They did not fit well either. They kept falling out because they were too small. He did not know what to do, so he kept climbing and found another berry — it was the one called Camp Robber's eyes.[1] He could see with this berry, but his eyes were red. He looked like a man but a person from some other place.

He came back down to his house, and he thought to himself, "Maybe I should paddle up river to see where they put my eyes." So he got his canoe and started up river. He was paddling along when he heard, up there among the big trees, what sounded like a lot of people laughing. He wanted to find out what all the noise was about, so he stopped on the bank and pulled his canoe up.

He started walking back into the woods. But when he walked back there, it was a portage, and there was nobody there. The noise was still heard in the woods, however. When he went down to the river [on the other side of the portage], he found a house. Before he came to the house, he put a bunch of spruce boughs in a pile. He spread them out, and then he defecated on it. When he did that, it became clothes.[2] He put these fancy clothes on. The mukluks were the prettiest. Then he put on another pile of spruce boughs and defecated again. Again there were clothes there. These he put in a bag. He carried them along as he walked.

He came down to a house by the river. There was a young girl there who did not go with the others. She was a single girl waiting for the right man to come along. She told him she had been asked many times by men to marry her but she refused. When Raven showed her the clothes that he had in the bag, she decided to marry him.[3] The girl told him, "I will marry you."

By this time, the people that were in the woods came back down. They saw Raven. They thought he was an odd stranger. The girl told them that she wanted to marry this person. The people told her to go ahead and marry him, so they got married.

In the daytime, the people went back into the woods to have fun, but the couple never went there. One day, Raven asked his wife, "What are those people doing back there?" His wife told him, "I don't know. But they are playing with something that someone said are Raven's eyes, which someone brought back. They sewed something over them so they do not look like Raven's eyes." So Raven found out that they were playing with his eyes.

The people came back in the evening, but in the morning they went back up and started to play with the ball. "Let's go up and see what they are doing," he told his wife. "I want to know what they really do." So they started up the trail.

As they were walking, they saw what looked like a big sandbar. It was a big area where there were no trees. That was where they were playing. He sat by the edge to see the game of ball they were playing. As he was sitting there, he watched the ball. There were two of them. Sometimes the eyes fell far apart. He wanted to get them, but there was no way. He really wanted to get his eyes back. He sat there wishing they would both fall where they were sitting.[4] As he wished, the eyes fell where they were sitting. He grabbed them and took them back. As the players reached for him, he flew off cawing like a raven. He became Raven again. He put his eyes back on himself and flew off, saying those were his eyes.

He landed on top of a big tree. The players were really mad at him. They were telling him how bad he was, and they told him, "Maybe we should hit you with an arrow." He sat there awhile and then took off. As he was going up, his wife, who was still standing there, her clothes became covered with Raven's droppings. They were all white with it. The clothes that she was wearing were very pretty before all this happened. Everyone was mad at Raven. He flew back to his canoe and became a man again. Now that he had his real eyes back, he threw away all those berries that he used for his eyes, and he came back to his home.

NOTES

1. Alpine bearberry *(Arctostaphylos alpina)*.

2. Raven uses his medicine power to make clothes.

3. The offer of a gift of clothing is a marriage proposal.

4. Raven has medicine power and uses his mind to cause events to happen.

Dotron' Suje Gona' No'iłtsenh

Raven Fixes Marten's Arm

Raven was living at this place. There were lots of people there. They were all kinds of animals living in one place. They were playing with a ball when more people came from upriver to play.[1] The local people kept beating the upriver people. The upriver people became angry.

They all started to play again. They were wolf people and grizzly people that came from upriver. They kept on playing, and then one of the upriver people tore off one person's arm. They took it back upriver with them. The downriver people did not know what to do. One of them was hurt, and they were unable to do anything about it.

They told Raven, "You are never beaten. Go upriver and get the arm. He [the person who lost his arm] is really sick." But Raven said, "It's impossible." The people kept insisting that he do something. Finally Raven said, "What will I do to those big people? I can't do anything to them. I know they have the arm hanging. They also have something that rings hanging by it. There isn't any way to get the arm back."

When Raven still wouldn't go, they fattened one dog for him because he was lazy. When it became fat, they killed the dog and cooked it. Then they brought it to him. When they brought it in, Raven was lying down on his back. "If we give this to you, would you look around upriver for the arm?" they asked him. Finally Raven moved his toes, "After I eat that I will try. When I paddle upriver, I will be gone awhile. It will be because I am trying to get the arm," he said.

After he ate, he started to get ready to leave. Then he told them, "If nothing happens to me and I return, take the hurt person to the riverbank and have the injured side facing the river."

Raven was leaving when Hawk Owl man spoke to him, "Uncle, I will go with you.[2] I will just keep you company. If you happen to leave the canoe behind somewhere, I could wait for you there." Raven took him along.

He was paddling along when he came to a portage. There was a trail. He stopped on a sandbar and turned over the canoe. He left instructions with Owl, "If nothing happens to me and I come back, throw the canoe back in the water. Have it ready so I will just jump in it." The Owl agreed.

Raven walked the portage. When he had walked a while, he stopped and picked some spruce boughs and set them in one place. Then he defecated on them and they turned into clothes.[3] When he put them on, he looked really good. They did not look anything like what the people around here wore. Again he put spruce boughs together. He did the same as he had done before, and they became clothes too. They were woman's clothes. He knew there was a single girl with the upriver people. The clothes were for her. He also knew the arm was hanging above where she sleeps.

He circled around and came to the house from the upriver side. When they saw him they said, "Where is that Copper Center person coming from? Only people around there dress like that. They use dentalium shells."[4]

They made him comfortable. They also gave him the single girl. He gave her the clothes and she put them on. He wished to himself they would put him under the place where the arm was hanging. As he wished, they gave him a caribou-skin mattress to put beneath the arm. There he stayed, but he was watched really closely. He couldn't touch the arm. He poked at it with a cane that he had and asked what it was. The girl said, "I don't know. The people that went hunting brought it in from somewhere. It has been hanging there since then." He poked it. When it swung, the things that were hanging around it rang. When they did, the people came running. "Who is moving it?" they asked. The girl told them, "This person is wondering what it is and poked it with his cane. He doesn't know what it is." They told Raven, "We have it there so that the person that owns it will not get it. He lives down river. We will never give it back."

As they went in and out of the house, he kept close watch on them. He watched even the girl who was given to him. He paid no attention to the thing that was hanging. He kept wishing he could get the arm. He was hoping everyone would leave the house. When that happened, he would poke it. The people always rushed back in, but he would be just sitting there doing nothing.

One day everyone left the house. He got up. It looked like he could get it. There was a smoke hole, and he thought to himself, "If I were to go up that way with the arm, I will get away." He grabbed the arm suddenly. The people came running in. He cawed and flew up through the smoke hole.[5] He ran through the portage, carrying the arm.[6] The people ran after him, saying, "We will catch up with you and kill you."

When Raven ran out on the sandbar, his canoe was still upside down on the sandbar. He kicked it, and it landed right side up in the water. His nephew, Owl, was sleeping right there. When Raven kicked him, he landed in the canoe sitting up. Raven rushed into the canoe and pushed out. Right at that moment, the people ran out on the sandbar. They said, "It is you again. We wish someone would tear you apart like this." As they were saying that, they were pulling out trees by their roots.[7]

Raven was out in the middle, staying in one place. He only moved his paddle once in a while. He said, "If you were out here, I'd do something to you too." As he was saying that, islands started coming out of the water.[8] "If you ever come near me, this is what I'll do. Don't ever bother me again," he told them. Then he paddled away, and so the people left. While all this was going on, the girl that wore the nice clothes had Raven's droppings all over her. The nice clothes had disappeared.

Raven came around the bend from where he was returning. He hollered to the people at his place, "Put the hurt man by the bank." They did that right away. While Raven was still in the canoe, he threw the arm at the hurt man. The arm went back in place, but it was a little stiff. The sick person could only move his arm back a little. That was a Marten person to whom this incident happened. From then on, his one arm is a little stiff. That is why when you see his tracks, one paw print is always a little bit further forward than the others.

NOTES

1. At that time animals had both a human and an animal form. They are referred to here as people because they are in their human form.

2. Animals in distant time had a kinship system that tied them together and patterned their behavior, just as people have today. They also lived in human form much of the time but could assume their animal form as needed. Hawk Owl is Raven's nephew.

3. Raven uses his medicine power to make clothing.

4. This indicates the direction from which the Upper Kuskokwim people received dentalium shells in trade and their view that the Ahtna people of the Copper River were rich in these shells and used a lot of them on their clothing.

5. Raven changes from his human form to animal form to escape.

6. He must have landed and changed back to human form.

7. Grizzly bears sometimes show rage by chomping their teeth and tearing up bushes.

8. Raven again demonstrates his medicine power by making islands appear.

Jezra

Camp Robbers

Once there were two old women.[1] Each had a cache of her own, which was full of food. They used fishnets to get fish. They also used snares to get rabbits. They used the skins to make rabbit-skin blankets.

One day one woman said to the other, "Let's eat only out of one cache. Maybe the food will last longer then. We'll eat from yours first." The other old woman agreed happily. They ate only from the one cache until there wasn't any food left in it.

Then the old woman who had planned it stopped giving food [from her cache] to the other old woman. The other old woman started getting weak. She would go in her cache and eat scraps of food like fish skins and even a fish-skin bag. She started to think about how she could trick the stingy old woman.

While the stingy one slept, she took out her best clothes. She dressed herself up like a man. Then she got some birch punk and put it in her bedding. She told it to snore and it started to snore.[2] Then she went outside. She acted like she had just arrived at the door. She was brushing herself off.

When the stingy one woke up, she heard someone at the door. She looked across to where the other one slept. She could hear her snoring. A man entered and sat down. He said he was very tired. The stingy one started rushing around for him, making him comfortable. She gave him her choice foods.

He told her he had traveled a long distance and had eaten up all the food he was carrying and was very lucky to have run into them. He told her that it would make him happy if she could give him some food to carry on the trail, so she went out and brought in her best dry fish. She put it in a sack for him.

The man was so grateful he told her he would pick her up in the spring. He will come back in a fancy-looking boat for her. This made her very happy. The man left, and she went back to bed. The other woman snuck back in after the stingy one fell asleep again. She put the punk back where it used to be. She hadn't eaten for a long time, so when she fell asleep she slept a long time.

It was almost spring when the food the stingy one gave her was running out. She had been eating it secretly. She had also grown stronger. The stingy one was waiting for breakup[3] so the man would return for her. One day she threw a piece of dried fish to the other one. It was hard and very dry. But it helped her to stay strong.

The stingy one kept talking about the man. Finally one day the other woman told her it wasn't true. "I tricked you because you were going to starve me. It was me that you thought was a man." Then there was a big fight. The stingy one ended up with a broken leg. After that, they lived there for some time, and then they became Camp Robbers and flew away.[4] That is what they say.

NOTES

1. This is the name commonly used in the Upper Kuskokwim area and elsewhere in interior Alaska for the Canada jay or gray jay *(Perisoreus canadensis)*, the large North American jay with black and gray feathers but without a crest.

2. The woman has some medicine power to be able to direct the birch punk to snore. All things in the Athabaskan world are considered to be alive and have personal spirits.

3. The standard Alaska/Yukon term for the spring thaw.

4. This story explains the origin of the Camp Robbers and some of their current behavior. Camp Robbers make it a practice to carry off food and cache it in secret places when it is available. They also frequently quarrel over food.

Ch'itsets'ina'

The Skull

Once a couple was living somewhere in a house. They had many children. Their last baby was a girl. She was their only girl. Time passed and she became a young woman. Men came from all over, wanting to marry her, but she didn't like them. The men finally gave up and left her alone.

Over a year later, visitors came to their place. They looked like downriver people. (From them there would come medicine people in the future.) There was a man with the group. That man also asked to marry the girl. The young lady said, "No." She hardly ever went out. She would usually spend all her time in the corner of their sod house. Her mother would get angry with her, but the girl wouldn't change her mind. When the visitors were leaving, the man said, "We asked her to marry our only son, but she refused. He would take good care of her."[1]

Summer passed and it was fall. Women were outside cutting grass. The mother of the young lady chased her out to join the women who were cutting grass. She started cutting grass with her knife. She was in the tall grass when suddenly she came upon the Head of a person. It was blinking its eyes. It startled her a little. As it passed by, she grabbed the Head. Then she stuck it inside her shirt and dashed back to the house.

From then on she was heard laughing every night in the house. After everyone was in bed, she would start laughing. Her mother started to wonder, "What is going on?" Once she went over and peeked at her daughter. She saw that her daughter was alone. (I wonder if she looked closely?)

Time passed and it was fall time again. The river had frozen over, so there was a water hole down there. One day the mother chased her daughter outside. She told her to go get some wood. The daughter was reluctant, but she did as she was told. She left but returned shortly. Inside she did something over there and then left again pulling a sled. [She had checked on the Head to see if it was okay.]

Her mother had been watching, and she knew something wasn't right. So she went over to the girl's bedroll. She looked in the blankets, but there was nothing there. Then she pushed the pillow aside, and there she found the Head blinking its eyes. When she saw it, she got mad. Over there was a stick that was used as a stove poker. One end had been burned to a sharp point. She grabbed that and poked the Head's eyes with it. Then she carried it to the door and threw it out. It fell to the ground and started to roll. It kept rolling straight down to the water hole. It rolled right in.[2]

Soon, the mother heard the girl return with a sled load of wood. She rushed in and went right to her corner. Her boyfriend was gone! She started to cry. The mother started screaming at her, "You don't like all the nice men, but you are keeping company with a Head?"

The girl went out and found a trail of blood. She saw where it had rolled out on the ice. She ran after it and jumped in the water hole. Her parents were sad. She was their only daughter. The father said to his wife, "You should have left her alone!" Then he cried.

When the girl jumped in the water, her ears started ringing. All of a sudden she felt like she landed. She was on land. The wind was blowing from the north, even though it was actually under water. She found the Head's tracks leading upriver and she followed it. The Head kept traveling. He would stop and talk to the people he ran into on his journey. Pitifully he would say, "My auntie did this to me," referring to his eyes, which had been injured. The girl kept following the signs he left. All the people she met would urge her to go back home. "He won't go back to you. He blames you for his injury."

There was a house up in the valley. She could see that he had entered it. She would have gone in too, but they wouldn't let her. She felt bad and started crying. But they said, "He doesn't want to see you." The girl said, "Please, let him out. I want to see him, just once more."

After standing there awhile, she finally gave up. Looking around, she saw this trail going up the mountain. She was going to go that way when the man came out of the house. He was covering one eye with his hand.[3] He told her that the trail was forked up a ways. "On the one side you will find a caribou-hair marker [from the long white neck ruff]. Go on that trail. On the other side you will find hair tied to something. Don't take that trail."

She took off and finally got to the place that the man had described. On the downriver side, she found the hair marker. The caribou marker was on the trail that was going almost straight up the mountain.

She decided to go on the downriver trail. (From her, people learned not to listen.) She was going along when she came to a big lake. Out there in the middle was somebody. He had dried twigs for hair. He was fishing. She just stood there watching him. When he lifted his hook, one side of her mittens was on it. She should have run away then, but she didn't. The man put the fishhook back in the water. When he took it out, the other side of her mittens was on there. As he continued fishing, her clothing began to disappear. Finally she was just standing there without any clothes. Then the man threw the hook back in, and when he pulled it out, he pulled out the girl. He put her in a boat. (It must have been summer where they were.) As he was paddling along, he said, "You'll see your older sister. She lives at my house." (I guess she used to have an older sister.)

Finally they came to a house. He went in and told her to come inside too. When she entered, she saw that there were bugs all over. Even on the face of the woman that was sitting there. The woman said to her, "What are you doing? You should listen when you are told to do this or that. Look at me. I didn't listen and now I am having a hard time."[4] Now, how can she sleep! All those insects!

"There is a path that goes up the mountain. You will run as fast as you can up that way," the old woman told her. "When you get way up there you will find another old woman. Enter her home. He won't follow you there."

She took off and was going as quick as she could when she heard someone running behind her. "Where will you go?" it said to her [implying that she wouldn't escape from him].

Then she saw smoke coming out of the ground [a house]. She was all out of breath from running when she stumbled in the doorway. Inside was an old lady. The girl said, "He's following me." The old woman answered, "He won't come in." They heard him coming. She hit the door with her hair (the old woman must have had real long hair), and when she did, there was no entryway. It became a solid wall. They heard him going toward the smoke hole. The old woman slapped her hair against it, and the smoke hole disappeared too.[5]

The girl stayed with the old lady. The old woman told her to sew. (The old woman must have had a lot of tanned skins!) She made a lot of things like hats, mittens, moccasins, and other fur clothes. She filled up a whole bag with that. It took her a long time. Then she prepared to leave. "Drop one item of clothing when he is catching up with you," advised the old woman. "Keep moving upward. You will come to another old woman's place. She has an unmarried son who lives with her."[6]

The girl traveled some distance when she heard someone following her. "You will not lose me," it said. She dropped one side of her mittens when he was catching up to her. She didn't hear him for a while. She ran for a long distance before she heard him again. Then she dropped the other side of the mittens. She dropped one piece of clothing at a time as she worked her way upward. When she dropped a hat, she didn't hear him for a long time. It was because he was looking for a pond. When he found one, he walked around the edge of the pond. He admired his reflection while he sang about how nice he looked.

She had dropped everything except for a small bag, which had red ocher [Alaskan paint] in it. By now she was very tired. She threw the bag as far as she could. Then she took off running again. Since she had thrown the last item, she ran as fast as she could. The man was gone a long time because he stopped chasing her to look for another pond. When he found one, he painted himself and sang about how nice he looked.

Then finally he remembered that he was chasing someone, so he took off after her. Just when he was catching up with her, the girl saw smoke rising from the ground. It was someone's home. She rushed inside. The old woman that was there said to her, "You should have listened to your parents. That is evil that is doing this to you."

They heard him coming. The old woman hit the door and the smoke hole with her hair. They became a solid wall. She told the girl, "This is the end. He will perish in a fire!" There was a spruce tree standing near the house. The man climbed that tree. From up there he told them that he would put an end to them. But the old woman said, "No, you won't do anything to us." Saying that, she blew on something, maybe her hair. She threw it at the spruce, and it torched up. She turned to the girl and said, "Now you may go out. He is no more." The girl went outdoors and looked where the tree stood. She saw the man burning with his arms wrapped around the spruce. From then on there was a clump of branches in some spruce trees.

The sun was going down when the old woman said, "My son will be returning soon." She made room for the girl next to her son's mattress. After a while they heard him dropping something outside. Later he came in. He was a big man. When he saw the girl next to his mattress, he grabbed it and moved it [he didn't like her].

The old woman went outdoors in the morning to take care of what her son had brought back. They were whole caribou, so she got busy and skinned them. She put the meat up and rendered the fat. She told the girl her son didn't like her because of things that she had done. Things that were not good. Then the old woman melted fat in a large birch-bark basket. She told the girl to get into it. The girl hesitated but did as she was told. Then the old woman started to skim off the top with her cane. A lot of stuff came to the top. Some dry fish, pieces of tanned skin, and other things. "These are the reasons why my son dislikes you. You stole them when you were small," said the old woman. Later she moved the girl's mattress close to her son's. "When my son returns, serve him some food," she told the girl.[7]

The sun was setting when the son returned. When he came in, the girl handed him a plate of food. He didn't touch it. His mother was disappointed. She said to him, "I will not always be with you. Here is someone who can help you, so you should accept the food." Her son did not answer her, but he finally ate what his mother gave him.

The next time her son left, she told the girl to stand in the melted fat. Again things rose to the top, like porcupine quills which they used for beads. She skimmed till there were no more coming to the top. That evening her son moved his mattress away from the girl's but not as far as before.

The old woman must have had a lot of tallow because she gave the girl a bath in more grease while he was gone. This time there was nothing in it. This time when the man returned, he did not touch his mattress. He left it where it was and sat on it. His mother gave him some food to eat. He ate part of it and handed the rest to the girl. He told her to eat. The old woman became very happy, thinking her son would get married.

In the evening after skinning she would go back inside. She would take out something that was round. She would look down through it. It entertained her. Sometimes she would smile. (What was she doing?)

The man and the girl were married by now. One day while the man was gone, the old woman said to her, "Do you want to look?" The girl agreed and looked. She saw her parents down below. It was summer and they were working hard putting up fish to dry. She got sad and lonely. The old woman said to her, "My son has started to like you. Now you want to return home. You still don't listen." After she said that, she brought in some sinew and told the girl to tear them into strands. Then she would twist them into threads. Later she braided them. She did this everyday while her husband was gone. The rope was getting long. The old woman would take it and put it through the hole. Then she would tell the girl to make more. She made a big bundle. Finally one day when the old woman measured again, it reached below. Then she told the girl to make some mittens that were lined [double-layered].

The old woman offered to take her to her parents, but the girl refused. When the old woman went back inside, the girl started climbing down the rope. It took all day. When her last pair of mittens was getting worn out, she reached the front of her parents' home. She stayed that night with them.

Later on the next day someone said there was an eagle out in a tree. The eagle started talking to them. "Send her out to me. If you don't, I will get rid of my mother.[8] After that you will never see your daughter again." They took out some arrows and started shooting at the eagle, but the eagle grabbed the arrows out of the air before they hit him. The people didn't know what to do. Finally they told the girl to leave. She didn't go though.

Night passed. In the morning when the sun was coming up, the sky was really red. The old woman had told the girl earlier that it would happen. It would be a sign that she had been killed. The girl felt bad and cried. The eagle came back and wanted the girl, but she wouldn't go. Time passed. They forgot about it. They never saw the eagle during that time.

One day the girl was walking to the riverbank. All of a sudden an eagle swooped down. It grabbed her dress and said, "Why don't you return to me? Because of you, my mother is gone." He carried her up to the sky.

Her relatives offered the eagle all kinds of fur for her, but he would not take the furs. He flew way up and then he let her go. She was falling close to the ground when the eagle grabbed her back. When he did, his claws went through her chest. He flew back up with her. This time he let her drop to the ground.

That is how it ended, they say!

NOTES

1. To turn down a request by people with medicine power can be very dangerous and may have played a role in the following events.

2. In the Athabaskan world-view, as revealed in stories, circles and holes such as a water hole or a smoke hole represent gateways to other worlds or planes of existence that are parallel to this world (similar to the rabbit hole in *Alice's Adventures in Wonderland*).

3. The Head has now become a complete person again but still has the injured eye.

4. Children are taught throughout life that it is important to listen because that is how you learn and prepare for the future. Failure to listen and to learn can lead to a life of misery and even to life-threatening situations.

5. The old woman has medicine power.

6. The girl is moving toward maturity and marriage.

7. To place a mattress near someone of the opposite sex and to offer food is a traditional way of proposing marriage. Sometimes gifts of clothing were also given.

8. The man she had married was really an Eagle person and now appears in his animal form.

12

Dena'ina

Speakers of Dena'ina occupied the area surrounding Cook Inlet in south central Alaska. Their territory extended inland across much of the Kenai Peninsula, northerly to the Alaska Range with the Susitna River valley, and westerly encompassing three of the major streams draining into the Kusko-kwim River and into Lake Clark and part of Lake Iliamna. Kari postulates waves of Dena'ina migration from west of the Alaska Range counterclock-wise into the resource-rich Cook Inlet. He also notes that some migration stories tell of a movement by the people from the Copper River area (much farther east) into the upper Cook Inlet region. Over the years, the people of this area have been given more than fifty names by European writers, but Osgood, following Russian scholars, solidified the use of the term *Tanaina* in the 1930s. *Dena'ina*, however, is a modern phonetic transcription of the same word, which means "the people." Occasionally in Alaska, one will still hear them referred to as Kenai Indians.

In Dena'ina, the stories of distant time were called *sukdu* and considered the basis of wisdom. A man without a knowledge of stories was considered to have a poor head. Often young men traveled to live with and work for noted storytellers, thereby gaining experience useful in later life. Both men and women told narratives, and often one or more persons at the gathering acted as commentator, correcting the storyteller when he or she made a mistake. As with other Athabaskan oral traditions, many stories included songs. Bill Vaudrin identifies three categories of stories told: narratives about historical events, "cultural myths" about spirits and beings, neither human nor animal, that inhabit the earth, and "legend stories" *(sukdu)*. Joan M. Tenenbaum establishes three different categories for *sukdu*: tradi-tional *sukdu*, Raven stories, and Mountain stories. The latter she identifies as stories told during the summer when the people are in the mountains fol-lowing subsistence activities. Rooth also notes the existence of Mountain stories, the telling of which, she suggests, is intended to procreate game and bring hunting luck. In her work, she observed a number of Dena'ina storytellers using a slow, elegant style and archaic vocabulary that indicate the existence of a high-language tradition in Dena'ina storytelling. She also describes some storytellers who used a highly dramatic narrative style.

Peter Kalifornsky was born on October 12, 1911, in Kalifornsky Village on Cook Inlet. His great-great-grandfather had founded the village after he returned from Fort Ross in Russian California. Peter's father, Nikolai Kalifornsky, lived there most of his life. His mother, Agrafena Chickalusion Kalifornsky, died in 1913, and when Peter was about six, he went to live with his uncle, Theodore Chickalusion, chief of the West Inlet Dena'ina people, at Polly Creek. Mr. Kalifornsky remembered his youth as a time of much traditional training. He was awakened for exercise and strength training and then taught subsistence living skills. During this time, he also learned many songs and stories. He returned to Kalifornsky Village and spent five years at the Kenai territorial school. While he engaged in subsistence activities such as fishing and trapping much of his life, he also worked on construction projects for the Alaska Railroad and in other wage positions that the Kenai area afforded. In the late 1950s he spent a year in Seattle, receiving medical care for tuberculosis.

In the early 1970s, he began to work on projects for the preservation of the Dena'ina language. Kari worked with him on a number of projects and helped produce two chapbooks of Dena'ina material. During this time, Mr. Kalifornsky also began writing in Dena'ina and English and translating Dena'ina. Fueled by an urgent sense to preserve as much of the Dena'ina language and culture as he could, he spent much of the last twenty years of his life engaged in teaching, researching, and writing about the life he had experienced in his youth. In 1979 he traveled to California, a trip that his biographer, Alan Boraas, says "gave him a broader perspective on his writing" and stimulated him toward further publication. Though largely self-taught, he produced an impressive body of material. His definitive work, *A Dena'ina Legacy, K'tl'egh'i Sukdu: The Collected Writings of Peter Kalifornsky*, edited by Kari and Boraas, was published in 1991. It assembles 147 pieces of his writing and won an American Book Award for 1992. Mr. Kalifornsky died in June 1993.

Katherine McNamara, who had numerous discussions with Mr. Kalifornsky in the mid-1980s, reports that he separates the stories he knows into four eras or cycles: the time when animals were talking to one another, the time when first laws and regulations were being made, the time when the people were testing belief for truth, and the time when things have been happening to the people lately. She emphasizes the analytical nature of Kalifornsky's stories, summarizing his comments on the way the narratives had been passed down through the ages to show the people how the world was composed and to put to the test the beliefs expressed in the stories. She cites Kalifornsky's belief that this testing was empirical and performed by actual experience, which often threatened or took the lives of serious investigators of truth and meaning in oral narratives.

"My Great-Great-Grandfather's Story" leads our selections from Kalifornsky's *Collected Writings*. This story mixes family history with the history of place names, but more importantly, it illustrates the nature of continuance in a changing world. "The One Who Dreamed at Polly Creek" is a good example of the many prophecies of the coming of Europeans that existed in Native America. "Beliefs in Things a Person Can See and in Things a Person Cannot See" is a didactic tale with a clearly cautionary note about how to treat the animals with respect. It also outlines some basic elements of Dena'ina cosmology.

"The Kustatan Bear" is a fascinating tale of shamanistic warfare and of the position and role of the shaman in traditional Dena'ina life. Christian religious belief and modern technology are gracefully intertwined with older assumptions about spirit power. "The Gambling Story" shows the nature of the relationship between the animal and the human worlds, and it emphasizes that the spirit world helps humans who act respectfully toward all living creatures and heed its guidance. In "Raven Story" the mighty Raven initiates the custom of singing songs. Songs, of course, are powerful forces that can influence the interaction of the human and the spiritual worlds. "Raven and the Geese" presents Raven trying to be something he is not; however, he learns he cannot live like the geese. The gluttonous Raven successfully tricks the whale, but he is unable to trick the humans and hoard his prize. And in the widespread story of "The Man and the Loon," the sin of hoarding is again introduced, and the spirit world intervenes to provide justice. Mr. Kalifornsky sees this story as addressing larger subjects related to spiritual awareness.

SUGGESTIONS FOR FURTHER READING

Kalifornsky, Peter. *A Dena'ina Legacy, K'tl'egh'i Sukdu: The Collected Writings of Peter Kalifornsky.* Edited by James Kari and Alan Boraas. Fairbanks: Alaska Native Language Center, 1991.

McNamara, Katherine. "A Talk with Peter Kalifornsky: *Sukdu beq' quht'ana ch'ul-'ani*, 'The Stories Are for Us to Learn Something From.'" *Alaska Quarterly* 4.3–4 (1986): 199–208.

―――. "'Then Came the Time Crow Sang for Them': Some Ideas about Writing and Meaning in the Work of Peter Kalifornsky." In *New Voices in Native American Literary Criticism.* Edited by Arnold Krupat, 488–504. Washington DC: Smithsonian Institution Press, 1993.

Osgood, Cornelius. *The Ethnography of the Tanaina.* Yale University Publications in Anthropology 16. New Haven: Yale University Press, 1937.

Pete, Shem. *Shem Pete's Alaska: The Territory of the Upper Cook Inlet Dena'ina.* Compiled and edited by James Kari and James A. Fall. Fairbanks: Alaska Native Language Center & The CIRI Foundation, 1987.

Rooth, Anna Birgitta. *The Importance of Storytelling: A Study Based on Field Work in Northern Alaska.* Studia Ethnologica Upsaliensia 1. Uppsala: Acta Universitatis Upsaliensis, 1976.

Tenenbaum, Joan M., comp. *Dena'ina Sukdu'a: Traditional Stories of the Tanaina Athabaskans.* Edited and translated by Joan M. Tenenbaum and Mary Jane McGary. Fairbanks: Alaska Native Language Center, 1984.

Vaudrin, Bill. *Tanaina Tales from Alaska.* Norman: University of Oklahoma Press, 1969.

Unhshcheyakda Sukt'a

My Great-Great-Grandfather's Story

My great-great-grandfather's name was Qadanalchen, "Acts Quickly" [literally "bounces up and out"]. This is my great-great-grandfather's story, and the reason why there came to be no more potlatches.

When they took him Outside [to Fort Ross, California, a Russian colonial post], they baptized him and he began to believe in God and to learn to write. When he returned, they gave him the name Kalifornsky.

And when he returned here from Fort Ross, California, his father, who had been chief, had just died. "You next, be chief in his place," they said to him.

But he said, "No."

"If you won't be chief, leave the tribe," they told him. So he took his relatives and founded a village at "Last Creek Down" *[Unhghenesditnu]* which they called Kalifornsky village, from his name.

When he was leaving, he told the people: "Keep on respecting the old beliefs, but there is God to be believed in; that is first of all things on earth," he told them.

And here on the Kenai Peninsula there was no longer a chief, and there were no more potlatches. And at Kalifornsky village they built a church, and also at Kustatan they built a church.

At that time, there were disputes over territory, and they say that great-great-grandfather of mine gave the people some advice: "If I were careless, I wouldn't be here now. If I were one to worry so I couldn't sleep, I wouldn't be here now. If my stomach were big [that is, greedy], I wouldn't be here now." That is what the old people told about him.

My grandfather, Alex Kalifornsky, and his partner, Nickanorga, too, died one after the other in 1926. After that there was no one at Kalifornsky village. The survivors moved to Kenai.

Recently, I found the graves there at Kalifornsky village. I set crosses over them.[1]

NOTE

1. In 1916 the United States Coast and Geodetic Survey established the map name of Kalifornsky as "Kalifonsky." For years members of the Kalifornsky family had the pronunciation and the spelling of their surname altered to conform with this map name. In 1981 the Alaska State Board of Geographic Names changed the spelling of "Kalifonsky" to "Kalifornsky." A year or so later the road signs on Kalifornsky Beach Road were also changed.

Qadanalchen K'elik'a

Qadanalchen's Song

Another dark night has come over me.
We may never be able to return home.
But do your best in life.
That is what I do.[1]

NOTE

1. Peter Kalifornsky's great-great-grandfather, Qadanalchen, composed this
song while he was at Fort Ross, California, sometime between 1811 and 1821. It is said
that he was not sure he would ever get back to Cook Inlet, and to ease his loneliness
he would sing this song. As he sang, he would take from a small bag a bit of soil he
had brought from his home village, and he would rub the soil on the soles of his feet.
This was a customary Dena'ina practice to ease the pain of homesickness.

Tałin Ch'iłtant Qatsinitsexen
The One Who Dreamed at Polly Creek

At Polly Creek there was a man who slept for three days. He woke up and he said, "Things will be different."[1]

"They go around on the land. In the water they have huge ships and they travel around in the sky.

"They talk different from us. Their buildings are large, and inside there is everything. Inside it is bright. Everything is there.

"There is an immense thing with smoke and fire. And the people were in two groups. Their movements look dangerous.

"There is one building where it is noisy. And those people are acting crazy. They are sitting on some kind of animal. And it is running around carrying them.

"And salmon are loaded in this boat that makes an exploding sound."

He went to sleep and did not wake up.

NOTE

1. This is a prophecy of the coming of the white man. Such stories occurred throughout aboriginal Alaska.

K'ełen Ił Ch'qghe'uyi Ch'u K'ech'eltani

Beliefs in Things a Person Can See

and in Things a Person Cannot See

The Dena'ina, they say, had some beliefs about animals. After they killed and butchered an animal in the woods while hunting or trapping, they would put the bones in one place. In the winter they would cut a hole in the ice and put the animal bones in the water. At home in the village, too, they put all the animal bones into the water, either in a lake or in the Inlet, or they would burn them in the fire. They did this so the animals would be in good shape as they returned to the place where the animals are reincarnated. They say they had that kind of belief about the animals.

There was one young man. The old men would tell stories about the animals, about how to take good care of them and treat them with respect. And this man listened to the stories the old men told and said, "Look, the old men are lying."

Later, that man went into the woods and built a brush camp and he killed a caribou. He took the caribou back to his camp and butchered it and cooked it, and he started to eat. Then a mouse came out and he clubbed it and threw it away. Then more mice came out and he clubbed them and threw them away, too. He was trying to eat but still more mice came out and he poured hot water on them and scalded them and threw them away, but still the mice kept coming out at him.

So he went back to the village and he went to the chief and he told him, "I'm in bad shape, I'm all tired out and I'm hungry." They gave him something to eat, and then he told the chief how the mice kept coming out at him after he had killed the caribou. He said that if the men would go with him, they could bring home the caribou meat that was still good. When they arrived at the brush camp, they found the mice had not touched the caribou meat; but when the man checked his traps, he discovered the mice had chewed whatever had been caught and he threw the meat away.

They returned to the village, and the man put his pack of caribou meat in a cache. A day or so later he went to get the meat he had brought home and discovered it was not usable because the mice had eaten on it and dirtied it with their waste. The chief told the man, "The mice are not bothering you for no reason. Maybe you treated the animals improperly."

At night, when the man went to bed, the mice ran all over him. Then, when he finally went to sleep, the man had a dream. He dreamed about an open country, no ridges, no mountains, no trees, as far as one could see. There were all kinds of people all around. And there was a lady seated in front of him there. "I know you," she said to him. There were people there, but their faces were made differently than human faces.

The woman was beautiful. She said, "The way you are now is bad, and as a result you will have a very hard time. You have smashed the animal bones and thrown them where the people walk on them. When the animals return here, they have difficulty turning back into animals."

And she gestured, and the place turned into a different country. It was populated by horribly disfigured animals. There were people there who were tending to them. "These are my children," she said. "Look what you did to them. You scorched off their skin with hot water."

Then she said, "Now, look where you came from — the sunrise side." He turned and saw that they were at a land above the human land, which was below them to the east. And all kinds of people were coming up from the lower country, and they didn't have any clothes on. When they arrived, they put on clothes, and when they did, they turned back into all kinds of animals again. The beautiful lady told the man that the animals were returning from the human people to be reincarnated. She told him, "The Campfire People have come. The Campfire People take good care of us. They take our clothes for their use and if the humans treat us with respect, we come here in good shape to turn into animals again. We will be in good shape if the humans put our bones into the water or burn them in the fire."

As she was talking to him, the woman was standing behind him. And when he turned to look at her, he saw a great big mouse sitting there. And the man got scared and startled and he woke up [from his dream].

He went to the chief and said, "You told me the right thing. You said maybe I had done something wrong to the animals. I want to tell my story in front of the people." And the people of the village got together and the man told them the story about the animals. He said, "The animals are on the west side of us, above us, and we are on the east side, below them, on the sunrise side of our country. The animals know whatever we are doing. The old men told stories about how to respect the animals, and I did not believe them. I would smash up the animal bones and throw them away. You people did not know it, but you were walking on the animal bones. And they [animals] knew it too." And then he told the people about his dream.

Afterward he thought a great deal about his dream, and, although he didn't exactly go crazy, he was not himself anymore.

Qezdaghnen Ggagga

The Kustatan Bear

A long time before my time there was a village at Old Kustatan, and there was a newer village on the north of the Kustatan Peninsula at *Tl'egh Diłchik* ["yellow sedge"] called the New Village of Kustatan, or New Kustatan.[1] Quite a few people lived at Kustatan. They were trapping all over that country, all the way down to Tuxedni Bay, and up into McArthur River, and all over in the mountains.

There were two brothers from Old Kustatan. They were trapping in Lake Clark Pass, and they went into the canyon up toward Lake Clark. They found a cache with some food and furs in it. They stole some of the food and furs and carried it back to where they had their camp at *Nutenq'a* [on upper Bachatna Creek].

In the meantime some people from the village of *Qizhjeh* came back to this cache and found their food and furs were gone. Instead of following the tracks to see who it was that stole their goods, they went back up Lake Clark Pass to their village.

In those days there used to be shamans. One man and his wife were big shamans [powerful shamans]. The *Qizhjeh* people paid them to track down the ones who stole the food and furs from their cache.

The two shamans wrapped bear skins around themselves. They went out and walked. They came out of Lake Clark Pass transformed into a bear and came upon the two brothers from Old Kustatan who were trapping. First the bear came upon the oldest brother, and, late in the evening, it killed him. From the camp they heard the shooting. The younger brother waited for his older brother to come back to camp, but he did not return. In the morning, as soon as it was daylight, he said he was going to see what his brother was shooting at and find out why he didn't come back. He went after his brother. He wasn't gone very long.

The oldest brother's wife and baby son were with them. She was pregnant. (The woman I am talking about came to be Mrs. Nickanorga later on on the Kenai side.) The old mother was with the brothers too. The wife wondered how come the brothers did not come back, it was almost mealtime, around noon. They should be real close by.

So she put on snowshoes and went to where she thought they would be. She found the men torn up by a bear. She went back to camp, took the baby and that old lady, and put them in a sled.

From their camp at *Nutenq'a* it took about four hours to reach Old Kustatan Village. She put the baby in blankets in the sled and pulled that sled all the way to near the mouth of Kustatan River. She pulled that sled with the baby and everything. She came that far. She was pretty exhausted. She built a brush camp and a fire for the old lady. And she went on for help.

She started running with her baby across the Kustatan River to Old Kustatan Village. When she arrived at her relatives' house, she opened the door and called for help. They knew something was wrong.

The young boys ran on snowshoes, following her tracks. She had passed out in the house. The boys ran to the brush camp, found the old lady, and brought her back to Old Kustatan Village. By the time she came to, the young woman was strong enough to talk. She told the story. She said, "A bear came to my husband and my brother-in-law and tore them up out there." The people ran to the village of New Kustatan and told them what had happened. They told the powerful chief of that area and his two brothers about the bear.

The bear did not follow the woman's tracks, but headed north through the lowlands and then cut off and went up toward McArthur River. Up by McArthur River there's a little point of a ridge *[Z'unishla]*. The bear went around it toward the south.

It happened that the Kustatan chief was trapping in the McArthur River area and was walking toward that very ridge. He saw the bear in a clearing, coming up toward him. He started running from the bear. He didn't shoot it. He ran all the way back to New Kustatan.

The chief's wife and some of the village women were fishing on the ice. They used to cut a hole in the ice when the Inlet froze, and fish for tomcod. He hollered, and they heard him. The women ran up the hill to the village.

Those people were prepared for things that might happen. They had fixed a smokehouse so it was animal-proof. They were expecting that bear to come to the village because they knew something was wrong with it. The bear came after the chief all the way into the village.

The younger boys were chopping wood to bring down to the village. As the woman ran up the hill from the beach, one of the boys ran to the chief's wife and found out what was happening. He ran to the people cutting wood and told them the bear was coming, so they ran back down toward the village. They saw the bear, and the chief started shooting it when it came up on top of the hill. The bear ran up in the woods toward where the people were and one of the men saw the bear coming and got excited and jumped underneath a windfall. The bear didn't see him under there and jumped right over him and ran past him. The man had a chance to get away and ran to the village.

The chief operated the Alaska Commercial Company store at New Kustatan. He sold many things, including guns and ammunition. The chief took some guns and cartridges from the store and went with some men into his animal-proof smokehouse. A woman with three children lived next to his smokehouse. The chief's smokehouse was well fixed so a bear couldn't break in.

The first night they shot at that bear all night long. The bear would try to get into the house, but they had guns ready all over the house so they could shoot at the bear from anywhere without reloading.

The next morning the bear went toward the woods to rest. In the evening it came back again. And again it tried to get into the house and they kept shooting at it.

On the second night it went over and broke into the woman's house next to the smokehouse. The bear broke down the logs covering the window and started to come through the window. She was ready for bed and one of the kids was sleeping under the table. The door closed from the inside. They were running out when she remembered the boy sleeping under the table. She ran back in and the bear was already halfway through the window. She grabbed the child and, with her other children, ran into her attached smokehouse. She slammed the door and locked it. A third room, a sweathouse, was attached to her smokehouse and she took the children in there and stayed all night. Meanwhile, the bear was wrecking her house.

Eventually the bear went back to the chief's smokehouse, and the chief and the men began shooting at it again. They shot at that bear all night long. In the morning the bear again went back into the woods.

In the morning the chief and his younger brother went to the woman's house. They hollered to see if anyone was alive. She answered from the sweathouse. They opened the door and she ran out holding the kids. It was wintertime and cold and it was a miracle they didn't freeze to death. They brought them to a house and took care of them.

Evening came and the bear came back. Again they shot at it all night until morning. They heard it making all kinds of racket in the woman's smokehouse.

[To rid themselves of the bear,] the chief at New Kustatan and his brother went to the church. They went into the church and took the Bible and a cross and some rifle shells. They burned incense and cut holes in the shells and put holy smoke into the shells. They sprinkled three shells with holy water. They took the Bible and the cross and went to the building where the bear was. They went around the building with the cross and the Bible. Then they climbed on the roof where the smoke hole was. They looked down and saw the bear. They shot the bear with the shells that had been baptized with holy water.

As soon as the bear was dead it swelled up, and they couldn't get it through the doorway. They went to work and tore the roof off the sweathouse. They took the bear out that way. They didn't want to say they had killed it; they weren't sure they had killed it yet. To be sure, they butchered the bear, skinned it, and put the meat in the woods. They built a rack to put up the meat and skin, and then they decided they had killed the bear. They took the Bible and cross back to the church, and one of them went to the village and told them the bear was dead.

The Kustatan chief had an aunt who was a shaman. They went for her and brought her to New Kustatan. She started doing shaman work and she could see a ring of fire around the house where they killed the bear. She saw two little people inside the house, a woman and a man. They were only as big as a finger. They couldn't get out because of the flame. She told them to make a bear intestine bag. If you clean it and blow it up, it looks like a clear bag. She took those two and put them into the intestine bag. They were two little people, the people that were in the bear.

Then the Kustatan shaman said, "Make me a dog." The villagers carved little dogs of wood and added pieces of the bear's skin. The chief and his brothers were not afraid of the bear for the three days they were shooting at it, but when they went back to the rack to get bear skin for the effigies, they were so scared that they walked backward all the way back to the house. That's how scared they were. But they got little pieces of bearskin for the dog effigies.

Then the Kustatan shaman said to bring her snow. They brought in snow. And she asked for one more thing, a leaf of tobacco. All this was to cure those two little people and send them home. She took all of the objects, the two little people, the little dogs, the snow, and the tobacco, and put them into the fire. She chased them back to their village at *Qizhjeh*. She kicked toward the fire and made an earthquake, a powerful magic to send them back home.

At the time the two people were sent back to their village, there was another shaman at *Qizhjeh* village. He was going toward Kustatan to look for them. The Kustatan shaman saw him with her magic power, coming toward her through a lake in the pass. He was sticking out halfway. She chased him back to his village with her power.

In the spring the wolves came to the *Qizhjeh* village like dogs. They ate all the food in the caches. The *Qizhjeh* people asked the shamans what could be done. "Leave them alone, they are our dogs," said the shamans. These were those little carved dogs. They cleaned up all the food, and the people had nothing to eat. The Kustatan people took the bearskins and threw them in the fire, along with snow for water. When the snow melted, the people of the village of *Qizhjeh* died off.

The Kustatan shaman had put a curse on the *Qizhjeh* people so those dogs would eat everything and starve them. If it wasn't for her power and the cross and the Bible, that bear might have destroyed both of the Kustatan villages.

Later on, around 1918, there was an influenza epidemic and most of the Kustatan people died. After the people had died, the chief took the cross and Bible from the church at Kustatan to Tyonek. They are still in the Tyonek church today.

NOTE

1. The principal incidents in this story have been historically documented as having occurred during the winter of 1895–1896. One of the men who killed the bear was Theodore Chickalusion, Peter Kalifornsky's maternal uncle with whom Mr. Kalifornsky lived at a later time. Maxim Chickalusion Sr., Theodore's son, recorded the story orally in English in 1981. After reading his cousin's transcribed narrative, Mr. Kalifornsky wrote it in Dena'ina and first published it in booklet form in 1982, with the English text identified as Maxim Chickalusion's and the Dena'ina text as Peter Kalifornsky's translation. For publication in *K'tl'egh'i Sukdu* (his *Collected Writings*) in 1991, Mr. Kalifornsky made further revisions. We have printed from this edition, where readers interested in further details about the history and publication may consult James Kari's introduction to the story. — Eds.

Qezdaghnen Ggagga Beghun

The Other Half of the Kustatan Bear Story

This is the other part of the Kustatan Bear Story.[1] There were three brothers; they were not shamans, but their spiritual convictions were strong. Because of their strong beliefs, this was what had happened. They had killed the bear in which the two *Qizhjeh* shamans had been residing, and that weakened the shamans' powers. Then the shamans from Cook Inlet [literally "from this side"] talked and sent the two shamans [who had been in the bear] along with the sickness [back to the other side] on the Cook Inlet people. And those shamans [from the Lake Clark area] and these shamans [from Cook Inlet] battled each other for perhaps thirty years.

These shamans [from Cook Inlet] sent their shaman power into the one who killed the Kustatan bear and he became like a shaman. They hoped they would figure out some way to end the shaman war. And various sicknesses broke out. Some of the shamans took the sicknesses into themselves. [They did this] to save the people.

The shamans from *Qizhjeh* caused the spirit of a Cook Inlet shaman to invade a moose to do evil. And that moose was sent after an old man [the chief] of Kalifornsky village. That old man was out hunting rabbits upland from the cemetery and the moose charged him. The old man was wearing snowshoes, and the moose chased him and stepped on his snowshoes, and he fell over. And the little dog he had with him jumped up and bit the moose by the bell [on its neck]. While the moose was trying to fight the little dog off, the old man escaped. From then on, every time the old man tried to go out that same moose would pursue him.

After some time, the old man told his partner, "I'm going out to get that moose in the morning." He got up in the morning and went to church and prayed. He prayed and placed three bullets on the cross. He sprinkled holy water on the three cartridges [that is, he baptized them] and he went fter the moose.

He went all over back behind the village where there were trails. He looked all over, but he could not find that moose. Then, as he was going near the gulch getting close to the cemetery, he came upon the moose lying down. When the chief saw the moose lying there, it got up. He took a cartridge that wasn't baptized and shot the moose from a short distance away, but the moose just shook himself. Then he shot it again, this time with a baptized cartridge, and the moose went down. It would get up and fall and try to get up again.

Then the young men from the village ran there and shot the moose in the head. Their bullets did not faze it and the moose got up. So the old man shot it with the second baptized bullet. He shot it in the neck. The young men cut off its head and set it down. It was still blinking its eyes at that old man. Finally, he shot it with the third baptized bullet and killed it.

It was just like mush inside the head. And the men went to work and they sliced off the front and back quarters and lay them separate from the body. The men butchered that moose and then they buried it in the ground just behind the cemetery. Then the Cook Inlet shaman [whose spirit the Lake Clark shaman had caused to invade the moose] said, "My head aches." And he fell down and died.

And more time went by. The one who had killed that moose had a big house at Kalifornsky village. The man didn't sleep in the bed. He slept on the floor. At this time he had a big black dog. The dog would lie by his feet.

One night the dog got up and started growling, looking at the bed. And then the chief got up, but he did not see anything. Then he saw a great big bear paw coming out from under the bed trying to reach over to get him. The big dog got between the chief and the bear paw.

The chief had a little table in the corner. He always kept it covered [with a clean cloth where he kept his icons, a Bible, prayer books, and holy water]. He grabbed some of these and the holy water and sprinkled that holy water on the bear paw. And that great big paw just disappeared back underneath the bed. Then the chief read from his prayer books and prayed and then sprinkled holy water all over the house. Somewhat later he got sick, but he got well again.

The chief from Kustatan with shaman powers continued the battle. Whatever [sickness] the shamans warred with, he took upon himself. His wife and the other Cook Inlet shaman also took the sickness into themselves. He took some porcupine quills and turned them into wolf effigies and he made war with them [by reversing the power of the *Qizhjeh* shamans]. He put the wolf effigies into the fire. And this caused death to turn back toward the other side. Then, whenever wolves howled, they would take sick and die. And those other shamans all died off and the Kustatan chief and those shamans from Cook Inlet all died off too. They inflicted the evil upon themselves in order to save people.[2]

NOTES

1. Peter Kalifornsky wrote this continuation of "The Kustatan Bear" in 1991 for inclusion in his *Collected Writings*. He wrote in Dena'ina and made his own English translation. — Eds.

2. In his introductory comment on this story, James Kari writes as follows: "Some events and tragedies of the 1918–1919 influenza epidemic were attributed to this shamanistic warfare. The death of Theodore Chickalusion, in about 1926, is seen in sacrificial terms as the concluding event in this sequence of incidents." — Eds.

Ch'enlahi Sukdu
The Gambling Story

The Dena'ina once used to tell stories. In this story, two rich men met and said, "Let's play the gambling game." One young man was a shaman. The other fellow followed the traditional beliefs [he was a True Believer, "K'ech' Eltanen"]. That shaman was winning everything from the rich man. He took all of the rich man's possessions from him. Then, all the rich man had left were his wife and children.

"What will you bet me?" the shaman said. He had his wife and children, one a small boy. He longed to keep them. The shaman had taken all of the rich man's belongings from him. He longed to keep the young boy and his wife. He bet his three girls, and lost. He only had his wife and young son left.

"Bet me your wife and boy against all your things and the three girls," the shaman said. Which one did he love the most, his wife or his young son? He bet his wife, and lost.

All his belongings and his daughters and his wife he bet for that boy. The shaman took the boy from him too. He had nothing. The shaman had won all that he had, even his last gun.

That young man went outside and walked a long way. When he came to a trap he had set in the foothills, a squirrel was caught in it. The squirrel was chewed up and only a small skin was lying there. He picked it up and put it in his pocket.

He walked a long way and then came to a big house. From inside someone said, "I heard you. Turn around the way the sun goes [clockwise] and come in." It was big inside. A big old lady was sitting there. "My husband is away, but he'll return to us," she said. Not long after, a giant came in. "Hello. What happened to you that you come to see me?" the giant said.

The man explained what the shaman had done to him. "The shaman took from me my daughters, then my wife, and even my young boy. And somehow I came here."

"Good," the giant said. "Rest yourself well and I'll fix you up." The man rested well, and then that little skin he had put into his pocket started to move, and it jumped from his pocket. It became an animal again. "Yes, you have come to us with our child," the giant said. "And I had searched all over for my child that I had lost. You said the one who gambled with you is a shaman. Good. I too have powers. I'll prepare you to go back to him," the giant said.

There were animal skins piled in the house. The giant cut little pieces from all of them and put them into his gut bag. He put down feathers in with them. "You'll return with this and sprinkle these down feathers on the gut bag when no one is looking at you. It will turn back into a large supply of animal skins. You will bet with these." And he lay down three sets of gambling sticks. He wrapped these up.

"The first time you play with the shaman, sometimes he'll win from you and sometimes you'll win from him. As you continue and he thinks, 'I'll take everything from him again,' you will throw down this set of gambling sticks. They will spin the way the sun goes [clockwise] and you will take back all your belongings and wife and children," the giant said.

"Then you tell the shaman, 'Do to me as I did to you. I went out and went to the one they call K'eluyesh. K'eluyesh resupplied me and gave me the gambling sticks. With them I won everything back from you.' Go to K'eluyesh and tell him, 'Give me gambling sticks,'" the giant said.

The True Believer went back. This is why the True Believer won everything back from the shaman when he gambled again. When he went to K'eluyesh, K'eluyesh blocked the shaman's powers by means of the pieces he had cut from all those skins. As the shaman tried magic, as he tried to transform himself, he couldn't take the form of an animal again. He failed at magic and left, and there was not any more word of him.

ABOUT THE GAMBLING STORY

In this story, the shaman's belief is in something tangible, that is, something he could see.[1] The other man's belief is *"k'ech' ghelta,"* that is, belief in something intangible that one cannot see. The story shows how one can have reversals in life because of bad luck. But the man is also a "True Believer" and that little skin represents how, through belief and proper attitude, one can rebound from adversity. In the end, it is the shaman who goes broke.

NOTE

1. This is Peter Kalifornsky's comment (written in Dena'ina, translated into English) appended to the story in his *Collected Writings*. The comment did not appear when the story was first published in 1974. — Eds.

Ggugguyni Sukt'a

Raven Story

A long time ago, they say, the Dena'ina didn't have stories and songs. Then one time Raven sang for them.[1] Before that time, there was only *"Di ya du hu,"* [a song loosely translated as "now, there, under, later"] to keep them together in time when they were working or moving.

So Raven was flying along the beach. And where a creek flowed out, there was a fish lying there, a dead one. And he looked up the bank, and there was a village there.

He turned himself into a human and visited them. There were only women at home.

"Where are the menfolks?" he said to them.

"They're in the woods, hunting," they told him. "Have something to eat," they said.

"I don't eat with strangers," he said to them. He was living on fish from the beach. So he asked for a dip net to go fishing, and he went down to the shore.

And there was a cottonwood drift log lying there. He took out one of his eyes and laid it on the log and told the eye, "If you see people, you holler 'Yu hu!'" Then he put on a bandage and went down to the fish and started eating it.

And then the eye hollered, *"Yu hu!"*

And he ran up there, but there was no one there. He spanked that eye and laid it back down. "If you see anybody, you holler 'Yu hu!'" he told it again.

He did this another time [the eye hollered], but again, when Raven rushed up the beach, no one was there. A third time the eye hollered *"Yu hu!"* but that fish just tasted so good Raven didn't want to go up the beach. Then after a bit, he heard people talking so he went up there and met them.

"What are you doing?" they said to him.

"I'm fishing, but there are no fish, only old ones lying there that something's been eating on."

"What happened to you?"

"Sand got in my eye."

"Let's see, maybe it's bad," they said to him.

"No," he said. "When I get hurt, I doctor it myself," he said.

Right then they saw that eye on the drift log. "Ah, that looks like an eye," they said.

"Oh no, don't touch it! You'll make a mistake! The eye brings you luck, it's looking out for you, for good fortune," he told them. "Only I know what to do," he told them.

He picked it up and threw it up in the air three times and sang to it: "We found something that will bring us good luck!" Then he pulled the bandage off his head and the eye dropped back into his eye socket, but it landed slightly crooked.

And then he started to sing: "*Ya la, ya la ah hi, ah hi hi yu!*"

Then he turned back into Raven. Three times he cawed "*Ggugh!*" and he flew away.

After that, the Raven's song became a song, along with "*Di ya da hu.*"

And they sent a messenger to another village to let them know what they had learned. Then they wished to camp when it got dark on the trail, and a boy tried to say, "Lend me an axe." He made a song: "Lend me an axe, *Du-gu-li shghu-ni-hish, ya ha li ya li ma cha ha, a ya ha a li, ya ha li.*" And with this, they now had three songs.

Then a young man wore out his moccasins. And a little old lady who was always prepared for emergencies cut out a piece of skin, and she poked holes around its edge, and she pulled skin strings through them, and he put his foot in the middle of it, and she pulled on the string and it tied up around his ankle. It became his new moccasin.

After that time, the Dena'ina came to have songs. They didn't know who he was, this Raven who visited the people. And they told stories about Raven, how smart he is, and how foolish too.

Some time later Raven visited Camp Robber and told him stories. "I visited the Campfire People," he told him. "They tell stories about me, with jokes and good times. And when they go hunting, I wish them good luck. And when they make a kill, then we ravens have a good dinner party."

ABOUT THE RAVEN STORY

This story describes how Raven can change his appearance to look like anything he wants to [and how he came to have slanted eyes].[2] It tells about contemplation of all kinds of things and about how wishes sometimes come true. In this story Raven is careful about what he eats, and that, too, is a lesson. There are many aspects to this story: to be watchful, to talk for yourself, to fool someone, to make songs. Raven transforms himself and then turns back to himself again. The story tells about how the people should learn everything about life, to help other people, to be kind, to be happy and have fun, to make gifts with potlatches, and to plan things with other people.

NOTES

1. Peter Kalifornsky usually uses the English word "crow" for "raven" *(Corvus corax)*. In this book [*Collected Writings*], however, we [Kalifornsky and Kari] decided to use the word "raven." Note also that the Dena'ina have a term, *chinshla*, for "northwestern crow" *(Corvus cavrinus)*.

2. This is Peter Kalifornsky's comment (written in Dena'ina, translated into English) appended to the story in his *Collected Writings*. — Eds.

Ggugguyni Ch'u Nut'aq'i
Raven and the Geese

The geese fly back in the spring, after winter, and in the fall they fly back south with their young ones. Once Raven fell in love with a girl, a white goose. "She should be my wife," he said. The geese said, "That's no good. You won't make it back with us. Our village is across the ocean," they told him.

"Well I'm pretty tough. And my words come true, too." And he flew around in different ways. He tumbled and fell doubling his wings. He was stunt flying.

In the fall, when the birds started to go south, Raven went with them with his girlfriend. Those geese were carrying the smaller birds. And as they crossed the ocean, his strength started to give out. And his geese brothers-in-law would transfer some small birds to their brothers. And they would carry Raven when he got tired. "You fly on your own," one told him. And then another one would carry him. "We aren't even half way over the ocean and we're all tired. You fly on your own," they told him. "We're getting tired out." And they left him behind.

So he had to turn back to the north. And he was flying slowly. His strength started to give out. He lost altitude and, flying above the water, he said "Let there be a place beneath me." And he landed on a rock sticking up. He rested.

But what was he going to do next? He flew again, and again he was losing strength. Near the water, he said, "Let there be some place for me."

And a whale surfaced and he landed on it. "Hey, friend, can you help me?" he said to him. "I'm really tired. I was helping the birds and the geese and took them halfway to their village. Can you ferry me back to the main-land?" So the whale started to swim him to the mainland. After he brought him to a point, the whale told him, "Farther upstream is not my territory. Maybe someone else can help you out." And he dove underwater.

And Raven flew up to the clouds but he got tired out again. And he descended, and nearing the water he said, "Let there be some place beneath me."

And another whale surfaced. He landed on it. "Friend, I'm exhausted. You are an old man and you don't look good without a mustache. If I put a mustache on you, will you take me to the mainland?" And he took out some tail feathers and made a mustache for him. "Yes, now you look like you have become a handsome old man."

And the whale started to swim with him toward the mainland. And Raven climbed into his blowhole and began to pick at him. "Ouch! What are you doing?" he said. "Well, I am picking out the worms and barnacles from your blowhole," Raven said to him.

The whale swam with him and when they were in sight of land, he said "This is too far for me. The water is shallow." Raven said, "There is still no land, but there is a sandbar. When I say 'swim fast,' you can slide over the sandbar." "Swim fast," he told him. And the whale swam fast and landed on the shore. And, being out of the water, he died.

And Raven was picking at its blowhole. And then Raven saw a person. He flew off into the woods. And the people came over to the whale and were cutting it up. Raven turned himself into a man and came up to them. "Be careful not to eat that. It died by itself. It might kill you."

And then he went to visit the people and stayed with them. In the morning he would sneak out to the flats and eat that whale. They were watching his movements. And one man went up to the whale, and all the others remained hidden. Raven went up to the whale and turned himself into a raven and flew inside the whale.

And the people came out to catch Raven, and he flew away. And the people said, "It must be good if the bird can eat it." And they butchered that whale.

That's a Raven story.

ABOUT THE RAVEN AND THE GEESE STORY

In this story Raven marries someone from another tribe.[1] Raven's ambition and his confidence in himself cause him to attempt something of which he is not capable. There are all types of travel in this story. Travel by air, travel by water, and even travel under water. When Raven travels with the whale, he must pay. There is inspection of food and a food shortage.

NOTE

1. This is Peter Kalifornsky's comment (written in Dena'ina, translated into English) appended to the story in his *Collected Writings*. — Eds.

Kił Ch'u Dujemi
The Man and the Loon

One man had a wife and a young boy. The husband became blind and they were hungry. People would give them some food, but that woman would not give this food to her husband. He was starving and beginning to lose strength.

He said to his wife, "Give me my bow." And she gave it to him. He said, "I whittled it down to make it easier to draw back the bowstring. If it shoots well, take me out hunting," he told her.

And they went out with their son. She took him to his brush camp. She built a fire.

And then a caribou appeared in the clearing. "Try out your bow," the woman said, and she pointed him toward it and he shot it. But she didn't tell him he killed the caribou. She would cut off a piece of that caribou and roast it for herself and eat it. And the man would smell it. When he said, "What do I smell?" she would say to him, "Those are only greasy rocks that have been heated."

One day she said, "Tomorrow I will take you out. Maybe we will find some game." And the next morning she took her husband out into the woods, and she told him, "You stay right here." And she hid his bow and left him to starve. And then she went back to the brush camp and roasted meat for herself and ate.

The man hollered out for her, but she was gone. And he began feeling around there, and he made a wooden cane for himself. And then he vowed, "I will survive, whatever happens."

He turned in one direction and walked that way. He heard a loon calling, and he walked in the direction of the loon. And he came out to the edge of the water. He felt the water with his staff. He stooped and he drank some water.

And Loon swam up to him. Loon said to him, "What are you doing?" and the man told him what had happened to him. Loon said, "Good. I will help you, but you will have to pay me."

The man said, "What can I pay you with? I am a poor man. All I have is this vest with dentalium shells."

"Good," Loon said. "I'll dive down with you three times. When I come back up with you, open your eyes and look closely."

The first time Loon surfaced with the man, he could see slightly. After the next time he could see better. The third time they surfaced he could see well.

"Can you recognize the places we surfaced each time?" Loon asked.

"Yes," the man said, "over there the first time, and there the second time, and over here the third time."

"Good," [Loon] said, "try to remember this place here. By this landmark you will return to your camp. From this place go that way, and you will return to your camp."

And the man left, and as he approached his camp, he began to crawl. His wife was roasting something again. She saw him. She said, "Loved one! I too had gotten lost and have just gotten back."

"What is that smell?" he asked her.

"It is just those greasy rocks."

When she said that, he said, "That is what I killed when we arrived here. And you did not give me anything to eat." And he grabbed a sharp, broken rock, and he pierced her eyes. And he said to that boy, "You love your mother more than me. You stay with your mother."

And he left them. He returned to the village and he told the people the story. He told them, "I paid Loon with a dentalium vest, a white beaded vest."

ABOUT THE MAN AND THE LOON STORY

This story describes how Loon is paid before he gave his help.[1] In helping the man, the loon points out three landmarks, which gives the man a spiritual understanding of his place. The man cannot see, and, in the end, neither can the woman. In this story, blindness is a metaphor for unawareness.[2] The man and the woman are each blind to one another at different points in the story, and, being incapable of being aware of each other at the same time, they eventually separate to seek happiness with someone else.

NOTES

1. This is Peter Kalifornsky's comment (written in Dena'ina, translated into English) appended to the story in his *Collected Writings*. — Eds.

2. The man regains his sight, or becomes aware, when the loon teaches him about his place.

13

Ahtna

As much as for any other Northern Athabaskan culture, landscape, language, and life merge for the Ahtna people. They believed that the various forms of life were not always as clearly differentiated as they have come to be, and their storytellers maintained, as de Laguna has paraphrased them, that "once all was man" ("Atna" 19).

'Atna' was the name (of uncertain derivation) of the principal geographical feature of the people's land—the Copper River; its great valley, lying generally north to south, was 'Atna' Nene'. The people have adopted the spelling Ahtna, and most of their villages stand along the course of the river at points where tributary rivers or creeks join it. Their territory, however, extends from the great Alaska Range in the north to the Chugach Range in the south, from the Wrangell Mountains and Chitina River valley in the east to the upper Susitna River and what is now Denali National Park in the west.

Four dialects of the language developed: Upper Ahtna, in the mountain passes of the northeast; Central, along the main course of the upper Copper River; Lower, along the Chitina and lower Copper; and Western, on the plateau between the two ranges. Distant-time stories are yenida'a in the Western and Central dialects, yanida'a in the Lower, and yanidan'a in the Upper. Historical stories, including biographical accounts and travel narratives, are ts'ehwtsaedi in the Upper dialect, ts'utsaede in the others.

De Laguna has identified a number of characters prominent in Ahtna yanida'a, including Little Old Crow, Kelya or Smart Man (the Traveler figure, said by the Ahtnas to be Fox or Lynx), Loon as restorer of sight, a boy abducted by Salmon for having offended them, Bears married to humans, giant Worms, and other, shadowy creatures such as "Bush men who come in summer to kidnap children or others who wander alone into the woods" ("Atna" 18–19). Ahtna storytellers generally concluded their yanida'a in a traditional way: "Let the winter be short. Let the summer be long."

Tellers of historical narratives and personal accounts imbue their *ts'u-tsaede* with a sense of place that is much more than establishment of setting. This sense becomes even stronger when the narrator has personal or family associations with the place — a village site, a creek, a river, an upland ridge, a mountain. For example, Nataełde (Roasted Salmon Place) resonates with special meaning in the *ts'ehwtsaedi* of Katie and Fred John because its connotations reach back to distant time, before humans lived there, and ahead to today, when humans no longer inhabit it, and the associations include significant history both of family and of Ahtna-Caucasian relationships. In the second of our selections, the Johns describe the first encounter between Ahtnas and the long-tailed creatures, *Cet'aenn*, who once dwelled in dens at Nataełde. Mrs. John concludes this narrative by telling how the people of the village that later stood on that site showed her mother, as a child, the caves where *Cet'aenn* had lived. In another account (not included here), Mrs. John artfully reproduces her mother's point of view in relating how Nelggodi (her mother), at age ten in 1885, watched as Lieutenant Henry T. Allen and his party of exploration entered the village at Nataełde and were fed by the chief, Bets'ulnii Ta' (in whose name Allen called the village Batzulnetas). Mrs. John's father, Sanford Charley, later built a house there (one of five that he had in Upper Ahtna territory) and became chief there in the 1930s. Nataełde, or Batzulnetas, was Mrs. John's home; as she herself puts it, "that is where I grew up." Although Batzulnetas has been abandoned for many years, fish, birds, and animals endure there, and the landscape and the lives both of those who inhabited the place and of those who only passed through remain in the language of *ts'ehwtsaedi*.

Kari regards Fred and Katie John as "tribal historians," and their own autobiographies are intimately and artistically entwined in the *ts'ehwtsaedi* they tell. In the first of our selections, they describe an incident believed to have taken place at the end of the eighteenth century in which Ahtnas killed a party of Russians who had intruded upon Nataełde, driven off the men, and held the women captive. A child born to one of the women, fathered by one of the Russians, became Fred John's grandfather. As a chief living at Shallows Lake Place half a century later, this man was instrumental in the killing of another group of Russians and persons of mixed heritage. His son, Chief John, became the next chief and lived until 1915, when his son, Fred John, was five years old.

Fred John's mother, Maggie, took her children to Mansfield, a village in Tanacross territory where they had relatives and lived for five years. They moved back to Mentasta (Shallows Lake Place) in 1920, and Maggie John did all the work of both man and woman to support her family — fishing, hunting, trapping, snaring, gathering berries and plants, rendering grease. At times they became migratory in search of food. Living off the land was hard. In his midteens Mr. John became *dzuuggi*, that is, a favorite child whom his mother instructed in the oral tradition and whom an older male relative taught how to trap. Married in his early twenties to Katie Sanford, he soon found himself in his mother's position of struggling to support a young family. He was helped by an uncle, Nabesna John of the Upper Tanana, who just a few years earlier had narrated stories for McKennan. Fred John had lost his luck in hunting, and Nabesna John first gave him food for Katie and the children and then, as a shaman, made medicine that succeeded in restoring his luck.

Fred John eventually became *Mendaes Ghaxen* (The Person of Shallows Lake), as the chief at Mentasta is called. Speaking at an elders' conference in 1984, he expressed a beautiful philosophy about the transitory nature of life in which the words of "the people of the past," nevertheless, link past, present, and future generations, even as the people themselves pass on.

One of those people to whom Fred John paid tribute in his speech was Sanford Charley, whose first wife, Nelggodi (Sarah Sanford), bore him ten children. Two of the younger were Katie John and Huston Sanford, another storyteller represented here. Katie John was born about 1915 in her father's house at Slana (a village on the Copper River near the point where the Slana River enters it). Early in life she, Huston, and their sisters and brothers learned the various trails that the family followed in their annual travels in search of game and fur-bearing animals.

In somewhat the same manner in which Fred John emphasizes language as the tie binding the generations, Katie John emphasizes the land and especially its trails: "Here are the people's trails, the people before us. They would pass by here . . . on foot where the trail is. I, too, went there when I was a child and that is how I know the trails. . . . We traveled there and I know all the trails, the people's trails."

Her brother Huston Sanford, some two or three years her junior, emphasizes the power of instruction, by precept from elders and by example in their stories, to show young people how to live worthwhile lives. In his narrative included here, *ts'ehwtsaedi* provides the frame for *yanidan'a*, the distant-time story within the autobiographical account. Mr. Sanford died on October 4, 1995.

Tatl'ahwt'aenn Nenn' (*The Headwaters People's Country*) is a remarkable collection of narratives by six speakers of the Upper Ahtna dialect. Kari, who had begun linguistic work with Ahtna in 1974, recorded these narratives between 1981 and 1984. Fred and Katie John told by far the greater number of stories, often in tandem, as illustrated by the two included here. Kari transcribed his tapes between 1983 and 1985, and Mrs. John worked with him in checking the transcriptions and in making the translations. The book was published in 1986.

Representing the Lower Ahtna dialect and traditional *yanida'a* is John Billum, two of whose stories are included here. He was born in 1913 or 1914 at Lower Tonsina Village, at the confluence of the Tonsina and Copper Rivers. His parents were Mariam and John Billum Sr., and his grandfather was Doctor Billum, who at one time used horses in operating a ferry across the Copper River at Lower Tonsina. Although John Billum Jr. had no formal education, he learned to run various kinds of heavy equipment and was employed by the Territorial Road Commission from the 1930s through the 1950s, then by the State Department of Highways in the 1960s and 1970s. He became a foreman on the maintenance of the Edgerton Highway between Chitina (on the Copper River) and the Richardson Highway. He and his wife, Molly, lived for two years in Anchorage but spent most of their lives at Chitina. They raised seven children. Mrs. Billum assisted her husband in his work as road foreman by writing his weekly reports. In the 1970s and 1980s she worked for the Copper River Native Association, teaching the Ahtna language in the Kenny Lake School. John and Molly Billum both died in Anchorage, he on February 15, 1995, she on January 20, 1996.

In the 1970s Millie Buck, an Ahtna Native and specialist in the language, recorded John Billum's narration of thirteen *yanida'a*. Mrs. Buck had participated, with Krauss, Kari, and others, in the first Ahtna Language Workshop, held at Copper Center in 1973; and she had joined Kari in compiling the *Ahtna Noun Dictionary* published by the Alaska Native Language Center in 1975. When Molly Billum transcribed her husband's stories from the tapes, Mrs. Buck worked with her. Then Mrs. Buck translated the stories and edited both the Ahtna texts and the English translations for publication as *Atna' Yanida'a* in 1979. For our reprinting of two of the stories, she has reviewed the translations and made certain corrections and changes.

In "Two Checker Players," Mr. Billum tells the same basic tale that Peter Kalifornsky wrote in his "Gambling Story." The central episodes, however, which concern the restoration of the unsuccessful gambler's luck, differ markedly. Whereas Mr. Kalifornsky has integrated another Dena'ina "mountain story," Mr. Billum has drawn upon a ritual-of-purification incident to be found in narratives of other Northern Athabaskan cultures (as well as in Huston Sanford's *yanidan'a*), and he has introduced the character of the faithful slave from still other narratives. In telling *"Xay Tnaey,"* his version of a widespread story about the Spruce Root Man, Mr. Billum emphasizes the unexpected — from the young man's choice of a helper to the ambiguous success of his adventure.

SUGGESTIONS FOR FURTHER READING

Billum, John. *Atna' Yanida'a (Ahtna Stories)*. Translated by Millie Buck. Anchorage: National Bilingual Materials Development Center, 1979.

de Laguna, Frederica. "The Atna of the Copper River, Alaska: The World of Men and Animals." *Folk* (Dansk Etnografisk Tidsskrift) 11–12 (1969–1970): 17–26.

de Laguna, Frederica, and Catharine McClellan. "Ahtna." In *Subarctic*, vol. 6 of *Handbook of North American Indians*. Washington DC: Smithsonian Institution, 1981.

John, Katie, Fred John Sr., Adam Sanford, Huston Sanford, Jack John Justin, and Nicholas A. Brown. *Tatl'ahwt'aenn Nenn' (The Headwaters People's Country): Narratives of the Upper Ahtna Athabaskans*. Fairbanks: Alaska Native Language Center, 1986.

Ruppert, James. "'Difficult Meat': Dialogism and Identity in Three Native American Narratives of Contact." In *Desert, Garden, Margin, Range: Literature on the American Frontier*. Edited by Eric Heyne, 143–55, 177–78. New York: Twayne Publishers, 1992.

———. "The Russians Are Coming, the Russians Are Dead: Myth and Historical Consciousness in Two Contact Narratives." *Studies in American Indian Literatures* 2.1 (1990): 1–10.

Tansy, Jake. *Indian Stories (Hwtsaay Hwt'aene Yenida'a): Stories of the Small Timber People, The Ahtna People of the Upper Susitna River — Upper Gulkana River Country*. Translated by Louise Tansy Mayo. Edited by James Kari and Millie Buck. Anchorage: Materials Development Center, 1982.

Lazeni 'Iinn Nataełde Ghadghaande

When Russians Were Killed

at "Roasted Salmon Place" (Batzulnetas)

The ones called Russians first were coming from down the Copper River.[1]
As they came up the Copper River they came [looking] for Ahtna people.
At the place they call "King Salmon Creek" [site where creek joins Copper
    River south of Drop Creek],
some Ahtnas were staying where long ago there had been a site.
They had a home there.
They [the Russians] arrived there and they asked for their [Ahtna] chief.
They brought him out to them.
They [the Russians] grabbed him and they whipped him.
He was sobbing.
From upriver at "Roasted Salmon Place" [Batzulnetas] a young man who
    was raised by his grandmother had traps set.
As he went back among the deadfall traps he heard him [sobbing].
He listened carefully and it sounded like a person.
He returned to his grandmother and he brought the news to her.
"It didn't sound like an animal.
I heard a person.
I heard a person sobbing," he told his grandmother.
His grandmother went over to the people staying nearby there.
"My grandchild was checking traps downriver
where people are staying and he says that you should be on guard.
Someone let him know that the Russians would be coming here.
And this is how the situation seems to be," and so she told the people.
Sure enough, in the morning Russians were approaching them.
They approached them and then they reached them.
C'uket Ta', "Father of Buys Something,"[2] asked, "Who are your chiefs?"
    they [Russians] said to them.
"He, he is our chief," they [Ahtnas] said to him.

"Bring the chief out to us," they said.

They brought him out to them.

They [Russians] lashed him to a stump that stood there.

They whipped him.

He was sobbing to them, that man.

"You are doing this to Yałniił Ta' 'Father of He is Carrying It.'[3]

Do you know you are doing this to someone who is vicious?"
    he said to them.

They [the Russians] couldn't understand him.

They asked C'uket Ta', "What is he saying?"

And he said, "He is sobbing. 'Ouch, Ouch,' he is saying."

C'uket Ta' did not tell them what he had [actually] heard.[4]

They entered his [the chief's] house.

"You [men] leave right away."

They took from them [the Ahtna men] all the bows and spears that
    they had.

They took their spears.

They drove them out so that they might freeze, those men.

Only the women, they took just the women.

They took the old women, too, as slaves.

They chased out only the men.

And then they [the Ahtna men] started upland from "Roasted Salmon
    Creek" [Tanada Creek].

They had been forced to go without [adequate] clothing so that they
    would freeze.

The Russians took those old women as slaves.

They [the Russians] killed some dogs and skinned them.

They gave them the skins, those dog skins.

They told them to tan them.

Then they [the women] chewed on them.

They chewed on them and tanned them, those dog skins.[5]

They [the Russians] didn't know that there were more people staying at
    "Small Salmon" [Suslota].

When they chased them out, they [the Ahtna men] went up above to
    "Small Salmon."

There clothing and food to eat were given to them.

Those who had come from down at "Roasted Salmon Creek" [Tanada
    Creek] were training [for war] among them.

They made medicine, and the old men made medicine.

They combined their medicine [powers].

The people trained with medicine.

The medicine men said, "You try to break the biggest spruce out there.

If blood and hair come out of it, then you will get your revenge,"

so the shamans told them.

So they did that.

Out there they charged against the largest spruce and they broke it and

blood, hair with blood, came out [of the spruce].

"There you have made revenge.

You will do like this. You will kill them," they told them.

The shamans told them.

Then they were trained.

It was said that they [the Russians] had appeared downriver, down the

    Copper River.[6]

They were fierce.

They were coming among them from downriver, those Russians.

They arrived down there at "Roasted Salmon Place" [Batzulnetas] and the

    weather was beginning to get cold [in the late fall].

That man [the interpreter], C'uket Ta', was a Tanaina they say.

He told them [earlier], "Don't do it [don't attack them now]!"

"It would be 'difficult meat' for us to kill them," they said.

"It would be difficult meat," they said.[7]

Then the chief [of Batzulnetas] went downriver.

He was taken and whipped with a whip.

Oh-ho-ho.

"Should you do this to one calling his own name?" he [Yałniił Ta'] said.[8]

[C'uket Ta' said], "Don't do it. It would be difficult meat.

Don't do it [don't fight them now]!" the Tanaina from the west told him.

C'uket Ta' told him.

Then he [a Russian] came back in.

"What is he saying?" he asked him [C'uket Ta'].

"He is just saying 'ouch,'" he told him.

After that then the Russians thought that he [Yałniił Ta']

had only said "Ouch."

They [the Russians] did not harm him [further].

They were afraid of them [the Ahtna men] and they chased them out.

They chased them out.

Well, up "Roasted Salmon Creek" [Tanada Creek] they reached the upland

    country [at Suslota].

Staying by the fire they trained [for war]. Oh!
Here they trained and they trained thinking that they would kill the
    Russians.
Then they were well trained.
They came back downriver to them [the Russians].
Ho-ho.

At night then, after they had finished training for war,
C'uket Ta' took the spears away from them [the Russians].
Then the fight started at night.
Ho-ho-ho!
They [the Ahtnas] came in to them.
To C'uket Ta',
they [the Ahtnas] said, "Pass the spears outside and we will take them from
    you."
"Are there spears there?"
He [C'uket Ta'] sat there and a noise was heard.
He shoved them [spears] out through a hole in the house.
Out there they took them away.
They took them [spears] away.
Meanwhile they killed the Russians here.

They [the Ahtnas] had informed C'uket Ta' and those women taken by the
    Russians about it [the plan of attack].[9]
They [the women] put sticks in the [Russians'] gun hammers so they
    wouldn't fire.
Many of them [the guns] didn't work.
The guns didn't fire.

Afterward one man [a Russian] grabbed something [a gun].[10]
"Don't! He took something," he [C'uket Ta'] said.
He [the Russian] stuck his head up out of the smoke hole and they killed
    him too.
They shot him with an arrow as they ran inside to him.
They killed him.

When they killed the Russians they did it at night.[11]
Then in the morning at daylight, as it was just getting light,
"Then they killed the meat, they killed the meat," [they said].[12]
In the morning they went back to them.

With the spears, bows, and weapons of war, with those they climbed up a
  hill.
Then they sang a war song to them.
I have forgotten some of it, just half [I remember].
They sang of what C'uket Ta' had told them earlier.
"It would be difficult meat. You should wait!" C'uket Ta' had told them.
They sang this again to them:
> Now it would be difficult meat.
> Now the meat has been killed.
> *Yaa 'aaaaaaa.*

The Ahtnas left from where they killed the Russians.
Only the corpses were left there.

The Ahtnas cremated them.
They chopped spruce for them and they built a fire in the middle of the
  area and burned them.
That is why this place is now called "By the Stumps" [site below
  Batzulnetas].
Stumps are there where the Russians were cremated.

Then there was one Russian half-breed who was wounded.[13]
They gave C'uket Ta' a set of clothes.
He started back away from them.
They passed "Rear River Mouth" [Slana] going downriver.
Then the guy who was wounded said,
"Oh-ho, I will tell on you Headwaters People.
You will not live in this country," he said.
Then they [some Ahtnas] came up beside him.
He tried to thrust a spear at them.
Then C'uket Ta' said, "You go back upriver to them.
I don't like what he is saying.
They ought to kill him," he said.
Then one guy ran back upriver to "Beneath Gray Sand" [point near Slana].
Up from there a fire started.
"How come [there is a fire while] it is still daytime?
Why are you building a fire?" [the wounded man asked].
"Well, we are tired and should stay here."
Ho-ho-ho.
In the evening from upriver [came] spears like frost crystals.
That wounded guy said, "I will tell on you Headwaters People."

Then they walked him out to the river flat with a spear [pointed at him].
He was stabbed with spears.
Only blood was left there.
Then C'uket Ta' said, "That is good that you did this."
Then they returned.
And then they had killed off the Russians.

NOTES

1. In his introduction to this narrative, Kari has marshaled the evidence (from historical documents, other Ahtna oral accounts, and recent scholarship) for identifying the Russians as the party led by Samoilov and for dating the event as most likely having occurred in the winter of 1794–1795. The first narrator we hear is Katie John. — Eds.

2. C'uket Ta' is the guide and interpreter, identified elsewhere in the narrative as Dastnaey, that is, a Dena'ina, whom the Russians had brought with them from the Lower Copper River or the Gulf of Alaska. — Eds.

3. Yałniił Ta' is chief of this territory. Here he calls out his own personal name, an act that is considered a very bold challenge.

4. This bit of mistranslation is the first evidence of collaboration between C'uket Ta' and the Upper Ahtnas.

5. The Ahtnas had never worked with dog skin before. It was 'engii, "taboo."

6. Fred John narrates the next segment of the story, beginning with this line. Kari notes that, in the recording sessions, Mr. John had told this portion prior to his wife's telling the segment just ended and that some of his details "duplicate Katie's longer version." — Eds.

7. Note that this term, "difficult meat," appears in the war song that was made after the battle.

8. Yałniił Ta', chief of Batzulnetas, says his name to himself as his ultimate challenge to those who are whipping him. In other words, "Who are you guys? Are your names of higher value than my own? I am the authority over this country." The use of Ahtna personal names is a matter of complex etiquette.

9. Katie John narrates this brief segment of four lines. — Eds.

10. Fred John narrates this segment of five lines. — Eds.

11. Katie John resumes narrating with this line. — Eds.

12. That is, they ended the war.

13. Fred John takes over here to conclude the narrative. — Eds.

Cet'aenn Nal'aen'de
When the Tailed Ones Were Seen

Let me tell about the ones called *Cet'aenn* ["The Tailed Ones"].[1]
By the water at "Mouth of Rear River" [Slana], there Ahtnas were staying.
They stayed there dip-netting for salmon.
There was a village there.
They did not then know of "Roasted Salmon Place" [Batzulnetas].
There was a young man, a young man.
Now this young man had gone off and he disappeared.
"I am going to go upriver," he said.
They knew that he had gone that way, that young man.
Upriver the *Cet'aenn* had moved to "Roasted Salmon Place."
There he came upon one.
A *Cet'aenn* killed him.

They [the Ahtnas] missed him and started to look for him.
"The man is smart.
What is he doing?" they said.
They sent a man after him.
They sent him.
He walked upriver alongside the river and he came up to "Roasted Salmon
    Creek" [Tanada Creek] and
here there were signs of some kind of life.
There were trails.
There were people's trails and
he looked down and there were stalks of grass across the trail [as a marker].
He stepped over it.
Then he walked ahead toward the place called "On the Hill" [hill south of
    Batzulnetas].

Ah-ha!

There were creatures with long tails!

Out there at "On the Hill" they were playing catch with that young man's
  head!

It was a man's head.

He was smart and he walked against the wind toward them.

Then he sat there watching.

Somehow it started sprinkling.

Oh-ho, they went back into their dens.

Then he counted them.

They had eight dens.

They disappeared into them

Then the wind shifted back toward them and

as he walked against the wind, they caught his scent.

They became excited.

Meanwhile, he ran away.

Then he returned home.

"It looks as if he was killed among them [the *Cet'aenn*].

The monsters were playing with his head," he said.

Then there were medicine people.

"What can be done?" he said to them.

"When it rains they go into their dens.

As the rain approached, they all rushed into their dens in a group.

Then there was no one at 'On the Hill,'" he told them.

Then the medicine people directed their thoughts toward rain.

They went upriver and off a distance [from "On the Hill"].

As they walked, they gathered together "brushy spruce" [parasitic growth
  in spruce].

They tied that onto the ends of poles.

Then they stopped off at a distance from them [the *Cet'aenn*].

Then came the rain that those medicine people had tried to make.

They had caused it to rain on them.

Then many of them went back into their dens.

Then they [the Ahtnas] set those "brushy spruce" on fire around their dens.

Those "brushy spruce" burned.

They threw the fire inside.

That stone *[bests'ae]* was then called "*Cet'aenn*'s arrowhead."[2]

Those [stones] exploded like rain from holes in the ground.

They [the Ahtnas] sat away from them.
They were not close to them.
Thus they killed them with fire.

Then they went down to the river.
Salmon were down there.
'*Ii!*
Here there were salmon.
At that time they were dip-netting only downriver [at Slana].
This is how that first became a village, because they had discovered the
    Cet'aenn.
"Roasted Salmon Place" [Batzulnetas] was then a village.
Now when was that?
Maybe one hundred years ago.
Probably longer than that.
Those *Cet'aenn,* I am telling how the ancestors used to tell us about those
    Cet'aenn.

From then on they never saw the *Cet'aenn* again.[3]
They say that the *Cet'aenn* looked like a human.
It had body hair.
There was no hair on its face.
They say its face was like a man's.
Its hands were like a man's hands.
It had a long tail.
They say that it was as big as a tall person.
That is what I heard about it.
They made their dens like bear dens.
They stayed down below the ground.
When my mother was a child, and first went there where the people used to
    stay [Batzulnetas],
they led her around it [the den area].
Because of them she saw the *Cet'aenns'* dens.
It still was not overgrown with brush.
It was still a cave when my mother saw it.

NOTES

1. Fred John narrates the greater part of this account. — Eds.

2. The stone called *bests'ae,* possibly obsidian, that exploded from the dens, came
to be known as "*Cet'aenn*'s arrowhead."

3. Katie John narrates the conclusion, beginning with this line. — Eds.

Dae' Ts'atk'aats

How We Were Trained

Ever since I was a child, my mother and my father would tell us stories.
They used to tell us so that we would be independent.
When it was snowing out there, we would shovel the snow away from our
    door.
We also gathered wood.
When we chopped down trees, "Clean it off good from the top!
If you do that you will become successful," they would tell us.
They used to tell us that in order to make us think about the ancient times.
"In a while you will be fasting," they would tell us.[1]
"You should train yourselves so that you can be independent."
When we were just waking up [they would tell us],
"You hurry outside just as the morning light begins.
At the doorway look up for it [the star-clock].[2]
You should look for it three times, and then you will be fortunate.
If you delay, you will forget about it.
After several days when you remember it again, you can run out for it.
Look up for it.
Then it will take care of you.
You will still remember it after three days pass.
From then on your life will improve.
Riches will come to us.
We will be in wealth.
We will be successful from it [the star]."
That is what our mother and father used to tell us.

They told us that long ago an orphan was blessed with good fortune.
Some time had passed since then and he used to tell them how he became
    blessed.

It was because of him that they [our parents] trained themselves, that
    orphan who was blessed with good fortune.

His uncles were keeping him and raising him.

All of a sudden he had become worthless and sleepy.

His uncle gave him a beating.

Later on he beat him a second time.

Then he did it a third time.

He beat him three times.

He [the orphan] got angry.

He went out under a tree and he cried.

As he stayed there crying he fell asleep.

Then all of a sudden he became blessed.

God spoke to him.[3]

"Why are you crying?"

"My uncle beat me."

"Why did he do that to you?"

"I am worthless [he said].

[Cutting] wood is hard for me and trapping is hard for me.

Sleepiness is starting to kill me.

That's why he beat me."

"Well, you should be blessed with good luck.

You should be blessed.

Turn toward me."

He [God] poked his [the orphan's] back with his cane.

Then he [the orphan] vomited, and vomited, and vomited.

When he poked him in the back the third time, he had vomited it all up.

"Well, it is because of this [impurity] that you have become so worthless.

It is because of this that laziness is killing you.

Now you go back in to your uncle," he [God] told him.

He went back in to his uncle.

He went to bed.

He woke up while his uncle was sleeping and he sneaked outside.

Up above he chopped up some wood.

He limbed the tree.

The morning light was beginning.

His uncle woke up.

He reached for him.

His nephew was not there.

He nudged his wife.
"Your poor grandchild, where is he?"
He dropped some wood outside by the door.
"Your grandchild is doing that! He dropped off some wood!"
All day he chopped wood.
He chopped up a load of wood and he came back in.
They cooked a little food for him.
They served him.
Then he [the uncle] spoke to his nephew.
[He said] "I spoke that way so that you would be on your own.
That was not out of dislike for you.
I love you even though I beat you."

That orphan child was blessed with luck.
Every day he packed skins back from the traps.
He gathered things together for a potlatch for his uncle.
"My uncle, I am going to make a potlatch for you.
Get your friends together for me."
The potlatch began.
He made a potlatch for his uncle.

Another summer and winter passed, and he went out trapping.
Then it started to be spring and,
"I should make another potlatch for you," he told his uncle.
He made a potlatch for his uncle again.
Again it happened the same way.
From then on he went back trapping, with deadfall traps.
Many many things [animals] were coming to him there.
He told his uncle, "I am making a potlatch for you again."
He made a potlatch for his uncle again.
He made a potlatch for his uncle three times.
Then he came in to his uncle.
"My uncle, had you beaten me four times,
then I would have made a potlatch for you four times," he told his uncle.

This is how the word spread throughout the country about them.
We grew up with this.
Our mother and father told us this so that we could be on our own.
Because of that I grew up and I became aware.

I started to think for myself.
The children who are growing up now can learn from me.
They can start to think about it.

NOTES

1. The puberty ritual was an important part of a young Ahtna man's or woman's training. They stayed in isolation, fasted, and observed many taboos. Similar rituals were also engaged in when a young couple had a child, or when an adult obtained spiritual power. The Upper Ahtna have extremely elaborate rules for counting days in this ritual cycle and for observing taboos.

2. Although not mentioned by name, the object looked for is the morning star that was used as a clock. The star is considered both a time referent and a source of luck.

3. The word *Nek'eltaenn* is now translated as God, but its literal meaning is "the one that moves above us." According to Katie John, before the white man's arrival, this word referred to a certain constellation of stars that looks like a man.

Demba

Two Checker Players

In far-off time, two families lived in a village. They were next-door neighbors, and they each had their own slaves. They had a very good year. Each family had fish, meat, spruce hens, ground squirrels, and berries of all kinds.

One day around midwinter, one of the families invited their neighbor over for dinner. They had a good time eating. After dinner, the man who did the inviting said to his guest, "Would you like to play checkers?"[1] The guest said, "Yes, I'll play with you." The checkerboard was brought out and they began playing. The two men were putting their property up for bets. It was not very long before the invited guest began losing. Soon he lost all of his personal belongings. He also lost his slaves,[2] his children, and his wife. The only thing he had left was an empty house.

The neighbor who had invited him told his slaves to go to the empty house and put out the fire and throw out everything that could help him to survive. There was one slave who liked his former master. When the other slaves began putting out the fire, this slave quickly took some of the hot charcoals and put them underneath a birch-bark basket. When the slave was passing by his former master, he whispered, "I put some charcoals under the birch-bark basket for you." The man went back to his empty house. He found the charcoals and started a fire. Soon it was warm. He found old pieces of fur, and he sewed them together for clothing. Then he went out to set snares to catch some rabbits. He was successful. He at least had rabbits to eat, and he survived through the winter.

Spring came and he prepared for fishing. He caught salmon and dried them until he felt that he had enough. So around the month of August, he went up the mountain and set traps to catch some squirrels and whistlers. Whistlers are animals that live and look very similar to the ground squirrels, but are much larger than the squirrels.

The man went back to check his traps the next day. Every one of his traps was empty. He did not catch anything. He felt so bad. He remembered all of the bad luck that he had. He thought of the game of checkers and how he lost everything. So he sat down and began to cry. Suddenly, he heard something behind him. He turned around and saw a very handsome stranger standing there with a cane in his hand. The man asked, "Why are you crying?" So he told the stranger about all of the terrible things that had happened to him. How he lost everything playing checkers with his neighbor, how the neighbor took over his family and everything he owned, and how he set traps to catch some whistlers but was unsuccessful. He did not catch anything.

The stranger touched him between the shoulder blades with his cane and caused him to vomit. The stranger said, "All of this is the cause of your bad luck in trapping. Go and check your traps tomorrow; there will be a whistler in every trap. Pick up all the whistlers but the one in the last trap. Do not touch it. Just leave it in the trap. Do not take it."

It happened as the stranger said. Each of his traps had a whistler in it, and the last trap had the prettiest one of all. But he did not touch it. So he picked up the ones in all of the other traps but did not touch the one in the last trap. Three days later, after picking up all the whistlers in the other traps, he came to the last trap and decided to take that whistler. This one had such a beautiful fur. He took it out of the trap and put it into his pack and started home. When he was almost home, the whistler jumped out of the pack and ran away. He ran after it right into its den. The den closed up behind him. In the den was the man who told him not to take the whistler that was in the very last trap.

The man said to him, "I told you not to take the one in the last trap." Then the man reached for a checkerboard. It was the fanciest checkerboard he had ever seen. The man invited him to play checkers, so they played and played until he learned to play checkers very well. Then the man said to him, "Take this checkerboard back home and invite the man who won everything from you to come and play with you. Do to him as he did to you last year." So he thanked him and began his journey home. He had lots of food and everything.

One evening he prepared a dinner and invited his neighbor over. The neighbor came. After dinner he brought out the fancy checkerboard, and they began playing. The neighbor thought he would win again as he did last year. But the other man, who lost all of his property in the checker game before, won every game until he won everything back of him and everything his neighbor owned. He ordered his slaves to put out the fire. The slaves did not leave any hot charcoals for this man, as one of them had done for his original master, because he was unkind to them. The neighbor went home to his empty house, and he did not survive. He froze to death.

May the summer be long
and the winter be short.

NOTES

1. Kari and Chad Thompson list *demba'* (checkers) among more than twenty Russian loanwords taken into Ahtna in the late eighteenth and first half of the nineteenth century. — Eds.

2. According to de Laguna and McClellan, chiefs or rich men acquired slaves by taking captives in warfare and sometimes by buying children either from destitute people within their own communities or from outside groups. — Eds.

Xay Tnaey

Spruce Root Man

In far-off time, many people lived in a big village by the seashore. They went out hunting seal, fish, and whatever they could find. One group of people went out and did not return. About three boats full of people did not come back. Only one lady was left in the village. She looked for her brother and relatives every day. She walked around looking.

One day she decided she was going to get some spruce roots to make baskets and dip nets. She started digging up some spruce roots, and she heard a baby crying. She listened, and it sounded as if it came from within the roots. She dug deeper, and here was a lump on the root, a large one. She was afraid to cut it open; she might cut the baby. As carefully as she could, she cut it open. There was the baby. She took it home and nursed it and cared for it, and the baby grew very fast.

In a couple of years, he became a man. One day he began looking around outside at the empty houses. He asked his mother, "Whose houses are those out there?" She did not want to tell him because she knew he would want to go find them. He kept asking. So one day she had to tell him, "Those are your uncles' houses and your relatives' houses."

He asked, "Where are my uncles and my relatives?"

His mother told him, "They went to sea to hunt, and they disappeared."

"Oh, I want to go look for them," he insisted.

"Oh, please don't go," she begged him. "You must stay with me or you too will disappear."

"Oh, I'll be back. I just want to know what became of my uncles and relatives," he said.

She could not hold on to him, so finally she let him go. Before he left, he told his mother to dig a great big hole because he was going to bring back the prisoners.

He made a bow and arrows for himself, then left in a boat. He went

around one bend and then around another, and there sat two old ladies, one
on each side of the river. The first old lady said, "Come over to me. Don't go
to that person over there. She will kill you the same as she did to your relatives."

The other lady said, "Oh, come here, my grandson. You finally came. I'm
so glad to see you. Don't go to that old lady over there." But Xay Tnaey knew
that this other lady was telling him the truth. So he told her, "I've got to find
out what happened to my uncles and relatives. I am going to her."

So he went to this bad old lady. She put her hands in the water. She had a
gaff hook. He had an arrow, and he threw the hook out of the water with the
arrow. "What are you doing with this?" he asked her. She used the gaff hook
to tip the boats over, and the people drowned. Soon he came into her house.
"What's your name?" she asked him.

"Xay Tnaey," he replied.

She laughed, "That's a funny name."

He asked, "What is your name?"

"Necaan Koldaeł Tnaey," she said.

"That's a funny name. Why do you have a name like that? It sounds like
you are eating people's guts," he said.

Then she asked, "Are you hungry? Do you want something to eat?"

"Sure," he said. She took a man's arm and put it over the fire awhile. Then
she put it in a bear-skull dish. She handed it to him. "Here."

He kicked it back to her, and it turned into a bear and growled and
bounced on her. He jumped into his boat quickly. He was rowing as fast as
he could. He looked back and saw her coming in a boat made from a man's
ribs. She yelled, "Wait for me, my grandson."

He waited as she talked. He saw she had her hand in the water with her
hook. He pushed it up with his arrow and said, "What is this? What are you
doing?" Then he took his bow and arrow and shot at the boat, and it broke in
two. She fell in the water. He took the gaff hook and hooked her by the jaw.

He brought the old lady home and asked his mother if she had dug the
hole. She had. He put the old lady in the hole. It was very dirty. He kept her
there for about a week or more, and then she made a deal with him. "If you
let me go, your uncles and relatives will come back here."

The Spruce Root Man said, "How can I know you are telling me the
truth?"

"Trust me," she said. "By midday tomorrow, your relatives will be back."
He let her out that afternoon, and she returned home.

By midday on the next day, they saw three boats coming. Everyone was
singing. "Oh, they're coming back," they said. They came back, and every-

one was happy. They were very glad to see them. They danced all night till dawn. Suddenly, it became very quiet. Xay Tnaey and his mother went to bed. The next morning they went out to see them, and they were all dead. Foam was coming out of their mouths. It was only their spirits that came back.

May the summer be long
and the winter be short.

14

Eyak

The Delta of the Copper River has for the past century been the final home of the Eyak people and their language. Today the language is all but extinct. The prehistory of the people is unknown, but they are believed somehow to have become separated more than three thousand years ago from ancestors of today's Athabaskans, possibly somewhere in what is now interior Alaska or the Yukon Territory. As a result of the separation, their language diverged from a related proto-Athabaskan language (from which today's Athabaskan languages are later descendants). Thus Eyak is not an Athabaskan language, and as observed by Michael Krauss (upon whom we have relied for our information here), it is no closer linguistically to Ahtna than it is to its most geographically distant relative, Navajo.

At the time of European contact, Eyak territory extended along the Gulf of Alaska from southeast of present-day Yakutat nearly to present-day Cordova. In this position, as a small coastal people, the Eyaks were vulnerable to their larger seagoing neighbors, the Tlingits and the Alutiit (inhabitants of the coastal lands westward who spoke a Yupik language). From the southeast the Tlingits moved onto the shore lands of the Eyaks and slowly assimilated them. The Eyaks pushed northwest against the Alutiit, taking the Copper River Delta and the lake, with a village site, bearing an Alutiiq name, *Igya'aq*, which they pronounced *Iiyaaq*, in English *Eyak*. It means "throat" in the sense of outlet from the lake into a river, now known as the Eyak River. The people themselves became identified by this name, but relations between them and the Alutiit remained hostile. On the other hand, although the Tlingit language bore an even more distant relationship to Eyak than did proto-Athabaskan, Tlingit and Eyak cultures had important resemblances, especially owing to Tlingit dominance and expansion.

Extant Eyak narratives appear to have been strongly influenced by Tlingit oral tradition and to a somewhat lesser extent by Alutiiq. Similarities between Eyak and Athabaskan stories may be ancient (from storytelling in the time of their common linguistic ancestor) as well as recent (from contact especially with Ahtna). The Eyaks distinguished between the two major genres, as Krauss has pointed out, in their language *tsahkł* (distant-time narratives) and *wəxah* (historical accounts). Prominent among *tsahkł* was the Raven cycle. Krauss has identified several other subclasses, including stories of animals only, of animals interacting with humans, of land otters ("which occupy a special place in Eyak folklore"), and of other beings not clearly human or animal. He also regards the short moralistic tales designed for instruction of children as *tsahkł* because they are developed with characters typical of the genre. The other major genre, *wəxah*, includes narratives of warfare, in particular nineteenth-century battles with the Alutiit, and accounts of shamanistic activity.

Anthropologists Kaj Birket-Smith and Frederica de Laguna were the first to collect Eyak tales, when in the spring of 1933, they spent seventeen days at Cordova. Old Man Dude, one of their informants, reported that all distant-time narratives were supposed to be sung. Galushia Nelson, their principal informant, added that they were supposed to be repeated word-perfect, but he did not remember which were to be sung. He also stated that each story had a traditional title. Mr. Nelson had been educated at the Chemawa boarding school for Indians at Salem, Oregon, and had lived away from Alaska for ten years. Because of his fluency in English, he was the ideal interpreter (in both senses) for Birket-Smith and de Laguna. In telling the stories, however, he appears to have relied almost wholly upon his wife, Anna, either through her prompting while he narrated or by translating orally (sometimes in writing) into English as she narrated in Eyak. Conversely, the exact nature of his influence upon the stories as recorded by Birket-Smith and de Laguna, who, of course, did not know the Eyak language, is not known. They published their detailed ethnographical study, including the narratives, in 1938.

Twenty-five years later, Krauss began his intensive study of Eyak with the few remaining speakers of the language. One of those speakers, who became his paramount collaborator, was Anna Harry, widow of Galushia Nelson (who had died in 1939), remarried to Sampson Harry, a Tlingit of Yakutat. Mrs. Harry herself had moved there, learning the Tlingit language, adapting to Tlingit ways, but remaining inherently, individualistically, Eyak.

She had been born on January 6, 1906, in Cordova, the last Eyak community. After seeing her pregnant mother murdered, she was raised but neglected in an Eyak family, sleeping by the fire beside dogs. She was twelve years old when she married Galushia Nelson, who had returned to his homeland six years earlier. Principally as a result of the four salmon canneries that had been operating in this region since 1889, employing five hundred or more Caucasians and Asians, who together outnumbered Eyaks in the area by about three to one, Eyak society had disintegrated. The young wife was at one time abducted by a cannery crew. Yet when her husband fell ill with tuberculosis, she had to work at a cannery to support their four sons, all of whom died in middle age or younger. These and the few other details of her life, as presented by Birket-Smith and de Laguna and by Krauss, illustrate both personal tragedy and, symbolically, the tragic fate of the Eyak people. Yet they illuminate the meaning and significance of her stories, told in a style that Krauss has called "cheerful and warm-hearted." She died on February 1, 1982, but, Krauss says, "Her spirit is indomitable."

Krauss recorded Mrs. Harry's narratives in Yakutat in 1963 and 1965, primarily on tape but partially in writing from her dictation. He transcribed the tapes in Cordova, assisted by Lena Saska Nacktan, one of the other last speakers of Eyak, since deceased. From 1965 to 1969 he edited the Eyak texts, made English translations and detailed annotation, and privately published the whole. Shortly after Mrs. Harry's death, he published ten of her sixty narratives in a commemorative volume, *In Honor of Eyak: The Art of Anna Nelson Harry*. As introduction to this book, Krauss has dealt incisively with Eyak history and compassionately with the author's life. He has organized the ten stories in sections corresponding to the major themes with which Mrs. Harry was concerned: greatness and smallness, good and evil, husband and wife, identity and conflict, and the beginning and end of Eyak history. Krauss has written interpretive headnotes to the thematic sections and, in the form of annotation, extensive commentary on linguistic, ethnographic, and esthetic features of each story.

Our three selections are from this book. To them Krauss appended for contrast the versions told thirty years earlier through the medium of Galushia Nelson's English translations, and we include these as well. (Krauss considers it a dual stroke of fortune that differing versions of these narratives by the same storyteller exist at all, in that Mrs. Nelson chose to tell them in 1933, and without specific prompting from Krauss to repeat them, Mrs. Harry told them again in the 1960s.) Mrs. Nelson had learned the stories, she told Birket-Smith and de Laguna, from Old Chief Joe, and in 1933 she narrated them in a traditional way. Our readers will see that in the 1960s she told them in a profoundly different way, the result, Krauss believes, of her lifetime's experience with the human condition and with the state of nations.

We follow Krauss in pairing "Lake-Dwarves" with "Giant Rat." In them, he sees Mrs. Harry's art as comparable to Jonathan Swift's in the first two parts of *Gulliver's Travels* (the Voyages to Lilliput and Brobdingnag). In each pair of tales, perspectives are played off against one another, but the author's own perspective comprises them all to reveal transcendent truths about human beings and their societies. Krauss suggests that only one born of and inspirited by a tiny nation could create narratives of such penetrating insight into the relative nature of size and importance of nations: for Swift, observing Ireland against the hostilities of England and France; for Mrs. Harry, the Eyaks between the Tlingits and the Alutiit; for us all, the nations of the future and whatever may be in store for us.

"Two Sisters" is another fine example of Mrs. Harry's art. With it she has seamlessly linked *tsahkł* with *wəxah* by making a girl who married a dog in a distant-time story the sister of a woman who took vengeance against Alutiit in a historical narrative. The development hinges upon ironic reversals and the use of spirit power in unexpected ways. But Mrs. Harry is doing much more than skillfully combining what were originally two disparate tales. Out of the devastating experiences of her own lifetime, Krauss believes, she reveals "that real life challenges our moral understanding, and that real morality often lies deeper than the surface we most easily see."

In recent reflections expressed to the editors, Krauss spoke of the utter uniqueness of Mrs. Harry's narrative art, an insight he has gained since he published these stories nearly twenty years ago. Her stories are atypical of any other oral art with which he is familiar. By the time Mrs. Harry was narrating the stories in the 1960s, her society no longer existed for her; she no longer had a traditional audience, so was freed from all restraints of adherence to traditional bonds and was, in effect, expressing her philosophical perceptions for listeners or readers in future times and other places. The three stories we present here, in their versions from the 1960s, Krauss regards as transcendental. Mrs. Harry's achievement of this transcendent freedom, however, was tragic, and she makes her narrative art serve as a warning for us all.

SUGGESTIONS FOR FURTHER READING

Birket-Smith, Kaj, and Frederica de Laguna. *The Eyak Indians of the Copper River Delta, Alaska*. 1938. Reprint, New York: AMS Press, 1976.

de Laguna, Frederica. "Eyak." In *Northwest Coast*, vol. 7 of *Handbook of North American Indians*. Washington DC: Smithsonian Institution, 1990.

Johnson, John F. C., comp. *Eyak Legends of the Copper River Delta, Alaska*. Anchorage: Chugach Heritage Foundation, n.d.

Krauss, Michael E. *Eyak Texts*. Fairbanks: n.p., 1970.

———, comp. and ed. *In Honor of Eyak: The Art of Anna Nelson Harry*. Fairbanks: Alaska Native Language Center, 1982.

Lake-Dwarves

A person it was,
he was going around.[1]
Just going around he was,
he came upon those who live around lakes.
They're dwarves,[2]
around lakes.
He stayed there,
watching them,
those lake-dwarves.
They were boating around in canoes.
Canoes,
little ones,
were simply full inside of them.
They were boating around,
two [canoes].

At that point a mouse[3] it was,
it came out.
That was a brown bear,[4]
a brown bear for them,
a mouse.
They saw it.
They got in a hubbub over it,
that mouse.
They were going to kill it.
Their bows-and-arrows,
they shot it.
Finally they killed it,

that mouse.
A mouse
lo,
they saw another one,
again.
They were going to kill it too.

The man was watching that,
"Wha-?
what is that?"
he was thinking about it,
people.

They killed that last one and then,
they all landed and,
they dragged them up the shore,
those mice.
Their innards,
they were butchering them,
they butchered them.
How,
brown bears are butchered,
they were butchering them like that.
Its skin,
they took it off.[5]
It was being loaded into the boats,
the meat,
the mouse-meat.
Quite a number of them were struggling with loads of it.[6]
Two [were carrying] a hindquarter,
they were carrying a mouse-thigh,
into a boat.
Its ribs,
its spine,
a mouse-spine.
That lesser little mouse,
a small one,
that was a black bear,
it was a black bear for them.

They were still bustling about over them and then,
that person took one of them,
he grabbed one of them,
the wee people.
He grabbed one of them.
While they were preoccupied with the mice,[7]
he grabbed one of them.
Then he stuck him down in under his belt.

Thus he said to him,
he said thus to the person,
"These, things I hunt with,
I'll give them to you,
if you let me go,
if you release me,"
he said to him,
to that person.
"Let me go.
You'll become a great hunter,
if you let me go."
He was begging him quite pitifully,
that little fellow.
So then,
he said to him,
"I'll show you,
this which we kill things with."
Thus he gave it to him.
It was the size of his thumb.
It was a leaf.[8]
Strawberry,
it was like a strawberry-leaf.
"This,
you shall put it inside your rifle.
When you're going to shoot anything,"
he said to him.
He let him go.

They were already about to leave in their boats.
They were waiting for him,

who had disappeared,
who had been missing from among them there,
they had missed him.
He had disappeared from their midst.
So then,
he let him go and he was running back along down there.
He ran back to amongst his kinfolk.
He was asked,
"Where are your weapons?"[9]
"I gave them away.[10]
That's how I managed to get back here.
A huge fellow,[11]
big as a tree he was,
grabbed me.
I paid him off.[12]
Forasmuch as I paid him with all my things,
he released me.
This is how I managed to get back here."
"Maybe it was tree-people,"[13]
they said to him.
"No,
he was a person.
He was the size of a tree though.
A huge person.
He was enormous.
He had clothes on.
He stuck me down in under his belt.
Then[14] I kept trying to pay him off so he'd let me go.
He let me go.
This that I shoot with,
I gave him my hunting-leaf.
For that it was he let me go,"
he said thus to his kinfolk,
"Quick, hurry up![15]
He'll come upon us again!"

They put out.
They got across the lake.
They boated home.

Goodness, how those women came running down![16]
Their little husbands[17] had come boating home to them.
They had killed a brown bear,
and they had killed a black bear.
They had brought them ashore.
They hung them up in the curing-house.
They did that,
right away,
those women.
It was already evening,
nevertheless they hung them up.
Just as is they hung them up,
that meat.
The next day they would cut it into strips.
They went to bed.
It was expected at any time,
that that man would come.
They had boated clear across the lake.
That man could not walk across the lake.[18]
It was too deep,
that lake.
It was deep.

He didn't go there.
He went home,
he too.
Just looking around he was for black bears,
he saw them,
lake-dwarves.[19]

NOTES

[Krauss has provided thorough, detailed annotation to this and the other stories.
Keyed to both Eyak text and English translation, the notes explain Eyak expressions
and the choices Krauss made in translating them, and they call attention to certain
features of the Eyak language that Mrs. Harry drew upon for satiric and other purposes. Since we reprint only the translations, we have omitted some notes and have
modified others. All notes appearing here are essentially Krauss's. Most are reprinted exactly as they appear in *In Honor of Eyak* and are not enclosed in quotation
marks. Those that we have modified identify the content as Krauss's by naming him

and use quotation marks around his words. Readers who make further study of these stories must consult the complete annotation in his book.]

1. Krauss notes that the Eyak expression, literally "is going around [on foot]," often means "hunting." — Eds.

2. Krauss points out that the Eyak word, used literally to mean the young of animals, is also used figuratively in the sense of "miniature" and that Mrs. Harry applies it to humans with comic effect. — Eds.

3. "Mouse" or "rat." I have arbitrarily translated it "mouse" throughout this tale, while in the next tale I have arbitrarily translated it "rat."

4. Note that Anna makes the same comparison between mouse/rat and bear in the next tale, but there we encounter a giant rat with hair "longer than a black bear's fur."

5. Krauss believes that Mrs. Harry has deliberately omitted from the verb the standard Eyak prefix used in referring to a skin or pelt and that her omission means "that it would be ridiculous to speak of a mouse-skin as a real pelt." — Eds.

6. Here her use of a prefix results in the literal meaning "were handling [puny] objects [and having a hard time]." The Eyak expression, Krauss points out, enables her to convey a derisive tone. — Eds.

7. Krauss notes that the greater part of the line in Eyak means, literally, "they were excited [in a hubbub, hurry] over the mouse/mice" and that a suffix (literally "behind, under cover of") adds the idea that the man could take advantage of this. — Eds.

8. A magical plant, Krauss notes. — Eds.

9. Literally "those things which you'll kill something/hunt with," standard term for "weapons."

10. Literally "I gave them to someone."

11. With awesome emphasis.

12. Agitated, partly breathless and distorted.

13. In Birket-Smith and de Laguna, Tale 20, there is an account of these beings, who eat people.

14. Krauss writes that the Eyak word means "literally both 'after that' and 'from there.'" — Eds.

15. Mrs. Harry spoke the latter part of the line, Krauss notes, in "a quickly fading, urgently hushed whisper." — Eds.

16. Spoken with high-pitched, resonant voice, only slightly dropping at end, as if very impressed or amazed, but here, of course, mockingly.

17. Krauss notes that Mrs. Harry here employs two suffixes "used for certain nouns referring only to humans, this time making extra-certain that they are treated as humans in her language." — Eds.

18. Anna starts by saying *k'aadi'daa* "never would" or "it would be pointless to,"

but changes to *k'udeedah* "impossible to," here wavering between the man's point of view and the dwarves', since only from their point of view would the lake be too deep to step across.

19. Whispered with practically no lung-air, barely audible, and, as I remember, with a slight smile and twinkle in her eye.

Giant Rat

They were boating along,
one man with her,
they were probably boating for berries.
They were boating along and the woman said thus,
— they were boating in front of that monster's place — [1]
"I wish we might see it,"
thus the woman said.
The man said thus,
"Don't ask for trouble!"[2]
He said thus and it emerged behind them,
that rat.[3]
The canoe capsized with it.
It emerged and the man [grabbed] the child,
he grabbed the child.
He jumped onto the big rat.
They had capsized.
It was they,
the woman of them had disappeared.

Then it went inside with them.
They went in with it and then,
he got off it.
They had gone into its hole with it.
It stuck its tail out over there.
Simply everything was sticking out.[4]
The child,
he held her.[5]
She was afraid of it.

Nevertheless he lived a long while with it,
with that monster.

When it got dark it would go out
— it would go hunting —
to hunt.
Seals,
it would kill them for them.
All these sorts of ducks,
it would kill them.
It would put them in under itself.
Thus it cooked them.
It cooked them for them.
It would lie down on top of them.
When they cooked,
it would give them to them.
Then they would eat them.
When it went out,
that person would try it,
those spruce-roots,[6]
to climb out there.
He had been living with it for quite some time and,
he tried it.
He climbed out there.
It hadn't come back here yet and he ran back there,
again.
He got back and then pretty soon it was coming in.
Inside it would straightaway look for them.
They were sitting right there.
It cooked for them.
It would lay it in under itself,
what it had killed,
it cooked it,
it cooked it for them.
Thus they ate it.

His child,
a girl-child,
wasn't big.

When it was pitch-dark it would go [out].
As it started to get light it would come back in.
Thus it did and then,
he put her on his back,
that girl,
and
he climbed out there with her.
There had come a little daylight and,
he had climbed out there with her.
Before he had gotten far,
he was going along with her and the rat came back home.
It missed them.
It started banging its tail around.
It knocked everything down.

He had gotten back there.
He had gotten back home to among people.
He got back with the child and then,
he said thus to people,
"Those young crows,
young ravens,
snare them.
Snare them,
lots of them."
So they were snared,
they were snared.

He would look there and,
the moon had become full and then,
they went there.
It wouldn't come out when the moon was full,
that rat.
It would stay right at home.

It would never go out.
They packed them on their backs,
those young ravens.
Young ravens,
they packed them there.

They sharpened them.
They sharpened them,
those knives,
axes.
They dumped them down,
they dumped those young ravens down there,
where there was a hole going down.
"Now then,[7]
throw the ravens down,
[to see] will they quiet down."
They clamored,
they clamored.
It just jerked it down,
its tail.
Not far.
They chopped its tail off.
They chopped its tail off.
Thus they killed it,
that big rat,
monster rat.

Halfway forward [out of] there it moved.
It moved halfway forward [out of] there.
Then,
they went back,
those people.
Then they killed it,
that big rat.
Then they went there by boat.
They were going to tow it forward to the shore.
They couldn't.[8]
They left it right there.
There was a big tide and it drifted forward out of there.

It was taller than a very big whale,
that monster rat.
Its teeth were long,
that rat.
The lower ones weren't, though.[9]

Its hair was longer than black-bear hair,[10]
that rat-hair.

It floated forward there.
It was washing around.
They towed it ashore.
They butchered it to get its skin.
They cut it open and then,
all sorts of things were in its stomach.
These people's bones were in its stomach,
people's bones.
People who had been disappearing,
they didn't know what had become of them.
They were the ones that big rat had been killing.
Some of them,
their skulls were in its stomach,
in the rat-stomach.
That's why they butchered it.
Already its hair was going,
some place[s].
Where it was good,
that part they dried.

They did thus to it and so,
then they called a potlatch.
People called a potlatch.
Then they exhibited it before people's eyes,
what had been killing their relatives.
Not just anybody could use it,
that rat-skin.
Only a high-class person,
a high-class person would sit on it,
that rat-skin,
monster rat-skin.
They had a potlatch and,
thus they said about it,
all the people,
"No cheapskate will sit on it.
Only those who are high-class people are the ones who will sit on it.
Too many people have fallen victim to this.

These poor wretches,
it has killed them.
That's why only high-class people will sit on it,"
they kept saying.

Then a different tribe at a different place,
they wanted it for themselves,
that skin,
that rat-skin.
They went to fight with each other over it.
They made war over it,
a different tribe,
inhabitants of a different land,
they made war over it.
It wasn't taken from their hands.
Many people died.
But it wasn't taken from their hands.
That high-class person who used to sit on it,
he was the first killed,
in the quest for that rat-skin.
Therefore there were some among them who would not abandon it.[11]
It didn't concern them how many would perish on account of it,
would be killed,
in the pursuit of that skin.

They had finished the battle and then,
that high-class person['s corpse] from among the other [dead] people,
they picked it up.
It was put inside the rat's tail.
They wrapped it around it,
and,
they burned it up with the rat-skin.

(In the old days they didn't use to bury one another.
They used to cremate one another.
Whoever died they used to cremate.
Their charred remains,
they used to gather them into a box.
Their bones,
they used to gather them into a box.

Into a little box,
they used to gather them.)

Thus they did to it.
Then that other tribe found out about it,
that that high-class person's bones had been gathered together,
into that box.
They threw it in the water.
They packed it on their backs up onto yonder mountain with those [bones
      inside it] and,
threw it in the water.[12]

Then there arose more trouble over it,
again.
There was another fight over it.
Those whose high-class person's bones were thrown in the water,
they wiped them out.[13]
They wiped them out.
Only the women,
women it was,
children,
they didn't kill them,
and old men they didn't kill.
The men in their prime,
they slaughtered them all.
Those people,
those who had thrown the high-class person's bones into the water,
thus happened to them.[14]

Then they grew up,
those children got big.
They wanted to get revenge for it but,
they didn't get revenge for it.
They got wiped out,[15]
those whose high-class person's bones got thrown into the water,
those of another land.

They were people just like each other,
though living at a different place,
living in a different land.

From Sitka here,[16]
as we live here at Yakutat,
they live.
Thus they waged war over a rat-skin.
People just like each other.
What good is a rat-skin?[17]
But,
they went through with that.[18]
They got wiped out and then,
nothing more could happen to them,
those others.
There was no way,
they couldn't wage war with anyone any more.
They got wiped out.[19]

That's all.

NOTES

[As with the notes to "Lake-Dwarves", the notes here are Krauss's, some containing our editorial modifications. Those reprinted verbatim from *In Honor of Eyak* are not enclosed in quotation marks. In those which we have edited, quotation marks enclose Krauss's words and square brackets enclose ours; reference to Krauss in a note without quotation marks but labeled as ours (note 12 for example) indicates our paraphrase of his content. For note 19 Krauss has added for this edition a second main clause, which did not appear in *In Honor of Eyak*.]

1. Krauss elaborates: "that is, offshore by where the monster reputedly had its hole. This apparently was in a cliff, with two entrances, one vertical at the top and one horizontal at the foot of the cliff." — Eds.

2. *Yǫxuh* — "don't!", an urgent command not to violate a taboo, which would bring disaster.

3. See note 3 to "Lake-Dwarves." — Eds.

4. Exact interpretation of this sentence not clear in general context. Anna apparently starts to mention *geets'* "spruce-roots" (in anticipation . . . [of her reference to spruce roots in lines to follow]), changes to *łi'q' yaayuu* "everything, all sorts of things."

5. For this and the next two sentences, Krauss notes, the grammatical subject "could be either the man or his little daughter." — Eds.

6. Unfinished, not grammatically connected to the rest of the sentence. There were, no doubt, spruce-roots hanging down from above, on which the man could climb up.

7. The idea here is that the ravens would be quiet if the rat was absent, but if the rat was there, their noise would wake and stir up the rat.

8. Compare the Lake-Dwarves tale, where the dwarves' great struggle to butcher and load the mouse-meat into their canoes is described.

9. Barely intelligible, rapid, and distorted.

10. This is the only explicit comparison of the Giant Rat with a bear, definitely tying it together with the Lake-Dwarves tale, actually told the following day. Nevertheless, the fundamental comparison is unmistakable if not explicit throughout.

11. Ambiguous as translated; it may be either the quest or the rat-fleece they are unwilling to abandon.

12. Krauss notes that the situation of something being thrown down from a mountaintop or of a person's plummeting down from a summit appears in a number of Mrs. Harry's narratives. — Eds.

13. This and the following line are "ambiguous, as translated," Krauss writes. — Eds.

14. Articulated in a barely audible whisper. This then clears up the ambiguity [of the earlier lines reading "they wiped them out"]. The tribe that had the skin in the first place and whose high-class person's bones were thrown in the water massacred the foreign tribe. But this is in partial contradiction to [the fifth line that follows].

15. Internally and externally contradictory. Those whose high-class person's bones were thrown in the water were not the foreign tribe, nor, according to [the last reference to this matter], were they the ones who got massacred.

16. That is, "There are people from Sitka living here at Yakutat just as we do," implying that "Though they are foreigners they are like us, and we live together in peace."

17. Anna chuckles.

18. Krauss writes that a literal translation would be "finished doing it to it," but that in meaning it is "something like 'to the bitter end' or 'fought to the finish.'" — Eds.

19. It matters not at all, of course, which side annihilated which in this bloody war over a rat-skin, and Anna is probably playing with the nonspecificity of Eyak third-person pronouns in Eyak grammar to make this point.

Maagudətl'əlahdəx̱unhyuu

Around-the-Lake-People [1933]

Dwarfs as big as a thumb used to hunt and fish around the country. They were found around Strawberry Point [on Hinchinbrook Island, near Boswell Bay] at the small lake there. The little women row; the little men hunt and fish. A human captured a little man who had become tangled in some roots. The dwarf gave the man all his hunting outfit — spears and bows and arrows — to let him go. One spear with an agate point he hated to part with.

When he was turned loose he returned home, but his people had gone outside the breakers. He hollered for them to come back and get him. One of his relatives came through the breakers for him. They all started home in canoes and on the way they saw a mouse, which was a brown bear to them. They all landed to try and kill him.

The little man without hunting implements was killed by the bear, for he had no way to defend himself. The other people killed the bear. The bear was cut up in small pieces and left there because he had killed one of their people.

They put the body of the dead man in a canoe without examining it at all. His relatives took the body home. The wife ran down to meet her husband; she didn't know he was dead. The skin of his head had been pulled off. The wife and children ran down to meet him. They were happy that their man was coming home.

The wife, when she saw her husband's head, tore a piece from the bottom of her skirt and bandaged his head. They took the body and placed it in front of the left front house-post. They left the body outside for eight days. On the eighth day they took the body inside.

Toward noon the body began to move. Only the wife was there. Right at noon he moved more and more until he lifted his head. He sat up and scratched his head. He asked his wife what had happened and she told him that a bear had killed him. He asked what they had done with the bear. She said they had killed it, cut it in bits, and left it there. He asked who had brought his body home.

He told his wife not to worry about him, and left, taking two men with him. They went to Yakutatik[?]. They were gone about a year. They came back at the time when the birds start to lay eggs. When the people saw them coming they were excited. Each man was coming in a separate canoe and all three were full of brown-bear skins. When they landed the people lifted them up and carried them to the house. The man was made chief of the tribe.

When they had finished eating, he said to his wife: "I guess I got even with those bears."

He gave his oldest daughter to a man. She knew everything — all about making baskets and keeping house. She had already promised to marry another man, but she had to obey her father and left the first man. The first man asked her husband to dig clams with him. They were digging as the tide was coming in. He made the husband stay on a sand spit. He was drowned there and they never found the body. He turned into a shrimp [or sand-hopper?].

The other man went home and told several different stories about what had happened. The drowned man's wife had a dream that the man had caused her husband to be drowned by the tide and in the dream her husband told her he had become a sand-hopper. People asked the man if that was true. He said yes. But they did nothing to him.

That's all. *Dəq'eedah q'ə'aw.*

[These dwarfs had many different tribes around the lake, like the different tribes of Indians.]

Łuundiyahsluw

The Big Mouse [1933]

Big mouse living under a cliff. He come out every time someone pass in a canoe. Kill them and eat them. He killed several people like that. There was one old man taking three women to pick berries. Old man knew the mouse's song. If you knew it he wouldn't bother you. Sing it when passing. Old man was singing.

The youngest woman said: "I wish we see this mouse."

Old man said: "Don't! What you say that for?"

Just a few minutes later, the water turned red under the cliff and spread out to the canoe. The old man was still singing the mouse's song. Mouse come out backward — halfway out. He put his tail out of water and dropped it on the canoe. The old man, when he dropped his tail, jumped on the mouse's tail. He hang onto the tail. The women were all killed.

Mouse went back under the cliff with the old man. He was saved. The mouse came into a big room under the cliff. The man went to the other side of the cave from the mouse. The man sang the mouse's song so the mouse didn't bother him. He got some feed for the man. The mouse only went hunting at time of no moon, when it's dark. When the mouse goes hunting — there was a root of a tree sticking down from the roof of the cave — he [the man] tried the strength of the root. Later he climbed to the roof. The mouse had a hole clear to the top of the ground where he stuck his tail out. Man climbed clear out but came down before mouse came back from hunting and sat down where he was before. When mouse comes back sometimes he brings back big seal or halibut. He puts it under himself to cook them. When it gets cooked, he bring it out and give it to the man. The man eats it.

At one time the mouse went out toward morning. The mouse was supposed to be home before the raven starts to make a noise. When the mouse left, the man climbed the root and got out. Before he got very far, the mouse came back. The mouse was making all kinds of noise in the cave because he missed the man. He stuck his tail out of the hole and swung it around. The man got home.

At full moon the mouse sleeps sound. When old man got home he told the young man to try to snare a crow. If they snare a crow in full moon time they're going back to mouse's den.

"Sharpen all that you use for your old knives, and sharpen all that you use for your old axe," the old man said.

When they caught the raven they have all knives and axes sharp. They go to where the mouse sticks out his tail. Mouse had his tail sticking out the hole when he's sleeping. (Tail was like a watchman.) The old man sneaked up on him with an axe. He chopped the mouse's tail twice before he cut it off. The mouse pulled the rest of his tail down.

The young man said: "Throw the crow down that hole!"

So the crow started to make all kinds of noise down there. The mouse started to go out under the cliff. He got halfway out before he died. After the mouse died, the old man went down on the root and looked at the mouse. When he found the mouse was dead, he came back up and told the other man. This young man would like to see it. So they went down and looked at it. When they came out, the mouse turned into a rock. The crow came back out of the hole, too.

[The hunter must rise before the crow makes a noise in the morning, or he will not get any game. All the animals are up before the crow. If the crow gets up before an animal does, the animal will die.]

[The Girl and the Dog] [1933]

There was a man and his wife. They had a daughter who was always playing around with the dog.

Her mother told her: "Don't play around with that bitch. Leave her alone."

They were going to move to another place. When they were ready to move, she was playing with the dog. So they left her playing with it. Before they left they tied the girl's head and the bitch's head together and left them like that.

They had a female slave, too.

The slave said: "Wait awhile, I forgotten my *weekshk* [woman's knife]." It was just an excuse to go back and cut the girl and dog apart. She told the girl: "Don't show yourself. I'm going to get a licking if they find I cut you loose."

The slave went back to the boat and they left. The girl was still crying. They went home to where they were before.

After a year, the girl's mother told the slave: "Go to our camp, and throw their bones out. Shovel them out."

So the slave went over there. The slave find the girl and dog. They were still alive. The house was almost full of things to eat. The dog was a good hunter. When the slave went over there, they fed her and gave her all she want to eat. She sneaked a piece of fat under her shirt for her son.

The slave says: "I'm going home now. I'm staying too long. They're going to get after me for it."

The girl said: "If they come back with you — when they land, you run in first. We're not going to let my father and mother in."

The slave got home.

The mother asked her: "Did you shovel the bones out?"

The slave said: "Yes."

That evening when they went to bed, the slave went to bed with her son and gave the fat to her son. After the son ate up the fat, he started to cry for some more, and called for fat: "*K'uq'əx̣dee!*"

The woman asked the slave: "What's wrong with your son? He never cried like that before."

"I tried to feed him with the breast, but it slipped out of his mouth. That's why he cried."

The boy still kept crying. The woman asked the same question.

The slave got mad, and said: "That daughter of yours that you tied to your dog got a house full of meat and gave me all I could eat. I hid a piece of fat for my son. After he ate it up he wants more."

"You want to get up early in the morning. We got to go there early in the morning. Try to stop your son from crying."

So next morning they started before daylight. When they land where the girl and dog were living, the slave grab her son, jump out and run.

The girl asked the slave: "Is that my mother and father?"

The slave said: "Yes."

The girl's mother started to run up, too.

She and her father said: "My poor daughter! My poor daughter!"

The girl pulled down a piece of fat that was hanging and threw it toward her father and mother, and said:

"You didn't think I was your daughter when you tied me to a dog." She said to the fat: "Turn into a glacier!"

It did — between her and her mother and father. The glacier got long, and the father and mother made a bird noise: "*Gak gak.*" It sounded farther and farther away.

Two Sisters

One time it was,
a woman,
sisters,
two of them.[1]
One of them,
however,
had no sense.
Nothing mattered to her.
The other one however was good.
She was a nice person.
A man liked her.
A man liked her,
because she was a nice person.
As for the other one though,
she wasn't thus.
She was a bad person.

She got married,
that girl,
that little sister,[2]
she got married.
She married into a big house.
She got married and then her father and mother,
they built a house.
They built a house.
They built a house.

The other one however not so.
She lived alone.

Her father and mother built a house and then,
they moved away from them.[3]
They moved.
They moved again.
She had a house in a different place again.
She had a big plot of land,
she acquired it.

She had two children and then,
she had children.
Children,
six children she had,
from her husband.
Her husband died on her and then,
she wouldn't remarry.
She didn't want that,
to get remarried.
She would never remarry,
because of those children of hers.
Her children,
she didn't want that,
that anyone should slap their faces and beat them up,
that anybody should beat them up,
those children of hers.
She didn't beat any of them up,
nobody.

Then they got somewhat big.
They had gotten somewhat big and then,[4]
their mother moved with them.
Their mother moved with them and then —
where at? —
Aleuts came upon them.[5]
An Aleut killed some of them.
Those Aleuts,
one boy and one girl,
they killed that woman's children.
They killed them and then,
a paddle,
they wrapped it around her hair,[6]

they wrapped it around her hair,
that girl.
They thrust it under with her [tied to it]
over there,
they thrust it under water.
Simply way under water.
By the hair they held her down.
They had tied her down to a paddle.

As for the boy however,
him they put in under a tree.
They stuffed something in him.
They stuffed moss in his mouth,
Aleuts.

She found out about it and then the mother,
for eight days,
she didn't eat anything.
For eight days she didn't eat.
She was going to cut something.
She was going to cut something,
because of that.
She was going along a long time and then
    on this eighth day she was going along.
She was going along early in the morning,
the mother.
Her children,
she hid them inside.

Then it was a magpie she came upon.
It flew off.
She didn't pay attention to it.[7]

Then,
she killed something.
She cut it.
She cut it,
that land-otter,
she cut it.
She cut a land-otter.

She cut it and then,
then it was,
her mind became like a man's.
Already ten days have passed for her.
Her mind became like a man's and then she boated off.
[For revenge] on them she had cut something.
[For revenge] on those Aleuts she had cut something.

She boated off.
She came upon them.
A woman she was.
She killed them.
Eight — seven Aleuts,
she slaughtered them.
She dashed their brains out.[8]
That woman it was did thus.
For that [revenge] it was she had cut something so,
because of that she became thus.

She killed them and then,
she went back.
Then she said thus,
to her younger sister,
"You should be married already.
You're just clutched onto the underside of dead dogs,[9]
for your senselessness.
You lie with men on housetops,[10]
you lie thus."

That's why that woman,
that sister — [11]
people went.
They were boating along.
They were going to move.
They were going to dry things.
Her old mother was still alive.
Her old father however had died.
Her old mother was alive and so,

her mother too went away.
They were drying fish.

The sister,
the one who didn't have any sense,
her child too,
went away.
They were going to move back from there and then she said thus to her,
"Abandon her right here.
She's too senseless."
A slave they had,
those who were going to dry fish.
She had an old slave.
Then,
They were going to boat back.
With a dog it was they tied them together.[12]
A dog,
with a dog,
they tied them together.
They tied them together and then,
that old slave however said thus,
"Already they're about to put out![13]
My heavens,
I forgot it,
my old ulu.
I'll go back for a moment to get it."
She ran back there.
Just to lie it was she said thus.
With the dog as they were,
she cuts them apart from each other,
that woman.[14]
With the dog their heads had been tied together,
so that they'd die.
Then the slave cut them separate,
with the dog.
She lived there with it and then the dog it was,
it came out of its skin.[15]

She ran back down to shore.
She immediately boated off.

They abandoned her there.
They boated off leaving them right there.

Then that old dog,
the dog it was said thus,
"I'll marry you.
I'll marry you.
I'll take good care of you.
I'll marry you.
I'll go around [hunting game] for you."
So then the woman in turn,
"If you'll take good care of me,
I'll live with you.
Alone this'll be we'll live here."[16]

So then a person it was it turned into with her,
that old dog.
Then the dog it was,[17]
it would go onto the mountains,
to get mountain-goats.
Any of these things,
fish,
all kinds of things,
it would bring in hauls of them.
All kinds of things,
it would drag them to her.
It would pack them to her.
So then the woman would prepare it nicely.
She dried it,
she dried it.

Winter had half passed and then,
to the old slave — [18]
summer was coming.
She boated there.
She was going to boat back there.
She boated back there.
"Shovel them out,
those bones,
shovel them out."

She boated there,
to shovel them out.
She knew it,
that nothing had happened to her,
that woman.
The dog also nothing had happened to it.
She boated there and then,
all sorts of things,
mountain-goat meat,
black-bear meat,
fish she had dried,
in seal-oil.
Mountain-goat fat,
she had dried it.
Then,
she boated back home and then,
she boated back.[19]
"I'm going to boat back,"
thus she said to her.
That woman [said],
"Don't tell it to my mother,
that I'm alive.
That I'm alive,
you won't tell her.
Be sure not to tell her that."

She went back,
she boated back,
and then she said thus,
thus she said,
"I already shoveled them out."

They went to bed and then,
a bit of fat apparently,
she had jammed it in her pocket for her kid.
So then she lay down and then she gave it to him.
Then that kid, though, cried again for some more,
for fat,
that mountain-goat fat be given to him.
Then she said,[20]

"Quiet down,
quiet down!
Where would I get any from to give you?"
Then someone said thus to her,
"What is it,
that he's crying for,
what?"
"It's those whom you tied together,
their house is simply bursting open,
from abundance of food.
It's fairly bursting open."
So then the mother said thus,
"Hurry,
hurry,
hurry!
We'll boat there."

They boated there and then,
the slave,
she jumped out.
She jumped out of the canoe,
and she ran up from shore.
She grabbed her kid and ran up from the shore.
They were coming up from shore and that fat was hanging up.[21]
She cut it down from there.
She threw it out.
A big glacier immediately, that fat,
it expanded by there.
Gone.
They didn't get to them.

Then,
he went onto the glacier,
onto the glacier the husband went.[22]
Then he fell down on the glacier.
He fell down and he died,
that husband.
She went to find him and then,
she too,
the slave too.

Then just owls,
they became owls.
They flew away.
They became owls,
those two,
the boy-child also,
the three of them,
owls,
they flew away.
Owls they were.

Since then one doesn't speak any further about them.[23]

NOTES

[The notes here are in keeping with those for the preceding stories: Krauss's notes reprinted verbatim are not enclosed in quotation marks; our modifications of his notes attribute the content to him and enclose his words in quotation marks. The second part of note 5 is our editorial addition.]

1. Literally "woman (or girl), siblings, two [people] (or twins)."

2. Literally "little sibling," but not necessarily the younger.

3. The father and mother (probably the bride's, according to the custom of matrilocal residence) built a separate house for themselves or for the new couple, or a new house for them all. The youngest sister was excluded from this arrangement. Now it seems that the young couple moved again, to their own house and "land" elsewhere.

4. Note that in smooth narrative style it is not uncommon at some points to repeat the last part of the sentence as the beginning of the next, as Anna does twice in a row here.

5. Krauss writes, "This might also be interpreted here that they came upon the Aleuts." He notes that the preceding line ("where at? — ") may be interpreted either as "where [did] they [move] to?" or "where [did] their [encounter take place] at?" The Aleuts are Alutiit, inhabitants of the coasts of the Gulf of Alaska, not Aleuts of the Aleutian Chain. The term *Aleuts* was historically applied to both groups, even though they spoke different languages and were culturally distinct. — Eds.

6. This sentence says that they wrapped a paddle around her hair, where it is surely meant that they wrapped her hair around a paddle.

7. This quest for shaman's power generally involved fasting in the woods for eight days, and cutting the tongue of an animal, especially of a land-otter. The meaning of the encounter with the magpie in the quest in this story is not clear to me, however.

8. Krauss also gives a literal translation: "Against something she kept banging their heads." — Eds.

9. Very strong version of standard Eyak expression for a promiscuous woman.

10. Very unusual, colorful, and powerfully effective grammar here, "you are in a constant state of lying repeatedly many times with men." The second instance of the verb here "to lie down with someone" is much more ordinary.

11. Anna breaks the sentence to go into how the whole family moved to summer fish-camp, then abandoned the "bad" daughter there when leaving.

12. The structure of these two sentences is evidently good Eyak, though not good English.

13. Krauss notes that Mrs. Harry, in character as the slave, spoke the line "with great urgency." Translated literally it means "they're about to go [by boat] out to sea." — Eds.

14. Again, good Eyak but not good English.

15. This sentence belongs after the next four sentences. Anna starts to go on to say how they lived together, then interrupts, remembering how the slave hurriedly rejoined the family that was abandoning the girl and the dog.

16. Very rapid and fading [ending in a whisper].

17. Voice style suddenly slow, deliberate, resonant, characteristic when Anna describes the abundant take of a good provider.

18. This was probably late winter or early spring, a lean time of the year, and the people probably very short of food. Someone is going to give the slave the command to shovel out the bones, finally given [beginning five lines] later.

19. This sentence belongs after the next [eight lines, at the beginning of the next verse segment].

20. Krauss notes that Mrs. Harry's delivery here, as the slave woman, is "very rapidly articulated, to express impatience and irritation." — Eds.

21. The rest were in pursuit. The slave is ahead of them, sees the fat, and transforms it into a huge obstacle.

22. Spoken in a rapidly fading voice.

23. The exact outcome is not certain. The girl who married the dog is not mentioned explicitly at all, but she is certainly one of those who ran away and became owls. Her dog-husband apparently perished in following her. The slave makes the second owl, and the third is the male child, apparently of the slave, already mentioned, there being no mention of any children from the marriage of the girl and dog. The horned owl is a sinister bird for both the Eyaks and the Yakutat Tlingits.

Source Acknowledgments

The following stories appear here by permission of the copyright holders.

Belle Deacon, "Deg Hit'an Gixudhoy (The People's Stories)," "Taxghozr (Polar Bear)," and "Nił'oqay Ni'idaxin (The Man and Wife)," were published in *Engithidong Xugixudhoy (Their Stories of Long Ago)* (Fairbanks: Alaska Native Language Center and Iditarod Area School District, 1987).

Catherine Attla, "Doz K'ikaal Yee Nogheełt'uyhdlee (The One Who Used to Put His Nephew into a Fishtail)" and "Dotson' Sa Ninin"atłtseen (Great Raven Who Shaped the World)," were published in *Sitsiy Yugh Noholnik Ts'in' (As My Grandfather Told It): Traditional Stories from the Koyukuk*, transcribed by Eliza Jones, translated by Eliza Jones and Melissa Axelrod (Fairbanks: Yukon Koyukuk School District and Alaska Native Language Center, 1983).

Catherine Attla, "K'etl'enbaalots'ek," "Dekeltlaal De'ot Etldleeyee (The Woodpecker Who Starved His Wife)," and "Ełts'eeyh Denaa (Wind Man)" were published in *Bekk'aatugh Ts'uhuney (Stories We Live By): Traditional Koyukon Athabaskan Stories*, revised edition, transcribed by Eliza Jones, translated by Eliza Jones and Chad Thompson (Fairbanks: Yukon Koyukuk School District and Alaska Native Language Center, 1996).

Katherine Peter, selection from "Gwichyaa Zheh Gwats'à' Tr'ahàajil (We Go to Fort Yukon)," and chapter 7 "Jalgiitsik, Tł'yahdik Hàa (Chalkyitsik and Tł'yahdik)," were published in *Neets'ąįį Gwiindaii (Living in the Chandalar Country)*, second edition, retranslated by Adeline Raboff (Fairbanks: Alaska Native Language Center, 1992). The stories appear here by permission of the publisher and the author.

Katherine Peter, "Shaaghan (The Old Woman)" and "K'aiiheenjik," were published in *Dinjii Zhuu Gwandak (Gwich'in Stories)* (Juneau: Alaska State Operated Schools, 1974).

Gertie Tom, "Gyò Cho Chú (Living at Big Salmon, 1930s and 1940s)," "K'ènlū Mǎn (Northern Lake, 1944)," and "K'ènlū Mǎn (Northern Lake, 1956)," were published in *Èkeyi: Gyò Cho Chú (My Country: Big Salmon River)* (Whitehorse, Yukon: Yukon Native Language Centre, 1987).

John Dickson, "Gédéni Gēs Gagáh Nédē (The Girl Who Lived with Salmon)," translated by Pat Moore, appears by permission of the translator.

Maudie Dick, "Dzǫhdié' Gųh Chō Dzéhhīn (Dzǫhdié' Kills the Giant Worm)," translated by Pat Moore, appears by permission of the translator.

Angela Sidney, "Getting Married" and "The Stolen Woman," were published in Julie Cruikshank, with Angela Sidney, Kitty Smith, and Annie Ned, *Life Lived Like a Story: Life Stories of Three Yukon Native Elders* (Lincoln: University of Nebraska Press, 1990; copyright © 1990 by the University of Nebraska Press).

Annie Ned, "Our Shagóon, Our Family History" and "How First This Yukon Came to Be: Crow and Beaverman," were published in Julie Cruikshank, with Angela Sidney, Kitty Smith, and Annie Ned, *Life Lived Like a Story: Life Stories of Three Yukon Native Elders* (Lincoln: University of Nebraska Press, 1990; copyright © 1990 by the University of Nebraska Press).

Kitty Smith, "Naakw: Devilfish, or Octopus, Helper," [To Build a Fire], and "The First Time They Knew K'och'èn, White Man," were published in Julie Cruikshank, with Angela Sidney, Kitty Smith, and Annie Ned, *Life Lived Like a Story: Life Stories of Three Yukon Native Elders* (Lincoln: University of Nebraska Press, 1990; copyright © 1990 by the University of Nebraska Press).

Mary Tyone, "Stsǫǫ Shyaan Ǫǫnign': Ch'aldzeek Shyii Dineh Gaay Na'ithädn (My Old Grandmother: The Little Man Standing in the Moon)," "Dlign Mba' Hehk'aayh Ts'ä̀' (When the Tree Squirrels Cut Fish)," "Ch'ǫǫt'üüdn Ch'aachin' Shyiit Eedah (When Horsefly Was Living in a Stump)," and "Taatsaan' Dzänh eh Ǫǫnign' (Raven and Muskrat Story)," were published in *Ttheek'ädn Ut'iin Yaaniidą̀' Ǫǫnign' (Old-time Stories of the Scottie Creek People): Stories told in Upper Tanana Athabaskan by Mary Tyone, Ts'ä̀' Yahnik*, transcribed and edited by James Kari (Fairbanks: Alaska Native Language Center, 1996). The stories appear here by permission of the publisher and the author.

Gaither Paul, "The Child Who Was Stolen by a Brush Indian" and "How Dentalium Necklaces Came to the Country," were published in *Stories for My Grandchildren* (Fairbanks: Alaska Native Language Center, 1980).

Peter John, chapter 1, "Stand for What Is Right" ("I Learned the Indian Way" and "Strong People"), selections from chapter 2, "Old Ways" ("I Belong to My Mother's Side" and "Try to Make Things"), selection from chapter 3, "Set Your Mind" ("Never Get Scared"), and selections from chapter 4, "Out on Our Own" ("Love Woods Life" and "I Don't Go Around"), were originally published in *Peter John: Minto* (Fairbanks: Spirit Mountain Press, 1986).

Miska Deaphon, "Dotron' Minagha' Sritonedak Di (Raven Lost His Eyes)" and "Dotron' Suje Gona' No'iłtsenh (Raven Fixes Marten's Arm)," were published in *Ni-*

kolai Hwch'ihwzoya', translated by Betty Petruska (Anchorage: National Bilingual Materials Development Center, 1980).

Lena Petruska, "Jezra (Camp Robbers)" and "Ch'itsets'ina' (The Skull)," translated by Raymond L. Collins and Betty Petruska, appear by permission of the author and translators.

Peter Kalifornsky, "Unhshcheyakda Sukt'a (My Great-Great-Grandfather's Story)," "Qadanalchen K'elik'a (Qadanalchen's Song)," "Talin Ch'iłtant Qatsinitsexen (The One Who Dreamed at Polly Creek)," "K'ełen Il Ch'qghe'uyi Ch'u K'ech'-eltani (Beliefs in Things a Person Can See and in Things a Person Cannot See)," "Qezdaghnen Ggagga (The Kustatan Bear)," "Qezdaghnen Ggagga Beghun (The Other Half of the Kustatan Bear Story)," "Ch'enlahi Sukdu (The Gambling Story)," "Ggugguyni Sukt'a (Raven Story)," "Ggugguyni Ch'u Nut'aq'i (Raven and the Geese)," and "Kił Ch'u Dujemi (The Man and the Loon)," were published in *A Dena'ina Legacy, K'tl'egh'i Sukdu: The Collected Writings of Peter Kalifornsky,* edited by James Kari and Alan Boraas (Fairbanks: Alaska Native Language Center, 1991).

Katie John and Fred John Sr., "Lazeni 'Iinn Nataełde Ghadghaande (When Russians Were Killed at 'Roasted Salmon Place' [Batzulnetas])" and "Cet'aenn Nal'aen'de (When the Tailed Ones Were Seen)," were published in Katie John, Fred John Sr., Adam Sanford, Huston Sanford, Jack John Justin, and Nicholas A. Brown, *Tatl'ahwt'aenn Nenn' (The Headwaters People's Country): Narratives of the Upper Ahtna Athabaskans* (Fairbanks: Alaska Native Language Center, 1986).

Huston Sanford, "Dae' Ts'atk'aats (How We Were Trained)," was originally published in Katie John, Fred John Sr., Adam Sanford, Huston Sanford, Jack John Justin, and Nicholas A. Brown, *Tatl'ahwt'aenn Nenn' (The Headwaters People's Country): Narratives of the Upper Ahtna Athabaskans* (Fairbanks: Alaska Native Language Center, 1986).

John Billum, "Demba (Two Checker Players)" and "Xay Tnaey (Spruce Root Man)," were originally published in *Atna' Yanida'a (Ahtna Stories),* translated by Millie Buck (Anchorage: National Bilingual Materials Development Center, 1979). Permission granted by Copper River Native Association.

Anna Nelson Harry, "Lake-Dwarves," "Giant Rat," and "Two Sisters," were published in *In Honor of Eyak: The Art of Anna Nelson Harry,* compiled and edited by Michael E. Krauss (Fairbanks: Alaska Native Language Center, 1982).

Anna Nelson Harry, "Maagudətl'əlahdəxunhyuu (Around-the-Lake People)," "Łuundiyahsluw (The Big Mouse)," and "The Girl and the Dog," were originally published in Kaj Birket-Smith and Frederica de Laguna, *The Eyak Indians of the Copper River Delta, Alaska* (Copenhagen: Levin and Munksgaard, 1938). Permission granted by Frederica de Laguna and National Museet, Copenhagen.

Index

LaVergne, TN USA
28 December 2010

210375LV00005B/33/P